NONE BUT THE BRAVE

A Novel of the Surgeons of World War II

ANTHONY A. GOODMAN

DEER CREEK
PUBLISHING GROUP

Published by:
Deer Creek Publications Group
www.DeerCreekPublicationsGroup.com
www. NoneButTheBraveNovel.com

Cover Painting: "Normandy Sabbath" by Lawrence Beall Smith, 1944.
Courtesy of the U.S. Army Center of Military History. Photo from U.S.
Army Medical Department Office of Medical History Website 2011.

Excerpts from: "A Survivors' Haggadah." Copyright 2000.
With permission from the publisher:
Jewish Publication Society
Philadelphia, PA

ISBN: 1463507984
ISBN-13: 9781463507985
Library of Congress Control Number: 2011930165
CreateSpace, North Charleston, SC

Also by Anthony A. Goodman

Historical Fiction

The Shadow of God: A Novel of War and Faith

Non-Fiction

Never Say Die. A Doctor and Patient Talk About Breast Cancer
With Lucy Shapero

Lecture Series with The Great Courses

Understanding The Human Body: Anatomy and Physiology

The Human Body: How We Fail; How We Heal.

Life Long Health: Achieving Optimal Well-Being at Any Age

The Myths of Nutrition and Fitness

Critical Praise for Anthony A. Goodman's Historical Fiction

The Shadow of God: A Novel of War and Faith.

Nominated for the prestigious *International IMPAC Dublin Literary Award.*

"So vividly rendered historical fiction fans will be crossing their fingers for a follow-up."

Publishers Weekly

To the memory of Dr. Alfred Hurwitz
Surgeon, Soldier, Teacher, Mentor

And

To the men and women who risked their lives day after day to rescue
the wounded and the dying of World War II.

Acknowledgments

My deepest thanks and appreciation to Dr. Richard L. Hurwitz, Susan Hurwitz and Tobey Hurwitz Isenstein for allowing me the opportunity to read the diaries of their father, Dr. Alfred Hurwitz.

My sincerest thanks to Dorothy Hurwitz for inspiring and encouraging me to write this book; and for supplying me with the books, photographs and stories of her husband's journey. She is greatly missed by all of us who knew her.

To my wife, Maribeth, who encouraged me to write this work and then guided and supported me through the many stages of bringing this book into being; and for her always helpful, tireless and important editing, suggestions and corrections. And, of course, inspiration.

My thanks and deep appreciation to Col. Ron Stevens, U.S. Army, Retired, for his help in editing and keeping me on the correct military path.

And to Mike Alexander, my long time friend who provided many colorful and accurate first hand accounts of life as a combatant in World War II. Thank you, Mike.

My thanks to Tommy Nardine for his excellent graphic design work.

D-DAY INVASION OVERVIEW

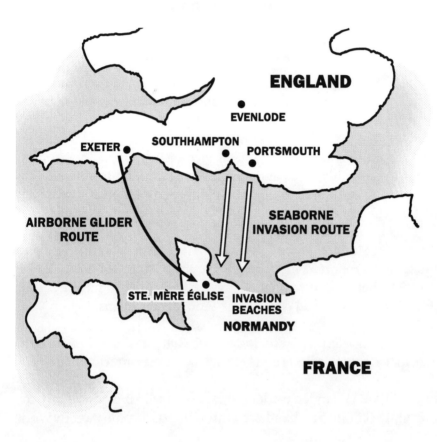

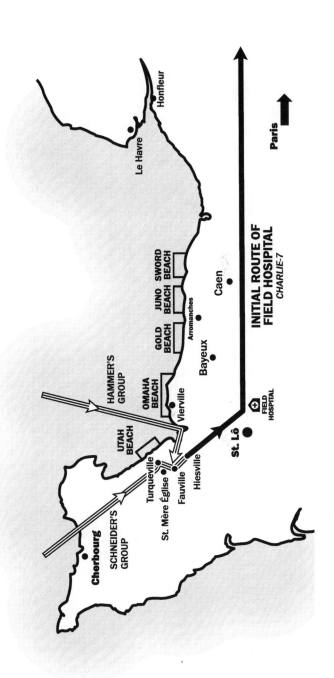

D-DAY INVASION
JUNE 6, 1944

Honfleur

Le Havre

Paris

SWORD
BEACH

JUNO
BEACH

GOLD
BEACH

Caen

Arromanches

Bayeux

HAMMER'S
GROUP

OMAHA
BEACH

Vierville

INITIAL ROUTE OF
FIELD HOSPITAL
CHARLIE-7

UTAH
BEACH

FIELD
HOSPITAL

St. Lô

Turqueville

Hiesville

Fauville

St. Mère Église

SCHNEIDER'S
GROUP

Cherbourg

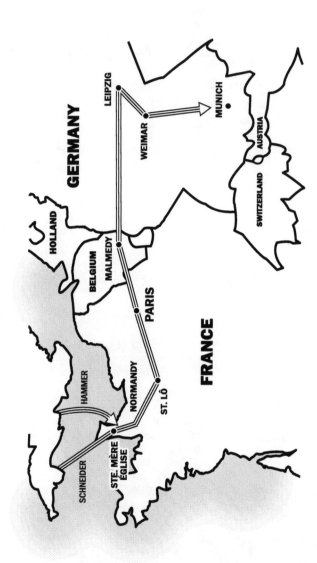

EUROPEAN CAMPAIGN
1944-1946

ROUTE OF FIELD HOSPITAL CHARLIE-7

Contents

Dedication   v

Acknowledgments   vii

Maps
D-Day Invasion Overview   viii
D-Day Invasion, 6 June 1944   ix
European Campaign, 1944-1946   x

Chapter One   1
6 June 1944, 0300 Hours
A Horsa Glider, Over the English Channel

Chapter Two   7
10 September 1942
Nearly Two Years Earlier
Operating Room
Philadelphia, Pennsylvania

Chapter Three   15
11 September 1942
Home of Steve and Susan Schneider
Philadelphia

Chapter Four   23
19 April 1944, 2330 Hours
Nineteen Months Later
The Fox and Pheasant Pub, Devon, England

Chapter Five   31
6 June 1944, 0330 Hours
LST 37-Baker, the English Channel

Chapter Six   39
6 June 1944, 0330 Hours
A Horsa Glider Over Turqueville, France

Chapter Seven   53
6 June 1944, 0630 Hours
Rhino Ferry 47-Fox, the English Channel, Normandy

Chapter Eight   65
6 June 1944, 0630 Hours
Near Turqueville, France

Chapter Nine   73
6 June 1944, 0700 Hours
On the Road near Turqueville, France

Chapter Ten   85
6 June 1944, 0800 Hours
A Concentration Camp near Weimar, Germany

Chapter Eleven   95
6 June 1944, 1340 Hours
Near Fauville, France

Chapter Twelve   107
7 June 1944, 0800 Hours
Dog White Section, Omaha Beach, Normandy

Chapter Thirteen   129
8 June 1944, 1700 Hours
Fauville, France

Chapter Fourteen   141
11 June 1944, 1100 Hours
Field Hospital Charlie-7, Fauville to Hiesville, France

Chapter Fifteen   151
11 June 1944, 2200 Hours
A Concentration Camp near Weimar, Germany

Chapter Sixteen   161
13 June 1944, 0200 Hours
Field Hospital Charlie-7, Hiesville, France

Chapter Seventeen   183
13 June 1944, 0600 Hours
Field Hospital Charlie-7, Hiesville, France

Chapter Eighteen   193
1 July 1944, 0800 Hours
Field Hospital Charlie-7, East of St. Lô, France

Chapter Nineteen   225
26 August 1944, 0600 Hours
Field Hospital Charlie-7, 100 Miles West of Paris

Chapter Twenty   265
1 December 1944, 1700 hours
Field Hospital Charlie-7, Belgium

Chapter Twenty-one   295
3 December 1944, 0530 Hours
A Concentration Camp near Weimar, Germany

Chapter Twenty-two   305
17 December 1944, 1200 Hours
Filed Hospital Charlie-7, Waimes, Belgium

Chapter Twenty-three   321
18 December 1944, 0200 Hours
Baugnez Crossroads, near Malmédy, Belgium

Chapter Twenty-four   331
8 May 1945, 0900 Hours
A Concentration Camp near Weimar, Germany

Chapter Twenty-five   339
8 May 1945, 1200 Hours
Field Hospital Charlie-7, Leipzig, Germany

Chapter Twenty-six   347
8 May 1945, 1300 Hours
Field Hospital Charlie-7, Leipzig, Germany

Chapter Twenty-seven   353
9 May 1945, 0700 Hours
Field Hospital Charlie-7, Leipzig, Germany

Chapter Twenty-eight   367
19 May 1945, 0800 Hours
A Concentration Camp near Weimar, Germany

Chapter Twenty-nine   371
20 May 1945, 2100 Hours
A Concentration Camp near Weimar, Germany

Chapter Thirty   395
25 May 1945, 2100 Hours
A Concentration Camp near Weimar, Germany

Chapter Thirty-one   409
26 May 1945, 0800 Hours
A Concentration Camp near Weimar, Germany

Chapter Thirty-two   415
15 April 1946, 1900 Hours
Deutsches Theater Restaurant, Munich, Germany

Chapter Thirty-three   429
15 April 1946, 2200 Hours
Munich, Germany

Epilogue   437
15 April 2004
The Home of Dr. Jacob Hammer
Philadelphia, Pennsylvania

Tribute   451

Author's Note   453

None but the brave,
None but the brave,
None but the brave deserve the fair.

Alexander's Feast
John Dryden

Cowards die many times before their deaths;
The valiant never taste of death but once.

Julius Caesar
William Shakespeare

He who would become a surgeon, should join the army and follow it.
Hippocrates.

Chapter One

6 June 1944, 0300 Hours
A Horsa Glider, Over the English Channel

octor Steve Schneider was still agonizing over what the hell he was doing in a Horsa glider scudding through the clouds high over the English Channel. The glider was approaching the coast of France and about to land in the dark behind German lines.

"Jesus Christ!" Steve muttered.

The glider shuddered and Schneider bit his tongue hard. He tasted his own blood trickling into his mouth.

It's not an airplane! It's an orange crate, he thought.

He wasn't far off. He was flying in a wood-and-canvas box held up by flimsy eighty-eight foot wings. It wasn't even metal. Just plywood and canvas, with windows only for the pilot. With no visible means of support, to Schneider it felt more like a coffin than an aircraft—a coffin dragged behind an aging tow plane at a hundred miles an hour. Schneider looked around at the silent commandoes and medical personnel around him. Thirty in all plus the pilot.

How the fuck did I do this to myself? Seemed like such a good idea at the time. I should have talked to Hamm before I volunteered for this one. Damn! Hamm would have talked me out of it.

Except his friend Hamm was getting ready to land on a beach somewhere in Normandy.

Back in England, the officer had made it sound so easy, so heroic. He had come to Schneider's billet shortly after dinner. Sitting there in his own warm quarters with a full stomach, Schneider had felt comfortable, almost safe.

"Why anyone would want to go in with the main invasion force is a mystery to me, Major," the officer had said. The man had not introduced himself. His insignia indicated that he was a major, like Schneider. They were equals in that regard. But that was where it ended. This man was all army, all the way. He looked twice Schneider's size— at least to Schneider. And his hair was cut to regulation. His uniform was starched and clean in spite of the dampness and the continuing rain. Even his boots were shined. Schneider wondered how the man had walked there and managed not to get mud on his boots. He smiled at the image that surfaced in his brain: an enlisted man carrying the major from the jeep to Schneider's billet.

"The main invasion force is going to be reduced to a mass of seasick grunts," he told Schneider. "They'll hardly be fit to fight when they finally hit that beach. Those who live long enough to land, that is. It's going to be a slaughterhouse."

Schneider just listened as the officer pointed out how strongly the Germans had defended the coastline.

"The Krauts have had years to build up their defenses. Doesn't matter that they don't know the exact location of the invasion—at least we don't think they do. Anyway, Major, we have a mission, and we want you to be part of it."

The mission was to land undetected behind German lines three hours ahead of the main invasion force.

Ahead of the invasion, Schneider reminded himself.

The commandoes were to secure the small town of Turqueville, just east of a German stronghold at St. Mère-Église. Schneider and his small medical group were to establish a forward aid station and then wait for the main invasion force to catch up with them. The main force would then bring in a larger medical group, supplies, and personnel. Then they would eventually become a full-fledged field hospital. At least, that was the way it was supposed to work. The commandoes were along to protect the unarmed medical group on the ground.

Schneider ran his now tender swollen tongue against the roof of his mouth as he thought back upon that conversation. He shook his head at his own naïveté. If it sounded too good to be true back then, it sure as hell was too good to be true now in the damned glider. The officer had made it sound heroic: volunteer for a mission to defeat the Germans and prepare the way for the guys who would be wounded in the invasion. Schneider had convinced himself that he was doing a noble thing, a brave thing, going in ahead of the invasion. Ahead of Hamm and the others. But, deep inside, though he could barely admit it to himself, he knew he was really trying to avoid at any cost landing on that beach under the guns of the Wehrmacht. He knew he could not face those guns and the slaughter they would create.

Schneider leaned forward to look out the front window of the glider. Over the pilot's shoulder he could just make out the tow plane's silhouette, and barely hear the engine noise. The tow plane pilot had just reduced power and begun a slow controlled descent as they crossed the northern coast of France. All the commandoes had eyes on the glider pilot, who was trying to maintain his position directly behind and slightly above the tow plane. The men in the glider were seated on narrow wooden benches bolted lengthwise along the walls of the aircraft. Their feet were tucked in and they faced each other across the small walkway.

The glider shuddered with each gust of wind. It was as if they were bouncing along a rough dirt road in an old jeep. Through the windshield Schneider could just make out a glow from the exhaust of the tow plane's engine. He wondered if the German ack-ack batteries could see the glow too. The plane was moving in and out of the clouds, and from their low altitude he caught glimpses of white caps on the surface of the English Channel below. Then the clouds closed again and plunged them into a deep gray darkness. Although being able to see out of the glider gave Schneider some comfort, he knew this was an illusion.

"If we can see the Krauts, they sure as hell can see us," he said out loud.

"Sir?"

Schneider looked to his right. It was Andy Marsh, his medic. He was all of nineteen years old and barely shaving yet. Schneider couldn't imagine what the hell a kid so young was doing here.

"Just talking to myself, Andy."

Could Marsh see his fear? He wondered.

Schneider's bladder was suddenly very full. He wondered when he would get the chance to pee. He tightened his muscles against the fullness and then tried to relax his mind, hoping he could relax the spasm deep in his pelvis. It never occurred to him that this would be a problem. The damned glider didn't have a toilet. Now he was flying into battle with a bladder ready to overflow.

"Crap." He looked at Marsh again and said, "Never mind." Schneider shuddered again, and squeezed his thighs together. He wanted to tell Marsh that if he wet his pants now it would be because there was no toilet—not that he was afraid.

It wasn't just Schneider who was having trouble. All the soldiers had full bladders by then. The minutes passed slowly for everyone, and the ride became bumpier as the aircraft descended closer to the ground. Here was where the English Channel met the French coast, driving columns of air upward that tossed the glider like a kite. His stomach knotted each time the aircraft lurched, his knees locked tighter together, and his fists clenched. He hated the turbulence, but if the rough ride were the only threat to his safety he could tough it out. If only there were not the additional risks of being shot out of the air, of burning to death in this wooden crate, of crashing while still alive into the trees of France.

Schneider looked out the window again but couldn't see any of the other gliders in their flight. He guessed that they were still behind him. Or too far off to the sides.

None of the other men seemed to be bothered by the turbulence. But Schneider's nerves had broken him into a cold sweat. Every time he adjusted his position, the droplets coalesced into a tiny creek of cold salt water between his shoulder blades. He was beginning to shiver.

"Cold, Doc?"

Marsh had called Schneider "Doc" from the first day they met in England a year and a half ago. Never "Major" or "Major Schneider" or even "Doctor Schneider." Just "Doc." It was the army way.

It was fine with Schneider. He didn't feel much like a major. Or a soldier. He was a surgeon. He carried just a heavy medical pack, and no gun.

Schneider smiled at Marsh. "No, Andy," he said. "I'm just scared shitless."

There! He finally said it out loud. Oh, man, did that feel good!

In all these many months and years, he had never spoken the words. Now he was admitting his fear to this nineteen-year-old medic he hardly knew. Well, why not? It was very likely that one or both of them would soon be dead. That made Schneider shiver again.

"What's there to be scared about, Doc? After all, here we are in a plywood and canvas airplane with no engine, no guns, no armament; flying over enemy territory at night with no lights; getting ready to land in the fucking dark, in a place with no fucking runway, in a place the Krauts've been fortifying for the last four years. So what the fuck there to be scared about? Anyway, they're not shooting at us. Yet."

Schneider didn't answer. He wondered if Marsh could actually put a sentence together without a "fuck" every fourth word?

Marsh went on, "Hey, it's OK I call you Doc?…uh…Major…Sir."

"Yeah. It's OK." Schneider said. Now he asks?

But anything, even this conversation about nothing, is better than thinking about what's ahead.

Marsh kept looking through the pilot's window. "I'm just trying to figure the odds of living through the war. Hell, I'm really wonderin' if I'll live through the night."

The young man shook his head. "It's going to be bad for us medics out there. That much I know. I just don't know *how* bad. My older brother, Bill, enlisted on his eighteenth birthday. Right after Pearl Harbor. Wouldn't listen to Mom or Dad. He was my big brother but…"

Schneider didn't say anything. He just listened.

"Then one day, about three months later, I'm sitting on my front porch with my mom and dad, and a taxi pulls up. I'm studying geometry—not very easy for me—and Dad's reading the paper. Mom is shelling peas. We watch an army officer in a uniform step out of the cab and pay the driver. I know now he was a captain, but I didn't know it then. Mom buries her face in her hands and begins to sob even before the cab pulls away. I don't know what's going on, but Mom's crying already, so I'm getting nervous. I look up at Dad, and I see, over his shoulder, the little flag hangin' in the front window with the star. It looks like a frame around Dad's head. Like a halo or somethin'. I can still hear Mom cryin'." Marsh shook his head, "I'm so fucking dumb, I still didn't get it.

"So the officer walks up and stands on the steps just below us. He was an older guy, maybe a few years younger than my dad. He took off his hat and spoke very quietly to us. He told us what happened.

"Billy was dead. Killed in action. He was a medic, and he was killed in the line of duty on some crappy Pacific island that none of us had ever heard of. I still don't know where it is. The officer gave Mom a medal in a little box. Said Billy was a hero because he died trying to save a wounded soldier. It was Billy's first action of the war. His first fuckin' day, can you believe it?

"A few weeks later, my draft board sends me a letter exempting me from active duty as the sole-surviving son. The next morning, I go downtown to the recruiting station and sign up. I'm not eighteen yet, so I forged my parent's signature and became a medic. Just like Billy." Andy stopped there, and just stared at the floor boards in the aisle.

As Andy finished telling his story, Schneider wondered if Andy was going to do any better than his brother, Billy. Or would he, himself, for that matter?

Schneider started to sweat again. His distended bladder was now becoming painful. He really didn't know if he could hold it.

Ah fuck, he said to himself. I had a deferment too. In writing, right in my hand. Everyone told me not to go. Everyone! So what do I do? I enlist. I fucking enlist! I can't believe it. I'm in this shitty glider, gonna take shrapnel any minute now, piss in my pants and embarrass myself just before I get killed. And I could have just stayed home with my girls and... Susan. Ah, shit.

Chapter Two

10 September 1942
Nearly Two Years Earlier
Operating Room
Philadelphia, Pennsylvania

Schneider backed away from the operating table as Marie, the circulating nurse, untied the back of his gown. He pulled off his gown, tossed it into the hamper and removed his rubber gloves. Then he stretched them taut, aiming as if he were holding a pistol, then fired the gloves at the trash can, missing by almost a foot. Marie shook her head and picked them up off the floor, dropping them with some flourish into the can. She started to say something to Schneider but stopped and shook her head again.

Schneider pulled off his mask and carefully dropped it into the white laundry hamper along with his surgical cap. He smiled, and Marie nodded a thank you.

He walked to the scrub sink outside the door and gave his hands a quick rinse with soap and water just as his partner, Dr. John Hammer, pushed through the OR doors. Hammer, or Hamm, as he was most often called, was a tall man, over six foot two. He was thickset with wide shoulders and strong facial features, particularly his broad, slightly bulbous nose. On a slighter frame, his face might have been almost coarse, but on Hamm it came off as authoritative, if not downright handsome. He had dark brown hair, combed over his fore-head, and a disarmingly ready smile for such a big man.

Right behind Hamm came a young orderly pulling at the foot end of the rolling gurney, while Dr. Ted McClintock, the anesthesi-ologist, pushed from the head of the gurney with one hand, bagging oxygen into the slowly awakening patient with the other. McClintock was a darker version of Hamm, also over six feet and heavily muscled. He had a thick neck that seemed to rise from the outer edges of his shoulders, recalling his college wrestling days at Duke. His dark hair and blue eyes made him a much sought after bachelor both inside the OR and out. He spoke with a disarmingly slow, North Carolina drawl. Beyond that outward persona, McClintock was an excellent doctor. He appeared to move more slowly than his colleagues from the North, but his precision and economy of motion were beauti-ful to watch. He wasted no effort. Lesser anesthesiologists were fool-ing around with IV lines and checking for correct placement of the endotracheal tube long after McClintock had the patient asleep and stable; ready to go.

Hamm held the patient's chart under one arm while he rinsed his hands at the sink. Then, he followed in McClintock's wake toward the recovery room.

"Nice one, Hamm. Very slick," Schneider said, waiting at the recovery room door.

Hamm laughed. "Yeah, after the first thousand they get easier."

Hamm had known Schneider all through their college and medical school years. They had been roommates freshman year and remained close ever since, graduating together and even working summer jobs together. Although they trained in different residency programs, they had come together again in Philadelphia when they began their prac-tices and often assisted each other in surgery. Their families socialized only occasionally, but the two men played squash two nights a week on the way home from the hospital.

McClintock and the orderly pushed through the recovery room doors, wheeling the patient into an empty space as a recovery room nurse took over the job of administering oxygen. The patient coughed a few times as she emerged back into the real world from her ether induced sleep.

"Take some nice deep breaths, Mrs. Collins," McClintock said, leaning over and talking right into her ear. "That's it. Your operation's over. You're going to be fine," he reassured her.

Schneider went over to the coffee pot and poured himself a cup, heaping in the sugar and cream. When he offered Hamm a cup, Hamm made a face and said, "Just black, thanks."

Schneider shrugged, brought the chunky white ceramic cups to the long desk, and sat down beside Hamm.

While Hamm was writing his operative notes in the patient's chart, Schneider took some order sheets from the stack on the table. He looked over Hamm's shoulder and copied the woman's name from the chart. He added the date and then began writing the post-op orders.

As the two surgeons wrote, McClintock saw to the now fully awake Mrs. Collins. He left instructions with the nurse. The recovery room nurse handed McClintock a mug of coffee. Black like Hamm's. Then the three men rose together, taking their coffee with them, and walked back to the surgeons' locker room to change.

Schneider glanced at himself in the locker room mirror, seeing how scrawny he was compared to the bulky muscular stature of Hamm and McClintock. Schneider was barely five foot ten and had never weighed more than one-sixty, and then only in college. Seeing the reflection of the three of them made Schneider wince as he remembered those college days with Hamm when their wise guy friend used to call the two of them Mutt and Jeff. Schneider was dark haired and dark skinned. He had brown eyes and chiseled cheeks. The girls used to call him Frankie Boy after Sinatra, and except for the eye color, the name was fitting. He did look like Frankie.

Schneider and McClintock sat on a ratty couch with yellowed stuffing escaping its edges and coffee stains making a Rorschach-like pattern interspersed with small cigarette burns. Hamm sat directly across from them, perched precariously on a battered wooden spindle chair, a relic from another century.

"What's up, Hamm?" Schneider asked. "You've been very quiet today. You barely said a word during surgery. What's on your mind?"

Hamm stared off into space for a moment. "Actually, yes. I'm very preoccupied."

"About what?"

"What else is there?" Hamm said, a hint of exasperation creeping into his usually placid voice. "The war. This goddamned war."

"And?" Schneider asked, setting his coffee cup on the side table.

Hamm sighed. "I've decided to volunteer."

"You're going to *volunteer*?" Schneider and McClintock said almost in unison.

"Actually, I already have," Hamm answered. "It's taken us so long to get into this war that we're taking a beating on *both* fronts now. We're losing thousands of GIs. How can I stay here taking out gall bladders and fixing hernias while our guys are getting torn to pieces over there?"

A tense silence followed. Things were going very badly in both the European and the Pacific theaters. Casualties were high, and the end of the war was nowhere in sight, perhaps years away. Rumors of German and Japanese atrocities were in the papers and on the radio every day.

"You talked this over with Allison?" Schneider asked.

"Yes."

"And?"

"And she cried. But she understood."

"She understood what?"

"She understood that I can't stay back here in safety when almost everybody I know is over there risking their lives. I've got neighbors with kids over there. Some of them are just out of high school. My uncle even signed up. He's fifty-two! They turned him down for combat, but he insisted on joining up. They put him in the Quartermaster Corps manning a supply depot. He'll let his wife run the business while he's gone. And that's not even unusual now."

McClintock stood and paced the crowded room. He said nothing. Both Hamm and Schneider could see something was really bothering him.

"Big decision, Hamm," Schneider said, turning from McClintock.

"Damn right it is," Hamm said. "But it's the right thing to do."

"Jesus," McClintock said.

"Allison is OK with this," Hamm said. "She cried, and she's scared. But she knows I have to do it. I really have no choice."

"Who have you signed up with?" Schneider asked, still sounding doubtful. "The Army? The Navy? Marines?"

"Army. There's a volunteer surgical group already mobilized. Mostly doctors and surgeons from the same hospitals or medical schools are joining up together to form their own groups. I'm joining one from here."

"Jesus, Hamm!" Schneider said.

"Yup. I leave in three weeks. I've got a hell of a lot to do: shut down the office, transfer the care of the patients. Three weeks isn't going to give me much time. Then a little basic training somewhere. Learn who I have to salute. Then I think we're going to England. After that I have no idea."

Schneider could hardly speak. His best friend was leaving and might never return; he might die some place no one had ever heard of. The radio and the newspapers reported terrible losses every day. Even the *Movietone News* showed scenes of carnage every weekend. Grainy footage of the real war came right into their neighborhood theaters, narrated in the deep, clear, familiar voice of Lowell Thomas.

It was crazy. Watching those grim awful newsreels, then going right into some *Looney Tunes* cartoon followed by *Bambi* or Bob Hope in *The Road to Morocco*. An all-afternoon show for twenty-five cents and five cents for candy. What a world!

"I'm going, too!"

Hamm and Schneider wheeled around, turning to McClintock, now perched uneasily on the windowsill.

"I am! Who the hell else will pass gas for Hamm? He can't operate without me."

Hamm said, "You better think this over, Ted. This isn't like saying 'Let's go to a Phillies game.'"

"What's there to think about? I've been thinking this over for three years. Three fucking years this war has been on—in Europe, anyway." He stood and punched his locker just hard enough to momentarily buckle the metal, then added, "Besides, I only stayed here so I wouldn't embarrass you guys."

No one laughed. Hamm turned to him. "It's a big decision, Ted." He stared directly into McClintock's eyes. "Please think this over before you jump in."

"Nothing to think over, pal," McClintock said. "You go, I go. I've got no wife or children. It's easy for me. The Philadelphia ladies'll get over it."

Schneider stared at them both. "Damn," he muttered.

Hamm turned from McClintock to Schneider. He said, "Steve, this has to be your decision. Yours alone. Don't go trooping off after me just because I decided to go, or after Ted here. We still need surgeons at home. People still get sick on the home front. No one is going to think any less of you if you don't sign up. You've got Susan and the girls to think of."

"So? You've got Allison and the boys," Schneider said.

Hamm didn't answer. He bent and tied his shoes very slowly, barely aware of what he was doing. McClintock gathered his watch and wallet from his locker.

Schneider shook his head again, stared into space, but said nothing. Then he started to laugh. He laughed so hard he collapsed onto the couch, shaking his head and wiping tears from his eyes.

"What?" McClintock asked.

"I've already *been* drafted! I got a goddamned draft notice two weeks ago. 'Greetings from you-know-who!'"

"Holy shit!" McClintock said. "Why didn't you tell us?"

"I thought it was a mistake. I'm technically 4F because of my asthma, and with my doctor's OK I can play that card. I can get a medical deferment."

"Well, 'technically' doesn't mean shit, Steve," McClintock said.

"I know, I know," Schneider said. "One of the Army docs told me if you're fit for duty as a civilian doctor you're fit as an Army doctor."

"Yeah, as long as what you've got isn't *rapidly* fatal," Hamm added.

McClintock laughed. "War can be rapidly fatal, boy. I think you should take the 4F."

"I'm damned if I know what to do. I'm not 4F. It's asthma for Christ sake. If I *really* want to go I can get my own doctor to sign off on it. Crap!"

The three of them were quiet again. Schneider looked at his two strapping friends and thought, Jesus, these two really look like soldiers. They'll fit right in. But how can I let them go without me, he thought?

"Alright, I'm with you. One for all, and all that shit."

"Steve, slow down here. Take it easy," Hamm said.

"No, I'm in. It's done," Steve replied.

Schneider put on his watch and wedding band. He started for the door, then turned to his friends and said, "Oh, shit. What am I going to say to Susan?"

Chapter Three

11 September 1942
Home of Steve and Susan Schneider
Philadelphia, Pennsylvania

The next morning outside his home in the Elkins Park area of Philadelphia, Steve Schneider kissed his little girls good-bye at the curb. Emily was eight, and Anna was six. Emily looked like Steve, with a slightly prominent nose and dark features. She wore her black hair in bangs, and she was quite sure she was her father's favorite. Anna had not grown out of her baby features yet. She had lighter hair and fair skin, more like her mother, though she didn't really resemble either parent. Anna, too, knew without a doubt, that she was her father's favorite. Neither of his girls gave much thought to their mother these days. Dad was the center of their young lives.

As the school bus idled next to the curb with its door open, the girls gave Schneider tremendous hugs, each trying to out-love the other. Then they laughed and scrambled aboard the waiting bus. Even before the door had closed, Emily ran to the nearest open window to wave, as if she were going away for years instead of just until three o'clock. Anna was already engrossed in animated conversation with her friends on the big back seat. Then, before the bus got too far away, she pressed her nose against the glass, spread her fingers wide on either side of her face and stuck out her tongue. Her image, except for her pink tongue, was quickly obscured by her warm breath clouding the cold glass window.

Schneider laughed, shook his head, and waved again as the yellow bus pulled off in a cloud of blue exhaust smoke. As he walked back to the house, he pulled a small bike and a homemade scooter from the dying grass and dragged them onto the wooden porch, tucking them in behind the low, gray clapboard wall.

It's a good neighborhood, he thought as he hid the toys from sight, but still....

He walked across the wooden porch, noting a little dry rot along the wainscoting near the front door. Always one more thing that needed doing.

He opened the front door and went back inside, the joy of his little girls rapidly fading as he crossed the broad hallway and returned to the kitchen to thrash it out still one more time with Susan.

Schneider didn't know what was going through Susan's mind that morning. She was pacing the kitchen clutching a paper in her hand, wrinkling it, worrying it. He walked over to the kitchen table and pulled out his chair. Then he sat with a weariness that should have marked the end of a long day, not the beginning.

Susan was almost as tall as Schneider. And she was as fair as he was dark; her hair as straight as his was curly. Even their eyes were at the extremes of the genetic scale: his dark almost to black, and hers a pale blue.

Schneider watched his wife cross back and forth in front of him, moving her head from side to side in an unconscious gesture of *No*. Her lips were drawn tightly across her teeth, turning them into thin lines of flesh, lines of anger and frustration. By this point, Schneider could not tell if the look on her face were anger or fear or disgust. Most likely all of them.

Although she was only in her early thirties, Susan looked haggard to Schneider. She had bags under her eyes from pure lack of sleep, not age. And, he knew, some crying, too. The two of them always seemed to be going to bed angry for the past few months, and waking up the same way. Even in their small bed, their bodies rarely touched, each sleeping on the very edge of their territory. He couldn't remember the last time they had sex.

"Why don't you sit down, Susan. I can't talk to you while you're pacing like that," he said in as calm and noncommittal a tone as he could muster.

"I can't sit down. I feel like I'm going to jump out of my skin."

"Look, there's absolutely nothing I can do about it. I have to go."

"No you don't, and you and I both know it," she said, throwing the crumpled paper on the table and stomping out of the kitchen. Schneider was sure she had thrown it *at* him, but the air intervened and the paper drifted harmlessly down on the table. He opened the letter, smoothing out the wrinkles with the fingers of both hands. Then he read it for the hundredth time.

Order to Report for Induction

The President of the United States to <u>Stephen N. Schneider</u>.

Order 86945

Greetings:

Having submitted yourself to a local board composed of your neighbors for the purpose of determining your availability for training and service in the land or naval services of the United States, you are hereby notified that you have been selected for training and service therein.

You will, therefore, report to the local board at Walnut Avenue, Philadelphia at 0900 on Friday, 18 September 1942.

DDS Form 105 (revised 15/1/41)

An illegible scrawl filled the signature space. He pushed the paper aside and took a sip of coffee. He reached for the sugar and stirred three teaspoons into the cup. Then he took a fresh milk bottle and pulled off the wire that secured the outer paper seal. He flipped off the cover and exposed the round cardboard cap. He picked at the little semicircular tab and marveled at how the simple task of removing the cardboard cap from a milk bottle could be so baffling to a skilled and highly trained surgeon.

It's a wonder anyone drinks milk, he thought.

When the milk bottle was open, he took great care not to disturb the three-inch layer of yellow cream that filled the neck, floating on top of the white milk like an ornament.

Next, he took a spoon and pressed down, making a small crater on the surface of his coffee, careful not to let any of the coffee float into the spoon. He slowly poured the cream off the top of the milk bottle, floating it from the spoon onto the surface of the coffee where it made a bright yellow puddle of pure cream. He removed the spoon slowly so as not to stir in the cream, then raised the cup to his lips, closed his eyes, and savored the moment, preserving just a few heartbeats for himself away from the turmoil with Susan. For those precious few seconds, he was not in his kitchen anymore.

He kept his eyes closed as he sipped his drink, feeling the contrast between the thick cold cream on top and the dark sweet hot coffee as they mixed in his mouth and rolled together across his tongue.

He smiled.

"God, Steve! How can you drink that stuff?" Susan said, barging back through the swinging kitchen door.

Schneider didn't answer. He kept his eyes closed and his mind focused on the pleasure of his morning ritual. He reached for the chocolate-covered doughnut on the table and dipped it into the creamy brew, then took a bite of pure sweetness.

Heaven!

After a moment more, he looked up, bringing himself back to reality. He turned to the clock on the wall, noticing the wrinkles in the wallpaper he had tried to hang when they had moved into this, their first real home. They had no money for renovations back then. So, he had papered the kitchen himself and marveled at what a bad job he had done.

It was approaching eight-thirty. He would be late for rounds and surgery, but this had to be finished. He knew that the operation couldn't start without him anyway, so he took another bite of the chocolate doughnut, ignoring the reprimand in Susan's eyes.

"Look, Susan, I'm going. I have to go."

"You don't have to go. You're 4F. You told me when you went for the physical that the draft board said you're 4F. So why do you have to go?"

Schneider sighed. They had been through this so many times in the last several hours that he just couldn't stand another rehash, another fight.

"The draft board screwed up. Doctors can't really be 4F. If I can perform surgery in civilian life, I can perform it in wartime. For Christ's sake, I'm only 4F for asthma! I'm not risking my life or any one else's just because I have a mild case of asthma."

"You can die from asthma! And they said you don't have to go."

Schneider took another deep breath. He felt as if he were talking to his little daughters, except that he knew he was losing his composure and felt a touch of hysteria creeping into his voice too.

"I'm not going to die of asthma, Susan. And I'm not going over there to die at all. This war is the biggest thing that's happened in our lifetime. The whole world is involved. The Germans are over-running Europe. The Japs are all over the Pacific. Everyone's fighting. You see the papers. You hear the news. They're doing something horrible over there to the Jews. My family came from Germany. I know I never go to temple, but I'm still a Jew. Susan, I can't just turn my back on this…on them. And, all my friends and colleagues are going—"

"So there it is. The real truth. You *are* making a choice. Your friends over your family. Just say it. Steve, you sound like a twelve-year-old. 'My friends are going to jump off the garage roof, so I am, too.'"

Again he sighed, barely holding his rising temper in check. Actually, he had jumped off the garage roof with his friends when he was twelve, and had broken his fibula. It was only a hairline fracture, but it still it hurt like hell sometimes. However, he wouldn't give her the satisfaction of admitting to that one right now.

"One more time," he said with condescending patience. "Volunteer surgical teams are getting together all over the country. They're forming surgical groups with the people they work with over here. I'll be with my own group from Philadelphia. I know I technically don't have to go, but I must go. How can I stay here safe in private practice while our guys are dying over in Europe by the thousands? Thousands! They need general surgeons more than anyone else. We're the most experienced part of the trauma team, Susan." He paused for a moment, sighed deeply, then added, "In fact, the truth be known, I'm looking forward to going."

There! He had finally said it out loud. The unthinkable: that going to war, going to a place where he might be killed, for Christ's sake, was better than the constant fighting with his wife. It would be a relief.

He said it, and he couldn't take it back. Susan looked as if she had been slapped. Her cheeks were red, and a tear formed in the corner of each eye, rolling slowly down her cheeks like the raindrops on a windshield, leaving crooked lines in their wake. She turned away for a moment, and when she faced him again, the tears were gone. Her neck and face were still bright red, now from anger, not hurt. She said nothing.

Steve took another sip of coffee and looked away. He began to fold the draft notice into a small ball. Then, when he could no longer make it any smaller, he tossed it toward the garbage can. It missed and fell on the floor. Susan looked at it lying near her foot then looked back at her husband without picking it up.

"I have to go, Susan," he said again with a weariness she had not heard since his days as a surgical resident, days when he came home after forty-eight hours of constant surgery and emergencies.

"So, we're not going to discuss this anymore—"

"No, no," he said, more softly now. "I mean I have to go to work. I've got rounds to make and a couple of big cases to do later this morning. And I have to assist Hamm with a case later on. We'll talk about it when I get home."

He finished the last of his coffee and put the cup in the sink.

"Steve," she said to his back, her voice calm and cool, without emotion. A chill moved through Schneider's spine, right down his legs. "What makes you think you can make it over there? They're not going to keep you in an operating room in England for the whole war, you know. What are you going to do when someone starts shooting at you?" And, dripping with sarcasm she added, "Who's going to protect you then?"

Susan had a look on her face that made Schneider's stomach tighten into a knot.

"You're going to bring that up again?" he said. "I was seventeen, Susan. It was no big deal."

"Wasn't it? I'm just asking you, Steve," she said, her voice hard, quiet. He had heard that tone only a few times in their marriage. "What are you going to do over there when someone tries to kill you?"

He shook his head in disgust.

"I'm going to sign up with the Surgical Group after work today," he said quietly. "I'll probably be late for dinner."

Susan's eyes narrowed as she folded her arms.

"Don't hurry," she said. "There is not going to be any dinner."

Chapter Four

19 April 1944, 2330 Hours
Nineteen Months Later
The Fox and Pheasant Pub, Devon, England

The smoke was making Schneider's eyes water, and the beer sat in his stomach like a puddle of gasoline. He never did care much for alcohol and always wondered what everyone thought was so good about it. To him, the Scotch whiskey the others were drinking tasted like tincture of iodine, and his beer like warm piss. But, there was precious little else to do there in that wet, remote place. The rain had been falling for weeks, it seemed. Even when it stopped, the sun never shined. The local roads were a swamp, though the Brits seemed not to notice. Nothing ever dried out, and the cold went right through to the bones. It was far worse than the bitter cold of Philadelphia's relatively mild winter. Schneider wondered how the Brits put up with it, considering the poor insulation and lack of central heating in their homes. It was absolutely primitive.

Schneider's surgical group had been in England for over a year. He was happy to be back with Hamm and McClintock after a few months of organization and basic training in the States at various bases. Then, quick weekend farewells. Susan and Steve were still deeply divided over his going. They barely spoke and didn't touch once during his three-day leave. Steve tried to put on a good face for the girls. They walked through the neighborhood together, Emily and Anna taking turns holding hands in the middle with their parents. At one point, Emily stepped aside and put Steve's hand in Susan's. You can't fool children. Emily's primal instincts cut through the bullshit in a way her parents could not.

So Schneider gave up his surgical practice just when he was finally putting away a few dollars after the poverty of his six-year residency. Just when things were looking up—at least financially—he threw it all away to go off to war with his buddies. At least, that was Susan's take on it.

Even though Steve and Susan put on a good show for their daughters, the strain in private was painful. They stayed as far as they could from each other, even knowing they might never see each other again.

Susan never did come around. She remained furious that Steve chose to go to war when he had every good reason to stay home with her and the girls. The asthma was real, after all. He was not making it up. But, for Schneider, there never really was any question of not joining the battle. All his colleagues were going. If he were going at all, he would go with them.

By the time he boarded the troop ship for the crossing to England, the marriage was nearly dead. Neither of them ever brought up the subject of divorce; there were the girls, after all. And except for Schneider's eccentric uncle in Brooklyn, neither of them knew anyone who was divorced. Divorce was a Hollywood thing.

The long and awful troop ship voyage from New York across a rough Atlantic Ocean was dreadful in every imaginable way. After six long days at sea, they arrived in Southampton where thousands of officers and men disembarked for various camps around the English countryside. Schneider had been seasick most of the way over. There was no shame in it as nearly three thousand men had been sick along with him.

During all of the long months away from home, Schneider had dutifully written letters, but he made sure to write to the whole family, the girls and Susan. This meant that he could avoid any talk of their marital problems and just keep it newsy and light. The girls would, he knew, insist on reading the letters by themselves, Emily reading the letters aloud to Anna.

More than a year and a half later, nothing had changed since the day he told Susan he was going off to war. Nothing.

Schneider looked at his watch. It was almost one in the morning.

"God, this is getting old!" Schneider said. "Same shit every damned day. Same drinks at the same pub with the same guys every night."

"You bored?" McClintock said. "You're actually bored?"

Schneider looked into McClintock's bloodshot eyes and shook his head. "Are you having fun, Ted?"

McClintock rocked his head back and forth. "Could be worse. We could be in the middle of the you-know-what."

"The invasion?" Schneider said on a stage whisper.

"Oooooh! Loose lips sink ships! The walls have ears…and all that." McClintock answered.

"Oh, right. Like the Jerries don't know we're coming. They're just sitting over there drinking Schnapps and enjoying the hospitality of the French," Hamm said.

Schneider looked at Hamm. "How the hell can the Jerries not know we're on the verge of the invasion? Christ! There are several hundred thousand men and women and machines piled so high they could sink this fucking island."

"But where, my boy? Where?" McClintock said. "They don't know where the invasion will be, and neither do we."

"Well, shit, I can give it a pretty good guess," Schneider said. "Dover to Pas de Calais is just a hop. But the Jerries are dug in up to their armpits over there. Normandy is a hell of a slog, but the defenses are lighter. Our guys are trying to fool them, and they are pretending to be fooled. We put phony-baloney men and equipment in one place, and they move their men to another place. It's like the Keystone Kops."

"Well, I, for one, would like to get it the hell over with," McClintock said. "I've had enough of this shit to last me awhile—the rain, the mud—and I'm drinking too damned much. The birds are OK though," he said looking at the young British woman sitting across from him.

Hamm looked at the woman and smiled softly.

"From what I hear most of the Brits are not real happy with us," Hamm said.

McClintock laughed. "Yeah, there's a hell of a lot of us here. The Brits think we're over paid, over sexed, and worst of all, over here."

"I can't blame them," Hamm said. "There's nearly two million of us in this little country not much bigger than Colorado."

Everyone knew that the invasion was only months away at most. All the soldiers quartered in England, hundreds of thousands of them, were straining to get off the mark and start the invasion that would, they were sure, end the war by Christmas.

"Hey, Hamm," Schneider suddenly shouted over the din, "I've gotta get out of here. I'm just dead."

"Me, too, I'm exhausted," Hamm said. "Let's go."

Hamm began to push his chair back but felt a restraining hand on his arm. He looked to his right, where McClintock was sitting.

"Don't go without me, guys. I need to get outta here, too." Although far from drunk, McClintock had been mixing beer and Scotch. Schneider knew this would translate into a very cranky anesthesiologist in the morning.

No one moved for a few minutes. There was an inertia settling into the group in everything they did. There was hardly any real surgery to do back at the base. The field hospital was set up for business, but most of their time was spent training to set up and tear down the field hospital as quickly as possible, training for the coming fighting in France. They practiced pitching their OR tents more than they practiced medicine. Schneider and Hamm were overseeing thousands of healthy young men who needed their attention only for the rare appendectomy or training injuries. The night before had been spent patching up a drunk private who lost control of his motor bike on a muddy back road trying to get in before curfew. Mostly cleaning out and sewing up a lot of lacerations while the oral surgeon came in to take care of a mouth full of broken teeth.

Then there were the routine training accidents. More lacerations and a few broken bones. Not to mention a sprained ankle or two in the spontaneous football games on base.

Take away their major surgery, and you have bored surgeons.

McClintock was single, so there was the diversion of the WAC nurses as well as the local British girls, many of whom, to the great annoyance of the locals, were very attracted to the Yanks. Being a tall, handsome and relatively rich Yank ensured McClintock plenty of distractions. He occasionally brought several women along on their nights out, but Hamm and Schneider kept a respectful distance. They all sat and drank together, but the two husbands went home alone.

The general buzz in the pub made it hard to talk, and Schneider's headache was now over the top. He nudged Hamm to get moving, and Hamm nudged McClintock. Using Hamm's arm for support, McClintock shoved his chair back right into the legs of a passing marine infantry captain. The captain's tie was undone, and the top of his shirt was wet with beer. His face was flushed and perspiring. The marine howled as the chair's crossbar nailed him across the shins.

"Fuckin' A, man! What the hell are you doing?"

McClintock dropped down in his seat again and said, "Sorry, pal. Didn't see you there."

With no warning, the marine lit into McClintock, leaning down and grabbing him by his tie. He pushed his face into McClintock's and said, "Listen, you little prick. Watch what the hell you're doing, or I'll shove your head so far up your ass—"

In a blur, without moving from his chair, McClintock reached up and, grabbing the marine by the hair, butted him in the nose with his own forehead. Blood spurted over McClintock's hair as he swung the marine's head downward into the tabletop with a nauseating crunch.

Everyone else pushed back out of the way as blood poured onto the wooden table. Although the marine struggled, McClintock kept him pinned there as he reached for the Scotch bottle in front of him. He took the bottle by the neck and smashed it across the edge of the table, coming up with a jagged glass sword in his hand. As the marine struggled, McClintock pressed the razor-like shards of the broken bottle against the man's cheek just below his eye, threatening to blind him if he struggled any more.

"Jesus, Ted," Schneider shouted, "take it easy!"

Ignoring Schneider, McClintock stayed calm and focused. The marine stopped struggling and became perfectly still. A trickle of blood started from just below his left eyelid.

Schneider sat frozen to his seat, his heart racing. He had never been so close to violence. As a surgeon, he saw the results of violence, but never the act itself. Sweat gathered in the groove of his back, sending a chill through his body and making him shiver with fear.

"Ted..." Hamm said in a whisper. "Don't do it."

Hamm leaned forward and placed a hand on McClintock's arm, the one holding the marine's hair, careful not to disturb the delicate position of the broken bottle in the other hand.

"Let him go, Ted. He got the message."

Without acknowledging Hamm, McClintock leaned close to the man's left ear, and whispered something no one else could hear. The man's eyes widened. He moved his head fractionally in assent to whatever McClintock had said to him. The marine's lips moved, and only Schneider saw him mouth the words, "Yes, sir."

McClintock slowly withdrew the bottle, the marine's blood already clotting along its jagged edge. The cheek was bleeding steadily and a bluish discoloration spread beneath the loose skin under the eye, blood diffusing into the delicate tissues. If nothing else, the marine captain was going to show up at assembly in the morning with a huge shiner and a jagged laceration.

When McClintock let go of the marine's hair, the man stood slowly and backed away. McClintock followed the retreat with the jagged bottle; then, when the marine was out of striking distance, he put the bottle down gently and pulled his chair back to the table. McClintock didn't give the marine another glance.

As soon as the marine was out of McClintock's reach, he turned and fled the pub. All eyes watched in silence as the door slammed shut. Several other marines silently followed their shamed partner out the door, humiliated that one of their own could be so easily defeated, and by a medical officer, no less. Then the entire room erupted in noisy jeering and cheering.

Ignoring the tumult of congratulations McClintock caught Schneider's eye. He read something there: a glint of admiration? Something...

McClintock leaned across the table to Schneider. In a voice that only Schneider and Hamm could hear, he said, "Don't ever even *think* about doing something like that, Steve."

"Why not?" Schneider said affecting a light bravado he didn't really feel. "It worked, didn't it?"

"Yeah," McClintock said, "But, I was ready to cut out his eyes if I had to. You wouldn't. I know it and so do you."

Schneider furrowed his brows, looking questioningly at McClintock.

McClintock said, "This ain't poker, Steve. There's no bluffing."

Then he pushed away from the table and threw a ten-pound note down to cover the damages.

McClintock walked alone to the door, steady as a rock. Hamm and Schneider followed. Schneider's knees shook so badly he could barely walk. The three made their way to their jeep and, with a sober Hamm at the wheel, drove through the cold misty night back to barracks.

Chapter Five

Hamm crouched in the lee of the ship's overhang, staying under the cover of the starboard gun platform. Icy water ran off the roof in a steady stream onto his helmet. He huddled as closely as he could against the steel wall, trying to keep the rain from running into his field jacket and down his neck. His shoulder muscles were already stiff and sore from the awkward position. In the darkness, he stared at his boots, which still showed the remains of his own fresh vomit.

The LST—Landing Ship Tank—was the military's name for naval boats designed for amphibious landings, capable of carrying huge numbers of troops, supplies, and vehicles and placing them directly on the beach.

"I don't know where it keeps coming from," Hamm said, looking up at his medic, Gene Antonelli. "I haven't eaten anything in hours. But it keeps coming up."

Antonelli looked at Hamm's boots and shrugged. As he did, water found its way into his own field jacket, sending a shiver of cold through his already wet body.

"I couldn't tell ya, Doc," Antonelli said. "You must've had a lot of chow down there to begin with. Still sick?"

"No, not really. Actually, after I throw up, I feel pretty good for a while."

Antonelli retreated further into his field jacket, huddling against the bulkhead and ducking out of the rain. He was a solidly built guy, dark and muscular, though he seemed very young to Hamm. Most of the time they couldn't keep Antonelli quiet; he showed a surprising enthusiasm for even the most awful tasks that fell to an army medic. But on the LST, even Antonelli had grown ominously quiet, as if aware of horrors none of the rest had yet considered.

They had been at sea for twenty-four hours. Five days earlier the ship had weighed anchor on the south coast of England and pulled out into the English Channel. Then the weather had worsened, and the ship returned to anchor; then back to sea and back to anchor again. Back and forth for five awful days, waiting for the signal.

But, the weather refused to quit. One rainsquall followed another. The seas grew calm for a few hours, cruelly tantalizing the officers and men, bringing hope that the worst weather was over. Then the wind would move in again and toss the whole fleet around like toys. Thousands of ships of every size and description dotted the horizon off the coast of England, just out of sight of Normandy. Twelve hundred huge fighting ships trained their guns on the French coast, jockeying in the rough seas to hold their positions. More than eight hundred U.S. and British transports carried more than one hundred and fifty thousand troops—almost all of them cold and seasick, all of them scared.

Four thousand landing craft hovered next to the troop carriers, waiting their turn to shuttle the men and arms ashore under the waiting guns of the German Wehrmacht. Day and night, destroyers hurried back and forth around the fleet, like sheep dogs worrying away the wolves. The wolves were German U-boats waiting for targets. Waiting for these men.

Back in England, twenty-five thousand more men and women waited for the weather to clear sufficiently, waiting for planes and gliders that would drop them into the darkness behind the German lines, just hours before the main assault would begin.

General Eisenhower and his staff at Supreme Headquarters Allied Expeditionary Forces (SHAEF) agonized over the final decision. To go, or not to go? Timing was critical. The invasion force required the longest possible daylight hours for air cover, favorable tides to clear the underwater obstacles the Germans had placed in front of the beach, and a full moon to light up the targets for the bombers. As the men waited on board the ships, the generals deliberated, the hours sped by, and a deadline approached that might postpone the entire invasion. It could be as much as a month before the conditions would be right again. In that time, the Germans might finally uncover the war's greatest secret, discovering the location of the real place for the landing and further fortify their positions. It was just too risky to delay.

In addition to all the power at sea, ten thousand warplanes waited to take flight and cover the attack. The biggest invasion in the history of humankind was about to begin. For those who survived, the most powerful and pervasive memory for the rest of their lives would be of vomit and fear.

It was cold for June. Wherever the men were unprotected, the rain inevitably found its way in, making everyone all the more miserable.

"Think it'll be tonight?" Hamm asked into the darkness.

"Beats the shit out of me, Doc," Antonelli said without raising his head from the protection of his field jacket. His voice was muffled and low inside his collar. "I'm just the lowly medic. Nobody tells me a fuckin' thing."

"Me, too," Hamm said. "I'm just the surgeon. Nobody tells me anything either."

Hamm was nearly old enough to be Antonelli's father, and as a major, he far outranked the young medic. Yet there on the LST, waiting in the miserable wet darkness and cold, a bond was forming that transcended rank and age. They might all easily die side by side in the coming hours. The bullets and the shrapnel would honor neither rank nor age.

They sat in silence a while longer. In the calm between squalls, Hamm took off his helmet and looked again at the red crosses painted in white circles on the front and back. He had studied it a hundred times, each time wondering if the German gunners would respect his position as a front-line surgeon, a non-combatant, a man without a gun. Or would they take aim at the white circle and red crosshairs? Hamm looked at Antonelli and saw the same red crosses on the medic's helmet.

A damned fine target, he thought.

When the downpour resumed, Hamm slouched down further, trying to shrink away from the rain, the vomit, and the fear. He thought about going below to try to warm up for a while, but his last trip below had been a bad mistake. It was stifling hot down there. All the toilets were full and overflowing. Soggy, feculent toilet paper hung draped from the steel toilet seats like bedraggled decorations from a drunken fraternity party. Even the fire pails were topped off with vomit. If he put down his helmet long enough, someone was bound to puke into it. The lack of any visible horizon or landmarks down there made it much worse below than topside. The endless groaning of his shipmates only made him feel worse. No, he thought, better to be cold and wet with a little fresh air in his face than to suffocate in the fumes from the excrement and the barf below. Hell of a way to go to war.

Hamm's thoughts were interrupted by a noise and some movement. There was a scuffling and a shifting in the darkness next to him. A big hulking figure pushed into the limited space beneath the overhang, edging Hamm nearer the downpour.

"Hey! Give me a break, will you, pal?" he muttered.

"Give me a break, my ass, Hamm." McClintock bullied into the place between Antonelli and Hamm, crashing down with a loud exhalation of air.

"Major Hamm, sir, to you," he muttered.

"Major Hamm, sir, my ass."

"Ah, Ted. Your mother would be proud."

Antonelli leaned over to McClintock and said, "Hey, Major McClintock. How ya doin'?"

"Great, Gene. Just great! I love this shit. I really do."

Hamm shifted again, trying to claim some more space under the overhang, making everyone move a little to stay out of the rain. The wind increased suddenly, changing the direction of the downpour from vertical to horizontal. The water slammed into their faces, as well as into everyone else's on deck.

"Fuck," said Antonelli.

"Fuck," said McClintock and Hamm.

Another figure moved into the shelter of the overhang, now making it impossible for any of them to stay out of the rain. Dick Higgenson, their second medic, shoved his tall muscular mass into the small gap between Antonelli and McClintock. Hamm slid over without a word and stared into the night. Antonelli looked at Higgenson but said nothing.

Higgenson was pure Middle America: He was a quiet guy, almost taciturn. Quite the opposite of Antonelli, the dark ebullient Italian. None of them really knew anything about Higgenson. He had been to college, but no one knew which one, how many years he finished, or what he studied. He was twenty-two. They all wondered why he had not gone to Officer Candidate School, why he wasn't an officer? He was certainly bright enough.

As soon as Higgenson was settled Hamm said, "Hey, Dick, how come you're a medic? I mean, why didn't you go to OCS?"

Higgenson laughed. "OCS? I'm a CO, Doc: a Conscientious Objector. A Quaker. My draft board looked upon my religious beliefs with a dollop of cynicism. My beliefs forbid me to kill, but my draft board still had the power to assign me to a noncombatant position. And they did just that."

As a medic, the draft board knew, Higgenson would be at greater risk than the soldiers around him; at greater risk than their own sons who were now at war. Higgenson's job would require him, like Antonelli and all the medics, to rush to the aid of the wounded under fire, to expose themselves to the same weapons that had found their targets in the wounded. It was unlikely that Higgenson or Antonelli would survive very long once the invasion began. The army had predicted a life expectancy for medics on the beach at about twenty minutes. If they made it off the beach, they might live a little longer.

McClintock could only shake his head. "Fucking draft board...."

Little by little, the men adjusted their positions on the cramped deck and shared the lee of the overhang as best they could. The rain and wind increased in intensity again.

It struck Hamm as funny that, with the thousands of men on the ship, there was still that urge to stick around the guys he knew, to stay with his group. He instinctively glanced around, looking for Schneider, half expecting to see him huddling behind McClintock under the overhang. He realized how much he missed his friend, and feared for Steve's safety.

Just before the invasion, Steve had volunteered for other duty. When he'd heard about it, Hamm had said, "Didn't anyone tell you never to volunteer? Jesus, Steve!"

But it was too late to back out, and now Schneider was gone. Hamm hadn't seen him for nearly two weeks before they embarked.

"Ted, what do you think got into Steve?" Hamm asked. "Volunteering for a mission like that?"

"Beats the shit out of me. Those guys are nuts going in ahead of the invasion. And those crates they're flying in."

"Bad enough out here," Hamm said. "But up there?"

"You know," McClintock said, "I don't even know how *these* poor bastards are going to fight when they hit that beach. They've been puking their guts out for days. I know they're not sleeping. They're a bunch of wrecks."

"Yeah." Hamm nodded. "I'd hate to think we're depending on them for protection from the Jerries."

"For that matter," McClintock went on, "they can't count on us for much either. When's the last time you slept, Hamm?"

"About an hour ago. Couple of minutes. Then I had to barf again. Look at my boots." All heads turned to look at Hamm's boots, though they all could smell what was there.

"Wouldn't worry about that, Doc," Antonelli said. "You're gonna get them cleaned off in the sea in a few hours anyway."

"You could wipe them with these French bank notes they gave us," McClintock said, holding up several soggy wrinkled French francs. "A lot of good they'll be when we hit that beach."

"I'll take yours, Major." Antonelli grinned. Wisely, McClintock put the notes back in his jacket.

Another soaking squall blew in. "When will they put us onto the Rhino ferries?" Antonelli asked.

"I think the big LSTs are going to tow the ferries into sight of the beach," Hamm said. "Then we'll board the ferries. I'd rather stay on the LST as long as possible. At least they're maneuverable, and there's some protection. We're going to be sitting ducks out there on those Rhinos. I don't think they can make more than three knots. How the hell can the Jerries miss them?"

"Well, the trucks have red crosses all over them," said Higgenson. "Must be thirty, forty trucks on board. And two Red Cross flags as well. They're not supposed to shoot at those."

"Yeah, right! Count on it," McClintock said.

Hamm said, "I don't know if we're better off with these red crosses or not. I don't trust the Krauts not to shoot us just for the hell of it. I've been hearing some awful stuff about what's going on over there," he said, nodding in the general direction of France.

"It's all bullshit," said Antonelli.

"I heard the docs and the medics in the Pacific are tearing the red crosses off their uniforms," McClintock said, "because the Japs never signed the Geneva Convention. They're shooting at the damned things."

"Well the Jerries did sign the Geneva Convention," Hamm said, "but I still don't trust them."

The squall intensified. None of the men moved. They just turtled their heads down into their collars and lowered their helmets against the storm. From where Hamm sat, the helmets of his little group looked like a small field of red crosses all lined up in a row, like a newly dug cemetery.

Chapter Six

6 June 1944, 0330 Hours
A Horsa Glider Over Turqueville, France

As Marsh and Schneider talked quietly together, Lieutenant Jim Sorenson, the senior commando officer, moved down the aisle. He was a big, dark-haired man, all business. The doctor in Schneider could see the remnants of a broken nose. It appeared to be an old injury either not fixed at all or fixed by a rather ordinary surgeon. Sorenson was regular army through and through. Schneider hardly knew him, but it made Schneider feel safer just to have him near.

With his big pack, and his rifle, and his Colt .45 on his hip, Sorenson exuded this don't-fuck-with-me air that made Schneider very glad he was on their side. Sorenson had a three-day growth of beard no matter when he shaved. He was rough and splintery, and all hard edges. Schneider noticed that Sorensen didn't even hold on as he moved about in the turbulent flight. When Schneider thought of the pictures of the German officers he had seen, all dressed up in their new, tailored uniforms with long coats and high collars, he decided he would take Sorenson over them any time.

"Hey, LT, enjoying the ride?" Marsh said as Sorenson passed.

Sorenson nodded to Marsh and to Schneider as he crouched behind the pilot and stared out the window. Then something dawned on Schneider, jolting him back into the moment.

Jesus. What if the invasion's called off? What if the shitty weather doesn't clear? Or gets worse? What'll happen to the advance elements like us? What'll happen to me?

"Shittyassratfuck!" he said under his breath.

"Sir?" Marsh was looking at him again.

"Nothing."

Schneider felt his gut tighten again as his bladder complained, insisting in spasms that he relieve the pressure. God only knew if he could hold it until they landed or, more to the point, crash-landed. He used to hate the makeshift army latrines with no cubicles for privacy. Men on both sides grunting and farting close enough to touch. But he would give anything for one of those now.

But, above everything else—even his bladder—was the fear. That same pervasive, nagging fear he'd had since he was seventeen years old was back to gnaw at him—the same one Susan had thrown in his face that day in the kitchen as they fought over his orders to report for duty. She just couldn't let it go.

Would he, after all, prove her right and disgrace himself in front of his men, his colleagues?

As he watched Sorenson, the light on the ceiling of the glider came on. Lieutenant Sorenson turned aft toward the men.

"Disengaging from the tow plane now, gentlemen. Seven minutes 'til touchdown."

There was a muffled thud. The glider jerked as the towline was released from the nose hook. The pilot of the C-47 added full power, and the tow plane climbed steeply to the right. The glider pilot eased the stick forward and began his descent to the left, angling away from the C-47 as far as possible. In seconds, the tow plane was out of sight, and the only noise was the sound of the air rushing over the glider's wings. Schneider found himself desperately wishing he were in that tow plane heading back to England to a warm bed, decent food and a clean toilet. And away from the fighting.

The last year and a half in England was looking a lot better from up here. Why had he been so anxious to get into battle? To volunteer! I must have heard a thousand times, "Never volunteer for anything!"

What an idiot I am to be here. I'm no soldier. I'm a doctor for Christ's sake.

In the darkness, the silent wooden plane felt suspended; there was much less turbulence now, the plane's movement barely perceptible except for the intermittent vibration of the wind on the wings. It was so quiet, almost peaceful.

Schneider saw it first. He thought it was a shooting star, but it was too bright. Too big. Too slow. Too close. Then Marsh's head popped up and he elbowed Schneider, pointing to the windshield. They leaned forward trying to see around Lieutenant Sorenson's bulky frame. White balls of light were streaking up from below. The lights moved in slow motion at first then appeared to rise with an acceleration that made a streaking blur across the sky as they passed the plane. An eerie glow reflected inside the aircraft.

Too close. Way too close! Schneider thought.

"Ack-ack," muttered Sorenson in an unconcerned voice that gave Schneider even greater concern.

The intensity of the antiaircraft fire increased until the sky filled with exploding light as they descended over the German ground batteries.

Marsh leaned toward Schneider and said, "The white ones are tracers. Every fifth round."

"So that means that there are five times as many bullets coming our way as I see out there?"

"Yessir."

"Great!"

As he spoke, a shudder passed through the glider. The pilot shoved his stick forward and to the right. The swerving of the plane threw everyone off balance, everyone except Sorenson, who was as calm as ever. Sorenson pointed to the right wing where there were several holes torn through the canvas. Shreds of tattered fabric fluttered in the wind. For the moment, Schneider was glad there were no wing tanks filled with gasoline to explode. However, the erratic movements of the glider were not from the hits on the wing, but were actually made by the pilot, who was trying to fly a zigzag pattern to elude the ack-ack batteries. Now, even Sorenson was holding on, albeit with just one hand.

After a quiet minute, more fire spewed upward at them from the ground. The glider shook violently as a ragged piece of the floorboard splintered inward ten feet aft of where Marsh and Schneider were sitting. The flak exited the glider through the ceiling, leaving in its path a whistling wind that sounded like someone playing an impossibly long and breathy note on a wooden flute. A moment later another shock along the fuselage, and more of the floor tore away, the flak this time exiting through the side wall. One of the soldiers opposite Schneider quietly slumped forward. Half his face and head had been torn away. A river of his blood circumscribed the exit hole in the glider, running onto the floor and pooling at the man's feet.

Schneider recognized the glistening gray particles on the splintered wall as pieces of brain. Marsh started to rise out of his seat, but Schneider put a hand on his arm and shook his head. Marsh hesitated, and then slumped back onto the bench.

Schneider knew immediately that the man was dead. One of the soldiers looked pleadingly at Schneider and Marsh. Both of them shook their heads and turned back toward the windshield.

Sorenson returned to his space on the bench for the landing. He looked with pity at the dead soldier slumped awkwardly half on and half off the wooden bench. His first casualty, and he hadn't even touched down yet.

At the command from Sorenson, the men locked their arms together and braced their feet against the opposite bench in preparation for the rough landing.

The ground was now only fifty feet below. Schneider was absolutely transfixed by the sight. He might have been in a movie back home. A detachment had come over him as if he were only a spectator to this bizarre scene. There, in a field ahead, were the remains of three burning German tanks, taken out by the Allies' bombing. The outlines of their long cannons were silhouetted by the orange flames. To his horror, he could now see that the glider was lined up for a perfect landing right on top of one of the tanks. He leaned forward, trying to alert the pilot, whose attention seemed fixed on something to the left. He leaned over and shook the pilot's shoulder. As the man slumped forward onto the controls, Schneider saw a small wound in his left temple that matched a ragged hole in the windshield. The exit wound was a jagged edge of steel in his helmet with pieces of brain and hair dangling out from underneath.

"Oh, shit!"

"What?" Marsh asked.

"Pilot's dead," Schneider said.

"Fuckin' A! Who's flyin'?"

But Sorenson was already there, pulling the pilot off the controls and trying, while standing over the dead pilot, to wrestle the craft back into a shallower glide path. An instant later, the glider stalled and dove in among the tanks.

With the impact, men flew through the air and landed in the field as the hard steel of the tanks shredded the plywood glider. Only a few men remained inside the tail section of the glider. Still strapped fast in his seat, the dead pilot looked as if he had brought his glider down to a safe landing and was now ready for the post-flight checklist.

Marsh and Schneider threw themselves through the side of the glider, precisely where the door had been. Neither struck any part of the plane as they flew out, but both landed hard against the ground. Mercifully, the landing spot was free of rocks or trees, so neither of them sustained more than bad bruises and, in Marsh's case, a sprained ankle.

Schneider knew only that he was alive, little else mattered. He tried to control the trembling and searched among the men scattered around him, wondering how many had survived. Who was hurt? Who could fight?

An unnatural silence followed the crash. The only sounds were the far-off reports of the ack-ack and the low moaning of the injured men in the field. The group appeared, for the moment at least, to have landed undetected by the Germans.

Schneider collected himself and crawled over to Marsh. "You OK?"

"Yeah. Yeah, I'm fine, Doc. I twisted my ankle, but I'm OK."

They lay low in the grass for another moment, trying to assess their position. Their drop zone was supposed to be near a place called Turqueville. But neither Marsh nor Schneider knew where they actually were. Schneider started to move, his bladder again insisting he take action.

But Marsh grabbed his sleeve and said, "Stay down for a minute, Doc. We need to see what the fuck is goin' on here, and where the fuck we are."

"Yeah. OK. You have any idea?"

"No. You?"

"No."

A rustling in the grass startled both of them. But there was nothing either of them could do to protect themselves. They were both unarmed. They held their breath as the grass parted. Schneider wanted to bolt, but his reason overruled his instincts. There was no place to run.

Lieutenant Sorenson broke through the cover. He was clearly in terrible pain. Blood covered his forehead, and his shoulders were stained with dry clots. He seemed to be pulling himself along the ground with his hands rather than crawling on his knees.

"I thought I saw you guys over here," Sorenson said through clenched teeth. "You OK?"

"Yessir." Marsh answered.

"You don't look so great, Lieutenant," Schneider said. "Let me have a look at you."

Suddenly, Schneider felt more in control. His fear dissipated as he began to work. Even his urge to urinate faded as he prepared to do what he knew.

"Where are you hurt, Jim?"

"My leg. Left leg. I'm pretty sure it's broken."

"How about that head wound?"

"Cut it when I went through the wall. It's just a scratch. Bleeding a lot, but I'm sure it's OK. Never lost consciousness or anything."

Schneider started to reach for Sorenson, but the lieutenant waved him off.

"Marsh," Sorenson said. "Start crawling around and see what you find. See how many of the men are alive. Find out who's well enough to fight and who needs the doc," he said motioning to Schneider with his head. "You know what to do. I have no idea if there's Jerries out there, but we need a perimeter now. Move out, but for Christ's sake, keep it quiet."

"Yes, sir!" Marsh whispered, and moved away across the field, crawling on his belly. He was gone in seconds. Schneider and Sorenson were alone. They hoped.

"OK, Lieutenant. Just roll onto your back, and let me look at that leg."

Sorenson rolled over, groaning as he did. His huge pack kept him from lying flat, but he did the best he could, never letting go of his rifle. Schneider leaned closer and placed his hands on the lieutenant's leg. He moved his fingers along the leg below the knee, feeling more than seeing anything. Keeping the pressure of his fingertips as light as possible, he sought out the injury while trying not to inflict any more pain. Sorenson surely had enough of that.

At a point halfway between the knee and the ankle, Schneider felt the deformity of the fracture. He stopped momentarily and leaned closer, trying to see in the darkness. There was a dark stain surrounding the bump in Sorenson's leg which looked black in the night. This was blood, the crimson color obscured by the combination of the dark pants and the lack of any real light. "Damn!" Schneider said, under his breath.

"What is it?" Sorenson asked, without any emotion. He might have been speaking about someone else.

"A minute more. I'll let you know for sure." Schneider reached into his belt and removed a small stiletto knife, an illegal souvenir given to him years ago by a policeman one night in the emergency room. He pressed the button to open the blade (the blade he had sharpened for hours while passing time at the airbase, waiting for the invasion to begin) and slit Sorenson's pant leg from the ankle to the knee. When he pulled the material aside, his fingers came away wet from a sticky fluid he recognized all too well. He could smell the blood that, as always, left a metallic taste on his tongue.

"Shit!"

"What?"

There in the dimness Schneider could see the white edges of an exposed bone fragment protruding through Sorenson's pale skin. The laceration was jagged and a steady ooze of blood was forcing its way out around the fragments as well as from within the marrow of the shattered tibia. Schneider couldn't see the much smaller fibula but suspected it was fractured, too. The two were usually injured together.

"It's a compound fracture. Bone came through the skin. Damn! How did you manage to crawl over here, Jim? That must have hurt like hell!"

In a voice lacking all emotion, Sorenson said, "Doc, I can't begin to tell you how much this hurts."

Schneider shook his head. "Listen, I need to dress this and get it splinted. Get you to a clearing station…if there is one."

"Hold on. I'm still in command of this group, and I need to be here with my men. Can't you just set it and get me going again?"

"You've been watching too many westerns, Jim. Look, I can't reduce this here in the field. You'd never stand the pain....Well, maybe you could. But it's a dirty wound. If I reduce it here—set it—the dirt and shit from this field will get pulled back into your leg. You'd end up with gas gangrene and lose that leg and probably your life. Then where would we be?"

"OK. OK. I get it. What do you have to do?"

"I'm going to clean it out with water, then put some sulfur powder on it. We'll pack it in a dressing and find something to splint it with."

"You got splints?"

"To tell you the truth, I don't have shit. Most of the equipment is scattered around the field. I need some of your men to help me round it up. Maybe when Marsh gets back. Meantime, I got some stuff in my own pack to get started."

"OK. Just do what you can. I need to command this group, or we're all dead."

There was nothing more to say. Schneider reached over and pulled his battered pack closer. He opened his canteen and began to pour water over the exposed bone and muscle tissue. Sorenson sucked air sharply in through his teeth.

"Oh, fuck that hurts!"

"Sorry, Jim. But this is the most important part. Grit your teeth. I'm not done."

"Grit my ass, Doc. But...goddamn it, just go ahead and do it!"

"When Marsh gets back, I can give you some morphine. He's got the whole supply."

"Not now. I need a clear head tonight. That stuff'll make me fuzzy-headed."

"Don't worry. With the kind of pain you're in for, the morphine won't touch your brain. You'll stay alert."

"Whatever you say."

Schneider poured more water over the wound. Sorenson gritted his teeth but didn't make a sound. Next, Schneider dug through his kit and pulled out a packet of sufanilimide powder, the crystalline antibiotic they carried in the field packs. Tearing off the top with his teeth, he sprinkled two packets of the powder over the exposed bone and the tattered shreds of muscle. Sorenson seemed not to feel it. At least he made no sound. Schneider dug out some more supplies, scattering them on the ground. He found a gauze dressing and applied it to the wound. He was feeling good now. Confident in doing what he knew how to do; what they trained him to do. The work took him out of the fear of combat and finally allowed him to focus on something he could control.

Placing Sorenson's hand on the gauze pad, he said, "Hold this down here while I find something to wrap it with. Press as hard as you can stand it. It'll help control the bleeding and the swelling."

Sorenson did as he was instructed, pressing harder than Schneider would have done, wincing even as he pressed.

"Easy, man! Easy! Don't *punish* yourself. Just hard enough to control the bleeding."

Schneider continued to search for the roller gauze to wrap the bandages, but there was none.

"Ah, fuck! Marsh has the roller gauze. We'll just have to wait for him."

In a few minutes they heard the staccato of small arms fire, though they couldn't tell the exact direction. Ominously, it seemed to be all around them. Schneider found himself shrinking into the earth, pressing his body lower, trying to disappear from the danger. Then, from nowhere, Marsh burst into the clearing. Sorenson grabbed his rifle and swung it around, nearly hitting Marsh in the chest with the muzzle. For a second, Schneider thought Sorenson might kill Marsh.

Marsh stopped dead in his tracks, "Whoa! Whoa! Whoa! It's me! Marsh!"

"Shit, Marsh!" Sorenson said, dropping the muzzle, grimacing as he rejoined his pain. "What the hell are you sneaking up on us for? You're gonna get killed you do that."

"Sorry, sir! It won't happen again."

"Bet your ass it won't happen again. Next time I'll fucking shoot you."

"Yessir."

"So, what's out there?"

Marsh moved closer and settled in next to Sorenson. "Well, sir, we seem to be pretty well surrounded. I don't know if the Krauts know our location yet. I couldn't see them from where I was, so I guess they can't see us either. There's a hell of a lot of random firing out there, though."

"How about our men?"

"There's ten dead that I can count. I don't know from which of the three gliders. Several more wounded and too badly hurt to move on their own. I gave them some morphine and first aid, but they need to be evac'd pretty soon. So I figure there's about twenty, twenty-five more fit to fight. They're doin' a little recon, and then they're gonna join up at the glider when they can."

Schneider cut in. "Hey, Marsh, how many morphine Syrettes you have in that pack?"

"'Bout three dozen, Doc. Maybe a few more. There's a lot in the main surgical kit, but I haven't found it yet. Must be around here somewhere."

"OK, give me a dozen Syrettes, some rolls of gauze and something to splint the lieutenant's leg here. He's got an open fracture. I need to get him back to a clearing station. Wherever the hell that is."

Marsh looked at Sorenson's leg and whistled softly. He saw the deformity in the limb and the ring of blood rapidly spreading through the pant leg.

"Got the gauze and morphine, but I don't have any splints, sir. They're all in the main supply kit. But I'll round up something from the field here. Be right back."

With that, he disappeared into the darkness faster than he had arrived. Schneider was about to call out after him for something else but hesitated to shout for fear of giving away their position. He turned back to Sorenson. "Let's get some morphine into you, Jim."

"You sure this won't fuck up my head?"

"No, no. You'll be fine. You'll be lucky if it does anything for this kind of pain."

"I've got to be clear-headed."

"Listen, these Syrettes have a standard dose of ten milligrams each. A big guy like you could take fifteen milligrams easy, even if you didn't have all this pain. With a fracture like yours, you'll be lucky if you get any relief."

Schneider took out a single Syrette, a hypodermic needle attached to what looked like a miniature toothpaste tube holding the dose of morphine. He popped off the needle cover with his teeth, and spit it away. He found a patch of skin uncovered by the torn pants, and stabbed the needle deep into the muscle beneath. Then he slowly squeezed the contents of the morphine dose into Sorenson's muscle. Sorenson looked at him and said, "Thanks, Steve."

It was the first time in all those months he'd used Schneider's first name. Schneider didn't know what to make of it.

They were both quiet for a moment. They stopped and listened to the night. The gunfire had ceased momentarily. They strained to hear the next shots and to try to assess where they were coming from.

"What now?" Schneider finally asked.

"Well, we got to get the hell out of here. But, I don't know where we are. That glider is our biggest problem," Sorenson said motioning with his head. "The Krauts'll know exactly where we are from its location, and they'll just zero in on it. It's gonna get very dangerous around here very soon."

It was as if the Germans were listening to him. As soon as he spoke there was the sound of a bottle whistling through the air. Only it wasn't a bottle, and both Sorenson and Schneider knew it. They ducked as a terrible explosion rocked the ground near the glider. Earth and rock flew up and rained down upon them. Schneider found himself pressing his face into the mud, his arms covering his head. Cowering would have described it better. He wondered if Sorenson were watching, or if he were doing the same thing.

"Fuck that! Let's get out of here now!" Sorenson said. "We need some distance between us and that glider." He tried to roll over and crawl, but the bolt of pain that shot through him literally knocked him back to earth more forcefully than the blast from the German mortar.

"Don't move. Let me do it."

"How the hell you gonna carry me?"

"I'm not. I'm going to drag you."

As Schneider moved to Sorenson's shoulders, Marsh burst through the brush again. This time, Sorenson made no move to get his gun. He was in much too much pain.

"Gotta get the hell outta here, LT!" Marsh said.

"Just do it," Sorenson said through his teeth.

Marsh moved in before Schneider could get a grip on Sorenson. He grabbed the lieutenant under the armpits and began to drag him off into the brush. Schneider quickly collected his own gear as well as Marsh's and followed the disappearing trail.

The morphine may have been changing Sorenson's experience of the pain, but he was still clearly in agony. As gentle as Marsh tried to be, the going was bumpy. There was no trail, only the path through the brush that Marsh was clearing with Sorenson's body. Schneider followed behind, trying not to become separated from the only real soldier in sight.

Finally, the firing stopped, bringing an ominous quiet to the night. Behind them, the remains of the gliders burned in the field, giving an eerie orange cast to the dark night sky. The only noise was the dragging of Sorenson's heavy body over the wet brush and grass. The three of them stopped near the edge of a clearing. From their position, they could see the land rise as it approached a small country road. They waited in the cover while Marsh rested and Sorenson collected his jangled nerves. He admitted to Schneider that in all his career as a professional soldier, he had never known such pain.

When he caught his breath, he whispered to Schneider and Marsh, "Now hear me. We're in a lot of shit here. The men are scattered. They don't know where we are, and I don't know where they are. God only knows where they scattered to since that mortar attack. So, keep your heads down and your voices down until we can regroup and find our way to our target. We don't want to go shooting each other. Well, at least you guys aren't gonna shoot anyone."

Schneider pursed his lips and just shook his head. Marsh laughed silently.

They sat in silence for a moment and watched the road. The night was slowly giving way to the coming dawn. Schneider looked at Sorenson and could see what he was thinking: If they didn't regroup by daylight, they would be slaughtered.

In the short time since the crash, Schneider had begun to feel the fear that had quieted down in the earlier lull, and was now welling up inside his core. He found himself giving way to panic. He wanted to run, to run far away to anywhere but where he was. He knew he couldn't because if he did he would be killed. But still the urge was there, and it took all his will to stay put.

To do something positive, Schneider drew his knees up under his abdomen, and unbuttoned his pants. Pointing away as best he could, he urinated awkwardly in that position, trying all at once to hurry the process while keeping himself dry. Marsh and Sorenson seemed not to notice, and Schneider wondered if they had already relieved themselves.

As the night ebbed, the quiet remained. The men all leaned back in silence and waited.

Chapter Seven

6 June 1944, 0630 Hours
Rhino Ferry 47-Fox, the English Channel, Normandy

Four wet hours after they left the LST, Hammer, McClintock, Antonelli and Higgenson were all huddled together again, this time in the lee of one of the ambulances on board Rhino Ferry 47-Fox. They had been off-loaded from the LST before first light, and Hammer was none too happy to be on board this slow tub of a barge. They presented too easy a target for the German 88s mounted high up on those cliffs.

Salt spray was coming in from windward, and the ferry was mushing along in the frothing waves at less than three knots. Their entire complement of sixty men was still vaguely green and, now that they were within earshot of the battle, overwhelmed with fear.

"Hey, Doc. We're not exactly racing into that beach yet, are we?" Antonelli said.

"Nope. Not exactly, Gene," Hamm said.

Earlier, at 0400 hours, the call had come for all navy personnel to man battle stations. Orders went out for the other groups to assemble at their pre-arranged positions. The men began climbing down into the thousands of assault craft that would take them to the beach. Hamm's surgical group mustered on deck and was transferred to the Rhino. The craft was a flat-bottomed barge with two large outboard motors to propel it to the beach after it was cast off from the LST towline. It was slow, unstable, and un-maneuverable. With only two feet of freeboard, the Rhino provided a trip that was more like swimming into battle than riding.

Though the night was still black, they had all watched the pre-assault bombardment with a mixture of awe and terror. When the big guns from the great battle ships and cruisers opened up behind them, it was hard to tell what was happening. The nearly continuous blast from the huge naval artillery dominated the sky, lighting up the bottom of the clouds with flashes of white and orange. Hamm couldn't imagine that anyone on the receiving end of that terrible barrage could survive. They all stared open-mouthed at the fury of the blast.

Earlier in the night, they could hear the deep-throated drone of the bombers and glider tow planes. Hamm wondered which of those planes might be carrying Schneider. He feared for his friend's life, and he sensed the terror that must pervade such a mission.

Aboard the Rhino, they were all glad not to be on the receiving end of that bombardment, though they knew full well that their safety was a temporary and relative condition. In a few hours, they would not only be treating victims of the coming carnage, but would be, for the first time in most of their lives, under fire as well. And the Germans had had a long time to prepare for them.

"Think this coxswain knows what the hell he's doing?" Antonelli asked.

"Why?" Hamm said.

"Well he's weavin' all over the fuckin' place. I could puke just watchin' our wake."

"I don't think he's got any choice. Those two outboards don't do much for him. This vessel is just not maneuverable."

"That doesn't instill very much confidence, does it?" said McClintock.

"It sure don't," said Antonelli.

The Rhino waddled in the chop stirred by the wake of the hundreds of landing craft scurrying toward the beach. Longer rolling waves threatened to crest over the sides of the ferry. A hundred yards to the right, another Rhino struggled to keep on course. Then they all watched in horror as, without warning, shells from German 88s high on a cliff bracketed the other Rhino. The first shell exploded about ten yards to the starboard side. The second was closer and to port.

"Oh, shit," Antonelli said in the dull monotone of inevitability, pointing to the Rhino. "Those poor bastards are done for."

Everyone strained to see what Antonelli was pointing at. To their horror, the third explosion landed directly in the center of the slow-moving target. Flames and sequential explosions ripped up and down the surface of the ferry as the gasoline tanks of the ambulances exploded. Men were hurled into the air, silhouetted against the yellow-orange flames. Others in the stern and the bow dived into the sea to escape the fire. Some of the men were already ablaze as they leaped into the churning ocean, their bodies silhouetted in the light of their own fires. Some disappeared under the weight of their packs; others clung to life jackets and floating debris. Burning gas and oil soon engulfed every man left in the water, and they, too, disappeared into the blackness of the water and smoke.

"Dear God," Higgenson whispered.

"You were wondering about the protective value of these red crosses..." McClintock said.

"No fuckin' way," Antonelli said.

Hamm could only stare, feeling a combination of rising anger and overwhelming fear.

Suddenly, the Rhino's outboards roared as the coxswain added full power. The craft responded sluggishly to the port helm, but it was too late. While their focus was on the Rhino ferry under attack, their own course had strayed into the path of another of the Rhinos. The two heavily laden craft slowly collided, port bow against starboard bow. The impact threw everyone to the deck. Metallic voices shouted angrily through loud hailers; orders flew back and forth between the ferries.

Their coxswain gunned his outboards in reverse, and after an eternally long response time, the craft shuddered, finally pulling off from its connection to the other Rhino with the scream of tearing metal.

"Fuck all! I told you this asshole couldn't drive," Antonelli said.

Hamm pulled himself to his knees. He was soaked with seawater up to his thighs. His boots sloshed in the bilge water, several inches deeper since the crash. The officer on the other ferry was still screaming through his loud hailer, but nobody paid any attention to what he was saying.

"Nice way start to our war, eh Hamm?" McClintock said, his voice calm.

"Yeah, great." Hamm glanced at him.

McClintock looked at his own drenched pants. "Y'all tell the cox I need to stop back at the hotel and have the valet clean and press these trousers."

Hamm laughed and shook his head. "Me, too."

They both started laughing. Antonelli sat in seawater up to his waist. Then he, too, began to laugh.

"Yeah. I think we should call this whole invasion shit off 'til we get some dry skivvies."

They were still laughing when an explosion knocked all three of them flat onto the deck again. Only their helmets kept them from suffering severe head injuries.

"What the fuck was that?" Antonelli yelled.

McClintock and Hamm stayed down, lying prone in the bilges. The seawater soaked into their ponchos and jackets, and they immediately began to shiver.

A shrill voice from the bow broke through the roar of the water and the engines and the explosions from the 88s.

"Medic! Medic! Help me!"

Antonelli, Higgenson, and Hamm scrambled forward together, all three on their knees, splashing through the oily bilge. More explosions from the 88s bracketed the boat. Several blasts of heavy ordinance struck directly on board, destroying at least one ambulance. Mercifully, no fire or secondary explosions followed.

"Medic!" the voice cried again.

They followed the sound, weaving their way between the rows of ambulances.

"There he is," Antonelli said.

The soldier lay in the bilge, nearly covered with water. He was shivering and still whimpering, "Medic!" when they got to him. All around, enlisted men sprayed streams of firefighting foam onto small fires spreading along the deck. Others sloshed seawater from the bilges, using their helmets as buckets.

"It's OK, pal. We're here. We're here. Where are you hit?" Higgenson asked.

"My thigh! Oh, Christ it hurts."

"Take it easy. We're here now." He turned to Hamm. "You wanna take this, Doc?"

Hamm looked down to examine the wound. Even in the darkness, he could see where the shrapnel had torn through the soldier's thigh and exited from the groin. His pants were torn open, a pulsatile stream of blood squirting from the wound. The bloody fountain trailed into the bilge water, making dark frills as it diluted away in the rocking of the ferry with seawater sloshing around the wounded man.

"Get some pressure on that wound, Dick." Hamm said. "It's the femoral artery. Probably the vein too. He's bleeding like hell. We've got to control that first, then we'll see what else we can do. Put some pressure on the wound with this. Here," he said, handing Higgenson a large wad of gauze from his pack. "Hold this tight as you can."

Higgenson wadded up the gauze and pressed it into the wound. The man howled with pain as Higgenson pushed down with the heels of both hands, his arms locked at the elbows, all his body weight on the wound. The bleeding slowed, but crimson streamers still flowed between his fingers.

Hamm started to get up. He turned to Higgenson and said, "Dick, try to focus the pressure on a smaller area. You won't have to press so hard. See if you can get your fingertips right on the artery and vein." Turning to Antonelli, he said, "Gene, come with me. I'm going to open one of these ambulances so we can work in there. We'll make a little operating room and get him out of this filthy water."

McClintock soon arrived and moved in next to the soldier. He said, "Get a couple of IV's started, Dick. You got any in your pack?"

"Yessir. But, you'll have to get it. I'm only just keeping up here with the bleeding."

"OK. I got it," McClintock said, rummaging through Higgenson's pack. He came up with a bottle of plasma, and some more morphine Syrettes. For the moment he was thrilled to see such abundance in the medication he was sure to need in great amounts.

He found some IV tubing, and a large-bore needle. McClintock fit the needle onto the tubing, placed a rubber tourniquet and found a vein in the man's arm. He inserted the needle and watched as the blood flowed back into the tubing, appearing black in the subdued light. He flushed the tubing with some of the plasma and hooked up the bottle. Then he taped the needle to the skin, making an extra loop to keep it from getting accidentally tugged out when they moved the man.

Higgenson was still applying pressure to the wound. The soldier had stopped screaming and was now moaning softly to himself.

"What's your name, soldier?" Higgenson asked, trying to divert the man's attention from his pain.

"Thomas, sir."

"You don't have to call me sir," Higgenson said. "I'm not an officer."

"Yes, sir."

McClintock looked around for some more help. Two figures appeared from behind the truck. They were carrying a litter. McClintock yelled, "Over here!"

The men hurried out of the darkness. They were both medics in their platoon.

"Get him on the litter," McClintock ordered. "Where's Major Hammer?"

"He's back in that ambulance, sir," one of the men said. "He's setting up an OR."

The three men placed the litter into the water and floated Thomas onto it. Higgenson continued to hold pressure on the wound. While the other medics lifted the stretcher, McClintock held the freely flowing plasma high overhead. They rose as a unit and made for the ambulance.

Meanwhile, Hamm and Antonelli were working fast. They set up a place for the litter in the middle of the floor. Then Hamm opened a small operating pack and was busy setting out the instruments and suture material he would need.

McClintock appeared in the doorway. "Hey, honey. We're home."

"Very funny, Ted."

Hamm and Higgenson lifted Thomas into the crowded space. McClintock moved to the head of the makeshift operating room.

"Well if it ain't Philly General Hospital!"

Hamm shook his head and said, "You think it's going to get better when we hit that beach?"

"I don't know if we're ever going to hit that beach. I just noticed that we're heading back out to sea toward the LSTs again," McClintock said.

Hamm turned momentarily to look out of the ambulance front window. He shook his head in amazement. "Jesus!"

McClintock went on, "That would suit me just fine. I don't think I'm going to like it much on that beach."

It seemed then that the very act of focusing on the familiar, of feeling in charge, took them out of their fear, even while their lives were on the line. With constant explosions raining all around them, and the 88s zeroing in on the toy-like boats carrying them into battle, the medical team focused on one man—their patient—whose life was slipping away. They gave him all their attention, in return for which he would take their minds out of the battle zone, if only for a few minutes.

Hamm kneeled at the right side of the litter, motioning Higgenson to the left to assist and hand instruments. A lantern glowed overhead. McClintock kneeled at the head of the litter and opened a can of ether.

"Gene, better switch that lantern off," McClintock said, "before we blow ourselves up with this ether. Get some flashlights and start the engine. We can use the dome lights once the engine's going."

Antonelli climbed into the cab and turned over the diesel engine. The vibrations shook the truck irregularly at first, sputtering and coughing before catching and settling into a relatively steady rhythm. The overhead bulb, dim as it was, added a bit to the light. McClintock began administering anesthesia. Soon the whole truck reeked of the familiar eye-burning odor of the open-drop ether. Hamm said,

"Better open the windows, guys, or we're all going to be sick in here pretty soon." The wind was wet and blustery, but it was better than the fumes, which had already begun to make everyone a little queasy.

"I hope we're not going to operate on our knees for this whole war," McClintock said.

"What do you want me to do, Doc?" Higgenson asked Hamm.

"Just keep the pressure on. You seemed to have stopped the bleeding...or at least slowed it to a trickle."

Hamm arranged a few more instruments. McClintock already had two big IVs running with plasma streaming into one arm and saline into the other. He was working on the second unit of plasma and wondered how many of these they would use before the war was over. The truth was that none of them could even begin to know just how many.

"OK, I'm set," Hamm said. "Dick, just let up the pressure really slowly. My side first so you expose the artery and vein to me. That's it."

Higgenson rolled his hands toward himself, showing Hamm the vessels. By now the gauze was a deep crimson wad of jellied blood, almost unrecognizable as a surgical dressing. But, the blood had clotted, and that was good. Higgenson lifted his fingers a bit more. Hamm saw the edge of the femoral vein.

"A little more. OK, stop! Right there. Hold it. There's a tear in the side of the vein. Let me fix that while you hold the artery."

Hamm loaded a suture-ligature and drove the needle carefully through the sidewall tear in the vein. Then he tied a series of square knots. Finally, he put a continuous running suture along the tear until the vein was closed. He tied another series of knots and cut the excess suture away.

"OK. Let up some more pressure."

Higgenson continued to expose the vessels.

"More. More. That's it. The vein's OK now. Let's look at the artery and...."

A blast rocked the boat, momentarily deafening everyone. The Rhino ferry shifted in the water then righted violently, throwing everyone in the truck off balance. Hamm braced his left hand against the floor to keep from falling over, making him plunge his sterile gloved hand into the filthy bilge water.

"Shit! What was that?"

"Another hit," McClintock said. "Let's get this operation over as quick as you can. We might get blasted again any minute."

"Well, I can't quit until I see what's with the artery. Move that gauze, Dick."

Higgenson removed the packing, and as the clotted jelly came away, blood from the tear in the artery spurted into the air. The column of blood hit the ceiling of the truck, and dripped back into the wound.

"Oh, shit!" Hamm said. "So much for goddamned sterile technique."

Hamm had just taken off the glove that had touched the truck floor. But now he knew there was no time for such luxuries as sterile technique, so he plunged his bare hand into the wound. He couldn't see anything as the blood filled the wound faster than Higgenson could sponge it out. They had no suction set up there as they would have in a real operating room.

"Watch out!" Hamm said, impatiently pushing Higgenson's hand out of the way. He placed his fingers into the puddle of blood, carefully feeling for the pulse of the femoral artery. He was grateful for the pulse, as it meant that McClintock was keeping up with the plasma volume replacement. But it also made for brisk bleeding. When Hamm found the artery, he used his thumb and index fingers as clamps, gently squeezing the artery shut just where it entered the wound upstream from the injury. The spurting stopped, but the back-bleeding continued to fill the wound from below the tear.

"Give me that vascular clamp," Hamm said to Higgenson .

Higgenson took a curved clamp from the small tray and handed it to Hamm, who guided it over his fingers, sliding the clamp over the artery and tightening its adjustable jaws. He removed his fingers, but the spurting continued. He gently tightened the jaws of the ratcheted clamp another click. The spurting stopped, but some bright red blood continued to seep into the wound.

Without waiting, he felt his way to below the tear and repeated the clamping process. All the bleeding stopped, allowing Higgenson to sponge it dry.

"If only we had a little suction," McClintock said.

"If! If! If my grandmother had balls, she'd be my grandfather," Hamm said impatiently.

"Cute," said McClintock.

Hamm didn't answer. He was staring into the ragged wound where he could clearly see the sutured femoral vein and the two clamps above and below the tear on the artery.

"OK, everything's under control now. Ted, make sure we're ahead on the plasma. He's lost a shitload of blood. I'm going to try to—"

Another blast rocked the ferry. And another. And another. They were bracketed. The overhead light went out, and one flashlight fell from its perch. The only light remaining was from a flashlight in the hands of Antonelli. Barely enough to see the wound, much less finish the operation.

"Call it, Hamm." It was McClintock. "Finish up now."

"OK. Wake him up. I'm gonna pack this wound open and leave the clamps in place. Hate to lose those vascular clamps; we're going to sure need them before long."

Still another explosion rocked the ferry. Antonelli held his place keeping the light on the wound. McClintock took the ether mask off the soldier's face, and let him breathe the cold damp air of the Normandy night. Soon the man started to moan. A frothy foam appeared at his lips, and he coughed several times. McClintock gently wiped the man's lips with a gauze pad.

"It's OK, pal," McClintock said quietly, wiping the froth away. "Take some deep breaths. Nice and deep."

"OK. The wound is packed," Hamm said. "Dick, wrap it with a heavy roller gauze, and make sure those clamps are covered so they won't get torn off when we transport him." Hamm turned to an enlisted man. "You know which way we're going?"

Another blast. Everyone ducked.

"We're heading back out to the transports, sir. Goin' to get on another Rhino, I guess. This one ain't gonna make it to the beach." Still another blast rocked the boat. It was a miracle they weren't on fire.

Hamm flinched with each blast. "I hope we make it back to the ships," he said. He envisioned the other Rhino ferry going up in flames, the men jumping into the water, the burning and the drowning, all the horrible ways to die. Hamm had seen death many times in his career and had often pondered the most terrible ways to go. He shuddered at the thought of first burning, then drowning in the sea. His two worst nightmares were coming true all around him.

The fear was beginning to overwhelm him, and Hamm began to shake. He squeezed his fists to still the tremor, to hide the fear from his friends. He realized that he needed more casualties to keep him busy, and he was ashamed of that thought. He knew, however, that as soon as they hit the beach he would have more than enough work to keep him occupied.

Higgenson finished packing the wound and binding it. He tore off his gloves and dropped them to the floor.

"What's going to happen to that artery, sir? To the leg?"

Hamm shrugged. It was all he could do to speak. Finally, the words came.

"If we can get him to a real OR in time—a couple of hours or less— we might be able to repair the artery. Or someone else will. Then he might keep his leg."

Hamm was so happy that the Rhino ferry had turned and run, heading back to the big ships and out of range of the 88s. He willed them out of range of the German guns.

"Nothing more we can do here with this shelling going on. We need to get him evac'd right away."

"Yessir," Higgenson said.

The wounded soldier coughed again and opened his eyes. He began to moan quietly.

McClintock leaned down and said softly, "It's OK, son. It's OK. The war's over. You're going home."

Chapter Eight

6 June 1944, 0630
Near Turqueville, France

As the trio kept watch, two human shapes appeared along the edge of the road. The men were moving silently, stealthily, carrying their rifles at the ready. Schneider exhaled when he saw the silhouette of the soldiers. He started to rise, to call out to the men to regroup with them there in the bush. A hand slammed into his mouth, knocking him backwards and cutting his upper lip. As he hit the dirt, he heard a distant voice from the road say, "Wo sind die verdammten Amerikannen?"

Schneider froze. He held his breath. Marsh's hand was still clamped over his mouth. Nobody moved.

An answering voice said, "Ich kenne nicht. Machen Sie still!"

As Marsh slowly released his hand from Schneider's mouth, he whispered, "Sorry, sir."

Schneider pressed his body deeper into the wet earth. He translated the German words to himself.

"Where are the damned Americans?" Then, "I don't know. Keep quiet."

The dark, bulky figures continued their stalking, looking from side to side, from the ground to the path ahead. The shadows drifted away from Sorenson and his men in the darkness until, finally, they merged with the trees and the sky and the night. And they were gone.

Schneider shivered as the dampness seeped into his undershirt. He wondered how long it would be before he would ever be warm and dry again. When would he ever stop shivering?

Schneider leaned closer to Sorenson, seeking protection from the lieutenant's massive frame. Then he realized what he was doing and felt ashamed. But he didn't move away. They waited a few interminable minutes more before daring to speak. He wondered how many Germans were out there—the ones they couldn't see.

Schneider relaxed into the earth, trying to regulate his breathing. He realized that it was not just the nearness of the German soldiers that had rattled him so. It was the thought of his own German heritage.

Both his parents had immigrated to America just before World War I. It was the combination of economics and anti-Semitism that had driven them from their homeland of so many generations. As Schneider grew up in America, his parents' German accents had been an embarrassment to him. Although his schoolmates rarely said anything—for lots of parents in his neighborhood were immigrants from somewhere or other—he did everything he could to avoid bringing his parents into contact with the families of his friends. He rarely had friends sleep over and never invited his parents to school functions. He struggled to make sure that his accent was always cleanly American.

Although he was fluent in German, which his parents spoke at home, he never let any of his friends or colleagues know it. Even as he grew older and supposedly more mature, he couldn't bring himself to be identified with his German heritage in any way. In high school and college, he chose to study French rather than continue learning German. Then, when Hitler rose to power and the Nazis became a symbol of everything evil, he found himself even more self-conscious about his parents and his name.

Now on this battlefield in France, he was haunted by his name and his ancestry. At home, he knew his parents were suffering from the universal hatred of all things German. They were confused and embarrassed. It was worse for the Japanese, he realized. They were being placed in internment camps. People of German descent were harder to identify.

His parents considered themselves to be as loyal to America as anyone native born. Didn't they, themselves, have their only son fighting on the battlefield against Hitler's Wehrmacht? Wasn't their very own child, born in America, risking his life to save American soldiers? Was there not a flag with a blue star hanging in their living room window? How could their neighbors think that they were anything but loyal Americans as well? They had left Germany decades before, long before the war. Who could doubt their loyalty? Schneider knew what they were suffering that very minute, and it made him ashamed.

Then there was the religious issue as well. They were Jewish. In the past several years, he had begun to participate in some of the rituals of Judaism. No, he was not a regular at services, but he wanted his little girls, Emily and Anna, to have a religious education, and he was still, after all, a Jew. The family celebrated the religious holidays, at least what were called "the happy holidays." Hanukah and Passover were great family gatherings and required very little in the way of serious prayer. Schneider found reasons to stay away from temple on Yom Kippur and Rosh Hashanah. Those services were too long. He claimed they bored the girls, but he was the one who became bored. Emily just went to sleep, and Anna played little games to pass the time. Susan was somewhere in the middle. Her parents observed most of the holidays, and went to temple when it wasn't even a holiday. That always confounded Schneider. The services were mostly in Hebrew, and though he understood the prayers, he found the ritual sterile and totally without meaning. But in the early years of their marriage, he went quietly—peace at any price.

So, Schneider now realized he had been the most disloyal of all to his parents and to his ancestors. He wondered what he would have done had he been born in Germany under the Nazis. He felt as bigoted as his parents' angry neighbors.

As the men lay agonizing over their situation, they heard a rustling in the bush. A few yards away, men were crawling quietly in their direction. Ignoring his own pain, Sorenson rolled carefully onto his side and positioned himself facing the noise. He unclipped the holster of his sidearm and handed it butt first to Marsh. Marsh looked at it as if Sorenson were handing him a rattlesnake. He took a deep breath then extended his hand to take the weapon. Schneider watched as if he were at the movies. He felt detached yet somehow involved, like a witness to a crime. The red crosses on his helmet and on Marsh's marked them as noncombatants. The same rules that should preclude the Germans from firing on them should have kept them from firing at the Germans. But, out of the darkness and the fear came a detachment, an instinct for survival that superseded the written rules of war. Schneider didn't have time to process the thoughts. He knew only that he was glad Marsh had the gun and that Sorenson was ready with his rifle. In fact, if he could have spoken at that moment, he would have asked for a .45 for himself, even though he knew nothing about how to use it. Instead, he pressed his body again more deeply into the ground, drawing upon the instinct of a worm to bury itself in the damp protective coolness of the earth.

Sorenson was as still as a rock as he trained his weapon on the approaching movement in the brush. Schneider could only admire the lieutenant's steel as he fought off his pain and controlled his breathing. The decision to fire or hold fire would be made in the instant the brush parted and Sorenson's brain processed the information in his sights. Schneider wondered about the effects of the morphine on Sorenson's reflexes and judgment. He needn't have worried.

Marsh and Schneider found themselves holding their breath again. Sorenson leveled his rifle, bracing his elbows against the earth as he squinted down the site. He waited, slowly exhaling his breath, pressing the fleshy tip of his finger lightly on the trigger. Once, his thumb went to the safety to assure himself that it was off.

Marsh watched Sorenson, and then he too felt for the safety on his .45 caliber pistol. Marsh's safety was on. He shook his head, feeling stupid as well as scared, he quietly thumbed the safety to the off position. Then he pulled back on the slide to make sure there was a bullet in the chamber. With what sounded to Marsh like a super-loud click, an unspent cartridge ejected and fell with a soft thud onto the ground as another round was chambered from the magazine. Surely the approaching men had heard the noise. Sorenson glanced at Marsh and shook his head.

They waited.

The movement in the brush slowly closed in on them. It seemed that four or five people were approaching their little clearing. Finally, the muzzle of a rifle parted the vegetation, and a weapon extended into their space. The muzzle inched slowly forward passing directly in front of Schneider's face. Without thinking Schneider reached out and grabbed the moist steel in both his hands, yanking it up and away. He lurched to one knee and screamed with the effort as he pulled the rifle, and the soldier attached to it, into the clearing. A single shot exploded in his ears as the fingers of the man involuntarily pulled the trigger. The man hurtled into the clearing and yanked on the weapon, which Schneider held firmly at the other end. Marsh propelled himself forward, dropping the man with a kick to the chest. He pinned the soldier to the ground, and rammed the muzzle of his .45 into the man's forehead. All this in the space of a few seconds.

The clearing erupted with soldiers struggling for position, weapons drawn, each afraid to fire for fear of hitting a comrade in the close quarters.

"Hold it! Hold it! Hold it!" Sorenson shouted. "Fuckin' A! Hold your fire!"

There was a moment of stillness as the soldiers recognized each other. All of them dropped to the ground and remained perfectly still, as if they might nullify the racket they just made. The only sound was of labored breathing, and then again, the silence.

There were four newcomers to the group. All of them were commandoes from the destroyed glider. Schneider released the rifle, and Marsh pulled back, releasing the cocked hammer of his .45. He realized how close he had come to killing Sergeant Frank Kelly. He backed away and then, reversing his grip, handed the weapon back to Sorenson. Sorenson clicked the safety on, holstered the weapon, and rebuttoned the canvas flap. Marsh felt around in the wet grass, coming up with the cartridge he had ejected from the chamber of the .45. He handed it sheepishly back to Sorenson.

Sorenson took the cartridge and turned to Schneider with a smile. "Nice job, Doc."

Schneider was still fighting off the temporary deafness from the blast so near his ears. He shook his head again and poked a finger into his ear. He never heard the compliment.

The men organized themselves into a tight group.

Sorenson rolled over onto his back. He was in terrible pain now, and it showed. The men looked at the deformed leg and winced at the thought of what Sorenson must be going through. It would be Sergeant Kelly, they thought, who would have to lead the platoon now. Kelly was still rubbing at his ribs where Marsh had kicked him. In any other situation but this, there would have been hell to pay. But Kelly was a professional.

Sorenson repositioned himself and said, "Kelly, what's going on? What's our position? Strength?"

"I don't know, sir. There's the four of us right here, and twelve more about a hundred yards west of here waiting in a little stand of trees near the road. We can regroup with them as soon as you're ready to move. But, I'm damned if I know where we are. This map's no good until we get an initial fix on something."

"Well, we'll have to make our way to the road and pick a direction until we can get some recon. Maybe find a house or a farm and get oriented. We should have been dropped in somewhere southeast of Turqueville, but who the fuck knows where we are, what with the pilot dead. First thing we need to do is see where the Krauts are. Kelly, you take these men and scout the area. See who's out there. Marsh and Schneider will make a splint for this leg of mine and take me to the rest of the men. Which way do you think they are?"

Kelly pointed to the west and said, "They should be right down there. Just go straight. Parallel the road, and you can't miss them. They'll be hunkered down in the tree line. But, let 'em know you're coming, or they might start shooting. Everyone is spooked after losing all those men in the glider. It's a fuckin' mess, Lieutenant."

"I know. But, we've got to get the doc to the clearing station at Turqueville. If there is a clearing station at Turqueville. If not, we'll make one, I guess. I have a feeling we'll have to fight our way there. There might be more of our glider groups around here. If we can link up with them, we might have a fighting force again. Let's get going. It isn't gonna get any safer here when the sun comes up, which won't be long."

Sorenson looked to the west for a moment and then at his watch. "They should be getting ready to hit the beaches just about now."

Kelly and his men crept off toward the road, while Marsh gathered some branches for a splint. Schneider organized the medical packs, taking out some heavy bandages to pad the splint. When they were ready, Marsh held the leg and Schneider lined up the stout branches.

They bound the leg from the ankle to the hip, keeping it as straight as they could.

"You think I'm gonna lose this leg, Doc?" It was the first time he had admitted the possibility to himself.

"No, I don't think so," Schneider said. "If we can get this cleaned up and debride—uh, cut out some of that dead tissue under anesthesia—we'll have a good chance to save it. We should get some of that penicillin, too."

"Some what?"

"New drug. For infections. An antibiotic. Kills a lot of these germs. We have a good supply of it with the field hospitals. We should get ten thousand units of that stuff into you as soon as possible."

"Well, let's go do it."

With Marsh in front holding the legs as carefully as he could, and Schneider in the rear supporting Sorenson's shoulders, they moved off along the edge of the road. The sun was now brightening the dawn, and the darkness receded from the east. Now they would see the enemy about the same time the enemy would see them. But only the enemy was in position to shoot.

Chapter Nine

6 June 1944, 0700 Hours
On the Road near Turqueville, France

Sergeant Kelly and his men were slowly gathering at the side of the road. There had been no enemy movement since they arrived at their new position. Kelly had deployed scouts and then tried to figure out his position on the map. But, there were no landmarks, no houses, no signs of a village. There was only a road without signposts.

After about twenty minutes of waiting, Kelly heard a low whistle from the scout just west of their position. Then he saw the figures of Schneider and Marsh struggling through the brush with Sorenson.

"Garcia. Fox. Go help with Lieutenant Sorenson," Kelly said.

The two privates scurried out of their cover, moving fast and low. They each grabbed a limb, and dragged Sorenson back into the cover of the woods. Sorenson made a muffled cry as one of the men stumbled, putting pressure on the fractured leg.

Moments later, Kelly and Sorenson were conferring over the map.

"Any idea where we are, Sergeant?" Sorenson said.

"I don't have a fuckin' clue, LT," Kelly said. "We could be anywhere."

"Any activity here?"

"Nothing in the last thirty, forty minutes. Not a peep."

"Well, we should just move out along this road. Choose a direction and go for it. We'll assume we were close to the drop zone, and go from there. If we're wrong, we'll soon find out, and we can back track. At least we'll be doing *something*."

"Yessir," Kelly said. "So, if we were dropped where we shoulda been, we're south, southeast of Turqueville. So we should make it north, northwest. That way," he said, pointing up the road.

"Where are all the road signs, Sergeant?" Schneider asked Kelly.

"Gone, Major. The Jerries probably took them down long ago."

Kelly's men had done the very same thing in England before the invasion. They had removed all road signs to confuse any possible German invasion. It was amazing, Schneider realized, how dependent they were on something as simple as street signs, even in their own neighborhoods. Now the Germans had done the same to them, and they were lost.

"OK. Let's do it," Sorenson said. "Get some of your men to make a litter for me, and we'll move out. Get some sturdy branches and canvas from the packs. You can't keep dragging my ass all over hell and back. Too slow. And it hurts."

"Yessir." Kelly said. Just as he was about to give the orders, Schneider looked up toward the road. He couldn't believe his eyes.

"Holy shit! Look at that!"

The entire group turned to see where he was pointing. There, in the early light, was a young boy of ten or eleven years leading a donkey-drawn cart. He wore torn, short, gray wool pants and sandals over ragged, black knee socks. His gray sweater was coming apart at the neck, and the sleeves were tattered as well. Empty milk cans clanged alongside the animal. The boy tapped the donkey's rump with a switch, unaware of the soldiers in the bush.

Schneider called out to him. "Hey! Pssst! Ici. Ici!"

The boy stopped suddenly, cringing against the side of the donkey. He stared into the woods, and then saw the cluster of soldiers. He started to back away, pushing still harder against the mud-crusted side of his donkey.

"Non! Non! Ne va pas! Nous sommes Américains. Amis. Nous sommes votre amis!" Don't run away. We're friends. Americans.

The boy stopped and stared. "Americains? Americains? Americains!" he shouted, jumping in place and hugging his animal. He turned to the donkey and told the animal, "Ils sont Americains!" He stood in the middle of the road excited, expectant.

"Schneider! Get out there and talk to him. Find out where the hell we are," Sorenson said. "And quietly."

Schneider began to crawl out of the cover, and ran up to the roadside in a crouch. Sorenson called after him, "And commandeer that cart for me. I'll ride in it."

Schneider acknowledged the orders with a nod of his head but kept moving. The little boy was jumping up and down in place. As he got closer, the boy thrust out his arm, and clasped Schneider's hand in a strong grip. He pumped up and down twice as if he were shaking hands with an old friend he hadn't seen in a long time—or trying to get water from the town pump. He said with great excitement, "Bienvenue! Bienvenue! Je m'appelle Claude!"

"Bonjour, Claude. Je m'appelle Steve. Nous sommes perdus. Y a-t-il un village près d'ici?"

" Oui! Certainement. Je vive la bas. Moins que trois kilometres. Á Fauville."

Sorenson called out in a stage whisper, "What's going on?"

"This is Claude. He lives in Fauville, less than three kilometers from here. Right up this road."

"Did you tell him…ask him…if we could use the cart?"

Schneider turned to the boy, who was squinting around Schneider to see the soldiers in the shade of the brush. "Claude, nous avons un officier blessé, très serieuse…uh…nous avons besoin de votre… uh… carte… non…uh… wagon…non… mmm…this..." he said, now pointing at the pathetic little cart. "Celui-ci."

Claude hesitated. Then his eyes lit up and he raised his eyebrows. "Ah, oui! Une ambulance!"

Schneider laughed and said, "Oui! Oui! Une ambulance."

At the sound of the word, ambulance, two GIs and Marsh hurried from their cover, carrying Sorenson seated across locked wrists. The rest of the men followed, surveying the surroundings as they ran. One whistled, calling in the outlying scouts. The platoon, or what remained of it, surrounded the cart. Claude was grinning and going from soldier to soldier pumping their hands and saying his name.

There were a few strands of straw in the bottom of the splintered wooden floor, but nothing that would give any sort of comfort to Sorenson's butt. He settled down painfully, grabbing the sides for support. Schneider placed his pack under the major's knee and added Marsh's pack at the side to keep the leg from moving around. It was a lot better than carrying him all the way to Fauville, but it still was not going to be comfortable. From Fauville they would try to find Turqueville and, hopefully, some help. Schneider looked at his watch. It was too soon for any more morphine. He looked at Sorenson.

"Maybe another hour, Lieutenant."

Sorenson nodded his head. He knew what that meant. Sorenson looked to his men, happy to see they were correctly deployed, and waved a hand forward. He was still in command, and he was going to remain in command until he could properly turn the platoon over to a larger force. Perhaps at Turqueville.

The little band proceeded toward Fauville at a pace dictated by the donkey, whose name was Charles. Schneider asked Claude if the donkey were named after Général de Gaulle. Claude shook his head but then saluted with his palm facing forward, and making a very dour face—a pretty good imitation of Le Général.

After they had gone about a mile, the sun appeared over the eastern sky under the remnants of the D-Day clouds. Schneider kept thinking about the invasion forces and hoped to hell they had landed and were fighting their way to join up with him. It was the not knowing that was killing him.

As they were starting up a gentle hill, Sorenson called to Schneider, who was walking along with the boy, chatting in French.

"Hey, Doc, ask the kid if there are any Jerries around here."

Schneider spoke to the child, who opened both hands wide, blew a puff of air through his pursed lips and said, "Les Bosches? Bien sûr! Ils sont partout! Partout!"

"Oh, shit!" Schneider said. He yelled back to Sorenson. "He says they're everywhere. Everywhere!"

"Even in Fauville? His village?" Sorenson was incredulous.

Schneider spoke to the boy again.

Claude said, "Mais oui! Depuis plusieurs années."

"He said, 'Of course! They've been there for several years.'"

"Whoa! Hold up. Shit! Why the fuck didn't he tell us that before we almost got ourselves into a fuckin' ambush? Jesus Christ!"

Schneider turned to Claude and slightly modified the major's question. The boy replied to Schneider.

"He says he was hoping we would kill them all as soon as we got there. Says he was going to ask you if he could kill some of them himself. Seems he has a few scores to settle."

Claude began to speak rapidly. It was way too fast for Schneider.

"Whoa. Whoa. Slow down, son. Lentement. Plus lentement. It's been a long time."

The boy caught his breath for a moment and then began speaking again at exactly the same excited pace as before. Schneider shrugged and smiled, and watched Claude's lips carefully.

He translated for Sorenson. "He says he hates the Jerries, and that he wants them all dead. Since they took his village—apparently they have a command post there—they execute a bunch of citizens every time a German gets killed or a rail line is blown up by the Resistance—the Maquis. One of them was his uncle; they shot him in the public square. The kid saw the whole thing."

"Well, gather 'round here," Sorenson said. "If he's right, we got a little planning to do. We have shit for a strike force here. Not enough to take out a whole town and a goddamned command post. We need to join up with some more guys from our side, then we can clean the fuckers out of that town. A whole bunch of gliders were supposed to have come down in this neighborhood. Ask him if he's seen any other Americans."

"I already asked him that. He hasn't. Just us. But he says there's a small farmhouse up ahead; we could hole up there until we have a plan. Maybe try to locate other groups in the area."

"He said that?"

"No. He told me about the farmhouse. I'm suggesting we hole up there and regroup. We're sitting ducks out here on the road."

"OK, let's do it. Talbot," Sorenson shouted, "take the point."

The odd little procession moved out again, commandoes fore and aft as well as flanked out along the sides as much as their small numbers would allow. Claude led the donkey as the cart bounced painfully along the rocky road. Talbot, on point, stayed about fifty yards ahead of the group. Claude asked Schneider if he could go up there with Talbot. Schneider told him, no, that it was too dangerous to go ahead. The man on point was likely to be the first killed in a firefight or an ambush.

"Better stay here with me and the lieutenant," Schneider said in French.

"Mais, je n'ai pas peur!"

"I know you're not afraid," Schneider told Claude in French. "But, we don't want to lose any more men." He emphasized the word "men." Claude puffed up, proud to be part of this man's army, the army that would soon liberate his little town, just as De Gaulle would soon liberate France.

Schneider was walking alongside the cart now, keeping tabs on his only patient. He thought it odd that after such a terrible crash, and the ensuing mortar attack, that he would have only one patient to care for. The rest were all dead at the site. Not a single wounded man had survived long enough for Marsh or Schneider to be of any use. He thought that by now he would be up to his elbows in blood, filling the aid station or field hospital with wounded and operating around the clock with the rest of his team. But, that was not to be. Not yet.

The day had begun to warm up a bit. With the sun brightening the day, the nagging fears that had gripped Schneider's bowels had disappeared. He felt some modicum of calm, though now and then, for no reason at all, he found his heart racing and the sweat of fear breaking out on his forehead.

Schneider smiled at the little boy who so bravely led the little force toward Fauville, toward his home. All these months, while Schneider and the rest of the invasion force—hundreds of thousands of men and women—were holed up in the relative safety and comfort of England, Claude and his family had been virtual prisoners of the Germans. They had lived the war every day for the past four years. They were short of everything: food, clothing, hope. Their captors shared nothing with them except an unremitting hatred for a centuries old enemy, the Germans.

Holy shit! Four years this little guy has been at war, while most of that time I've been drinking warm beer and cooling my heels in England. Schneider wondered where he would have found the strength. What would he have done at Claude's age in such a situation?

Schneider couldn't help but marvel at the extreme bravery of the ordinary citizen caught up in the horrors of this war and how they lived every day as if it could be their last, hostages to the capricious cruelty of the enemy. Villagers all over France, all over Europe for that matter, waited for rescue by the coming of the Allies. Schneider was struck by the extraordinary bravery it must have taken to walk down the street in your very own village under the guns of the Nazis.

"Quel âge as tu, Claude?"

Claude answered that he was ten, and soon to be eleven.

Schneider shook his head in wonderment as he looked at little Claude, now a proud part of the army of liberation.

They soon came off the long low hill and onto a level space surrounded by woods, stone walls, and hedgerows. Marsh had wandered up to the point and was talking with Talbot. The rest of the men spaced out along the road.

Schneider was almost enjoying the walk into the emerging light as the sun warmed the air, his mind fleeing the battle for a few seconds at a time. Then he heard the sound of a coarse zipper being drawn shut, except that the sound was amplified a hundred times. Even Schneider knew it was no zipper.

Talbot, the point man, seemed to fly backwards then sprawled awkwardly on the ground. The morning air filled with the sound of automatic weapons and rifle fire. The commandoes hit the ground. Marsh quickly dropped into a drainage ditch alongside the road. Sorenson grabbed his rifle and went scrambling over the side of the cart, dragging his useless leg after him. Schneider flinched as a spray of wood splinters flew into his face, momentarily blinding him. He stood there wiping his fingers at his eyes. Sorenson grabbed at Schneider's ankles, jerking him to the ground and dragging him under the cart.

Schneider recovered his vision and wiped the remaining splinters from his cheeks. His hand came away with blood on it. He knew that he hadn't been shot, only cut by the sharp bits of wood.

Then he remembered Claude.

"Claude! Claude!" he shouted, and scrambled to get out from under the cart. But, he couldn't move. He was pinned down by Sorenson's strong arm, a fist holding the collar at the back of his field jacket.

"Hang on, Doc. Hang on," Sorenson said quietly. Too quietly.

Sorenson nodded in the direction of the front of the cart. There in the dirt, the donkey lay on its side, struggling in its traces to get back to its feet. Its braying was lost in the din of the fire fight still raging around it. The blood trailing from its back indicated that the animal had been shot in the spine and was paralyzed. Schneider wanted to shoot the beast and put it out of its misery. But, of course, he had no gun.

Then he realized that he still couldn't see Claude. He thought the boy had taken cover in the roadside ditch with the rest of the men. Schneider crawled deeper into his place under the cart with Sorenson, then saw a sandal protruding beyond the donkey's neck. The sandal was worn and torn and had been repaired many times with thread and tape. It was barely holding itself together even then. Schneider thought how easily he could fix it for Claude with just some canvas and some heavy surgical stay-sutures. He was, after all, a surgeon and had fixed things for Anna and Emily just like this. Then he saw the blood. Then the hand.

Schneider looked around the fallen donkey. There was Claude, eyes open, staring straight at him and Sorenson. The eyes were already drying in the sun, but tears remained wet on the child's cheek. He was pale. So pale. A minute ago he was flushed with pride and hope. He was part of an armed force that was going to liberate his village. He was going to be a hero. He was bringing Les Americains home. And now, this. Schneider's own girls' faces appeared where Claude was lying. Emily was just about Claude's age, and Schneider continued to see her face in place of Claude's. He struggled to hold back his tears.

The firing continued. The commandoes deployed around the cart, moving into the roadside ditches. Within minutes, they established a defensible cordon, now systematically destroying the German positions. Although they had no estimate of the strength of the enemy force, the commandoes went to work in a professional, almost detached, way. There was no use in thinking about the possibility that they might be hopelessly outnumbered. That only led to panic and inevitable defeat. They just picked targets and fired. One at a time.

Sorenson and Schneider stayed under the cart. After a few minutes, Schneider decided that there was no way he would leave his patient, and there was no safer place for Sorenson at the moment anyway.

Sorenson needed to make himself useful. With the greatest of difficulty, he rolled onto his side, and positioned his rifle across his left forearm, winding the canvas rifle sling into place. Schneider watched with a deep admiration as Sorenson picked out one target after another, firing but a single shot at each. It was as if each bullet were his last. He was completely in control, and Schneider envied his cool professionalism under fire. If it were necessary, Sorenson would go down taking the enemy with him. By Schneider's count, there were already four. Four dead Germans from four of Sorenson's bullets.

Schneider also realized that his own professionalism would be the only thing that would keep him functioning like Sorenson. He would treat one patient at a time, as Sorenson would kill one German at a time, for however long it took.

Five. Six. Seven. There were eight killed or wounded when Schneider stopped counting.

He turned back to Claude. Flies were now gathering on the boy's face. The tears had dried to little trails of white salt. Nothing of the lively little boy remained. Schneider began to cry. Quietly at first. Then, in ever increasing sobs, until his body shook. Sorenson took a moment to put his hand on Schneider's shoulder, squeezed it, then returned to his work.

Crack. Crack. Crack.

Nine. Ten. Eleven. Eleven dead Germans.

The firefight lasted a little more than twenty minutes. When the firing stopped, Sorenson and Schneider held their positions. Neither could tell if it were a lull in the battle or if one side had decimated the other. And which side?

They waited.

Then they heard the shouting. In English. One after another, voices checked in, telling their comrades that they were OK, and their sector was clear. The Germans were either all dead or had retreated.

Sorenson and Schneider watched as the men in their group reappeared. One by one, they gathered around the cart, while Marsh ran to help Talbot. Schneider pulled Sorenson from his place next to the rear wheels. He propped him in a sitting position against the wheel. Schneider scurried over to Claude, placing his fingers on the boy's neck, hoping against any reality that he might feel a pulse. But there was none.

Then they began to count the men as they returned: a roll call of the living.

One—only one—was missing. It was the point man, Talbot, who had been cut down in the first enfilade of the ambush. He lay where he had fallen, face up in the middle of the road.

Schneider rose and jogged down to the front of the line, his eyes searching the brush and the trees for possible snipers. But, he saw none. He found Marsh kneeling in the dirt next to Talbot. From Schneider's perspective he saw Marsh's shoulders moving up and down as if he were laughing. Then, as he got closer, he realized Marsh was sobbing. Schneider approached very slowly, in part so as not to startle him, and in part not to intrude on his grief.

When he got close to Talbot's body, he knelt directly across from Marsh.

"You OK, Andy?"

Marsh quickly collected himself and with a small movement wiped both his eyes, turning his face away from Schneider.

"Yessir."

"Can I...?" Schneider began, but was interrupted by a pouring forth of words—a deluge of story and sorrow and anguish—from Marsh, interspersed with sobbing and tears.

"I did everything they taught me, sir! Everything! I put pressure on the wounds; I lifted his legs; I tried to stop the bleeding, but nothing I did stopped it. It just ran through my fingers... Look. Look!" And he held out his hands, still covered in rapidly drying blood, the cuffs of his field jacket stained crimson nearly to his forearms.

Schneider scrambled around the body and took Marsh in his arms. He cradled and rocked the young medic while Marsh poured out his grief. Schneider stayed silent for a long while, until Marsh's sobbing ebbed and then finally stopped.

Then Schneider said, in the quietest voice, almost a whisper: "Listen, Andy. There was nothing you could have done. Almost every single wound was potentially fatal. Put them all together, and Talbot didn't have a chance. He was as good as gone the minute you got to him. I promise you, if he had been shot like this in the middle of an operating room, he would have still died."

Marsh started to protest. "But—"

"But nothing. I wouldn't lie to you. If I had been the first one here instead of you, nothing would have changed. I would have done what you did, and he still would have died. We don't do miracles. We just do our best. If you're going to be any use at all, you just have to do your best. Can't do more than that."

Schneider opened his arms and released Marsh's shoulders. He backed away and sat back on his haunches.

After a few more minutes Schneider and Marsh slowly struggled to their feet, their knees stiff from kneeling.

The two men walked back up the hill to where the rest of the men had gathered, and joined the group.

No one spoke, the braying of the donkey was the only sound.

"Kelly, shoot that donkey," Sorenson said quietly.

The paralyzed donkey was still trying to move. Three men gently took Claude's body away from the animal and placed it next to the cart. Kelly nodded to a private standing next to him. The private walked to the head of the donkey and placed the muzzle of his M-1 right behind the animal's left ear. There was a loud report. The animal bucked once and was still.

Sorenson wasted no more time.

"Kelly! Deploy another point man. Get Talbot's body back here to the cart, and give me his dog tags. Put the boy in the cart as well. We'll take him home to his family."

Kelly dispatched several more men, then took his knife from its scabbard and began cutting the worn leather traces that held the donkey. Six men dragged the animal to the side of the road. Marsh and Schneider gently lifted the boy's body into the cart. Only now could they see the pattern of bullets that had stitched their way across his abdomen and chest, making a trail from his right hip to his left shoulder. Mercifully, Schneider thought, his little face was untouched.

Schneider took some water from his canteen and wet his handkerchief. Then he carefully wiped the salt tracks from the boy's cheeks. He took the khaki blanket from his pack and wrapped Claude's body. He put the body along the inside of the cart, keeping a place for Talbot. After both bodies were in place, he helped Sorenson into what little space remained. Four men took up the worn wooden drawbars of the cart, and two more pushed from the rear. Schneider injected another Syrette of morphine into Sorenson's thigh. Then the band of men set

off again on the road to Fauville with what was left of the medical supplies and the bodies of their two dead comrades, Talbot and Claude.

Far behind, scattered somewhere in the fields and brush, lay the
remains of twenty commandoes killed in the crash of their glider.
Marsh's uniform jingled as he walked. Unknown to the rest of them
at the time, he had risked his life by taking the time to retrieve all the
dog tags from his fallen comrades.

It was seven o'clock in the morning. The D-Day Invasion was one
hour old.

Chapter Ten

6 June 1944, 0800 Hours
A Concentration Camp near Weimar, Germany

Dr. Meyer Berg was trying desperately not to shout. He held back his anger with all his strength, but he was close to losing his temper, and he knew it.

And that would be dangerous.

"If we don't find a place to isolate these patients," Berg said, "the typhus will spread through the camp like a wild fire. The dead will pile up, and in time there will be no survivors."

"My dear Herr Doktor Berg, it is of little consequence to me exactly how they die, only *that* they die," Standartenführer Himmel said to Berg, his voice dripping with Weltschmerz. "In fact, this epidemic might be just what we need."

Berg stepped back, assaulted by the words of the Waffen-SS colonel. He looked at the ground, assuming the position of subservience that he had developed so well in his four years in the camp: hands at his side, head down. No possibility or suggestion of resistance. Anything to survive just one more day. Anything.

Himmel's uniform was spotless, as usual. Clean and black and perfectly creased. It stood in stark contrast with Berg's ragged white coat, torn and stained with dried pus and old blood. Himmel wiped an imaginary speck of dirt from the glistening toe of his tall black boots with a clean white handkerchief. He leaned back in the rickety wooden chair, *Berg's* chair, and said, "My problem right now is the disposal of the bodies, not the killing of them. Burying takes too long, the ovens are overloaded, and I am short of manpower at the moment."

Himmel rose to go. He turned away from Berg and started for the door. "In any case, there can be no changes right now. None!"

As Himmel opened the door, Berg stepped toward him.

"Some DDT perhaps? Just some DDT?" He tried not to plead. "If we don't control the spread among the prisoners, then everyone will be at risk—even the *SS*."

Himmel hesitated then walked out into the gray morning, still talking with his back to Berg. He did not deign to look at Berg as he spoke.

"Yes, yes, then," he said with a wave of his hand. "See the Ober-leutnant. But make sure that all my men are deloused first. All of them. Then you may treat your own kind." He left without closing the door.

Berg walked wearily to the doorway and looked out into the day. My own kind, he thought. Doctors? Jews? Vermin?

The mud was getting deeper, and the skies showed no suggestion that the intermittent rains would end soon. The prisoners would be cooped up for yet another day. One more day of crowding and, with the crowding, the sharing of lice, and with the lice, the typhus. And with typhus, almost inevitably, death. If they were stronger, better nourished, more might survive. But, the way it was, the typhus took nearly everyone it touched.

Berg was barely holding himself together these days, as he had lost nearly forty pounds since he came to the camp. He was one of the lucky ones. There were always extra rations for the prisoner Herr Doktor. It had been four years. Four years inside the walls where Arbeit Macht Frei. Work would set them free. And in a way, it did, for his work as a doctor kept him alive, gave him a reason to survive. Forty-eight years old now, though he was sure he looked decades older.

And almost every day of those four years the trains came with the new prisoners. Thousands of them. They were disgorged into a siding, and there they saw the sign:

Arbeit Macht Frei

The great black Gothic letters arched over the curved portal.

That same day, fifteen hundred wretched souls would be deposited at the train platform. Of these, thirteen hundred would disappear into the gas chambers and from there into the open pits or the ovens. The "selection" would be made as soon as the prisoners emerged from the boxcars. The SS would give them a cursory glance and point left or right. To the left was death, and to the right was life, if it could be called that.

Most of the women and young children were killed right away. The old and the infirm were also killed. Only those with skills such as the doctors and the nurses or the mechanical engineers were spared. Also, of course, the very strong who could be useful doing hard physical labor in the camp. Those chosen to be factory workers usually survived three months, if they were lucky. In the mines and the quarries, a month.

Every day for four years, Berg watched from the hospital window as the living bodies moved this way and that, wandering the muddy yards. They all looked the same to him now. No color. Just a gray world of gray people. After they disappeared through the doors of "the showers," their bodies and their souls would rise into the air as gray smoke from the tall brick chimneys of the crematorium. Some of the inmates told Berg that they could tell from the smoke who was being burned that day. There was a different smell and a different color depending upon how much fat was left on the bodies fed into the ovens. Berg avoided dwelling upon that unhappy distinction.

The SS would get complaints from the German citizens living in the nearby town. The ashes, they said, were ruining their laundry as it hung out to dry in the sun.

"How awful for them", Berg sneered aloud.

For the past year, Berg had stopped learning the names of his patients. He would not listen when they told him of their families, of their lives. He didn't want to know them. He didn't want to like them. So many would die no matter what he did. How could he continue to share their pain by caring? He began to wonder how different he now was from the Waffen-SS who ran the camp. If the Jews weren't people, weren't individuals, it didn't quite hurt so much to lose them. He heard the German officers talking one day. They said that an inmate who arrives at this camp is already dead. So, killing them wasn't murder. You couldn't murder a dead man, after all.

It was just about four years ago to the day, he realized, that he had returned home from his clinic in Berlin. He had been working steadily since the early morning, seeing his post-operative patients at the hospital, then returning to the clinic after lunch. There had been no surgery that day, which was unusual for Berg. He had a busy practice and was well admired and respected by his peers. Considering the lingering effects in Germany of the Great Depression, his family wasn't too badly off. That he was a Jew didn't help. But, somehow he had gotten by until....

One day a colleague of his, Joseph Stein, a pediatrician, did not show up for work. No one had called to say where he was. A rumor circulated that he had disappeared. Nothing more. Then another man failed to show up for work, and another, all Jews.

Until it became clear that the rumors were true. But these rumors were almost benign at first. There were whispers of the arrests of political prisoners. Of jails. Of deportation. But, no one ever described this place.

For no one who left ever came back.

If anyone had described the conditions—the torture, the murder, the inhumanity, the bodies stacked thirty feet high like cord wood—who would have believed them? No one, surely. Not even Berg. No stretch of the imagination could accept such a terrible tale.

So Berg had continued his work at the clinic. Surely nobody would come for him. He had not spoken up for his missing comrades. He had not gone to the authorities. Better to stay silent and invisible, his wife Rachel advised him. Better to be a rabbit. Rachel had an understanding of these things. She was so often right.

Besides, he wanted to believe her, for in his heart, he was afraid. It would be better not to disturb the status quo. And safer. Surely Rachel was right.

No, they would never come for me. My family has been here for more than three hundred years. Not for me, surely. I'm a Doktor. I'm not political. No, they will not come for me.

If only he had known. Much of his family, his sister and his younger brother, had left for America years earlier. They implored Berg to join them, but Berg refused.

"You are being irrational," he told his sister. "Yes, things are bad, but they will get better. This madman will fall, as have all the madmen who tried to rule the world. Besides, what would I do there? I would have to retrain before I could practice surgery again. I would have to start all over like a new graduate. I'm too old for that."

His sister and his brother had pleaded, literally begged him to join them. But he wouldn't hear of it.

Eventually, of course, the Nazis did come for him, too. It was in the night, as always. Beating down the door while everyone was still fuzzy-headed from sleep, they dragged away his wife, screaming and sobbing, and jammed rifle butts into the ribs of the protesting children, his two little boys, Max and Aaron. Six and eight years old. Berg had married late, and his boys were mere babies.

Out into the streets in his nightshirt, he was dragged through the mud. No explanation. No charges. No dignity. He was thrown into an open truck filled with other men, all of them shouting and arguing with the Nazis.

"There has to be some mistake."

"They could not have meant to arrest me."

Then it struck him with such force that he nearly staggered with the weight of the realization. They were all pleading the same cause of innocence, hoping to be the one who was spared, willing to let the others go to their fates. None of them were joining together. None of them were helping each other. No one argued to save his neighbor. The guards weren't listening to anyone anyway. They stared at the prisoners as if they were nothing. Even the occasional rifle butt to a chest or a head was delivered with a carelessness and detachment that paralyzed Berg with fear. From now on, he too was nobody. He had no past, and he would have no future.

They were delivered to the railroad yards; not the Bahnhoff where the passenger trains were, the commercial yards where they shipped freight and cattle. Yes, cattle. This was the second of his revelations. They were to be slaughtered like cattle, and again they would not resist or band together but rather submit like dumb beasts of the fields.

The Germans unloaded the trucks and jammed the prisoners into the cars. By the time the doors were closed and bolted, nobody could sit or lie down. At one point, Berg could lift both feet from the ground and not fall.

And so the journey began. So long ago.

No one would tell him what happened to his wife, to his little ones. Only the silence and the violence. And the cattle cars. And the camp.

Berg moved back into the little room and closed the door. The wind found its way through the ill-fitting jamb, keeping the room nearly the same temperature as the outside air. The moisture penetrated the scant clothing of the inmates, piercing the skin until constant shivering was a normal way of life. Berg walked to the side door and entered the ward. Fifteen double-decker wood-frame cots crowded the small room. It was nearly impossible to walk down the center aisle. The cots were so close together that the patients had to squirm sideways to get out of bed. Three of the cots were shared by more than one patient. But, here in this pitiful little hospital ward, there were few who were capable of walking anyway. These beds were reserved for the very sickest of the prisoners. These were the dying, not the curable. Berg had long since been reduced to a caretaker of the terminally ill. Virtually none of his patients left the ward alive. This was no longer a hospital but a way station on the road to death.

Over the years, somehow, the fear had diminished a bit. Berg didn't know whether this was because life as he was living it might not be better than death. What, after all, could be worse than this? When the Nazis took away everything from a person, they created someone who had nothing to lose, someone for whom any extreme was acceptable.

Yet Berg didn't give up. That was what puzzled him so. Why did he struggle to do his job every day? The odds were hopelessly against him. There were no real successes. Yet he went on every day, seven days a week, for four years with almost no rest. What was it, he wondered, that drove him and the thousands around him to struggle to survive until the next awful day?

In the early days, he had actually been able to operate on a few patients. For a short while, there had been a bit of ether and a few vials of morphine smuggled in by the doctors and nurses who had been arrested and sent to the camp. These were given directly to him to use on his most pitiable patients. There were some needles and sutures. But it had been at least two years since he had the luxury of even the most rudimentary medications. Now, he washed wounds with a tattered cloth and warm water. There was hardly ever soap. Oh, there was soap in the camp. Yes, they had small bits of soap in the "showers." The soap made it look as if the showers were real. Only after they were locked in the room, and the hydrogen cyanide gas, Zyklon B, had begun to pour through the shower heads instead of water, did the poor souls realize they had been tricked; only when they began to scramble for the barred exits and trample one another in their desperate and useless flight from the vapors of the Zyklon B, might they have realized that the soap was not for them; only when it was too late.

When the gassing was over, the guards would find a pyramid of bodies in the middle of the room where, in their terror, the prisoners had scrambled and clawed their way struggling in a desperate last attempt to get to the top, nearer the light coming from the glass in the ceiling. Anything to get away from the gas. Anything to survive a few more seconds.

So, every morning and afternoon Berg played doctor the only way he could. He made rounds. Rounds were all he had to give now, and all that gave structure to his own days. With no medicine, no surgery, he gave only his time and his attention. Kindness was his whole store of medical supplies.

Berg walked down the narrow aisle, stopping at the foot of a cot. He squeezed between two beds and managed to sit on the edge of the nearest. In this bed, an old woman (he had no idea of her actual age because they all looked at least ten or twenty years older than their real age) lay awake, the ragged blanket pulled up to her chin. She was shivering, even as the beads of sweat coalesced on her forehead. Her hair was matted and damp. Berg took her hand in his and turned it palm up. There, he saw the little red spots covering most of her hand. He didn't need to look at her other hand, nor the soles of her feet. It was all too clear what her problem was. He had made the diagnosis of typhus the moment she was carried into the clinic. What surprised him was that she had lived so long.

He put his hand to her forehead. At least one hundred and four. The last fever thermometer had broken a year ago, when a patient's fever-driven chattering teeth had bitten through it. But, he could still tell. For him, there were only three categories of temperature: no fever at all, a mild fever, or a high fever. The actual numbers were of no significance. Still, after so many years as a scientist, a doctor, he found himself needing to put a number on it.

Yes, at least one hundred and four.

He took a ragged piece of cotton and wiped the sweat from the woman's forehead. As he did, she opened her eyes and gave him a smile. This would be the highlight of his day today: a patient conscious long enough to know he was there—and a smile even.

"How are you, my dear?" Don't use her name.

"Better, Doktor. A little better."

"Could you eat something?"

"No. No…. I'm not very hungry. Perhaps later."

We are such wonderful liars now, he thought. I pretend there is food, and she pretends she has no appetite.

"Very well. Maybe later. Rest now." He rose from the bed and patted her hand. She nodded even as her eyes were closing, and then fell instantly back to sleep. Berg wondered if she would open her eyes again in the afternoon. And what would it matter?

Yet, I do matter, he thought. It matters to these souls that there is a hospital and a doctor. When it comes time to die, this is still a little better than dying in the crowded noisy barracks where everyone's suffering fills the air; where a cot of one's own is a luxury beyond reach. No, it is better to have a few days of quiet in the hospital in a bed of one's own, to hear a kind word from the Doktor, to close one's eyes to life in a place of silence, and to have someone who could recite the Shema Yisroel and the Kaddish for them.

Berg finished seeing all his patients just before dark. He would not return to the barracks in the evening. In fact, it was rare for him to go back there at all. The small luxury of a private space was worth the discomfort of having to sleep in a wooden chair. For him, anything was better than having to go back to the barracks and sleep in rows on a shelf like so many dead fish in the market. It was a small benefit of the job. He knew that he led a privileged life; that his position as a surgeon had put him at the upper levels of society before the war. At least, that was true until the Nazis had risen to power and singled out the Jews, the teachers, the businessmen, and all of the professionals in society who by nature were an anathema to Nazism; those whom

Hitler proclaimed to be the cause of all of Germany's problems. Now, he felt ashamed of his passion for privacy, for his need even to wash his hands when water and soap were in such terribly short supply.

At night, he would often dream of his days in the operating room, where nothing was spared for the welfare of his patients. He would dream in sensuous detail of his days in surgery with a full team of nurses and assistants. Early on in his imprisonment, the dreams had been of food and warmth and sex. Sex was the first to disappear. He had to admit to himself that he missed those dreams of making love to his wonderful Rachel. Occasionally it wasn't necessarily Rachel, but who would know? It was just a dream, after all.

Then with the gradual starvation, an obsession with food dominated his sleep, and what felt like hours would pass at fine restaurants at tables laid with expensive china and silver. There were platters filled with roast chicken and warm breads. Butter melted on his plate, and waiters refilled his wine glass over and over again until he had to tell them to stop.

Later, the dreams that comforted him most were the ones of sitting in front of his fire, a fine knitted rug over his knees, and a wonderful book in his hands. He was smoking his favorite old meerschaum pipe (the one he never took out of the house for fear of breaking it), filled with his own mixture rich with Virginia Burley from America and Latakia from Turkey and Perique from a small parish in Louisiana, while Rachel put the children to sleep.

Now, for some curious reason, he dreamt only of the operating room and never of anything else. He thought this must come from his powerlessness, his inability to do anything—anything—for his patients. Now his greatest fantasy was to be back where he could do some good, and only his dreams made that so. Only in his dreams.

Chapter Eleven

6 June 1944, 1340 Hours
Near Fauville, France

Schneider's mind continued to wander as the hot June sun beat down on his helmet. He could not let go of the fact that he had been responsible for Claude's death. Had he not called to the boy, had he not included Claude in their group, Claude would be alive right now. He knew it to be true.

Damn! What an asshole I am! How could I let a little boy join a combat team? I should have asked directions, commandeered the cart for Sorenson, and sent Claude to somewhere safe.

But what was safe? The Germans were everywhere. And they were nowhere in sight. Still, the boy had survived all these years with the Germans in his back yard. He had been safer with them apparently than he was with his American liberators. Schneider knew he could reason this out all day long for the rest of his life, and he still would never be sure. Only this was certain: Claude was dead.

Sorenson was sleeping in the cart. His brain had finally given in to the rocking motion, and to the morphine, and to the emotional exhaustion from the events of the past night and day. Marsh was alongside the cart, keeping an eye on Sorenson, trying to stay awake himself as he walked. The fragment of their weary platoon made its way carefully toward Fauville. They still had no idea at this point whether allied commandoes had taken the village, or whether the Germans were still in control. They didn't even know where they were in relation to the village. There had been no definite landmark on which to take a compass fix since they had crash-landed. Fauville was out there somewhere. They knew that only from the directions Claude had given them.

But now Claude was dead. And no farmhouse was in sight. So, although they were probably on the right road, going in the right direction, the platoon was still technically lost. The next few miles would tell the story.

Schneider's mind kept trying to put this whole thing into some frame of reference, some clear focus. The war against Germany had been going on for years now, but everyone assumed it would come to an end with the Allied invasion. Schneider had been cooling his heels in England for so long that none of the war seemed real. The Blitz was real enough. The nightly raids over London were something nobody who was there was ever going to forget. Schneider had been stationed far away from London. But every night he could hear the voice of Edward R. Murrow coming through the radio static as Murrow roamed about in the Blitz.

"London is burning. London is burning," Murrow told them as explosions roared in the background, intermittently drowning out the reporter's voice. Yet even that had in some ways become routine. It was hard to explain, but short of hiding under a bed for the duration, or in an air raid shelter like some mole in a tunnel, the English simply went about their lives as if each day were just another normal day. They lived with the shortages, the danger, and the deprivation with the most stoic attitude. Their proverbial stiff upper lip was no myth. Schneider found himself hoping that Americans could bear adversity so well should it ever come to that. After all, except for the fleeting "Day of Infamy" at Pearl Harbor, Americans had not witnessed armed conflict on their soil since the Civil War eighty years before.

All these memories, some of which were only a few days old, reminded Schneider that he still had a family at home who knew almost nothing of his new life. Susan, Emily, and Anna, knew absolutely nothing of what was happening to him, good or bad. His letters took so long to get home that, by the time he got an answer in the mail, he had forgotten what he had written. He never mentioned the fear and the anticipation of the invasion. There was no need to worry them.

His mother and father were living in their own personal hell. They suffered with him, and they suffered for the family his mother had left behind in Germany so long ago. His father's family was, mercifully, all in New York. It was worse for his mother, for she still had her "baby" brother somewhere in Germany. He was a surgeon like Schneider, except older. Schneider visited him once, taking a train to Munich and spending some wonderful time with his uncle. Schneider's German began to improve soon after he arrived, and his desire to follow his uncle's path into surgery was strengthened by the visit. His uncle became a role model for him even from so far away. He was a man of great integrity and devotion to his patients. Schneider felt he could do a lot worse than grow up to be like his uncle.

Munich was a wonderful city back then, even with the strife created by the rise of Hitler and his thugs. Schneider went hiking with his relatives in the Bavarian Alps, taking picnics of local wines, breads, cheeses, and salamis. His uncle was a great hiker and often left Schneider in the dust, laughing and teasing him about his misspent youth. Schneider could barely keep the older man in sight on the steep green slopes of the mountains.

They wrote often after Schneider came home, sharing hospital stories as the uncle followed his nephew's career through medical school and residency. But, he never visited Germany again, as the political climate rapidly worsened and Schneider was too busy and too poor as a surgical resident to return to Germany. His mother begged her brother to come to America. Jews were beaten in the streets, their businesses wrecked by the Hitler Youth, their wives and daughters abused in public. Nonetheless, Uncle said that they must not worry.

"As all the other plagues in the world's history have passed," Uncle wrote, "so, too, will Hitler."

Then, abruptly, the letters stopped. Some time just after the start of the war, they heard nothing more. They flooded Germany with letters and telegrams, often through intermediaries such as friends or neighbors. They tried diplomatic channels as best they could, but it was all to no avail. Communication between America and Germany became nonexistent, and in the silence, his favorite uncle disappeared from Schneider's life.

Now, along this road in France, on the first day of the invasion, Schneider felt like an emissary sent by his family to find his beloved uncle. It was as if his role in the war was to heal the wounded and to find his mother's baby brother. He didn't know which was the more important, let alone the more dangerous or more difficult. Walking along the dusty road in France, with the bodies of Talbot and Claude in the cart and dozens of corpses in their wake, it was hard to imagine that he could ever find his uncle, much less survive the long fight to Berlin and eventually Munich. How many more lives, he wondered, would be wasted before this terrible war was won? He never doubted that the Allies would defeat Hitler and his Thousand Year Reich. But, at what cost?

Sorenson woke with a start as the cart's wheels struck a rut. The pain resonated through his whole body. He looked as if he were going to vomit. He wiped the sweat off his face with a khaki handkerchief. Then he looked with dismay at the bodies lying next to him. He remembered that he was hitchhiking in a hearse.

Schneider looked at Sorenson and moved closer to the side of the cart.

"How are you doing?"

"Oh, I'm all right I guess. The pain's pretty bad, but I don't want to go to sleep again until we're in a secure place. Got any idea how far it is to Fauville?"

"Not a clue. Claude said three kilometers from where we met him. But, who knows? Just that it's in this direction. Must have been walking distance, though. I just wonder who's going to be waiting there for us when we arrive."

"Hell of a good question, Doc. Beats the shit out of me. Guess we'd better be prepared."

Sorenson propped himself higher in the cart and looked ahead, squinting into the distance. "There! There! Look!" he said pointing straight down the road.

Schneider raised himself to his full height from his walking slouch and squinted into the glare of the sun.

"Son of a bitch! A town. That must be it, Lieutenant. It's got to be."

"Hold up," Sorenson ordered. "Let's get tightened up here and make a plan."

The platoon stopped and regrouped around the cart.

"I want you two," he said pointing to the men at the rear of the cart, "to form up and relieve Miller and Brady on the draw bar. The doc is gonna stay here with me, while you two spread out and scout ahead. That village may be in allied hands by now, but I need to know for sure before we go waltzing in there. The rest of you spread out along the sides, and for Christ's sake don't bunch up! If there's Krauts there, let's not make it too easy for them."

The soldiers went right into action, two men pulling the cart slowly ahead, straining with the heavy load now that the others were gone. Marsh moved up and down the line, hoping to be in position if there were to be more casualties. Schneider walked warily alongside the cart, keeping his eyes dead ahead in the middle distance. From time to time, he scanned the sparse cover at the side of the road. He felt a tightening in his abdomen, an old reminder of his struggles with fear. He took purposeful deep breaths in an effort to clear his mind of the possibilities ahead of him. Now and then he had a terrible urge to pee, but there was no time. No place.

Am I going to live with an aching bladder for the whole damned war? he wondered?

He appraised the terrain. The woods had given way to open rolling hills where there was less chance for an ambush. Less chance for cover as well.

The lead scouts disappeared ahead. Within a few minutes, Sorenson and Schneider were nearly alone: a wounded officer, two dead bodies, and an old wooden cart pulled slowly along by two ragged GIs, all guarded by an unarmed surgeon with a full bladder.

Nearly thirty minutes passed before the village came into sight again. The terrain had dipped so that the low hills obscured the view of Fauville. Then the slope flattened, and the houses came into view once more. There was silence in the midday heat. Dust settled slowly on the road, suggesting the recent passage of someone or something.

Sorenson and Schneider noticed the dust at the same time, and both wondered whether it had been caused by their own men or the Germans. Without warning, a soldier scrambled from the side of the road and ran up to the cart in a crouch. The crouch seemed unnecessary, since the cart was plainly visible. The others were all standing straight up.

Sorenson whispered, "What'd you find?"

"Not much, sir. We're in position just outside the village. Took cover in those trees. Not much cover, but some. Don't see anything really. No people. No animals. No Krauts."

Sorenson's eyes narrowed, making little creases that added ten years to his appearance. Or was it the invasion that had aged him overnight? Schneider wondered.

"OK. Give me time to get up there with you, and then we'll see. Tell Kelly to keep his men down and out of sight."

"Yes, sir!" the soldier said and moved quickly back toward the village.

Sorenson signaled to the GIs as the cart moved slowly forward again. As they approached nearer to the village, the fear suddenly expanded in Schneider's chest like a mass of rising dough. It became difficult to breathe. It was the glider all over again: no cover; an enemy who might be waiting for them in ambush; and, of course, he had no way to defend himself—the curse and blessing of being a doctor, a non-combatant, a man without a gun.

"Shit!" he muttered.

When they reached the edge of the village, Sorenson found his men and settled in behind the sparse cover of some trees. Kelly knelt down beside the cart and said, "I sure don't like this one, sir. Can't see a fuckin' thing. The houses are all boarded up. Shutters closed. No animals. No people. Just not right for a normal village in the middle of the day. There's gotta be Krauts in there somewhere waitin' for us. I think they've already made us and are just waitin' for a better shot."

"Yeah," Sorenson said. "Listen. Deploy the team in force. As much force as we've got left. I'll stay here and cover any retreat. Stay as a group. You don't have enough men to spread out too much. Then just clear the village the old fashioned way, house by house. We'll find out soon enough how many Krauts are in there."

"Yessir." Kelly moved quietly back to his men and began assigning tasks. Schneider couldn't hear what they were saying. But, in a minute, he saw the men crouch low and begin to enter the village, using whatever cover they could find to hide their movements.

The minutes crept by. A fly or two began to buzz around the bodies of Talbot and Claude. Schneider knew the flies could not disturb the dead, but still he found himself instinctively brushing them away. Sorenson reached out and took Schneider's wrist. He held it still for a second, and then shook his head.

Movement, Schneider thought. He's afraid that movement will give us away. Someone's probably got his sights on me right now, aimed right at the red cross over my forehead.

A few minutes later, a shot rang out. The solitary crack of a single rifle broke the silence, followed by a distant cry of pain. Schneider hit the deck, covering his head with his arms. Sorenson looked down, then back toward the village.

It had been a single shot. A sniper's shot. Sorenson tried to see what was going on. Then there was an answering burst of automatic weapons fire. Then more silence. Scuffling noises floated up from the village. Almost immediately, two GIs appeared dragging a body through the dust. They got to the cart, and lay the stricken GI down in the cover of the cart away from the village.

"Sniper, sir," one of them said to Sorenson. "Fired from the little church up there. Kelly got him."

"Any more?" Sorenson asked.

"I don't think so. The doors and windows are starting to open, and people are peeking out. Couple of minutes, we're gonna have a crowd out there. That must mean they knew there was only one sniper in the village. I think the rest of the Krauts have pulled out already and left that guy behind to do whatever damage he could. He was just an expendable Kraut."

Schneider and Marsh were busy tending to the wounded soldier, hearing only a little of the conversation. The wound seemed to be a through-and-through chest shot.

"You gonna need a chest tube, Doc?" Marsh asked, rummaging through his medical pack for supplies.

Schneider pointed to the GI's chest wound.

"Look, there's no bubbling coming from the entry wound." He rolled the man partially onto his side. "And, see? None from the exit hole on his back either. And he's not having difficulty breathing."

They rolled the man onto his back again. Marsh took out a stethoscope and shoved it inside the man's field jacket. "Damn! He's got good breath sounds. Both sides."

Schneider flicked open his knife and slit the GIs field jacket. Then he saw the reason. Traced around the man's chest was a huge purple welt, nearly encircling the right half of the body, tracking from entry to exit. The bullet had struck a rib at an angle, and zipped around the man's body just under the skin before exiting from the back. Except for the pain, and a little bleeding from the skin edges, nothing much had happened to him. Marsh began cleaning the wounds, applying a little bit of Sulfanilamide powder to the entry and exit wounds.

The GI was silent, more aware of the danger of his position than the pain of the wound. Then he whispered, "You guys think we should get outta here?"

"Probably a good idea," Schneider said. "We'll be finished in a second.

Just as they were finishing, Kelly appeared, running from the village, but upright, taking no precautions. He scooted up to the cart and knelt next to the wounded GI. After he caught his breath, he said to Sorenson,

"That's it, sir. One fucking sniper. Gets off one shot and hits one man. Shit!"

"He's OK, Sergeant," Schneider said. "Just a flesh wound. As they say in the westerns, 'winged 'im.'"

Sorenson broke in. "Secure the village, Sergeant. Make a house-to-house, room-to-room search. Don't forget the basements and the outhouses. I don't want any more surprises. These villagers will probably tell us what's up, but don't take any chances."

Kelly rose and ran back to the village. As he did, a small crowd began flowing out of the little square. A noisy welcome filled the air. Voices. French voices. French cheers drifted up to where Sorenson and Schneider were waiting in the cart. Schneider helped the wounded soldier into the cart, which was becoming precariously overloaded now. As he turned back, he was nearly bowled over by the rush of the villagers coming out to greet Les Américaines.

Leading the pack was a little man in a very formal, if somewhat disheveled, waistcoat. He wore a black, silk top hat and across his chest a red, white, and blue sash—or rather blue, white and red as Schneider knew the French would say—bearing some sort of honorary medal. He wore a waxed mustache, looking for all the world like a character out of a French comic novel. He was carrying an open bottle of wine, offering drinks to all the GIs. He approached the cart, face smiling, cheeks rosy and flushed with happiness.

"Bonjour! Bonjour! Bienvenue, mes amis."

Schneider figured he was the only one who understood the welcome, so he took a step in his direction and greeted the man. "Bonjour, Monsieur. Comment vous appellez-vous?" he said, asking his name.

"Moi? Je m'appelle Noah le Dauphin. Je suis le Maire de ce village-ci."

Schneider turned to Sorenson and said, "This is Noah. He's the Mayor."

Before he could go on, Noah walked to the cart and addressed Sorenson in very passable English. "You are the Chef? The commander?"

"Yes," Sorenson answered.

"I am Noah le Dauphin," he said again. "You are very welcome in my village." He handed Sorenson the half empty wine bottle and continued in English, "Of course you are a little late, but…" He tilted his head and, in a very French gesture, blew some air through his pursed lips, just as Claude had done. "But welcome! Welcome!" Then he turned and passed the bottle to the rest of the GIs.

In a moment, the Américaines were surrounded by thirty or forty men and women dressed in shabby farm clothes, jumping and cheering. More wine was opened and passed around. Schneider tried to speak with them, but their French was so fast and so excited that he could catch only a few words. There were hugs and kisses for the liberators, and curses, kicks, and spittle for the dead Bosch sniper that some of the men had carried out and thrown on the ground at the feet of the Americans. The German sniper lay in the dust next to the cart, all but ignored after some of the obligatory kicks, the spent fury of the liberated townspeople.

Schneider knelt down in the road and placed two fingers over the man's carotid artery. He looked into the dead man's eyes to make sure he was, in fact, dead. Only then did he notice that the sniper was barely a boy. His blue eyes, now drying in the heat, were staring straight back. Tufts of thick blond hair fell across his smooth forehead.

Just someone's little boy.

"The master race!" Schneider muttered softly, shaking his head slowly from side to side. "They send their boys out to fight us."

"Well, this boy nearly killed one of our men," Marsh reminded him.

Soon the jostling and the exuberance subsided. Schneider found himself in the prolonged embrace of two farmers who held him tightly to their chests. Their grizzled gray beards rubbed his cheeks. He was embarrassed at the familiarity, the smells, and the closeness. Before he could pry himself free, he found himself immersed in silence. The two farmers released their grip and backed away. Their eyes were fixed, staring straight ahead.

They had recognized Claude's cart. Then, as reality registered, they saw the covered bodies lying next to Sorenson. It was the small blanket-wrapped body of Claude that had gotten their attention.

Schneider backed away, scanning the crowd that was now forming around them. The crowd parted, moving away from a woman standing in their midst as if there were something wrong with her; as if she had something they did not want to contract.

She was dressed in a black peasant dress, ragged and soiled. Her hair was tied up in a black shawl. It was as if she had come dressed for a funeral, but this was the dress she had worn every day for the last two years. It was the only one she still owned.

At first she looked startled as the others turned to face her. One old man who had been closest to the cart, one of the two who had hugged Schneider, rushed back and took the woman by the shoulders. He tried to lead her back to the village, but she shook him loose.

Schneider didn't know what to do. Finally, he reached into the cart and lifted the body of Claude, still covered with his khaki blanket. The blanket fell partially away and Claude's head hung back over Schneider's arm. Schneider tried to correct its unnatural tilt with his biceps. He walked toward the woman, realizing that it looked as if he were bearing some gift, some terrible awful gift. The blanket slid free as he approached, completely uncovering Claude's face, now pale and dry.

The woman gasped, rushed forward, reaching for her son. She stopped, her arms still out. Then she crumbled where she stood, collapsing to her knees and sobbing into her hands. The men helped her to her feet and supported her trembling body. Schneider continued walking, carrying Claude past the woman and down the hill into the boy's little village.

Chapter Twelve

7 June 1944, 0800 Hours
Dog White Section, Omaha Beach, Normandy

The Rhino ferry was rocking dangerously in the surf fifty yards off Omaha Beach. The approach was treacherous, even though the firing from the German batteries had decreased somewhat since the start of the invasion. The danger now seemed to lie as much beneath the surface of the ocean as it did from the shelling above. Underwater obstacles—steel and concrete pilings—threatened to tear out the bottoms of the landing craft as the tide eased.

Antonelli, McClintock, and Hamm huddled miserably against the steel bulk of one of the bulldozers. Higgenson was resting in the driver's seat of the medical supply truck assigned to their group. None of them had slept more than a few minutes in a row for the past several days. They were disappointed not to have landed on D-Day itself, though there was still enough danger to go around on D-Day Plus One. Now, on their second attempt to land on a new Rhino ferry, they felt no safer than the day before.

"That beach just looks too quiet," Hamm said, staring and squinting into the misty morning.

"Mmm," Antonelli agreed.

"Too quiet for what?" McClintock asked.

"Too quiet for what we were expecting. I mean, yesterday it was hell. There was shelling everywhere, and nonstop barrages, and machine gun nests. At least, that's what they told us on the way back out to sea."

"And?" McClintock asked.

"And now there's just scattered firing," Hamm said. "An explosion here and there. Nothing like yesterday. At least from here."

"Well, just count your blessings, man. When we land it might be a hell of a lot hotter."

"I guess."

The Rhino wallowed closer to shore. The coxswain, a new guy they hadn't seen before, maneuvered the clumsy craft slowly through the choppy waters, trying to minimize the wash coming in over the low gunwales.

They felt it first, a few seconds before they could hear it: a shuddering, a tearing, and then a low grinding sound coming from beneath the deck. The Rhino ferry shivered, stuttered and decelerated, all at the same time. Their forward movement slowed so fast that everyone grabbed for handholds to keep from being thrown off balance and into the bilge again.

"Fuck!" cried the coxswain.

"What happened?" Hamm shouted to him.

"We're fucked, sir!"

"What?"

"Underwater obstacle. Steel railroad track or some damned thing. We're impaled. Look." He was pointing to the center of the craft where the deck was now bulging in an unhealthy way.

"Jesus," Hamm said.

"We gonna sink?" Antonelli asked. Nobody answered.

There was a flurry of activity as the crewmembers aboard the ferry ran for their vehicles. The bulldozers were lined up in the bow since they were supposed to be deployed first when the ferry landed. But now it seemed they were still too far from shore. Lots of questions raced through everyone's minds. Was the water shallow enough for the dozers and the supply trucks? How far down would the ramp go? Or was it going to be yesterday all over again?

"Make ready to lower the ramp!" the coxswain shouted above the roar of the truck engines. The dozers rumbled and shook like steel behemoths as their big diesel engines coughed to life. The coxswain had tried to back the ferry off the obstacle, but the small twin engines were impotent against the steel impaling the hull, especially with the heavy cargo on board.

"Lower the ramp," he cried, and the bow ramp dropped into the surf. The dozers revved their engines as the first of the hulking machines climbed slowly to the bow. Diesel fumes wafted back into the faces of the crew, making eyes water and starting a chorus of coughing. The ferry wallowed, scraping against the steel impaling her hull as the dozer driver pushed his machine over the lip of the bow and onto the ramp. He edged the huge machine over and downward, causing the inch-thick chain links holding the ramp to strain and scream. As the weight of the big machine came fully onto the incline, the port restraining chain snapped suddenly, canting the ramp to the left. The dozer door opened, and the driver clung to the frame, trying to decide whether to stay with the machine or jump.

Finally, the starboard chain snapped as well, and the ramp slammed down, followed by the great mass of the dozer plunging nose first into the sea, the driver with it. The eyes of all the soldiers on board searched for the soldier, but he was nowhere in sight. The dozer sank immediately in a spume of bubbles and froth. The sea lapped around the rear of the huge machine, protruding from the surface while the nose and blade were buried in the soft sand of the ocean floor.

Antonelli and Hamm rushed to the open bow and scanned the sea. After a terrible wait, the surface was broken by the driver's flailing hands clawing the air for something to grip. Antonelli jumped down onto the submerged portion of the ramp and grabbed the broken end of the chain that was dangling free over the water. With his other hand, he grasped at the now exposed shoulder of the driver, pulling him to the ferry. Hamm knelt down beside Antonelli, and together they heaved the sodden soldier onto the deck, where he lay gasping and coughing up seawater.

The man heaved and coughed some more then looked up at Hamm and Antonelli and said, "Thanks."

"Any time," Antonelli said.

The coxswain again gunned his engines in reverse, but it was no use. The Rhino was impaled and would stay there for the duration.

"We're sitting ducks here, Major," the cox said to Hamm. "It's FUBAR!"

Fucked Up Beyond All Repair.

"What're you going to do about it?"

"Let's get on the loud-hailer and get you guys evacuated. Either that or you just get the hell off this tub and wade ashore."

Hamm turned to McClintock and said, "What do you think?"

McClintock looked toward the shore and said, "I say we go for it. If we go back to the ships, God only knows when we'll get in here. They really need us on shore, Hamm. We were supposed to have set up a clearing station yesterday. Guys are dying just over there," he said pointing to the beach, "while we're stuck out here. Shit, the dozer is sticking out of the water. How deep can it be?"

"What about the supply trucks. The equipment?"

"The trucks won't make it. No way. But *we* can. Let's just get what we can carry, and go from there."

"That means no big equipment. No autoclaves for sterilizing. No major surgical packs…"

"Yeah, and no anesthesia machines either. But, I've got some open-drop ether, and if I can get them asleep, you can do the surgery until we run out of supplies. So, let's get the hell off this fucking tub before some Kraut zeroes in on us again."

"Right." Hamm turned to the cox and said, "We're going in. We'll take a minute to get some supplies off the trucks, and then we're going to wade ashore. You hold it steady as you can right here, and then get yourself on to another craft and get the hell out of here."

"Aye, sir. But I don't need to do anything about holding this steady, sir. It's goin' absolutely nowhere."

Hamm turned to his men and said, "Everyone get into those trucks and pack whatever you can carry into your gear bags. Get rid of whatever personal stuff you don't absolutely need. We can resupply your skivvies and socks later. Make as much room for the surgical supplies as you can."

He turned to Higgenson and said, "After you get your gear in order, watch over the other medics and make sure they're carrying absolutely everything they can, especially plasma. Lots of plasma."

"Yessir."

McClintock and Hamm separated and entered the waiting trucks. Hamm went straight to the surgical operating room packs. He opened one and decided that the whole pack was much too heavy to carry.

All that steel would sink him to the bottom the moment he went over the side. He took out the heaviest and least important instruments. They were all made of stainless steel, so everything was heavy. First to go were the big Deaver and Richardson retractors. There were almost twelve of them in each pack, arranged by size.

This is going to be really gross surgery, he thought, as he took only one set each of the biggest retractors in the pack. Then he made sure he had adequate clamps to stop all the bleeding he knew he would be treating.

"Big surgeons make big incisions," he muttered to himself, "and that means big clamps and big retractors." He realized that he was talking to himself and looked around, embarrassed.

Next he packed up a variety of needle holders for all the different kinds of sewing he would encounter: giant needles wider than a hair curler, to close the entire abdominal wall with a single throw; fine needles for the intestinal suturing; and still finer needles and sutures, almost as thin as spiders' webs, for the vascular surgery. He stopped to think for a moment. Hamm had never done this kind of inventory before. Usually the operating room nurses prepared the surgical packs. He wracked his brains, trying not to forget anything. Then he snapped his fingers and rummaged through the pack to make sure he had some chest tubes and drainage bottles to re-expand collapsed lungs from penetrating chest wounds.

"Catheters!" He found some urinary catheters for draining the bladder for soldiers with urinary tract trauma and for the shock patients to monitor their fluid replacement. He stuffed them into his kit as well. He strained to think of what he might have forgotten.

The suture packs are in. Towels. Gauze. Sponges. Drapes...Something's missing. Something....

Hamm shrugged and began to bind up the pack before stuffing it into his duffel bag. As he got to his feet it struck him, almost a physical blow.

"Jesus Christ. Knives! I forgot the knives...."

He reopened the pack and took a dozen scalpel handles of varying sizes, and boxes of blades to match. He paused and then scooped up all the blades that remained. He put it all in the duffel, taking out his extra dry clothing to make room. He slung the web belt over his shoulder and stood. Staggering under the weight, he was shocked at how heavy it all was. And this after leaving most of the instruments and clothing behind. He eyed his diaries, leather bound and heavy. He just couldn't leave them, so he wrapped them in his poncho and stuffed them in with the surgical gear. Then he hoisted the duffel higher on to his shoulder and jumped down from the truck, hoping the duffel might have some buoyancy once it was in the water.

Hamm met McClintock coming from around the corner; they almost knocked each other down. McClintock was weighed down with an equally heavy duffel.

"You got a whole theatre in there, Hamm?" McClintock asked, using the British term for operating room, a word he had adopted after so many months in England.

"Just the bare minimum. You?"

"I'll just bop them on the head and hope they'll wake up when you're done."

"Right. Let's go."

They made their way toward the bow, picking up Antonelli and Higgenson on the way.

"You got everything?" Hamm said to them both. He couldn't believe that their packs were even bigger and heavier than his and McClintock's.

"Yup," said Higgenson, hefting his load.

Antonelli just kept moving forward. The men gathered at the bow, looking over the damaged ramp. Hamm noticed that the dozer had settled farther into the sandy bottom. He remembered the way his feet used to sink into the sand at the beach as the rushing water eroded his foothold. Still, the dozer blocked the way. They would have to go over the corner of the broken ramp and make their way around the big machine. With waters as roiled as they were, nobody could see bottom. Only the height of the water above the cab of the dozer gave any clue as to the depth. And that didn't look good.

The rest of the medical team gathered behind Hamm and McClintock. The infantry were forming up as well.

"OK," Hamm shouted to everyone. "Let's do it."

Hamm tried to put on a confident face. But his heart was racing and he was sweating. The prospect of drowning was foremost in his mind; being shot or blown up was just a flicker away. He swallowed hard to suppress the lump forming in his chest as a man appeared at his side.

"Sir, I think my men and I should go over first." A lieutenant stepped forward. Davies, Hamm read on the nametag. He was leading a platoon of infantry. "We need to secure a part of the beach and find some place for you guys to work."

"OK, Lieutenant. Go for it," Hamm said, very relieved not to be going in first.

The firing from the beach had intensified again, and the water's edge was alive with the splashing of bullets as they struck the surf. Many more LSTs and other landing craft were now going ashore to follow up the initial invasion. Some of the bigger guns were still pouring fire into the landing craft, and the men on the Rhino ferry were waiting uneasily for someone on the cliffs to take aim at the ridiculously easy target their impaled boat made. Splashes were not yet bracketing the ferry, but everyone knew it wouldn't be long.

"Hey, Cox!" Hamm shouted toward the stern. He couldn't remember the guy's name. "Why don't you come ashore with us? You're out of the war here, and sooner or later the krauts are going to nail this tub. Come on."

"Thank you, sir. But I'd better wait for a lift back to the ships. They'll give me another boat as soon as they get me off here. And, anyway, why the hell would I want to go in there with you guys?"

"OK." Hamm shook his head. The guy was right. Why would anyone want to go ashore who didn't have to? They'd soon be the sitting ducks.

"Good luck to you, Cox."

"Aye, sir! And to you too." The ensign saluted, and Hamm returned the salute. Then he made ready to go into the water, waiting for the infantry to go over the side. Davies mustered all his men, and gave the word.

"Let's go. Get off this tub as fast as you can, and get onto the beach. Rendezvous at that barrier," he said pointing to a cluster of steel erected to impede the landing of the tanks and trucks. "Follow me!"

Davies went right over the side. As soon as his feet hit the water, his platoon watched in horror as he sank from sight like an anvil. His gear, his gun, his whole person disappeared without a splash. A trail of bubbles rose to the surface, the only residue of the lieutenant's entry.

There was a short pause while numerous disconnected voices commented on Davies' disappearance.

"Holy Fuck!"

"Jesus Christ."

"Oh, shit…"

A variety of GI vocabulary filled the air for a second or two. There was barely a soldier who saw the lieutenant go in who did not have at least one word to say.

Except Higgenson. He was closest to the bow and, without a word or hesitation, dropped his pack to the deck, and disappeared into the churning water as quickly as had Davies. The bubbles stopped, and the water became still at the spot where Higgenson's body had momentarily calmed the surface. The men on deck froze. There was total silence, all the meaningless vulgarity ceased. The only sound was the uneven staccato of the German machine guns in the distance and the occasional whoomph of the 88s still firing at the invasion force on the beach and at sea.

Forever passed, and the water roiled again as it had before either Davies or Higgenson had gone in, wiping away any sign of their entry. A moment of silent calm; then, like a whale breaching after a deep dive, Higgenson flew from the depths, waving his arm for help, coughing and choking at the same time. Two arms flashed out from the boat, grabbing the big man and pulling him nearer the bow. But his bulk and his water-logged clothes made him even heavier. It took several more men grabbing at Higgenson's sleeve and field jacket to drag him up and out of the sea. Beneath him, like a fish snared in a net, lay the body of Davies, inert and limp, his rifle still slung over one shoulder and his pack still dangling from the other.

Higgenson had one hand clamped tightly to Davies' collar. It seemed as if he might strangle the lieutenant before they could get him out of the water. But he held on tightly, his fist white with the effort, even as he continued to cough and spew seawater from his own mouth and nose.

Hamm lay down flat on his stomach and reached out for Davies. He grabbed an arm with one hand and the front of the field jacket with the other. He heaved on the limp body, but the body didn't budge. Then Antonelli reached down and grabbed another fistful of clothing. The two of them heaved again and managed to get Davies onto the deck, even while Higgenson was still in the water. With the weight suddenly gone, Higgenson looked up, trying to see if he had lost his grip on Davies. When he saw the body disappearing up over the edge of the deck, he let go, surrendering the body to the others. Three more men helped pull Higgenson out, and the group all fell backwards to the deck. Higgenson coughed for a few more minutes, and then, gasping, drew himself to his knees to see about Davies.

Hamm rolled Davies onto his back, while McClintock scrambled to his side. It might be necessary to insert an endotracheal tube to aerate Davies' drowned lungs. Hamm got himself to his knees and took a position at Davies' right. McClintock scrambled to the head, his usual place as anesthesiologist. Antonelli moved opposite Hamm, the three of them automatically taking their places as if they were in the operating room. The others on the deck formed a shield around them and stared.

The 88s and the machine guns stepped up their barrage, a percussion background to the little drama.

And then they saw it. Somewhere, somehow, a random bullet had taken Davies through the throat. The entry hole on the right side of his neck was clean with hardly a bruise. The exit to the left was jagged and larger, but also washed clean by the sea. There was no froth. No blood. Davies had been killed as he went into the water. The sea ritually washed his body clean before returning him to the surface.

Higgenson had, without thought or hesitation, risked his life for a dead man.

And it wouldn't be the last time.

By late morning, the Rhino had been towed once again back out to sea. The entire medical group, along with its complement of infantry, transferred to an LST. The supply trucks and ambulances were loaded onto another landing craft and would head in right behind the main team. Again, they would make for Dog White Beach, avoiding the error of landing on Dog Green, as they almost had done yesterday. Hamm really didn't know what difference it would make, since they all would surely be up to their elbows with the wounded almost any-where they landed.

They were huddled against the side gunwales of the LST wonder-ing what would happen on this, their third try to get ashore to help the wounded.

"I feel like we're snake bit," Antonelli said. "I mean, Jesus! Davies getting it like that. Bad enough to drown as soon as you hit the beach, but to get shot in the neck at the same time. I mean, holy shit! He never had a chance."

McClintock stared ahead, though he couldn't see the beach over the raised ramp of the landing craft. After what happened to Davies, none of them lifted their heads for a peek.

"I wonder what that means for the rest of this sorry outfit," Antonelli said. "I've never been superstitious, but three strikes and you're out, man. Out!"

"Look, we're going in now," Hamm said, trying to restore calm to the jittery outfit. "If anything, this late landing may have saved us a lot of grief. I mean, not getting in on the first or second waves. Look how quiet the beaches are, now, compared to yesterday. It's almost eerie right now." He sounded strong and confident, but his heart was still racing.

"I wouldn't say that too loudly, Hamm." said McClintock. "We're not there yet, and God knows what the Jerries have in reserve. We could get there just in time for their big counteroffensive. Let's just see what happens. I'm getting superstitious, too." McClintock looked around and asked, "Where's Dick?"

"Right here, Major," Higgenson answered. "Right over here."

Higgenson was huddled near the bow, not yet dry from his swim. He was shivering slightly, but said nothing about it.

"Hell of a thing you did, Dick. Fucked if I could have gone in there just like that. Not a hesitation. My hat's off to you, man." McClintock touched the brim of his helmet.

"Thank you, sir. That's what they pay me to do: bring in the bodies so you can fix them up. I'm just sorry I couldn't bring him in alive for you."

"You never had a chance, son," McClintock said. "But you sure know how to do your job. That was a hell of a brave move. Anyone ever mouths off about conscientious objectors to me again, he'll be pulling my boot out of his ass."

"Amen to that," said Antonelli.

"Gene," Hamm said, "I want you and Dick to stay together. You make a fine team. And watch out for each other."

"Yessir," said Antonelli.

"Yessir," said Higgenson.

"Stand by!" a metallic voice came over the makeshift PA system. "One minute!"

The whole team gathered their things closer about them and secured their web belts. They had made their loads slightly lighter since Davies had demonstrated how heavy a pack really was when you are trying to swim with it. None of them had slung the packs across their shoulders either. They wanted to be able to dump them quickly, if necessary.

The LST approached the beach. Suddenly, there were grinding noises on the bottom of the craft. Most of the crew tumbled forward slightly with the deceleration. They regained their balance just as the boat stopped. The ramp dropped away, and the infantry went down into the water first. Most were able to walk in the chest-deep surf, arms and rifles held above the water line, white condoms protecting the muzzles of the rifles from the seawater and sand. Hamm smiled at the jokes that kept coming to mind. Several men stumbled but were helped up by their comrades. Next, the medical crew piled off the ramp, following the infantrymen into the shallowest parts of the beach. There was sporadic fire, and a few splashes as bullets struck the water. But none struck too close. Very few heavy weapons still fired from the cliffs.

McClintock and Hamm hit the sand at the same time, stumbling over the soft footing while trying to make their way as far inland as possible before stopping. They struggled forward, encountering very little in the way of firing. Then they were stopped. Not by German guns, but by what they saw around them.

Hamm fell to his knees behind a truck lying on its side, still burning slightly. McClintock fell down next to him.

"Holy shit, Hamm! Oh, dear God!"

Hamm said nothing as he shook his head in disbelief. He had expected the destruction: the wrecked vehicles, the fire, the craters, the scorched sand, the debris of unnamed and unnamable military gear.

But the bodies! He had no idea there would be so many bodies. Hamm had seen his share of trauma in the emergency room: the damage done by five thousand pounds of a steel car colliding with a hundred and sixty pounds of human flesh, or by an ounce of lead entering the body at a thousand feet per second, or by four or five drunks in a brawl.

Nothing in the world could have prepared him for this.

All at once, Hamm's stomach tightened. Even with all his experience in the many ways humans can destroy other humans, he knew he was going to be sick. His breathing increased until he was panting like a puppy on a hot day. But he couldn't stop. He knelt there in the bloodied sand and puked up the last of what remained in his stomach. He looked at McClintock, who had the same expression on his face and was puffing away as well. Then, Antonelli and Higgenson crashed in and fell down alongside the truck.

"Oh, Jesus, Doc. Look at this. Jesus!" Antonelli said.

Higgenson was, as usual, silent. His face said it all. There was no obvious fear. No revulsion. A quiet resignation was written there, a terrible sorrow for all the fallen men. For the first time in Hamm's life, he envied another man's complete faith in God. His own faith fell far short. He could see it in Higgenson's eyes, and he was sad that he did not have similar spiritual support as he entered this modern-day Valley of Death.

The lifeless bodies of not hundreds but thousands of men littered the wet and bloodied beach. They lay in every imaginable pose. Were it not for the uniform and the rifle, some could have been asleep in the sand on a chilly June afternoon, their faces cradled in the crook of an elbow. Others lay face up, in a pose of surrender, like a sleeping baby with one arm extended and the other cocked behind an ear. Still others were in pairs, and threes, and fours, victims of a single blast from a mortar shell or machine gun burst. Others hung like laundry from the steel beach obstacles and barbed wire. Those men, suspended in the air, did not look as much at peace as those nestled in the sand. Then there were the others, or the parts of others, mixed and spread over the sandy floor without order or reason. Hamm thought of a junk yard filled with used car parts, and he shuddered.

He could not tell which limb belonged to which soldier—sometimes even which head. The ghastly panorama, the remains of the first day of the invasion, was so bizarre, so grotesque, that the impact was at first nearly lost on him.

Can the pieces all fit together to make a man again? he wondered. A terrible thought. The sheer scope of the carnage swept over him with the realization that these were the men that they had come to save; had they arrived sooner, some of these souls whose bodies littered the sand might still be alive. He was ashamed of the frail safety that the crippled Rhino ferry and the LST had afforded him while these young men were dying there on Dog White Beach.

Several GIs flung themselves down in the sand alongside the wrecked truck, blocking Hamm's view and interrupting his thoughts.

"Who the fuck are you guys?" asked the sergeant who knelt gasping in the sand. He looked at Hamm's insignia of rank and added, "Uh, sir?"

He set down the end of a litter bearing the body of a wounded GI. At the other end of the litter, a medic was also gasping, trying to get a brief second's rest. A third man carried a plasma bottle, holding it high in the air while maintaining pressure on blood-saturated gauze against the GI's upper chest.

"Well, we're supposed to be a field hospital in a little while," Hamm said. "A clearing station right now, I guess." He quickly looked over the wounded man and moved to the side of the stretcher. The man was pale and breathing with difficulty. His breath came in short panting gasps as if starving for air, as if he had been carrying the stretcher himself.

"What've you got here?" Hamm said.

"Chest wound," the sergeant replied. "Got to get him back to the LSTs, ASAP."

"He ain't gonna make it to that LST, Doc," Antonelli said to Hamm, already clearing away the bloody dressing and taking fresh supplies out of his own kit.

Hamm moved nearer the chest and looked at the wound. He tore open the GI's field jacket and pressed his ear to the man's chest. Bubbles were coming out of the hole just above the nipple on the left side.

"He's got a sucking wound of the chest, Sergeant," Hamm said. "He needs a chest tube right now, like this minute, or he'll never make it off this beach."

Anthony A. Goodman

Hamm turned to Antonelli, who was already pulling a thick rubber tube out of a sterile cloth wrapper. He handed it to Hamm, who grabbed a large curved Kelly clamp from the pack. He held it in his bare hand—no time for sterile technique there on the beach. They could deal with infections later. Seconds would count on this one.

Hamm grabbed the tip of the tubing with the tip of the steel clamp, skipping an incision, and shoving it forcefully through the bullet hole in the man's chest. Pretty crude stuff. The man cried out with pain, arching his back and rising off the stretcher for a moment. Then he relaxed and fell back.

A large volume of blood poured from the tubing onto the stretcher and the sand, clotting and making a puddle of crimson jelly next to Hamm's knee. He forced the air out of the soldier's chest with one hand, while Antonelli put the open end of the tubing under the water in the man's canteen, sealing it from the atmosphere. Bubbles appeared in the canteen as the air left the man's chest, the water sealing off any reentry. Then Hamm ripped open a paper pouch with his teeth and sprinkled the wound with Sulfanilamide powder. Antonelli taped the chest tube to the top of the canteen, while Hamm secured the rest of it to the soldier's skin with more tape. No sutures. It all took less than two minutes.

The man was looking pinker already as his lung expanded, but he was not nearly out of the woods yet. Along with the air bubbles, telltale traces of blood were also coming through the tube and into the canteen. He was bleeding internally.

"OK, sergeant, get him out of here and back to the ships. He still may need that chest cracked," Hamm said. "And give me his first aid supplies: tape and bandages, sulfur powder. He's not going to need them now, and we do." The sergeant handed over the man's entire pack.

"Hang on a second," said McClintock putting a hand on the sergeant's arm. "Let me see if he needs to be intubated." McClintock took out his stethoscope, slipped it under the torn shirt, and listened to both sides of the man's chest. Out of habit, he held up a hand for quiet as he listened for the man's breath sounds. It was a ridiculous gesture there on the beach with guns blasting away from both sides.

Hamm chuckled to himself, looking up to see if the Germans would stop the shelling so that McClintock could hear the man's breath sounds.

"OK. Breath sounds are great. Well, not great, but good enough. No need to tube him. Get him out of here."

The sergeant and the medic struggled to their knees, then to their feet. Crouching low, they ran toward the water and the LST that had just delivered the medics to the beach.

"Now what?" McClintock asked.

"I'd say we have to get off this beach and set up a clearing station somewhere. And get our supplies—wherever the hell they are."

"I haven't seen one damned truck on this beach with a red cross on it, have you?"

Hamm looked around. The beach was littered with bodies and craters and the smoking debris of burning vehicles. It looked like a wasteland.

"No. Nothing. Where do you think they might be?"

McClintock looked back toward the water and motioned with his head. "Back there, I guess. Underwater."

McClintock and Hamm remained kneeling in the protection of the smoldering wreck. Neither spoke for a moment.

"Sir," Higgenson said, "there's an antitank ditch about a hundred yards inland and to the right. I passed it when I was lookin' for bodies."

They all looked in the direction Higgenson was pointing.

"You won't see it from here because it's completely dug out and level with the sand. But it's deep and wide: deep enough to stop a tank from crossing it, and wide enough, too. We could set up in there."

"In a ditch?" McClintock said.

"Yessir."

McClintock looked at Hamm and said. "It ain't the Philly General Hospital, man, but it's protected. I think Dick's got a point. We can't stay here. We can't even do anything here. Might as well try for the ditch. At worst, we can hole up there until we get some supplies. Maybe even do some good."

Hamm shook his head from side to side, smiling. "Let's do it. "

They crouched for a minute as they assessed the intensity of the firing from the German gun emplacements at the top of the hills along the beach. Small arms fire was sporadic, but didn't seem to be threatening them. The few heavy guns left were concentrating on the landing craft.

Higgenson took off, leading the way. McClintock and Hamm raced after him, with Antonelli bringing up the rear. The four ran in a crouch, stumbling over debris and body parts. From time to time, one of them would stop and kneel beside a body. He would roll the body onto its back and feel for the carotid pulse in the neck. The battle gear made it impossible to get to the chest. Radial pulses at the wrist were often hard to feel in the wounded if they were in shock, even if the heart was beating. The first ten bodies they examined were dead and had been dead for several hours. Then Hamm saw Higgenson stooped at one body a few yards away. He could see Higgenson do a double take as he felt for the pulse.

Hamm scrambled over to them. The soldier was pale with the waxy dry-eyed stare of the dead. His skin was cold and clammy. To Higgenson's surprise, he felt just the faint suggestion of a throb under his fingertips. Nothing certain. Just a hint. He tore open the man's field jacket, noticing as he did so the blood coming out of a small bullet hole in the upper chest on the left side. The blood was moving! It was not the clotted dark color of an old wound, but real blood flow. Such bleeding should have alarmed Higgenson, but it made him smile.

"Son of a gun! You're alive, man!"

He tore open the man's shirt and put his ear to the chest. "You've got a heartbeat! Hey, Doc, he's alive! Barely."

He looked for Antonelli, who was still stopping at body after body, running hundred-yard, low hurtles as he careened toward the tank ditch.

"Hey, Gene! Over here. I've got one! A live one!"

Antonelli stopped. He turned, trying to figure out what Higgenson had said. One look told him. There was Higgenson opening up his field pack and rummaging through the contents. Nothing else but a live GI could make him do that. In that very instant, the beach around them erupted, driving sand into their eyes and faces. They flattened against the sand, impotently covering their heads with their arms. The sand continued to fly, and they realized at once that they were bracketed.

Hamm flattened out in the sand behind a small mound of dead GIs and waited. Antonelli got to his knees and set up like a sprinter in the starting blocks. Then he burst forward screaming as he ran.

"You dumb motherfuckers, don't you see the red cross on my helmet?" He dodged and weaved as he went.

"Shittyassratfuckingcocksuckingkrautassholes!" he called to the German gunners, never stopping to catch his breath. He covered the distance to Higgenson, drawing fire as he went. For a moment, Hamm thought he might be endangering all of them if he kept going in their direction.

Hamm took a deep breath, then rose and sprinted to where Higgenson was working with the GI's body, in the direction Antonelli was running.

Higgenson rose slightly and dragged the body toward the cover of some anti-tank hardware a few yards away. When Antonelli was only yards away, the German firing ceased. He tumbled into a depression in the sand and took shelter behind the crossed steel beams.

Hamm tumbled in seconds later, practically on top of Antonelli. He shook the sand from his face and nodded to Higgenson. "What've we got?" he said, gasping.

Higgenson held a pressure dressing hard against the entry wound in the man's chest.

"Just a single shot through the chest. But he's pretty shocky. I'm gonna hold pressure here. Gene, you start some plasma, then we'll get him to the ditch. What else, Doc?"

Hamm quickly evaluated the situation. "Keep on doing what you're doing," he said. "I'll get my gear out."

Antonelli quickly started an IV line, attaching one of the two bottles of plasma he carried in his own pack. He had no idea where he could get any more. But now it was first come, first served. They had a patient who needed the plasma—maybe all of it. They would worry about the next wounded man when the time came.

Hamm tried to start another IV in the other arm, but there were no veins to be found.

Antonelli grabbed the strap of the plasma bottle in his teeth and using both arms, hoisted the GI by the legs. Higgenson took the man under the armpits, holding the compression dressing with his left hand. At an eye signal, they both lifted and began to run and stumble their way to the tank ditch. Hamm followed, dragging all the rest of the gear behind him. Unencumbered by the heavy body, he moved a lot faster than the medics could.

McClintock was just tumbling into the ditch as Hamm got there. None of the four had come across a single living soldier except for this one.

As they settled into the ditch, Hamm was shocked at the size and depth of it. It was several hundred feet from end to end, parallel with the ocean, and almost twelve feet wide. It was dug down to more than seven feet in depth, with seawater in the bottom.

"Jesus H. Christ!" McClintock said. "Look at this place, will you?" They immediately began to unload their packs. Suddenly, there was a shower of sand as Antonelli and Higgenson scrambled over the edge of the ditch, dragging the wounded GI behind them. They slid down into the wet bottom of the ditch pulling the man with them, then cradled the wounded GI across their knees to keep him out of the water.

"Hey, Doc," Antonelli said to McClintock. "Look what we found."

"Looks dead," said McClintock.

"Unh unh," said Higgenson, shaking his head slowly and gasping for breath.

Higgenson and Antonelli cradled the GI's body across their knees, and opened his field jacket to expose the entry wound in the left upper chest wall. They all could see the chest move slightly. It wasn't much, but the man was trying to breathe, trying to live.

"Ted, break out whatever gear you've got," Hamm said as he opened his own pack.

"I haven't got much," said McClintock. "I'll do what I can with an IV morphine drip to start. But let me get him intubated first."

McClintock took out a steel laryngoscope and an airway from his field jacket pocket. There wasn't going to be much sterility for a while. He put the blade of the scope down into the man's mouth and, pushing the tongue down, searched for the vocal cords. When he could see them, he slid the tubular airway between the cords and into the trachea, more by feel than sight. He taped the tubing in place then squeezed the black rubber respirator bag, breathing for the young GI. The chest moved up and down. It was only air: there was no pure oxygen or anesthetic to use at the moment. But, mercifully, the man was unconscious and felt nothing.

Hamm felt again for the pulse. Then raised the soldier's eyelid and looked for a pupillary reflex. He didn't see many signs of life.

"He's got no volume, Ted, he's almost bled out." Hamm said. "I've got to get some plasma into this guy or he's dead."

The plasma wasn't dripping. The one puny IV was not going to do it. Too slow. Hamm looked carefully at the two IV lines.

"It's blown. Must've come out while you were dragging him."

"What do you want to do?" McClintock asked. "His veins are all collapsed."

"I'm going to crack his chest and try to control whatever's bleeding. Otherwise, the plasma's just going to run in and right out the hole again. You've got the airway covered. I can't think of anything else."

"You're gonna crack him in a foxhole? Right here?" McClintock was incredulous.

"What have we got to lose? He hasn't got much more than a couple of minutes anyway. He might even be brain dead already," Hamm answered, lifting the man's eyelids and looking at the pupils. "Pupils are equal and reactive though. Let's go."

He rummaged around in his pack and found a large scalpel handle. As Higgenson worked to clean off the chest as best he could with water from his canteen, Antonelli made ready another bottle of plasma, pulling out the useless IVs.

With the scalpel blade loaded on the handle, Hamm drew a long incision across the man's right chest, cutting deeply into the space between the ribs. Ominously, only a small amount of very dark blood flowed from the incision. As his blade entered the chest, a soft hiss of air came from the injured lung. McClintock's artificial respiration just kept up with the leak.

Hamm inserted a large steel chest retractor between the ribs and quickly cranked it open with the ratcheted handle. There was a loud sound of two ribs cracking

"Look at that, guys."

Hamm was pointing to the heart, where there was a shrapnel tear in the right auricle. Blood was clotted around the heart muscle edges, but more blood was streaming from the hole in the heart itself.

"Give me that IV tubing, Gene. This ought to put the plasma where it's needed."

Antonelli handed Hamm the tip of the IV tubing attached to the second plasma bottle. Hamm took it and shoved it inelegantly through the ragged hole in the auricle and into the right atrium of the heart. He held it in place with his fingertips and said, "Open her up wide, Gene."

Antonelli raised the plasma bottle high in the air. The whole volume was delivered right into the heart in just a few minutes. "That's my last one, Doc. You got any?"

"Nope."

Higgenson reached into Antonelli's medical pack and fished around, looking for some more plasma. His hand exposed a pile of morphine Syrettes.

"Holy cow, Gene! You got enough morphine to zonk the entire platoon."

Antonelli pulled his pack away from Higgenson and closed the cover.

"You'll be glad I got so much of that shit before this day's over."

Higgenson reached out with his free arm and handed Antonelli another full plasma bottle from his own supply. Antonelli quickly exchanged the empty one for the full one and again held it high as the plasma ran into the wounded GI's heart. After the complete supply of plasma was exhausted, six bottles in all, the four men just sat there and watched.

As the last of the plasma entered the right auricle, the strength and force of the cardiac contraction increased rapidly. The heart rate sped up, and a pulse could be seen in the vessels leaving the heart. The man's color improved, and as the GI's blood pressure climbed, some bleeding began to show along the wound edges where Hamm had opened the chest.

Hamm laughed.

"Will you look at that!" He took a heavy suture in his right hand and held the tubing in place with his left. Then he placed a purse-string suture around the tubing and tightened it into place, securing the IV right into the heart itself. Antonelli replaced the plasma with a bottle of saline solution, which was all he had left now, and slowed the drip slightly. It wasn't over yet.

Hamm let go of the tubing, now held securely by the purse-string, and began to look for other sources of injury. The hole in the lung was small, so he was able to stop the air leak with a few sutures in the pleura, the shining, thin covering of the lung.

McClintock tested the suture line by inflating the lung forcefully with the anesthesia bag. The sutures held. There was no air leak. Then he backed off the pressure and kept the lungs only full enough to aerate the man's blood, but not enough to get in the way of Hamm's exploration of the chest. They had always been a good team. They hardly ever needed verbal communication.

"I think that's all it was," Hamm said to everyone. "Let's just wash this out and close him up.

McClintock shook his head slowly back and forth. This show of incredulity was rapidly becoming a habit.

"Anyone going to believe that you just did open heart surgery in a tank ditch?"

"Pretty crude surgery," Hamm admitted.

"Pretty tough patient," said McClintock.

"Good work, guys," Hamm said to Antonelli and Higgenson.

Hamm took some adhesive tape and put it across the man's forehead. Then he took out a pen, and on the patient's forehead wrote "MS (morphine Sulfate)." He wrote the date and the time of the dose. He looked up at Antonelli and Higgenson and said, "This man's going to see a lot of different doctors in the next few hours and days. I need to keep the medication records where they won't be missed!"

The two medics nodded. They were still trying to bring order to their little ditch hospital, even as they, themselves, served as the operating table, IV stand, and assistants, with the patient still lying across their knees.

Hamm smiled. "Very nice indeed. Let's close."

Chapter Thirteen

8 June 1944, 1700 Hours
Fauville, France

Sorenson's platoon of commandoes and medics spent a busy forty-eight hours after they killed the sniper and moved into Fauville. They set up a perimeter and organized the locals to help patrol some of the weak spots.

As soon as Sorenson was settled into his makeshift command post in the Mairie, the little town hall, he called for Kelly to organize the care and feeding of his own men and the locals as well.

"Round up all the food you can find, Sergeant, and make sure there's no hoarding. Everyone's gonna get fed here with whatever we have."

"Yes, sir. But these people have almost nothing. The Krauts pretty much took it all when they boogied."

"Do the best you can. We'll have to share our C-Rations and K-Rats with them until we can hook up with some resupply."

Kelly did the best he could, and the French villagers were very cooperative. They were so happy to see the last of the Germans that the Americans could do no wrong.

The troops methodically cleared the houses one by one, looking for any more snipers, then for booby traps. But, none were found.

Schneider stayed so busy tending to the villagers' various ailments that he had almost no time for anything else.

The situation stabilized by the morning of the second day. Schneider made many house calls to Sorenson's command post. In the early morning of the second day, he found Sorenson asleep, glad that the Lieutenant had slept without needing any more morphine. Still, he needed to wake him.

"Sorry to get you up, Jim," he said as he gently touched Sorenson's shoulder.

Sorenson awoke with a start, reaching for his rifle, then grimacing in pain from the sudden movement.

"Jesus, I'm sorry," Schneider said.

"It's okay, Doc. I'm still on high alert, I guess. Even asleep!"

"Sit tight, here. I just need to look at that wound."

Sorenson lay back against his makeshift cushions of his field pack and local blankets while Schneider undressed the wound and washed it with water. Then he applied some more Sulfanilamide powder and clean gauze. Finally, he re-splinted the whole leg.

"Looking good, Jim," he said. "I'll be back later. Need anything for pain?"

"No, Doc. What are you doing out there?"

"Ha! It's like being a GP and a gynecologist and a surgeon and a psychiatrist all at once. I've never been so busy even in my own practice. These people are starving for medical care. The Krauts did nothing for them. I'm just afraid I'll run out of supplies and have nothing for our guys when the fighting heats up again."

"Do what you can. I'm thinking we'll link up with a field hospital soon. At least I hope so."

For the next day, the men stayed busy patrolling and helping the locals when they could. Kelly sent out several small patrols to secure the area and try to make contact with American troops. But to no avail.

Sorenson felt better after the village was cleared and under his control. But they still hadn't joined up with the main body of the surgical group, and worse still, they hadn't joined up with any significant fighting force. They had no supplies to speak of. Pretty soon the team would have trouble treating a hangnail with what was left in their packs: no plasma and only a handful of sterile supplies, most of which went to keeping Sorenson's wound from turning gangrenous.

Schneider was still incredulous that he had taken such a great risk dropping into France, at night, behind enemy lines, so that he could have an aid station up and running to receive the inevitable casualties. *What was I thinking?* However, it gave him great satisfaction to treat the locals, and a sense of pride at both how much basic medicine he remembered from medical school as well as his rapidly improving French language.

Still, when he wasn't busy treating patients, his mind was teeming with questions and recriminations.

Shit. What have I gotten into, he thought? *And what's happening to Hamm? And McClintock? Jesus, those poor guys are landing right into the German fortresses. Festung Europa, Hitler called it.*

He couldn't help imagining that the rest of the invasion was foundering just as badly as his part. It wasn't a pretty thought. He was also agonizing over his decision to sign up at all. He didn't have to go. How much of it, he wondered, had to do with his need to get away from Susan, even at the cost of leaving his little girls as well? Or the fact that all his colleagues had joined up? And how could he have looked Hamm's family in the face if he had stayed behind? Or more important, Hamm himself? And how much was determined by his guilt over his German heritage? And his orthodox Jewish parents? And, not the least, his hope to find his uncle? Was his uncle even alive? So many questions.

When Schneider wandered up to the command post again, Sorenson was talking with Sergeant Kelly and two other soldiers. Sorenson had moved up from Claude's cart to a more stable vehicle. The Germans had abandoned a small trailer used to carry supplies. It was made of steel and had rubber wheels. The ride was better, but without a jeep or truck to pull it, there was no way they were going anywhere: it was way too heavy to be pulled by his men for any distance on the flat, and uphill not at all.

Schneider walked over toward the small group and listened from a distance as they made plans for the defense of Fauville. Sorenson was still trying to set up a protected perimeter, but there just weren't enough men to go around. For the time being, he had no idea if the villagers would be of any use to them at all in a fight. Another group of GIs was dispatched to find out if there were any French Resistance fighters in the neighborhood who might help. So far in the two days there, not a single Maquis had turned up.

"Hey, Doc. Come on over here for a minute, will you?" Sorenson said.

As Schneider joined the small group, he noticed that the dressing on Sorenson's leg was bleeding through again. The wound had remained fairly clean, but he was now concerned about the continued blood loss.

Sorenson was probably losing significant blood though the open bone marrow, and that really had Schneider worried. He was in no position to fix anything under these conditions without supplies. He didn't say anything to Sorenson because, for the last several hours, Sorenson had adamantly refused to let Schneider do any more with the leg. He was fully engaged with the defense of the group, and he would waste no more time or supplies on anything as trivial as an unset open fracture; never mind the unremitting bleeding, the possibility of tetanus, gas gangrene, and loss of limb or life.

"Listen, Doc. Exactly what can you do here in the way of setting up an aid station? I mean, are we doing any good?"

"We may as well not even be here, Major. I have shit for supplies; I have no support personnel other than Marsh. He's damned good, but he's still just a kid with a high school diploma and a few months of on-the-job training playing doctor. We need to link up with the main medical group and set up a field hospital as soon as possible. And I don't have to tell you that we need some more warm bodies to defend us. I mean the Jerries may have pulled out of this town, but God only knows when they'll be back."

"God may not know, but I do. They're going to be back through here just as soon as they regroup in sufficient strength to blast our asses. That could be any time now."

"Well, then shouldn't we move out of here and find some friendly faces? Your guys and mine."

"Listen, Major. Leave that to—"

Before Sorenson could finish, Marsh began shouting and waving.

"Hey, LT, Doc! Look. Look. Quick."

Marsh was pointing and shouting at the same time. He stood at the crest of the small rise at the edge of town. Schneider trotted up to

Marsh, while three of the GIs struggled to drag Sorenson's trailer over to join them.

As Schneider pulled up, he could see, off in the distance, a cloud of dust rising from the surface of the earth, looking for all the world like a big brown caterpillar. It undulated and slithered along the brown dirt road, coming slowly and steadily in their direction. Marsh continued to stare straight ahead. He handed Schneider a pair of binoculars. Schneider adjusted the focus and zeroed in on the vehicles at the leading edge of the caterpillar. What he saw was just too unimaginably wonderful. There, less than a mile away now, and moving toward them at a fast pace, was an American military convoy led by khaki-colored jeeps and trucks, the first three of which were armed to the teeth. Moving through clouds of dust behind them were jeeps, trucks, and ambulances emblazoned on every surface with red crosses set in bright white circles. By Schneider's count, more than fifteen of them, followed by many more jeeps and troop transports.

The cavalry had arrived.

Sorenson was pulled up next to Schneider, his men sweating and puffing at the exertion of getting the steel trailer the few yards up the little hill. Sorenson lifted his war-battered binoculars to his eyes.

"Holy shit! Look at that!"

It was only seconds more before all of them were cheering and hugging and jumping up and down in place. The villagers, who had been milling around the outskirts of their little town, saw the commotion and began running to see what was happening. When they arrived at the observation point, they too began cheering and hugging each other. Everyone began waving at the convoy. One of the French villagers had unfurled the French tricolor flag, the Bleu, Blanc, et Rouge. After a moment, the members of the convoy spotted the hilltop as well. The three armored lead jeeps accelerated aggressively up the dirt road in the direction of the crowd, brandishing three large tripod-mounted machine guns as they came. When they were about five hundred yards away, it appeared that they could see the American uniforms, and they too began to wave, slowing down the jeeps and elevating the muzzles of their menacing guns to a safe position.

"Looks like our prayers have been answered, Doc. Here comes the cavalry," Sorenson said quietly, as if this were just what he had expected. They had all watched too many westerns.

"Sure does, Lieutenant. But now that we have some protection, I think we need to set up closer to the fighting. Nothing's going on around here. What good is all that equipment, if there are no casualties for us to treat?"

"We're not out of the war just yet, Major. We may be up to our asses in casualties in short order here. Let's just see what these guys know. They must have some radios and information. And a god damned map!"

"Where are Hamm and Ted right this minute? Are they even alive?" Schneider said to himself.

Schneider and Sorenson waited, not so patiently, as the medical caterpillar made its way up the slope to their position. After being alone for so long, it seemed forever before the rescuers arrived. The jeeps came up the hill first, the muzzles of their machine guns all now aimed safely at the sky. Several of the soldiers jumped down and immediately mingled with the troops. An officer—another lieutenant—came directly up to Sorenson, who was still holding court from his German trailer.

The lieutenant saluted Sorenson, more of a friendly gesture than a stiff military salute, and said, "Nice ride you got there, Jim." Then he looked down at Sorenson's leg, and his expression changed. "Oh man, what the hell happened to you?"

"Fell out of a glider," Sorenson said. "It's sure as hell good to see you, Jack. Where'd you come from? And who's with you?"

"We're just comin' up from Utah Beach. Been movin' in this direction since the invasion. We got hooked up with these medics as soon as we got off the beaches. Got orders to bring them inland to set up a field hospital at Hiesville, about six miles southeast of here. We secured Ste. Mère Église early this morning. Bad shit, that was. Very heavily defended, but we sure did kick some Jerry ass back there. Heavy losses on both sides. Then we rounded up these medical guys and their supplies from Omaha Beach and were ordered over this way to find you. So? What's left of you?"

"We got the shit kicked out of us, Jim. Crashed and burned most of the gliders. Lost about half my men right there in the field the first night. We just made it here. Jerries cleared out except for one dumb fuckin' sniper, just a kid, who managed to wound one of my men before Kelly nailed him. But the doc here's ready to go. Oh, Doc, this here is

Lieutenant Jack Bender. He and I went to OCS at Benning together a long time ago. We go way back. Jack, this is Major Schneider."

Bender reached out to shake hands. "Pleasure, Doc."

Schneider shook hands and nodded.

"Glad to see you guys, Lieutenant. Who've you got for a surgical team back there?"

"Got a whole surgical group for you, Doc. Surgeons, anesthesia, medics. Operating tents. Generators. All kinds of good equipment. You'll be happy as a pig in shit. No nurses yet, but they should be along after a while."

As he told Schneider the good news, the convoy of trucks swept up the hill and descended into the town. Bender waved them past and pointed to the village. The trucks passed in a cloud of dust, leaving everyone coughing and wiping the grit from their eyes. But, oh, were they happy to see those red crosses all lined up on the doors and hoods and roofs of those ugly khaki trucks. It was as if all their wishes had come true at once; it was like a birthday with presents for everyone.

Schneider immediately started looking for his team, especially Hamm and Ted. Also, he couldn't wait to get his hands on those supplies. He knew that his very first task would be to get Sorenson under anesthesia, debride his fractured leg, set it properly with a real plaster cast, and pump him full of some of that wonderful penicillin. This time, he would not be taking no for an answer. Bender's presence meant that they could take Sorenson out of the line of fire and get him back to a safe place where he could recover from his injury. He might even live to fight another day, walking into battle under his own power.

Wouldn't that be nice? Schneider thought. Or maybe Sorenson could just go home. That would be even better.

Suddenly, Schneider couldn't stand it any longer. He waved to Bender and Sorenson, spun on his heels, and began to run down the slope in the dusty wake of the caterpillar convoy. The trucks had stopped outside the village square and were lining up under the direction of one of the sergeants. Men poured out of every vehicle: jeeps, trucks, half-tracks. Combat soldiers were forming their protective groups, creating a perimeter while the medical teams unloaded supplies and erected tents. The apparent chaos was in reality an enormously complex machine building itself into a full-fledged army field hospital. All Schneider's worries and the visceral fear that had clung to his intestines ever since he took off from England two days earlier evaporated. He was going back to work. At that moment, he was just proud to be part of this organization.

Hidden beneath the seething movement of hundreds of men and machines was a plan. An organization. A well-rehearsed play. The two years that they had spent in the English countryside had not been wasted after all. The mind-numbing drills that went on rain or shine— mostly rain—day after day, month after month, were now evolving into one of the most important engines of modern warfare: a highly mobile army field hospital.

Schneider stood for a moment about fifty yards from the village and watched as the tents went up and crates of materials were carried to their proper place, continually scanning the bustle for Ted and Hamm. Generators were set in place and filled with diesel. Power lines were connected. Latrines were dug away from the tents but close enough to fall under the protective eyes of the commandoes. The whole operation was a thing of beauty. After so many hours of helplessness and disorganization, of being lost and fired upon by superior forces, of being totally unable to do his job, Schneider just wanted to sit down and cry with joy. But he didn't.

The canvas of a medical tent tightened in the sunlight, and his curiosity had the better of him. Who were the other surgeons, if not Hamm? Did he know any of them? Might they know him? He had to admit, there was always that time when new postings got the better of him. Even as a student, when he rotated from service to service in medical school: from gynecology to psychiatry, from surgery to medicine. Each time he felt he had to prove himself all over again. He would have to show the new teachers, the new nurses, the new colleagues that he was someone to be reckoned with. Later, during his surgical residency years, it was the same. For every new rotation (almost every three months) there was a new team and new teachers, all of whom were watching to see if the new surgical resident knew anything, could do anything, could even operate at all. When those six years were over and he had finished his twelve months as Chief Resident, he went out into practice and realized it never ended. There would always be someone else there to judge him. At every new hospital, with every new operating team, all eyes would be on him to see if he could cut it. Literally. Yes, even each new patient had the same skeptical look in his eye.

Can this guy help me? Have they sent me to the right surgeon?

Here he was again, faced with a whole new bunch of medics and surgeons and soon some nurses, who would all want to know the answer to the same damned question: Was this guy any good? Could he cut his way out of a paper bag?

Of course he could.

Schneider took a deep breath and walked up to the first of the medical tents. He looked at the big red crosses painted on the roof and the sides. He was home.

He pushed the flap aside and walked inside. The room was filled with equipment and wooden boxes. The technicians were getting the lighting in place. As he stepped inside, the engine of a generator sputtered and coughed from somewhere outside toward the rear. It kicked in and settled to a steady background hum. The lights flickered and glowed and filled the tent with a yellow brightness that reflected off the white walls. Someone somewhere up the line had realized that, while the outside walls of the tents needed to be camouflaged, the operating room would require less lighting if the interior walls were white. A small thing at home, perhaps, where lighting was plentiful. But not so small out here.

A group of medical officers were huddled around a folding table at the rear of the tent. They were pouring over several sheets of paper which outlined the procedures and the check lists for setting up their field hospital. Their backs were turned to Schneider as he approached. Schneider started to say something when one of the officers turned at his approach.

"Steve!" Hamm cried out.

"Holy shit!," Schneider shouted, with the biggest grin his face could hold. "You're finally goddamned here!"

They shook hands for a moment. Then they broke down and hugged—great strong bear hugs that took their breath away. Schneider just couldn't believe it.

"Hey," Hamm said, letting go of Schneider and spinning him around by the shoulders, "look who's here!"

Ted McClintock rushed from the shadows of the tent, and shoved Schneider in the chest.

"Holy crap! It's Old Home Week," McClintock said.

Schneider shoved back. "Shit, Ted, I'm even glad to see your ugly puss! You gonna pass gas for me?"

"Damned straight!" McClintock said "So, how the fuck did you get here ahead of us?"

"A shittyassedratfucked glider. Pilot killed in midair; crash-landed about five miles from our target, long before your asses ever touched the beach. Lost half the men. It was a nightmare. I nearly shit my pants. God damned! I am so glad to see you guys."

Schneider hugged Hamm again, then stepped back to look at his friend. Hamm opened his arms and said, "Will you look at this shit." His khakis were still covered in dirt and wrinkled beyond repair. There were blood stains all over his pants and field jacket, and he wore no socks.

"We've been digging in here for a couple of days," said Steve. "What the hell happened to you on that beach?"

Before Hamm could answer, McClintock began to spill it all out. He just couldn't stop talking.

"We went back and forth on the god damned LSTs and fucking Rhino ferries. Seemed like we'd never get to the beach. Then we land in a nightmare of bodies and body parts. God, Steve, it was a living hell. Took us forever just to find a live GI to save. Then your pal here opens this poor guy with a gun shot wound to the heart! Can you fucking believe it! We're operating in a ditch up to our knees in salt water and sand. The medics are pouring in fluids. Hamm opens this guy's chest and sews the goddamned IV tubing right into the auricle! Right into the auricle! And the guy survives. Jesus. And that wasn't the half of it."

"Holy shit, Hamm…" Schneider said. "And then what?"

"Well, we…" Hamm started to say.

Again, McClintock interrupted.

"We've been on the move ever since. Never stopped. It took the rest of the day to get off that beach." McClintock's voice started to crack. He stopped talking for a second to take a breath. Then in a slower, more measured voice he said with great sadness, "So many bodies, Steve. I've never seen anything like it. All those young kids…."

Hamm put his hand on McClintock's shoulder and said, "It was a nightmare. Thousands dead, I think. We took care of most of the wounded right there on the sand, but there weren't a lot of them alive. Most of them who were still on the beach by the second day were dead. So we moved inland and caught some rides with these guys," he said pointing to the soldiers setting up the field hospital. "And here we are."

"What's happening with the invasion?" Schneider asked.

McClintock said, "The Krauts seem to be retreating, but we hear they're regrouping further inland to the east and we should expect a counter attack pretty soon. This little lull isn't gonna last long. No idea where the front line is, though."

Then all the men were silent. Their heads were lowered and their eyes on the ground. Schneider made circles with his toe in the dust. He was embarrassed now. He had thought his adventure was the nightmare of all wartime nightmares. But he realized that his own group's losses were a pittance compared to what happened on the beaches.

For the longest time, no one moved or spoke.

Finally Hamm said, palms up and shrugging his shoulders, "Let's get to work. Let's do what we came here to do."

The team spent the rest of the day and all that night setting up the field hospital. Marsh, now working with Higgenson and Antonelli, took over organizing the medics. The organization was a thing of beauty. When all the tents were up, the operating rooms were physically attached to separate pre-op tents where cases were evaluated and prepared for surgery. There was a post-op recovery tent, attached to the operating room on the other side, where the patients recovered for a few hours and stabilized before moving to the post-op ward. The patients would remain in post op until they could be evacuated to the rear. This established a nice flow from pre-op to operating room to recovery room to post-op.

Their living tents were a little farther off, separated from the medical area and close to the latrines. The mess tent was at the far end of the compound. The whole place was guarded by two platoons of infantry whose sole task was to keep the medical teams safe. The medical teams could forget about security now and focus on their job: saving lives and getting soldiers back to the front to fight or back to the rear for evacuation to England.

They were doctors again, and they loved it. Home again, among family.

Chapter Fourteen

11 June 1944, 1100 Hours
Field Hospital Charlie-7, Fauville to Hiesville, France

Schneider and McClintock had been up working at different tables all night and into the morning. There were many new surgeons coming and going almost daily, but Hamm's group managed to stay together at least in the same field hospital. Hamm just came off a nice two-hour nap and was feeling remarkably fit, considering that he was getting even less sleep than he did as a surgical resident. It wasn't the long operating hours so much. Those, he could handle. But being so close to the battle lines got him down. He couldn't imagine how the medics at the front lines were holding up. The Germans weren't supposed to shoot at them, but they seemed to be damn well trying to kill as many medics as possible. Hamm thought about these young men, taken from ordinary towns all over America. They had been taught that it was wrong to kill, and that the world was not supposed to be filled with people trying to kill you. Now they were dug into foxholes with no way to defend themselves near some town they'd never heard of, their friends dying all around them, and people were shooting at them in spite of their red-cross arm bands and helmets. It amazed Hamm that everyone wasn't shell-shocked or suffering from battle fatigue. That would have been the sensible reaction to the constant violence and fear. Behaving the way these men were—following orders, holding unholdable positions—those were the crazy choices. Going crazy would have been the sane thing to do. But they didn't.

Still, with all the pressure and the chaos, Hamm did manage to get Sorenson onto an operating table. It really should have been Schneider's case. Schneider had done the work in the field, and he had become close to Sorenson. Hamm knew that Schneider wanted to be the one who got Sorenson on the road to recovery. But, Schneider was busy with critically wounded men, who always came first. Hamm just happened to have an open table when Sorenson's semi-elective case came up, so he took over. No sense waiting for Schneider and risking Sorenson getting bumped to the end of the line again. They never knew when it would get busy, only that it would get busy again, and soon. Anyway, Hamm had more orthopedic experience than Schneider did. He had spent more time in his residency in the orthopedics rotation by choice.

Sorenson bitched and complained all the way to the OR.

"How am I gonna command my men? Who's gonna take my place?"

Hamm didn't argue with him because, in medical matters, he outranked Sorenson. When they finally got him into the surgical tent, Hamm nodded to McClintock, who shoved an ampoule of Pentothal into Sorenson's IV, and that was that. Sorenson stopped talking in mid-sentence—he was still bitching—and his eyes rolled up in his head. Out he went. Peace and quiet except for the background shelling and machine-gun fire.

Hamm cleaned up Sorenson's wound. There was a lot of dead muscle around the fracture site from all the rough movement, but mercifully there was still no evidence of gangrene or any other infection.

He's sure made of good stuff, Hamm thought. He filed down the sharply fragmented ends of splintered bone and put everything back together as close as they had been in nature. It was too dirty a wound to use any hardware or a primary closure, so he covered the exposed bone with healthy muscle and fascia, and left the skin open with several rubber drains in the wound.

"Let's pump him full of penicillin, Ted—God bless that stuff."

"Yup, I already gave him 10,000 units."

Then Hamm splinted the leg from Sorenson's toes to his upper thigh, leaving two little windows in the plaster cast to observe the wound and to make sure his toes stayed pink and warm. Sorenson got a first-class ticket to the evac hospital now in business near the secured beach at Normandy. The Germans were long gone from the area, and LSTs were landing there hourly with still more personnel and supplies. On the return trip, the LSTs evacuated the wounded back to hospital ships or to England. Hamm didn't know exactly where Sorenson would go, and Sorenson never woke up in time for Hamm to say good-bye. Hamm wanted Sorenson evacuated as soon as possible, so he ordered him into the first available ambulance. Sorenson slept like a baby all the way to the ambulance trucks, where he was loaded into the racks built along the side walls. There were three men stacked on each wall of his particular truck. Hamm tucked the records into the stretcher with him and silently wished him well. He didn't think Sorenson was likely to make it back into this war. Not unless the war went on a lot longer than anyone dared imagine.

After only a short time at Fauville, orders came down to pack it all up again. It would soon become maddening how often and how quickly they had to tear down the hospital and then set up again only a few miles away, so they could be as close as possible to the fighting. But being close to the fighting was what saved lives in the time saved to get the wounded to medical care. It was a sight to see: officers and men running around, looking for all the world as if they were confused and lost. However, behind the illusion of chaos was an orderly system functioning the way it was designed. In an hour, that whole field hospital could be packed up and on its way to where it was needed.

One hour, Hamm thought. Amazing! Like to see them do *that* in Philly.

"Hey, Doctor Hammer. Where's Doc Schneider?" It was Marsh. He was busy packing up, too, but he never seemed comfortable when he was too far away from Schneider. Something about surviving the glider crash and subsequent battle together seemed to have bound their souls. It was almost as if Marsh had taken responsibility for Schneider's well-being, a teenaged guardian angel.

"I'm not sure. He was operating a while ago. Did you look in the OR tent?"

"Yup. Not there."

"Then he might be in town. I think he went back to see one of the locals. Something about Claude?"

"Oh...," Marsh's eyes fell. He turned away and started walking back to the tents.

Hamm didn't know what that was about, but Steve would tell him when the time came.

Before Marsh was too far away, Hamm shouted: "Hey, Marsh. I just operated on Lieutenant Sorenson. I think he's going to be fine." He pointed and said, "He's in that ambulance over there if you want to say good-bye."

Marsh brightened up and ran in the direction of the ambulance pool. Hamm had never actually seen Marsh walk anywhere.

The medical team finished packing the gear and the trucks and loaded themselves into several of them. The doctors almost never rode together in a single truck, in case there was a land mine, or an artillery strike or an ambush. The army didn't want to lose a whole medical team in one shot. Still, they labored under the delusion that the big red crosses emblazoned on the trucks gave them an umbrella of protection: that they were protected by the Geneva Convention and its rules against firing on non-combatants. They would learn a lesson about that shortly.

Once the surgical supplies were packed and counted, Hamm headed back to his tent to gather his personal things. Not much of them to pack. He was going to need a resupply of socks and underwear before very long, and he had no idea when that would be.

"Hey, Major!" It was Marsh, still running. "I saw Lieutenant Sorenson, but he was still out like a light. Hope that leg's gonna be okay."

"He's going to do great, Andy. You took good care of him from what Major Schneider told me."

"I hope so."

"Hey, is it my imagination, or are these convoys just getting bigger and bigger?"

Marsh looked around.

"Starting to look like one of those circus caravans used to come to town every summer. We get so many new surgeons and medics every day I don't who's who. Barely know who to salute. Must be thirty trucks in that caravan now. All full of wounded too."

The ride was slower than the one from the beaches at Normandy. After D-Day, there had been little resistance once the army plowed inland, and those trucks could race flat out to get to the front lines. The Germans were in a full-out retreat and had not yet regrouped or coun-terattacked in any force. That situation was changing now as pockets of German resistance began to flare up all around them. They never knew which direction was safe. One moment their rear was covered by marines or commandoes; the next, there were Germans all over the place. Meanwhile, the casualties poured in. It was hard to guess when they would pack it up and leave an area to head for safety or to follow the fight. And that made it impossible to know which wounded GI would have to wait until the next stop for his surgery, if he could survive that long. Tough decisions were part of every day for the whole war.

Hiesville was supposed to be in friendly hands when the auxiliary surgical group arrived. They had heard there were some good build-ings in which they could set up their hospital and living quarters. Hamm fantasized about a real bed and a big old bathtub—maybe the kind with claw feet—and lots of hot water. It would remain a fantasy for some time. In the few days since they had landed, the tents had already grown wearisome, and a solid floor and plumbing would have been welcome. Not to mention that the tents were useless at stopping bullets and shrapnel, whereas some of the old villas and châteaux had thick stone walls.

The medical group was approaching Hiesville, with the armed jeeps leading the convoy. Hamm could hear a firefight ahead as they approached, but no one knew its magnitude or who was winning. The trucks slowed to a crawl. Then they finally stopped altogether. The medics opened the back doors to try to get a better look, but a marine sergeant waved them back.

"Stay in the trucks, and keep down. We'll be done here in a few minutes."

No one liked the sound of that very much. How close was this fighting?

Soon enough, though, the firing ceased, and a few minutes later the trucks began to roll again. Within ten minutes, they were climbing out at their destination. Or nearly so.

When Hamm bailed out of the truck, he was about a hundred yards from a classic old French farmstead. It was built of a light beige stone with a slate roof and dormer windows on the third floor. The house looked like something off the label of a wine bottle. As he walked closer, he could see the pockmarks of bullets all over the walls.

"There must have been a hell of a firefight at some point to have made all that damage," he said to the driver.

About fifty yards further up, soldiers had taken cover in various positions around the house. Sporadic small arms fire broke the calm of the countryside, but Hamm couldn't tell where it was coming from, or where it was going. The soldiers around him showed no concern, but the troops closer in kept their heads down, crouching behind jeeps and trucks.

Hamm asked one of the GIs what was going on.

"Sniper, sir. In the barn to the left. We can't see his position. He opens up every now and then with a single shot, and then moves to somewhere else. He's like a ghost. I don't know if there's only one or several. Can't get a fix on him."

"Has he hit anyone yet?" Hamm asked.

"Yes, sir. We've got two down already. Medics are up there with them." Then he looked from Hamm's major's oak leaves to the caduceus on his collar and said, "Maybe they could use you up there too, sir."

He pointed to a ditch behind a jeep, a lot closer to the stables than Hamm cared to think about being.

Hamm let out a breath, picked up his pack, and started running in a crouch as fast as he could toward the jeep. No shots rang out, but he could just feel his chest in the cross hairs of that sniper's scope. He had heard that hunted animals feel the presence of the hunter; that experienced hunters don't look directly at the prey until they are ready to pull the trigger. Hamm felt the heat of that sniper's scope on his chest, and the hairs on his neck stood against his shirt collar as he ran.

He made it to the ditch and tumbled down next to the two soldiers and a medic already there. Hamm lay panting in the bottom of that little hole, grateful that he was alive and that the steel of the jeep was between him and the sniper

"Doc! What the hell you doing here?" It was Antonelli. Hamm hadn't seen him since the day before, when he was busy bringing in the wounded at Fauville.

"I work here, Gene. What's up?" he said, trying to lighten his black mood.

"Leg shot. This guy's got a pretty bad wound in his thigh; bullet seems to have fragmented when it hit the bone. Still bleeding pretty good, too."

The man was lying at the edge of the ditch in the most awkward position imaginable. His legs and pelvis were nearly face up, allowing Antonelli to tend the wound. But, the upper body was twisted almost prone, with the man's chest elevated to the earth at the edge of the ditch. He was holding a rifle and aiming at the stables.

"Roll over here a minute, soldier. We need to see this leg," Hamm said.

"Can't, sir."

"Well, why the hell not?"

"Just can't."

As Hamm spoke, his left ear was shattered by a blast. He ducked and dropped deeper into the ditch with Antonelli right on top of him.

"Got 'im! I fuckin' got 'im!" The soldier was shouting and squirming around the ditch.

"God damn it! Hamm said, shouting over the momentary deafness in his ear.

"Sniper, sir! I fuckin' nailed him!"

"Jesus Christ!" Hamm said. "Give me that damned gun."

He yanked the weapon from the soldier's hands and threw it to the ground. "What the hell do you think *this* is?" he said, pointing to the red cross on his own helmet. You're wounded, and we're medics. We're here under a red cross. We're not supposed to be shooting at anyone. Now drop it 'til I'm finished!"

Hamm took the wounded soldier by the shoulders, pulled him down, and rolled him onto his back. The man moaned with the pain from his wound. "Be still, soldier! I need to get a look at this leg, and don't even think about reaching for that goddamned gun!"

"It's a 'rifle,' sir... not a gun," the boy said.

"And don't give me a damned grammar lesson! Jesus! You want me to fix this leg or not?" With that, he cut the soldier's pant leg from the cuff to the hip to expose the wound."

"Well, I got the son-of-a-bitch that shot me! He shot two other of our guys, Major!" the young man shouted.

"Son, if I hear one more word about—Ah shit." He looked at the boy and a sadness swept over him. He couldn't believe he was scolding this teenager who had just been so badly wounded.

Then he said more softly, "Just take it easy, son. I'll be finished here in a minute. Then we'll get you out of here."

The soldier reluctantly relaxed his body and gave in to Hamm's care. Antonelli put the rifle out of reach next to the medical packs. Only now did sensation seem to make its way from the man's shattered femur and torn muscles to his brain. Before, while he was still in combat, the gates to his consciousness had been closed, his senses focused on killing the sniper who had shot him. Now, all at once, a tear formed at the corner of his eye, and this killer became a scared little boy.

"Gene, give him a Syrette of morphine and hand me some sulfur."

Antonelli injected the painkiller while Hamm sprinkled the sulfur powder onto the wound.

"Dress it up and get him to pre-op. If there is one. If not, I'll go set one up right now. I don't think this is the last we're going to hear from Jerry snipers."

Hamm pulled himself out of the ditch and slung his pack. There was no more firing, and the men around the farmhouse were slowly getting to their feet and coming out of cover. Hamm walked past them on the way back to the medical trucks.

One GI shouted to him: "Nice runnin', Doc. You can play for our team."

Hamm smiled and waved. Boy jokes.

By the time he got to the trucks, the engines were running. They drove the final yards toward the house. Then, the whole process of men and machines kicked back into gear. In less than two hours, they had Field Hospital Charlie-7 up and running again. By nightfall, the cots were nearly full, and all the operating tables occupied, including his wounded GI from a few hours before. Schneider and Hammer were up to their elbows in blood again.

Everything was the same. Just a new address.

Chapter Fifteen

11 June 1944, 2200 Hours
A Concentration Camp near Weimar, Germany

It was hard to stay awake so late. Berg's eyes burned. His hands began to shake, and they shook more and more as the night wore on. He sat in his office waiting until the guards had grown sleepy. The officers headed to bed with their women—some willing, some not. By midnight, the chances of Berg being interrupted were very slim. This timing had served him well for four years, but luck was a big part of it. And luck, he knew, could run out.

Finally, Berg had free reign in his miserable little kingdom. He could make all the decisions necessary to run his hospital (if the unheated, decrepit wooden shack could be called by such a lofty name). He may have had no supplies, but he did his best.

The SS officer in charge, Standartenführer Himmel, liked to visit Berg during the daytime. The SS doctor in charge, Sturmbannführer Grau, never came by after dark. Grau puzzled Berg. He was a well-educated physician from München, very much respected from what Berg heard. He specialized in heart diseases and taught at the university as well.

How did this man fall in with such a mob of butchers? How did he forget the oath he swore to care for the sick? What happened to this man that he could join the Nazis and their madness?

It was inconceivable that a man could practice medicine his whole adult life and then, in a moment, become a killer, a man entirely without conscience.

Grau's job was to oversee the day-to-day operation of Berg's hospital. He never got his own hands dirty except when it came time to treat one of the German staff or his own SS officers. This would prevent Berg from administering a poison or purposely making some surgical blunder that might put a German out of service. Berg never actually thought of doing such a thing until it became clear that this was the very reason Grau was standing over him. But Berg was not sure he could do it, even if he were given the chance.

So, Grau was there as a guard in a way, but his main job was to conduct and oversee the experiments that the Nazis had designed even before the war had started. It was a gruesome idea, experimenting on living people. But the Nazis said that these weren't really people anyway; they were Jews, Untermenschen. *Underpeople.* Not people at all. By the very fact of their being in that awful place, they were dead already, so what did it matter? Most died within three or four months of arriving there.

And Hitler is an antivivisectionist! And a vegetarian as well. Imagine that? Berg often marveled at the madness of it.

The various experiments, if you could call them that, were appalling. Some patients were placed in vats of ice-filled water to determine the effects of freezing temperatures on the body. This was supposed to teach the Nazis something about pilots shot down in the North Sea. Few of the prisoners survived even minutes of immersion. Everyone knew what would happen to the pilots. If you survived the crash, you had about two to three minutes in the water before you died. Everyone died. So, why experiment? Why? Because it was so cruel. Berg witnessed not a single experiment that could be justified even in animals, much less humans. Nothing useful could be learned except how to inflict more pain and more misery on people who were nearly beyond further suffering.

Joseph Mengele, Berg had heard, was injecting blue dyes into the eyes of living patients to see if eye color could be permanently changed, could be made into the pure blue of the Aryan race. Most of these poor souls went to the gas chambers blind for their troubles. Jewish women were the subject of experiments to increase the efficiency of sterilization procedures. Caustic and toxic chemicals were injected through the cervix and up into their fallopian tubes in an attempt to scar and mangle the organs so that fertilization could not occur, so that no more Jews could be conceived.

Of course, there was no anesthesia to spare the victims the pain, no narcotics to help them through the post-operative days before they inevitably died of infection or chemical peritonitis, an excruciatingly painful inflammation of the lining of the abdominal cavity.

In the early years, Berg escaped participation in the terrible ordeals. But, as time wore on, the SS became shorthanded, so Berg was conscripted. They forced him to perform mass sterilizations of both men and women. The Nazis did not want the Jewish vermin proliferating. In a way, it gave Berg a chance to do something of value. Jewish women who were pregnant or became pregnant while in the camps were immediately gassed. So, whenever he could, he performed abortions under the guise of sterilization procedures before it became evident to the guards that the woman was carrying a child. It broke his heart to destroy these lives, but it saved mothers who might still survive the camps to bear children in a better world. Berg did not believe in life after death, but he still believed in life after the camps. Perhaps not for himself, but maybe for someone.

Later, the participation became more egregious, and when Berg resisted, the threats to him and his patients became very real. Grau made no bones about it. He came into Berg's little cubicle one afternoon just after rounds. He did not sit, for Jews had sat in the only other chair in front of Berg's desk, and Grau would not contaminate himself. He feared the lice, and from the lice, the typhus.

"Berg," he said, "the time has come for you to take part in our scientific research."

Berg dropped his book to the desk and stood. The man could not be serious.

"I don't understand," he said, though, of course, he did.

"Sit down!"

Berg sat.

"Nothing to understand. I need more manpower to cope with the increased load of patients coming into the camp. I cannot do all these procedures by myself, and the assistants I have now are incompetent. I need the kind of manual dexterity that only a surgeon such as yourself, or a heart specialist such as I, possess." He was almost smiling, expecting Berg to be flattered to be included in this world of abominations.

"What procedures Sturmbannführer?" Berg could barely say the words that would lead to Grau's defining Berg's role.

"I have received orders to increase the numbers of people who will be…how shall I put this?"

"I know what you are saying, Sturmbannführer. But how am I to be involved in this?"

"We are in short supply of Zyklon B, and it's dangerous to transport and to use. There have been some accidents already. Berlin wants us to see if there is an efficient and more humane way to dispose of the prisoners who are about to die anyway."

Berlin wants. Such an easy way to lay the burden of guilt elsewhere, Berg thought.

Zyklon B was hydrogen cyanide in pellet form. When exposed to the moisture in the air, it became a gas that was almost diabolical in its efficiency. Cyanide poisoned the system by blocking respiration at the cellular level. All the cells of the body are instantly suffocated from within. The very first breath sends a signal to the brain demanding more oxygen, forcing the person to take deep involuntary gulps of air, which in turn takes in more of the cyanide gas. Death occurs in seconds, or at most, a few minutes. The sensation of total suffocation must be awful during those last conscious moments, though there are no survivors to attest to it. A few minutes could be very long. And Grau was correct, it was very dangerous to handle.

"What do you want from me, Sturmbannführer?" Berg asked again, with increasing dread in his voice, his calm demeanor beginning to fall apart.

"We will try another way, a kinder way, to bring these prisoners to their end. We will be injecting solutions of phenol or of sodium Evipam directly into the heart. We'll see which works better. This should send the drugs directly to the coronary arteries and to the brain in seconds, painlessly stopping the heart and the brain function at once. Much kinder, don't you think?"

Oh, dear God, that I should be part of this killing machine!

"Well?"

"Don't ask me to participate in this, Sturmbannführer. Anyway, I'm needed here. There is always more work than I can do." Berg was pleading, and Grau was enjoying it.

"My dear Berg. Can't you see what a good thing you will be doing? You will save these people from the showers. You will be helping them with your skill in getting the drugs directly into the left ventricle. Why, none of the Kapos or the unskilled laborers could do such a good job. They would miss the ventricle and get an intramuscular cardiac injection. Painful and slow...." He wrinkled his nose and shook his head as if he had just swallowed an objectionable medicine.

"But—"

"No buts!" Grau shouted. Then in a calmer voice, as colleague to colleague: "You will join me in the operating room tomorrow morning at nine. Without fail."

Grau turned on his heels without another word and left Berg alone. As he stepped out into the compound, he nearly ran into one of the prisoners coming into the hospital.

"Schwein! Get out of my way you vermin!" Grau sidestepped to avoid any contact with the possibly typhus-infected Jew.

Joseph Meyer climbed the two steps, turning to watch Grau disappear from sight. The little climb took his breath away. But he was relieved that all he received was a few choice words, and nothing worse.

"Hello, Doktor Berg," Joseph said, as he eased himself into a chair. Joseph was a walking skeleton, not much different from most of the inmates. He was fifty pounds lighter than when he had arrived, and clearly burdened by many chronic diseases at this point.

"Guten tag, Joseph," Berg said. "What do you need?"

'Me? I need a vacation. And something good to eat. What was the Sturmbannführer, that piece of shit, doing here?"

Berg shook his head.

"Careful, Joseph. You might talk too loudly one day," Berg said. "You won't believe this but he wants me to help him kill more inmates. For science!"

"They're not killing enough already? They better be careful. They might run out of us one day. Then what would they do?"

"They'll find someone else to torture and kill." Berg snuck a peak at the door to be sure no one was near by listening.

"Why do you let them, Doktor. Why don't you fight back?"

"Me? How can I fight back. Why don't you fight back?"

"It would be useless. There's nothing I can do before they'd kill me. But you...."

"Me, what? What can I do?"

There must be many ways for you to hurt them. You have patients dying of contagious diseases, don't you? Couldn't you find a way to share them with The Master Race? Typhus? Syphilis? Dysentery? They could just shit themselves to death. Something? There must be something you could do. I would help you."

"You? You can't help yourself fart, Joseph."

"Think about it, Doktor. I'll think, too. Between us maybe we could kill some of them. Even just a few. Even just one."

Joseph hunched down into his pitiful coat and left the room. Berg watched as the little man made himself almost invisible walking through the compound. Best not to be noticed.

Berg sat down at his desk. His face saddened as he realized that a new line would soon be crossed. In the next days, Berg would become part of the Nazi killing machine.

Berg never slept that night. Pictures drifted through his mind; horrible visions of patients convulsing as the deadly phenol traveled into peoples' brains. Not peaceful deaths, nothing like a falling off to sleep, but deaths punctuated by spasms and rigors of involuntary muscular contractions, of fecal and urinary incontinence, of frothing at the mouth with eyes wide in terror.

How can I participate in this? Is it time for me to commit a prisoner's ultimate act of rebellion? Should I walk into the compound and throw myself onto the electric fences that surround my world?

This was the time-honored way of committing suicide within the camp where no weapons were available other than the very fences that imprisoned them. The irony was that a camp rule specifically forbade inmate suicide—and the punishment for breaking the rule was death! Only the Nazis could have dreamt up that one.

Berg sat at his desk in a fugue state for an hour or so. He thought for the thousandth time of all the missed opportunities to leave Germany before it was too late. He berated himself for not following his family's pleadings to go to America. Relatives in America as well as those in Germany had seen this coming. So why hadn't he? Was it hubris? Was he so proud of his skill and his importance to society that he could not see what was in front of his face? How could he even contemplate exposing his family to such unthinkable danger, let alone actually do it?

It had been so long since he last saw his Rachel. The night they dragged him away, they took her too, but at least they both were taken to the same camp. He could see her through the wires from time to time. He knew she was all right. He even took to bribing the Kapos— prisoners who worked for the Germans inside the camps, and were known for their brutality—with cigarettes he stole from dead and dying patients. He could not believe that he had been reduced to stealing from the dead! At first the Kapos would smuggle notes and sometimes food or medicines to Rachel for him. He would watch from the doorway of his clinic to make sure they got to her. She would glance his way and smile to let him know she was all right. He would nod.

But this little glimpse of assurance lasted only a few months. It had been years now since he had seen or heard of her. He didn't know if she had been sent to another camp or if she had become part of the smoke drifting from the chimneys of the crematorium. His heart ached every day the smoke rose across the yard. The Kapos stopped accepting his notes and gifts. He begged them for information, tried to bribe them for just a word, but they said they knew nothing. So, every night and every morning in his prayers, he asked God to watch over her and to send her back to him after the war had ended.

Berg's hope lived only in his children now. Before Rachel disappeared, she wrote to him on the back of cigarette papers that she paid the Kapos to smuggle back to him. It took several messages, but he learned what happened after he was taken away. Rachel was kept in the local jail for a week. When she was released, she went home for another week. She found the children hiding in the basement of one of their neighbors' houses. They had been beaten in the streets the night Berg was taken, but they were left there and not deported to the camps. Their neighbor, Frau Meissner, took the children to her home and cared for them. She hid them in her basement and then, a few days later, she took them to a place in the country. Relatives had a farm, so the children and Frau Meissner stayed with them, away from the city where it would be too difficult to hide. Then Rachel was arrested again and sent to the camp because she would not tell the Gestapo where the children were. Finally, Rachel disappeared from the camp, and that was the last news he had of the children. That was four years ago.

When he thought of the terrible tragedy that his people now faced; when he was overwhelmed with hatred for the Nazis and the SS and the Germans who did this to him; when he wanted God to painfully destroy each German remaining on earth, he had to remind himself every single day he was in this camp that Frau Meissner risked her life and the lives of her family to save his children. Not to save her own relatives, but rather the children of people who happened to live nearby: neighbors whom she barely knew. A friendly nod as they passed in the street. Nothing really more than that.

And Frau Meissner was not Jewish. To think that Frau Meissner and her entire family, if they were still alive, must live in fear every minute of every day for the crime of saving Jewish children. Who knew if any of them were alive?

Berg yawned and stretched, trying to work those old stories out of his head. Then he went into the ward. It was quiet and dark, the only noises the rasping breath of the nearly dead. He could hear the fluid bubbling through the airways of patients in their last throes of typhus. He tried to ignore the suffering about which he could do nothing, but he couldn't. Instead, he tried to focus on his one small act of disobedience, of rebellion, against this monster regime; the only step he could take to ensure justice after the war, whether he survived or not. Frau Meissner and her family had made their stand, and he would make his.

He walked to the end of the ward and stepped into the smaller room reserved for the most contagious cases, those with tuberculosis and other deadly infectious diseases. There were no windows, no ventilation; the air was heavy and pungent. He could smell the sepsis. Small miracle he had not been infected yet. Perhaps he had developed some immunity after all these years of exposure.

In the far corner, the place least likely to be visited by the SS because of the risk of contamination, there was a wooden container marked with the words:

Achtung! Gefahr! Entzündete Gegenstände nur!

Attention! Danger! Infected Objects Only!

Berg opened the lid, carefully removing the pus-soaked rags and bandages, using a wooden stick that he kept at the back of the container. Beneath these was a layer of cleaner rags and a box wrapped in waxed parchment. He lifted the box from the bottom of the container and replaced the cover. Unwrapping the box, he took from it a leather-bound book whose leaves were barely held in place by the worn and cracked glue of the binder. He sat on the floor behind a table and opened the book on his knees. About half of the pages were filled with his writing, first in ink and lately in pencil. There was no more ink in the camp now, so he guarded the last pencil as if it were priceless. To him it was.

He opened the book to the next clean line and began to write in his own handwriting—the only part of his identity that might survive him in the camp. He had no typewriter, of course, but even if he had, he wanted this to be written in his own hand so there could be no mistake about the authenticity of the authorship.

Halfway down the page, he wrote:

11 June 1944. 2300 hours.
Sadie Rubenstein. Age: about 35.
Admitted following a broken mandible sustained two weeks ago:
struck by Kapo Stein; Unable to take fluids or solids by mouth.
Cause of Death: starvation/dehydration

On the next line he wrote,

11 June 1944. Abraham Ragovski. Age about 42.
Admitted with pneumonia secondary to broken ribs sustained in
beating by SS guard Anton Hochschuler.
Cause of death: Respiratory failure.

And on and on and on. He listed the deaths in his hospital. He omitted no one. He could not list the names of those who were gassed, except for the very few he knew of personally, and in those cases he did so. But most went to the showers with no one there to record their deaths. As many as ten thousand could be gassed in a single day. However, only thirty-two hundred people a day could fit into the four ovens. The cremations blanketed the camp and the surrounding countryside day and night with a gray ash that fell like filthy snow.

To accommodate the rest, the SS dug huge open pits and dumped the bodies into them, using bull dozers to cover them with lime when it was available. Not everyone was dead when they went into the pits; some of those still alive might be shot for target practice by the SS guards. If the victims were not so lucky, they were crushed to death or suffocated by the bloated and putrefying bodies heaped on top of them as the graves filled.

What a sad and pathetic attempt at justice was this little book, he thought. Somehow he hoped, that after he died there, as surely he must, his book would be found at the end of the war when these monsters were defeated, as surely they must be. Perhaps his documentation of these killings, like a deathbed confession, would lead to a justice in some way he could not envision now. So, this is what he did. For, little as it was, it was all he could do.

"Thank you, Frau Meissner," he said as he wrote the last entry for the day and closed the book.

Chapter Sixteen

When Hammer and McClintock came back into their tent, Schneider lay facedown, still deeply asleep. The fourth cot had been empty for two days. New surgeons were rotating in and out of various field hospitals at a fast rate now that the action was escalating and the casualties increasing.

They had been in Hiesville only three days, and it was already beginning to feel like home. Schneider was sorry to have missed the chance to operate on Sorenson, but he knew Hamm had done a great job, and he was happy Hamm could squeeze the case in before the next onslaught of wounded. Schneider hadn't been able to say good-bye to Sorenson before the ambulance took him back to the LSTs. He wondered what the beaches must have looked like by then. Were all those bodies and body parts still there? Had they identified the dead yet? Hamm's descriptions would remain with him until the day he died; which, the way the war was going, he thought, might be sooner than he wanted to imagine.

Schneider enjoyed working with his team together again, though they liked to needle each other. Especially McClintock; he never let up on Hamm. It must have had something to do with the ongoing relationship between anesthesiologists and surgeons. It was a curious thing. Something in the relationship seemed to irritate. Surgeons liked to feel in command, and, like the captain of a ship, their word is law. Or should be. Anesthesiologists rankle at this, so the conflict never really went away.

The farm was now a full-fledged field hospital, running as smoothly as could be expected. They were short of almost everything except patients, but they had grown used to that. They all just made do. None of the autoclaves ever made it ashore—or at least had not caught up with them yet. So, instead, they set up big pots and tubs of boiling water day and night to sterilize instruments, sheets, drapes, gowns, and just about anything else that might touch the inside of a patient. There were never enough surgical drapes or linens. They appropriated bedding, curtains and towels to use instead. They did have almost enough surgical instruments, with more showing up on a truck within a few days of their arrival. Plasma was always in short supply but, for the moment, there was just about enough whole blood, which turned out to be better for the wounded GIs anyway. How long the supply of type-specific blood would last was anyone's guess. They weren't counting on it for very long. Besides, they had a lot of O-negative, the universal donor, to keep them going.

The snipers kept them busy every day. As the soldier had told Hamm, they were like ghosts. They might strike from anywhere. There was no pattern. It might come from the woods, the surrounding trees or rocks. Anywhere. Often from so far away that it took a few shots before they knew where death was coming from.

Schneider was taking a break one night, sitting on a log with some of the staff and enjoying a moment of quiet, when out of nowhere a shot rang out. The man next to him silently crumpled to the ground with a bullet wound through the head. Dead on the spot.

Schneider's gut tightened into a knot. He instinctively dropped to the ground. It was like a conscious faint; he had no control over what his body was doing, but he was aware of what was happening.

Schneider couldn't tell where the shot had come from because of the echoing. Might have been from the woods, but it also might have been from the house itself. Soldiers were pointing in every direction, but no one really knew where the sniper might be. A search followed: the woods, the stables, the trees. They never found him. The sniper had done his damage and departed. A ghost.

One day later while Schneider was operating alone on a GI with multiple gunshot and shrapnel wounds to his abdomen, a young GI ran right into the operating room and shouted, "Hey, Major Schneider, we got another one!" He meant that they had killed a sniper.

Schneider said, "Great! Keep it up!" A few seconds after the young man had disappeared, he said aloud to no one in particular, "And next time wear a mask when you come in here for Christ sake." Schneider looked to the tent flap as it closed behind the young GI. God, they're all so young, he thought. Then he went right on operating. He had to keep operating, keep focused. Otherwise, he knew he would be taken away in a straitjacket.

And young they were. The surgeons were in their thirties or forties because it took four years of college, plus four years of medical school, and about six years of residency to train a surgeon. That was fourteen years after high school. The surgeons went out into the world at about thirty-two years old. Compared to most of these GIs, whose average age was about eighteen or nineteen, the surgeons were old men. In the real world, the GIs would be calling them 'sir' even if they weren't officers.

A few minutes later Marsh wandered into the operating room, tying his mask on as he moved through the door.

"Hey, Major. Lot's of action out there. It's a madhouse in Pre Op."

"Then it's sure to be a mad house in here before long. Want to scrub in with me, Andy?"

"Yes, sir. Oh, yes sir! You bet," he said puffed up with pride.

Marsh disappeared, and was back in flash, now scrubbed and ready for some action. He was gowned and gloved by Fred—Marsh didn't know his last name—the circulating nurse, and then stepped up to the table.

Schneider handed Marsh some retractors and positioned them into the wound so Marsh could keep the edges apart and the incision open.

"It's all about exposure, Andy. Without exposure you can't see and you can't operate. Then you're just dangerous."

"I can see great, sir."

"That's because you're giving me great exposure. So don't move an inch unless I tell you to. Just remember that I'm the one who has to see in there, not you."

"Don't forget that, Andy." McClintock said. 'Surgeons believe that they are the top of the heap."

"Well, we are. You ever start a case without us?"

"Y'all go on ignoring the facts of life. Makes you feel good," McClintock said. "Doesn't bother me."

"What facts, Ted?"

"When y'all are operating down there on your side of the drapes, don't forget that I'm the only one really taking care of the patient. I'm the only one taking care of a live patient. Down your end it's just meat. You're just cuttin' and sewin'. You're the technicians, and I'm the doctor. Don't forget that when you're laughing and making jokes about the gas passers."

Schneider looked at Marsh. Then at McClintock.

"Sorry, Ted. Never thought about it that way."

"Your heartfelt apology is accepted. Now go on and finish this damn case so y'all can save another life."

Schneider continued to operate in silence for a few minutes, carefully running the bowel—examining each inch of the small and large intestines—which amounted to about forty feet altogether, for any bullet or shrapnel hole that needed to be sutured. Missing even a small one would very likely prove fatal to the young GI on the table. As he closed the last of the holes with Marsh now cutting the sutures for him, he looked up and stretched his tight aching neck. Too much time standing around with his neck bent over still one more casualty.

"You know, Andy, you're getting a hell of an education here. When this war's over, you could go to medical school. You'll be way ahead of the rest of them."

"You think so?"

"I do. Why waste all this on-the-job training you're getting for free?"

"OJT's gonna take me only so far, sir."

"But you'll have all the basics. Look, take what we're doing here every day. It's not that hard. Trauma surgery's always the same. The wounds may differ, but the procedures never vary. That may mean racing around in a state of emergency all the time, doing the same thing over and over again with very little imaginative thinking required. But the procedures don't change. You've seen that."

"Yeah."

"It seems very complicated and dramatic. But you already know what you're going to do every time you help another wounded GI."

Schneider began pulling the large gauze laparotomy pads out from the GI's abdomen and handed them to the scrub nurse, who passed them off to the circulator for counting.

He went on.

"The airway has to be cleared first, because if the patient isn't breathing, it doesn't matter if the heart's beating or not. Then you've gotta deal with the heart, and for me, most of the time the easiest way is to take a knife and open the chest and pump the heart by hand. You know, open cardiac massage. After all that, we'll deal with the bleeding, or the sucking chest wound or the collapsed lung, or the guts hanging out of a bad abdominal laceration, or the bone fragments from the blast of a land mine, or the brain injury from a mortar, or the neck wound from a single bullet or...whatever needs attention. But, the airway, the heart, and the blood volume replacement always comes first, fast, and all at once. That's why we need so many of you guys."

Schneider made one last thorough exam of the abdominal cavity, then washed it out with sterile saline. He nodded his approval to himself and said, "Okay, let's close. Let me have some stay sutures please."

There was no on-call schedule at the field hospital. The medical team worked all the time, sleeping when they could. There were about twenty-four surgeons and a dozen anesthesiologists at the field hospital by then. It was impossible to keep track of all the personnel, in part because of the rapid turnover, and practically speaking, because most of the time in the OR, all their faces were covered with masks and caps—only their eyes showing through.

As in civilian life, there were rush periods and quiet times, though the quiet times were never long enough. Here they all grabbed snatches of sleep and quick meals, and then they went back into the OR at all hours of the day and night. It was a matter of need, and need ruled their lives.

Hamm and Schneider were expecting the arrival of a few truck-loads of Women's Army Corps nurses in a few days—the WACs. That would ease the load considerably, they knew, and brighten up the scenery, too. They had gotten pretty tired of looking at those unwashed, unshaved men day after day. Although they looked forward to the nurses' arrival, at the same time they feared for the safety of the WACs so close to the front. Schneider didn't know why he thought men were the only ones who should expose themselves to death in war, but he did. Chivalry came out in the most curious ways, and keeping the women safe at home had always seemed right. But the WACs were on their way, so the scuttlebutt had it, and the men weren't all that unhappy about it.

Hamm and McClintock came back to their quarters—a tent with a canvas floor close to the barn wall—after two in the morning. Both were looking pretty bad. They had been at it all day and much of the night. Their faces were grizzled and their eyes bleary and red.

Schneider had been snoring loudly. "What's up?" he said. He knew exactly what was up. He had slept only two hours, enough to make him groggy and cranky, but not enough for sufficient rest and refreshment.

"You," Hamm said. "You're up, and you're needed in the OR, stat."

"What is it?"

"Chest and abdomen. Shrapnel. He's stable right now. They're just getting his blood volume up, so he'll be ready to go in about fifteen minutes. You ready for an all-nighter?"

"I have a choice?" Schneider said as he fumbled for his boots.

No one answered. McClintock was asleep in his clothes already, and Hamm was off to the latrine before his nap.

Schneider got back into some warmer clothes—the nights were chilly, even in June—and walked over to the OR tents. There were usually fifteen to twenty operations going on at any one time, day and night. All the operating tables and beds were full. There was never enough room at the inn. But, unlike the famous inn, the field hospital turned no one away.

Schneider's walk from his bunk to the OR tents felt surreal: A crisp June night in northern France, a starry sky above and a charming farmhouse at his back. Nearby, a creek made lovely, burbling sounds. Old poplar trees stood silhouetted by the starlight. Napoleon's plane trees lined all the roads. It could have been heavenly. Instead, in the background, artillery whistled steadily, punctuated by the whoomph of mortars. Machine guns stuttered nearly nonstop. Occasionally, Schneider would involuntarily duck as low-flying German aircraft buzzed their position. It read like fiction, but it was all too real.

Schneider fretted that he had yet to gain control over his fear. If he weren't totally focused on a surgical case, his mind filled with the possibilities of sudden death or painful injury. Every wounded GI he saw could be him the next moment.

He quit stargazing and made his way to the operating tents. The area was dark, but he knew the path by heart and didn't risk the danger of turning on his flashlight.

Snipers.

The outside of the tents were the usual army khaki, with red crosses set in huge white circles painted four feet high on both halves of the slanting roofs and on each of the four walls. There was a little vestibule at the front door for several reasons. It made a good air trap so that contamination from the outside (like dust and flying insects) wouldn't get into the operating room. It also helped maintain the heat inside the tent. But, most important, it provided a buffer for the lights which were kept bright inside the OR itself.

Schneider pushed open the outer door and shut it before going inside into the OR area proper. The comparative brightness momentarily blinded him. He stood squinting for a few seconds. It was a noisy place, he noticed. Ten operating tables lined each side of the tent, with a walkway down the middle. Each team had a surgeon and assistant (usually another surgeon or a medic), an anesthesiologist, a scrub nurse, and a circulating nurse. They usually called them the sterile nurse and the dirty nurse, but naturally those names got misinterpreted and so reverted to scrub nurse and circulating nurse.

Schneider walked over to the changing areas, exchanging nods with members of the various teams as he passed their tables. Although there were a lot of personnel there, he had gotten to know a lot of them. They did, after all, eat three or more meals every day in the same mess tents and changed their clothes in the same pre-op area; they did their laundry in the same washhouse and used the same latrines But, most of all, just hung out together when there was any hanging out to do. They were too near the front for movies, restaurants, or theaters. Their only entertainment was each other.

Schneider hung up his khakis on a peg and put on some clean white scrubs. Then he walked over to the pre-op room to find his patient. It didn't take a genius to figure out which one was for him. At the entrance to the pre-op area stood a cot surrounded with personnel. Three IV bottles hung from high poles fed whole blood into a patient, and a fourth ran plasma. The medics had raised the poles high to make them run faster. A medic was changing one of the empty bottles. No question the young GI had suffered much blood loss. Schneider made a mental note to be alert for clotting and bleeding disorders he might develop after so many transfusions.

He walked to the bedside, where the little crowd parted for him. Antonelli was holding pressure on a Vaseline gauze pad wrapped around a chest tube protruding from the soldier's left chest. The drainage bottle sat on the floor, quickly filling with blood.

He looked at Antonelli and said, "You bring him in, Gene?"

"Yessir."

"What's he got?"

"Well, he's got a number of through-and-through wounds of the abdomen and the left chest. A large number!"

When Antonelli said someone had a large number of bullet wounds, Schneider paid attention. Gene was no hothouse flower. Even though he was only eighteen, his last few weeks had pushed him right up there with the most experienced combat medics.

"Anything else?" Schneider said.

"No sir. Just the bullet wounds, but they're enough."

"How we doing on the volume?" Schneider said to no one in particular.

One of the pre-op team answered: "His BP is back up; he was in shock when he got here, though. Pulse is down below a hundred now, and the BP is about one hundred over fifty. Not great, but I don't think he's going to do better than that until you get in there and stop whatever's bleedin'. Look at it running outta that chest tube!"

"I see. Any urine output?"

The same man said, "Yeah, about thirty cc's since he got here—about a cc per minute. Not great, but it's urine."

"OK," Schneider said. "Where are his films, and where are we going?"

"You're at Table Six, with Major Page. He's setting up now. He's new. Just arrived, so he's plenty fresh. Mahoney is scrubbed and waiting, and Dallas is circulating. Films are on the light box already."

"Great job, guys," Schneider said as he started toward the OR. They did a great job every time, but Schneider never failed to thank them. "Let's go."

The team followed, pushing the wheeled stretcher. Antonelli held one of the blood bottles high overhead, at the same time pressing on the dressing over the chest tube to prevent any air leak.

They got to their space at Table Six and positioned the gurney next to the operating table. Page immediately took over, holding the GI's head as the rest of them slid the unconscious man over from the gurney.

"Hi, I'm Dan Page," the anesthesiologist said. You Major Schneider?"

"Yeah. Steve Schneider. Good to see you."

The two men reached across the patient and shook hands.

The patient was already intubated—Page had placed an endotracheal tube in the pre-op area as soon as the man had arrived—so he transferred the tubing to his own anesthesia machine, which was pumping out pure oxygen. Since the GI was still unconscious, they wouldn't need any anesthesia until they began to operate.

Schneider looked around the table. "Who's assisting?"

Page shrugged. "We seem to be a little tight just now, Steve. Can you do this one alone, or should we send someone to go wake Major Hammer?"

"No. Let him sleep. Hey, Gene, you want a battlefield promotion to surgical resident?"

"Sir?"

"Come on and scrub. I just need someone to hold hooks for me."

"Yessir!" And just like Marsh, Antonelli turned and literally ran from the OR area to get into a scrub suit, hat, and mask. When he came back, barely three minutes later, he had his hands out and waited for gloves.

"Not so fast, pal," Schneider said. "There's the little matter of scrubbing."

Antonelli laughed and reddened a little. He was so excited at the thought of playing surgeon, he forgot to scrub. He actually wanted to get started before a real surgeon arrived and bumped him off the case.

Schneider and Antonelli stood at the scrub sink together and washed their hands with soap and wooden scrub brushes. The soapy water ran off their elbows, making wet spots on the canvas floor.

"You take off your wedding ring when you scrub, Doc?" Antonelli asked, pointing with his chin at the gold band on Schneider's left ring finger. Strictly speaking, it should have come off before he scrubbed.

"Nah. I'm afraid I'll lose it one day, and if I do that, I may as well not even go home."

"Your wife wouldn't like that, eh?"

"No, she wouldn't. Nor would I."

Schneider did not elaborate. He was thinking that the ring was not what might keep him from going home. For a long time since he'd left, he felt as if he were always walking on eggshells. Nothing he could do was right with Susan. If he fell asleep after dinner on the floor of the den, she'd be on him for not playing with the girls. Never mind that he had been up for forty-eight hours. He felt whipped, and he didn't like it. None of that helped their sex life either. It was hard to be passionate and loving when he was on the verge of a fight all the time.

When he left for basic training, Susan had not even seen him off at the station. She barely looked at him as he hugged his little girls good-bye. Now he wondered if Emily and Anna were all that was holding his marriage together. If they'd had no children, would he stay with Susan?

"What's your wife's name, sir?"

"Hmmm? Oh, Susan."

"You miss her?"

"That, I do, Gene."

They finished scrubbing and walked to the table. Mike Dallas, the circulating nurse, opened a pack of towels and dropped them onto the sterile field. Pete Mahoney, the scrub nurse, draped one over Schneider's hand and another one over Antonelli's. They dried and gowned, and Dallas tied them in. Schneider stepped to the right of the table, as Antonelli took his place at the patient's left. The GI was already positioned and draped; Dallas had washed and disinfected the skin while they were scrubbing. Mahoney had made a window in the draping towels along the midline of the abdomen and another over the left side of the chest, exposing both the bullet wounds and the incision area.

"Everything stable, Dan?" Schneider said, looking at Page.

"Yes, you can start," he said.

Schneider was glad to see a calm and confident anesthesiologist at the helm, just like McClintock. That was where the likeness stopped. Page didn't have any of the slow, North Carolina drawl emerging as it always did when McClintock sought to slow and calm the waters in the sometimes frenetic operating room. Page was all business with a definite speedy clip and efficiency. His accent had no regional give-away, but Schneider bet on somewhere in the Midwest. Page was short and stocky with wisps of curly blond hair peeking out from under his knitted surgical cap. He looked very athletic, with arms that bulged tightly into the short sleeves of his scrub suit. He had deep blue eyes. Schneider would have to wait until after surgery to see the rest of his face, now hidden under the surgical mask.

Schneider made a quick catalogue of the wounds, and then opened the chest. Sure enough, the left chest cavity was full of both liquid and clotted blood. Schneider placed a self-retaining retractor and spread the incision wider. Then he began scooping out the blood with cupped hands. It wasn't very elegant, but it was fast. The suction apparatus would have become clogged with blood clots. Schneider plopped the clots into a basin, which was quickly filled to overflowing. Then, when he was down to liquid blood, he asked for the suction and handed it to Antonelli.

"Suck this stuff out and keep sucking until I find the bleeder."

Page deflated the lungs slightly to give Schneider more exposure. Schneider knew he would enjoy working with the New Guy.

Antonelli was busy sucking out the blood and enjoying himself greatly.

Who knows, Schneider thought, after the war, this kid too might just be inspired to go to college and then medical school. Wouldn't that be nice?

"Hold this," Schneider said to Antonelli, handing him a wide flat malleable metal retractor covered in gauze to protect the lung. Antonelli retracted the lung and exposed the hilum where the major vessels were and where the bleeding seemed to be coming from.

"Look at that, Doc," he said.

Right at the place where the major vessels entered the pleural cavity from the heart was a tear in the left main pulmonary artery. The artery was the size of Antonelli's thumb and bleeding out fast. It was a tribute to the laws of evolution that the GI had survived this long.

Schneider put his thumb against the tear in the vessel and the bleeding stopped. "How are we doing on volume?" he asked Page. He could, if necessary, wait with his finger in the dyke until the blood volume was restored.

"We're just about caught up, Steve. Don't wait for me, I'll take care of his pressure and volume. Just go on ahead and sew him up."

Schneider took his finger off the artery, and placed a small vascular clamp across the edges of the tear. The bleeding stopped again. Then he took some fine vascular sutures and closed the tear.

When the tear was closed, he irrigated the chest cavity with several liters of saline solution until it was clean and shiny and good as new; that is, as good as it could be with about a dozen bullet holes visible in the chest wall. However, none of them were bleeding, and the pre-op x-rays showed no evidence of any bullets or fragments left in the chest or the lungs or the heart. There were a few holes in the lung itself, but they were easy to repair with some fine sutures.

When everything was the way he wanted it, Schneider asked Mahoney for a chest tube and some stay-sutures for the closure. Gene had begun to take out the self-retaining chest retractors, as Schneider instructed him, while Schneider made a hole between the ribs for the chest tube.

The kid was stable now.

Schneider had just said to Page, "We're closing the chest and going to the abdomen," when their whole world imploded.

Schneider didn't hear the noise itself. There had been so much background war noise since D-Day that no one paid any attention to what went on outside. So, when he felt the shock wave, he had no idea what was happening. There was a terrible pressure and pain in his ears, and the room went dark at the same instant his hearing went away. Then he was swept to the ground as the entire operating tent came down.

Buried beneath the tent, he couldn't tell whether or not the generators had gone out. Whatever was happening, Schneider was helpless beneath hundreds of pounds of canvas and tent poles. He couldn't breathe, and, in his panic, he struggled like a swimmer trying to get to the surface. But, there was no surface. It was like drowning under the ice with no place to escape. Instead of calming himself and breathing slowly to conserve what air he had, he lost all control over reason and began to struggle and thrash and use up what little oxygen was circulating in his blood.

His head ached, feeling as if it were growing larger, as if it might explode. He grew more confused and thrashed frantically, clawing at the canvas, trying to tear his way to the surface with his fingernails.

A temporary rescue came as something knocked him closer to the overturned operating table, where a small pocket of air had been trapped under the canvas. Somehow, he was on his hands and knees again, and in this position he had accidentally established a small air space beneath his body.

Schneider used all his strength to stay up on his knees, to preserve that precious volume of air beneath him. He had visions of a malevolent tent willfully pressing him into the ground as the air seeped from beneath its folds to be wasted on the outside of the canvas.

He might have been in that position a few seconds or a few minutes. However long it was, he felt himself losing the battle, slowly sinking beneath the unremitting weight of the surgical tent.

His precious air was slipping away.

As he lost the last few inches beneath his abdomen, his face pressed into the rough canvas floor, there was a sudden pressure on his back, strong enough to hurt like hell. It was as if someone was walking across him with boots on. And that was just what was happening.

Schneider wanted to cry out for help but could not. He wanted to shout to them to get the fuck off his back! But he could not. He found himself losing all grip on reason, slipping into helplessness, giving way to the coming of death by suffocation.

And he began to cry.

Suddenly there were more boots stomping on his back, driving more air out of his lungs. He became angry and afraid at the same time. He wanted them to leave him alone, to get the hell off his back so he could breathe again.

But there was nothing to breathe. There was no air left in his world.

He opened his mouth to cry out, to scream at them, but nothing came out of his mouth. There was no air left in his lungs. He could not even call for help.

His head swam, and in the darkness—a darkness he recognized as the coming of death—he saw flashes of light against his closed eyelids. What was left of his rational medically trained brain told him these were the random firings of oxygen-starved brain cells in his visual cortex. Hallucinations. The last things his brain would see before he died.

The pressure on his back suddenly released. The boots stepped off him, and he could take a small breath. A very small breath. A tearing sound raced past his ear. Hands—how many he didn't know, but many—grabbed at him. Cold wet air swept over his face. He gulped at the sweetness of the first breaths, coughing and choking.

Strong hands pulled at his arms, legs, head, and chest. It felt like a coordinated effort to tear him apart. He was twisted and turned and dragged as the rough canvas scratched his face.

In a moment, he was through the hole in the canvas, and there were stars in the black sky, and people running and scrambling everywhere, tearing holes in the ruined tent and pulling bodies out from underneath. It was like an anthill that had just been stepped on, with small dark creatures swarming out to meet the attack.

Just as Schneider was about to turn to his rescuers, a hand cradled his cheeks and turned his face upwards. He was staring into the eyes of some dark stranger who released his hold, allowing his head to fall back against the outside of the tent. His head banged on the ground, as Schneider heard the voice say, "He's OK! Let's go!"

And they were gone. Like the Masked Man and Tonto. That's what Schneider thought anyway. Just like that.

Schneider got to his feet. He was bent double at the waist, hands resting against his knees as he took deep breaths of the cool night air. It was crisp and fresh and wonderful, and it made him cough. He couldn't get enough of it.

When he had gathered his wits, he stood and looked around.

Where the hell are Gene and Dan Page? There was an army of men running and crawling across the downed tent, now in shreds, probing and cutting and pulling bodies from underneath the heavy suffocating folds. But he could not find Gene or Dan. With all his senses restored, perhaps keener than ever, Schneider joined the search for bodies, crawling along on his hands and knees, feeling for shape, for movement. He knew there were others who were suffocating just as he had been and he needed to get to them quickly.

It reminded him of the avalanche he witnessed years ago while skiing, all of the rescuers crawling across the cold white rubble of the huge avalanche field, probing and poking the snow and ice and rocks for bodies, for life. On that day, there had been none. Three people had died, and it took hours to find the corpses. None had sustained serious injuries, it turned out. They had all suffocated in snow compressed into facial masks of ice.

But tonight there was life under that mass of canvas, and he was proof of that. After a few moments, he found a mass moving slowly just under his knees. Remembering how it felt to be trampled by the boots a few minutes earlier, he carefully backed off, feeling for a free space near the body. He tried again and again to tear the cloth, and only when his fingers were slipping in the blood from his own finger tips did he realize he was doing no good. Even the nail that had torn off his index finger had not caused enough pain to slow him down. He was holding his breath as he struggled, as the man beneath him might be holding his. Schneider nearly cried in frustration at his inability to get through the thin barrier of canvas—the thin barrier between the air and some poor soul's life. His precious switchblade knife was back in his tent!

Then, two GIs scampered past him. He called out to them.

"I need a knife! Give me a knife! Please!"

Without stopping to speak, one of the GIs unsheathed a bayonet and tossed it to Schneider. He grabbed it by the blade and cut his hand. For an instant he was put out by being handed a bayonet. He wanted a surgical knife.

A scalpel, for Christ's sake! Not a bayonet! he thought.

He sawed through the canvas, making as big a slit as he could, trying not to injure the man beneath him with the bayonet. When the hole was big enough he reached in and grabbed at some clothing. He pulled and struggled and kicked backwards from his sitting position until he finally got the man out, hauling on his shoulders and sliding him out onto the canvas headfirst.

Schneider and the man found themselves sitting on top of the giant white circle with the blocky red cross in the middle; the red cross that was supposed to protect them from low level bombing runs like this.

Those fucking Krauts bombed our hospital!

It made him so furious he wanted to scream at someone. But there was no one. Just this poor, nearly-suffocated GI.

Schneider tried to examine the man, but he had rolled onto his side and was clutching at his abdomen. Schneider wasn't able to get him rolled over, but even in the dimness of the night, he could see a trail of black liquid pouring from between his fingers.

Oh shit, I stabbed him with that bayonet.

Schneider was horrified that he might have killed this man in his panic to get him out of the tent.

The man remained doubled over on his side in the fetal position. Finally, he relaxed and let Schneider roll him onto his back. However, Schneider's relief was very short-lived as he realized that the GI had not acquiesced, but was now in hemorrhagic shock.

There was very little time left.

Schneider pulled off his undershirt and stuffed it into the wound. He couldn't believe it. The man was going to die in his care from wounds suffered at Schneider's own hands. He wiped the abdomen clean with the shirt, and before the field filled up with blood again, he managed to see the ragged torn edges of an entry wound. It was not the clean linear surgical slit of a bayonet, but rather the jagged path of a large caliber tumbling bullet.

The fucking Krauts strafed us at the same time they bombarded us, and this poor guy caught one in the belly.

He looked around for help shouting, "Medic! Medic!"

But there was no response. There was no spare help. Everyone was busy trying to help someone else.

Then Schneider saw their second operating tent standing untouched only twenty yards away. The bomb that had obliterated his tent had spared OR Tent Number Two except for a few shrapnel tears, which emitted spears of white light into the darkness like a movie projector. People moving inside the tent caused the light to flicker, making it even more like a projector.

Schneider grabbed the man by his wrist, and from a kneeling position slung him up onto his shoulders in the classic fireman's carry. With his other arm between the man's thighs, Schneider staggered to his feet, wobbling across the uneven surface of the downed tent. He ran the gauntlet between the squirming bodies still beneath the canvas and the swarms of GIs trying to rescue them. Although he no longer had the bayonet, he was in no position to help anyone else anyway. He needed to get this man to surgery.

One patient at a time.

Schneider made it to the tent with the GI on his shoulders. He crashed though the double set of doors, and all the OR tables were full. He tried to gauge who would be finished first, so he could get this guy on the table and opened up.

There were no free cots in the pre-op area, so he lowered the man carefully to the floor. Schneider's shoulders and abdomen were covered with the dark crimson jelly of clotted blood. He expected to see a river of bright red blood issuing from the center of the man's abdomen, but there was none, and that worried, rather than reassured him.

Schneider gathered up IV supplies from the locker: plasma bottles, IV tubing, needles, gauze, and tape.

"Hey, Doc. What do you need?" It was Higgenson.

"Oh, thank God. Here, take over this IV and get some fluid into him. Much as you can. I'm going to find a Lap kit and open this guy right here."

Higgenson took the supplies and sorted through them. Then he tied a rubber tourniquet around the man's left upper arm and looked for a vein. These young muscular GIs were usually teeming with veins, but there wasn't a single one Higgenson could get a needle into. He slapped three fingers against the skin at the inside of the elbow joint, but there was still nothing. He kept slapping and slapping, looking for anything that might take a large-bore needle. Still nothing.

Maybe he didn't want to know, to admit the truth, but he kept at it. He had no idea how long he persisted. Finally, he sat back on his haunches, and looked at the wound. The blood in the wound had clotted, and there was no up-and-down movement of the belly or his chest.

Schneider came back and dropped to his knees across from Higgenson. "Got a table for us. No anesthesia, but this kid won't need any."

Then he made a quick visual assessment. He wiped away the clot. There was no fresh bleeding. Finally, he took out his penlight and pried open an eyelid. He shined his light in the right eye and then the left. No response. The pupils were fixed and dilated. He put a finger on the carotid artery on the left side of his neck, then on the facial artery where it crossed the jaw, then the temporal artery. He never bothered with the heart, for his stethoscope was still buried under hundreds of pounds of shredded OR tent.

He looked at Higgenson, whose face had grown old and sad.

"Ah, crap! Jesus," Schneider said in a whisper.

He took the GI's cold hand in his and a saw a high school ring on the fourth finger of the left hand. There was a faceted crimson stone covered with little scratches all over it. In an oval around the stone were the words "Ridgedale High School." On the two sides of the ring were inscribed the numerals **19** and **43**.

Schneider turned off the penlight and, for the second time since his landing in France, he began to cry.

It would not be the last time.

Before dawn the chaos had subsided, replaced by the orderly rebuilding of their field hospital. A new operating tent was on its way, they were told, and in the meantime thirty combat soldiers cleaned out rooms in the farmhouse to serve as ORs.

After Schneider recovered, having found Antonelli and Dan—at about three in the morning—he later ran into Hamm and McClintock at their operating tables. They had been awakened from their sleep by the chaos of the bombing. Unbeknownst to Schneider, both were among the many GIs scampering over the folds of the ruined OR tent looking for survivors. At dawn they were back in the OR as if nothing had happened.

Hamm pointed Schneider to the pre-op area indicating to him there was plenty of work to do. Schneider could see in their eyes that he must still be showing some of the shock from the night's terror. Schneider nodded to Hamm and made his way to pre-op to triage a few cases. Then he selected the most seriously wounded soldier he thought he could save and prepped him for surgery.

Schneider spent the rest of the next hours putting the boy back together.

As dawn cleared the sky and the sun peeked over the trees on the low hills to the east, the encampment became very quiet. Everyone was exhausted. More than that, the bombing and strafing had created a sense of a new vulnerability. They had passed many days pretending that their status as non-combatants, healers—men without guns—would somehow protect them from the enemy. Surely, the Germans would respect the red crosses on the tents, trucks, helmets, and armbands. Instead, during the night they had lost their collective virginity, and the reality of their new world scared the hell out of them.

Schneider finished his last case and checked the pre-ops. Nobody else was waiting for surgery, and the medics seemed to have things under control. He was just getting out of his bloody scrub suit and washing his hands when he heard a commotion outside the tent. Then he shook his head and ran outside where there was fresh air and room to run. No way would he be buried under another tent. He was sure they were under another attack from somewhere.

He looked to the sky, and screamed out loud to no one in particular. "Where the fuck are they?"

But there was no sound of airplane engines, no noise of close combat.

His ruined tent was already gone, only the shallow bomb crater remained nearby to remind him of the night's events. A crowd of shouting GIs lined the entry road. As Schneider drew nearer, he realized that they were cheering. He thought reinforcements or supplies must be on the way. Red Cross packages, perhaps. But, no, it was none of that.

A hundred yards away was a slow-moving convoy of canvas-topped trucks, all bearing red crosses on their sides and roofs, even on top of the hoods. He still couldn't figure out why all the excitement. The four trucks came into the courtyard, escorted by several jeeps with machine-gun mounts armed and ready, and circled to a halt. A sergeant major strolled up to the first truck and spoke with the driver. Then he went to the rear and pulled down the tailgate. He extended his hand up to the back of the truck, and to Schneider's complete amazement, a beautiful white hand reached out and took the sergeant major's fat, hairy paw. A leg stepped out, bare to the skirt hem. The sergeant major extended his arms and lifted a WAC nurse by the waist and gently lowered her to the ground. She wore captain's bars on her shoulders.

The WAC officer stepped back as the sergeant major snapped a crisp salute. She returned the salute and then waved to the back of the truck. In a moment, the crowd of GIs surged forward and began helping the WAC nurses down from the trucks. There must have been sixty of them in all, and to the tired medical group they were as creatures from another world. Their uniforms, both enlisted and officers, were crisp and clean, and their shoes were still shined.

Schneider walked closer. He did not want to miss a moment of this. He stood among them, not speaking but drinking in their presence. Their hair was washed, and he could smell the soapy fragrance of them. As they walked by laughing and smiling and greeting everyone, he just stood there. He simply could not move. He could not believe the whiteness of their skin, the softness that emanated from them. In the few minutes since their debarkation, his world was once more transformed. He was grateful that they had not arrived earlier, to be there for the bombing of the tent. He shuddered to think that some of these young women might have died in the night; then he realized to his horror that inevitability some of these young women would die here in the next days or months or years. For better or for worse, with their arrival, life would never be the same again.

Schneider stopped his staring and sniffing. He fought the urge to sweep up one of these creatures into his arms. Instead, he wiped his hands on the khaki towel he had unconsciously brought with him and started toward the changing tents to get out of his bloody scrubs. Before he got more than a few yards, a voice called to him, and somehow he knew, without turning, that it was she.

"Good morning...uh...?" she said.

Schneider turned and looked into the eyes of the first WAC captain he'd watched descend from the truck. She looked at Schneider quizzically, and he realized that she had not finished her sentence because he was out of uniform, so she did not know his rank.

"Schneider," he said. "Steve Schneider."

He put out his hand, but she still had that puzzled look on her face.

"Oh," he went on, his hand hanging in the air, "Major Steve Schneider."

She saluted, a courtesy he returned feeling very silly. Then she held out her hand and shook his. Her hand was the softest thing he had ever touched. At least it felt that way to Schneider. He flushed with embarrassment, sure his pleasure showed in his face. Worse still, this simple touch of a woman's hand, after so very long, gave him an erection. In a scrub suit, standing out in the open, that was not a good thing. He quickly dropped her hand and continued drying the nonexistent water from his hands, keeping the towel well positioned in front of his fly.

She smiled widely—so widely that her wonderful teeth and red lipstick were all he could take in at one time. It was a moment later before he finally noticed her emerald green eyes and flaming red hair.

"I'm Captain Ferrarro. Molly Ferrarro."

"Welcome to our field hospital, Captain Ferrarro," he said.

"Thank you. And Molly is just fine with me, Major."

"And Steve will be fine with me. We rarely refer to rank here." Schneider looked around. "Oh, and we generally don't bother with saluting. Not necessary, and it might let a sniper know who's an officer. Anyway...what have you brought for us?"

"We're a surgical team. We have scrub nurses, circulating nurses, recovery room nurses, ward nurses. Just about any job you could need done, we can do. We're here now to free up the surgeons from the scut work, so you can do your jobs. We'll move with the hospital wherever it goes." She reached into her shoulder bag and started to take out some papers. "I have my orders here—"

"No, no, no. You've got the wrong guy. I just work here. I'm a general surgeon. You want to give those to the CO," he said, pointing to the house. "He's over in that building."

"Thank you, Major," she said and started to salute again.

"It's still Steve, and ditch the salute."

She laughed, and said, "Perhaps tomorrow. We're a little new at this."

They said good-bye, and Schneider made his way back to the changing tent. Ferrarro made a beeline toward the farmhouse, walking right past the khaki rags and debris of what was left of the operating tent without even seeing it.

It was a whole new world now. Schneider walked slowly back through the crowd of mingling men and women—boys and girls really—the chatter and the nervous laughter. He might have been at a high school prom. Or a college mixer. But it wasn't a prom, and he wasn't in high school any more, though most of these kids weren't far from it.

As he entered the tent, he tossed his towel in with the dirties and glanced at his wedding ring.

Chapter Seventeen

13 June 1944, 0600 Hours
Field Hospital Charlie-7, Hiesville, France

Schneider stood next to McClintock at the head of the table, watching Hamm finish his operation. When he related what had happened to him, the hair literally stood on the back of Hamm's neck. McClintock and Hamm listened, riveted, as Schneider recalled the night's events. Although he tried to underplay the terror, it was clear to everyone that Schneider was badly shaken by it.

"Listen, Steve," Hamm said, "why don't you go on back to your bunk for a few hours and leave the OR to us. It's pretty quiet. I'll call you if I need you."

Schneider said, "Yeah, thanks. I'll do that. Not sure I can go to sleep, though. Maybe I ought to get some chow and then settle in." He turned and left the OR tent. Hamm didn't see him again until nearly noon.

Hamm finished three more cases that morning, all shrapnel or gunshot wounds. There was one burn case left that occupied a lot of personnel, but the medics had it under control by the time Hamm got there. By then another surgeon was free. So, he dropped his dirty scrubs into the hamper and changed into his khakis. His boots were starting to look like hell, and he wondered whether they would last the war... however long that was going to be.

Hamm walked over to pre-op, delighted to find the place nearly empty. He had operated on more bodies in the past eight days and nights than he had in all his years of civilian practice. He couldn't remember the names of the wounded GIs, their injuries, or just about anything. Sometimes he got to the end of the shift, and when he went into post-op to see how they were all doing, he had to look at the chart to remember what he did to a particular GI. That was a little scary.

Everyone kept saying "Home for Christmas," but he didn't buy it. The Germans might be on the run now, but they were still putting up a hell of a fight.

He detoured to the showers before lunch. The shower trucks had just arrived, and the lines for them were not yet long. There was only lukewarm water, but plenty of soap, and he was feeling particularly dirty. The food could wait a bit longer.

After he got cleaned up—although clean was a relative term by this time—Hamm strolled over to the mess tent, enjoying the lull in the arrival of the battle casualties. For some reason there weren't even the usual sounds of distant gunfire. The sun was trying to poke through the mist that typically shrouded the morning. He passed the final resting place of their Number One OR tent and shook his head. He didn't know what he would have done had he been trapped under there as Schneider had been. Hamm had always been a little claustrophobic. Actually, a lot claustrophobic. It even took him a while to learn to be comfortable wearing a mask over his nose and mouth all day long in the operating room. The mental image of suffocating to death under the canvas folds of an OR tent made him shiver.

He walked through the flap of the mess tent and was stunned by what he saw. The place teemed with people. It looked like Saturday night at a dancehall. The WACs had arrived in force and were sitting with all the officers and other men. This close to the front, they didn't have the luxury of separate mess tents for officers and enlisted personnel. A good thing, Hamm thought; the logic of separate mess tents eluded him. They were, after all, fighting for the same thing, and it didn't seem reasonable to separate officers and WACs from the enlisted men in battle. Just as people did in civilian life, everybody in the medical and surgical teams understood the chain of command.

He grabbed a metal tray from the stacks and proceeded through the mess line. Lunch was Sloppy Joes and an undistinguished soup that too closely resembled the scrub water that ran off his elbows as he prepped for surgery. He took a Sloppy Joe and some coffee and passed on the soup. Then he looked around for some friendly faces in the mob and spotted Schneider sitting at the far end of the tent at an almost completely full table. He pushed his way through, trying not to spill his coffee, and found a seat at the edge of the bench next to Schneider.

"Shove over, pal," he told Schneider, "make room for a friend."

"Hey, Hamm."

At the table were Schneider, McClintock, Antonelli, and five WAC nurses. No wonder the tables were packed, Hamm thought. What a refreshing addition these nurses were to their dreary lives. Schneider made the introductions.

"Hey, everyone, this is Major John Hammer—Hamm to all of us— an old and dear buddy of mine." There was a chorus of welcomes from the WACs.

"Hamm, this is Captain Molly Ferrarro," Schneider said, gesturing to the very attractive woman at his right. Hamm did a double take. The Captain was one hell of a stunning woman. He figured her to be about thirty or so, with shocking red hair and green eyes that nearly made him light-headed. Her skin was a creamy white, and her face just beautiful. The picture didn't fit with the name Ferrarro, but with a first name of Molly, Hamm assumed she was Irish and had married someone Italian. But most prominent in Hamm's consciousness was the inappropriate tingle he felt just being near her. Inappropriate for a married and faithful man.

Schneider woke Hamm out of his trance-like state and continued with the introductions.

"And this is Ruth, Betty, Alice, and Mary. I'll get all the last names later."

Hamm noticed that Steve had barely taken his eyes off Molly as he made the introductions of the others. He could see a look in Schneider's eyes that hadn't been there before. It made Hamm very uneasy. Both of them were married, and while Hamm had no designs beyond window-shopping, he was afraid from that very moment in the mess tent that Steve would get himself into a difficult situation.

Hamm smiled and nodded to everyone. Antonelli was practically salivating, and McClintock looked very peaceful. He talked with each of the WACs at the table, one by one.

"So, Ruth. It is Ruth, right?" McClintock said.

"Yes," she said. "You're good at names I see,"

"I'm good at lots of things, darlin'," McClintock drawled. His accent was markedly ratcheted up for this social moment.

Schneider and Hamm groaned.

"And you are…mmm… Betty?" McClintock went on. It was obvious to everyone he was making a mental address book. He was staring deeply into the WAC's eyes directly across from him.

"Actually, I'm Alice. But nice try, Hamm."

"Actually, I'm not Hamm, I'm Ted," McClintock said. A bit of his bloated ego sagged.

"Actually, I know who you are. I was just pulling your leg, Ted. And I'm Betty. She's Alice," Betty said, pointing to the dark haired woman seated on the bench right next to McClintock."

The whole group burst into laughter, but without a beat, McClintock leaned toward Alice, their thighs touching and their faces very close. He said, "Hello, Darlin'. I'm Ted. But you already knew that."

The happy group continued their banter. Names exchanged and quick biographies given. The war was so far away for them all just then. And no one was in a hurry to return to battle.

Only Schneider appeared nervous, but Hamm put that down to his terrifying experiences of last night. It had been a very close one. But maybe it was more than that.

"So," Hamm said to Steve, not wanting to ignore everyone else, but wanting to know the score, "you recovered from last night?"

There was a silence for a moment as all eyes fell to their food plates. Hamm felt as if he had touched on something unspeakable.

"Yeah, I'm OK. But there were no operative survivors from that tent, Hamm," Schneider said. "When the tent crumpled, the weight of it pretty much disrupted all the connections. IV lines were pulled out; anesthesia machines toppled and disconnected from the airways. Most of the patients had their chests or their abdomens open, and they were just knocked to the floor off their tables, spilling their guts while they were still under anesthesia. I hate to say it, but until we were pulled out, it was every man for himself. I mean, there was just nothing we could do to help the poor bastards."

Schneider looked at Captain Ferrarro and said, "Excuse me." Then he went on. "It was the worst nightmare you could ever imagine.

Everyone trying to claw their way out. Bodies all over the floor, overturned equipment...and the darkness...."

Schneider paused as the recollection of his terror swept over him like a shadow. Then he shook his head. "There was no air. I could smell the anesthesia leaking from the overturned machines...."

Schneider looked away, again suppressing the resurgence of fear that welled up in his throat at the memory of it all.

"Jesus," Hamm said. It was all he could say.

The new WAC nurses were silent, some of them appearing to be on the verge of tears. Captain Ferraro had her head cocked, and her brows wrinkled. She was following Schneider's description intently, probably trying to figure out how she was going to keep her girls from falling apart.

Hamm focused on the reality facing these young women. Here in the middle of a great world war they would be as exposed to danger as every other GI. But they looked so damn young and fragile that Hamm couldn't help himself. He thought of them as girls, young and frail and afraid.

McClintock said, "What happened to your scrub team?"

"Most of them are lying down over in their tents," Schneider said.

"Maybe I'll go on over and check in on them. I'm not very hungry anyway," McClintock said as he rose and nodded to the WACs. "See y'all later, ladies."

He got up and left, leaving his full tray on the table. It was the first time Hamm or Schneider ever saw McClintock walk away from food —let alone a table full of women.

"So, there weren't any survivors at all?" Hamm said.

"None from the operating tables, anyway. Most of the staff and the pre-ops got out; that is, got rescued. Nobody could have gotten out without help. Whoever cut me out of there...well...."

Captain Ferrarro cut in. She was ashen, and the hand which held her soup spoon in midair was trembling, as was her voice.

"How could they do this? How could they bomb a hospital? Dear God! What are they?"

Schneider put a hand on her shoulder and said, "You're right, Captain. We can't believe it either. But their snipers have been shooting at the medical personnel, too. And we hear worse things than that. Scuttlebutt maybe, but, I'm beginning to think it's true. We—you—

have to assume that you're a target, and be very, very careful. Don't rely on your noncombatant status to protect you. It won't."

Schneider shook his head sadly and returned to his coffee. He hadn't touched his food. Suddenly, Hamm wasn't so hungry either.

"So...? How do we protect ourselves?" Molly asked. "I mean, if they're willing to strafe and snipe and bomb hospitals—clearly marked hospitals—then why should we think they'd hesitate to overrun us right here. And who'll protect us then?"

"Well, you're absolutely right, we're unarmed," Hamm said. "And we're supposed to be unarmed. Not that a gun would do me any good. I have no experience with firearms. And you don't either, do you, Steve?"

"Me? I'd be more of a danger than an asset. Might shoot myself or my friends. I've never even held a gun."

"Well, I have!" All eyes turned to Molly. "I grew up in the country with four older brothers. I learned to shoot when I was six. Twenty-two's and deer rifles. Pistols. Even my dad's .45 automatic—though we generally didn't tell him when we borrowed his gun. By the time I was ten, I could outshoot all my brothers. Not that they were very happy about that."

Schneider cut in. "Well, we're very glad you're on our side. Too bad there's no deer rifle for you. Maybe we can scrounge one up. Along with a deer or two. I'm sick of sloppy Joes."

Molly smiled. "Maybe...."

Mercifully, it quieted down for a few days after the WACs arrived. There was still a steady stream of casualties, never a complete lull, but when no seriously wounded were coming in, the medical team had time to go back and do some cleanup surgery. They debrided infected wounds . They cut away any dead tissue that was not apparent on the first go-round. They did some of the unending paperwork, too. Everyone hated that part—all those forms. But different doctors would be treating these wounded GIs at every stop on their way home. Those doctors needed complete records to know what had been done earlier.

Then there was the triage tent. Whenever Hamm had the time, and sometimes even when he didn't have the time, he made his way over to triage to talk to the dying—to give them something, anything.

And again on that day, Hamm walked over from the mess tent and pushed his way through the double blackout doors of the triage tent. There were about ten men in there now. Actually, they were boys to him. At his age of thirty-nine, they all looked like teenagers. The stretchers covered almost all the floor, and the men were covered with layers of blankets up to their necks. They tried to keep the wounded warm and pain free with lots of morphine. There were wounds that were so bad, it was impossible to save them, and they couldn't waste valuable resources that were needed for men—boys—who could be saved. But they did have a hell of a lot of IV fluids to keep them from feeling thirsty and enough morphine to keep them in never-never land.

So that's just what they did.

The triage ward was very quiet. Most of the men were nearly comatose anyway. They wouldn't last long. Maybe hours. And the trucks heading back to the beaches for evacuation to England or to hospital ships were constantly filled with seriously wounded men—but men who could be saved if they reached help in time.

Hamm could do little from a medical standpoint, but he felt an obligation to give them, if nothing else, the comfort they deserved. When he was in training, one of the surgeons told him that he always spent time with the dying whenever he could. Even if it was just to sit at the bedside and hold a hand or talk to the families. His teacher had said that the gall bladder patient you did that week didn't need you so much. He was going to get better and go home soon, no matter what you did. It was the hopeless patients who really needed your care, even if that care was not going to help them to survive. Hamm thought it was some of the most important advice he had received in all those years of training.

He found one young kid who was awake enough to know Hamm was there. Like many of the soldiers who end up in the triage tent, he had third degree burns over 90 percent of his body. Parts of the burned skin hurt like hell. Nothing on earth short of a miracle was going to save this poor kid, and there just weren't enough miracles to go around.

Hamm sat down on the canvas floor next to the stretcher and touched the boy on the shoulder. "Hey, Private," he said softly, "how're you doing?"

The boy looked up at Hamm through a narcotic haze and said, "Oh, hey, Major. I'm OK...I guess."

There was that look in his eyes that told Hamm the boy knew very well that he was not OK. It was almost a state of peace. Or resignation. There seemed to be no fear in this young man, who hadn't yet lived long enough to know much about anything.

"You need anything? Anything at all?"

"Yes, sir. I need to go home. Soon as possible," he answered with a little laugh. "But I guess that ain't gonna happen too soon."

"Not just yet, son."

What am I going to say, that he's going home in a casket? Jesus!

Hamm was suddenly having a hard time getting his breath. He had to resist the urge to flee. He could take the bleeding and the shrapnel and the torn and bloodied bodies of his patients. At least he had a chance with those. But this....

"Well, now that you ask, sir, I kind of need to take a pee."

Hamm looked down to make sure the boy had a catheter, and seeing the tubing leading from the bottle up under his blanket, said, "Actually, it only feels that way. There's a tube in your bladder to empty the urine so you won't have to go."

He didn't tell him that there was no urine coming out anyway because his burns were sucking up all his fluids and plasma faster than the medics could pour it in. His kidneys were failing rapidly because the decision had been made not to give him the valuable plasma. Just salt water to keep the boy from being too thirsty.

"Funny, it sure feels like I have to pee."

"Yeah, I know. The catheter is irritating your bladder. Makes it feel that way. Maybe a little more medicine will make that go away."

Hamm flagged down the solitary nurse who had just arrived this morning and was already on the job in that awful place.

"Up the dose of morphine for this young man, will you please?" He wrote down a frighteningly large dose on the order sheet, but the nurse never flinched. "And a belladonna and opium suppository for his bladder spasms, as needed," he added.

"Yes, Major Hammer," she said. She wrote quickly and finished saying "…and a B&O suppository PRN."

Hamm nodded.

How did she know my name so soon? I don't know hers. He wondered if she were one of the nurses at the table and felt a little ashamed that he had forgotten everyone's face and name already.

A hand touched his shoulder, and there standing over him was the only nurse he hadn't forgotten. Truth be known, it was not possible to forget Captain Molly Ferrarro.

"Hello, Captain," he said. "Pull up a pew."

Molly knelt down next to him and turned immediately to the young soldier.

"Hi…" she turned over his dog tag and read, "James. Do you need anything?" But James was sound asleep now from the IV morphine he had just been given. They stared at him for a few minutes, and each wondered how the flames had failed to touch his handsome young face. Odd. Even with no time to shave in the field, his skin was smooth as a baby's. The boy slept deeply. Hamm and Molly both noticed that his breathing had slowed to a dangerous rate. It was the morphine, they knew, and that would be both his salvation and his end. He could die a respiratory death under the merciful smothering of Morpheus, the Greek God of dreams.

Hamm choked back the sorrow that was building in him. He took a deep breath. It was time to leave. He didn't want to be there to pronounce the boy dead. Just two or three sentences with him had been enough to get too close. It was better when they came in unconscious; he operated on them, and they went out to post-op still asleep. He didn't know them then. Now, he knew James too well. He hadn't even asked him his name. Molly had. He didn't thank her for that, but Hamm knew it was the more courageous thing to do.

Molly could see the pain in Hamm's face. She reached out and took his hand in hers. As she tightened her grip, Hamm looked into her eyes and saw the tears forming there. His own eyes were tearing too. Then, he pulled his hand away, and turned from her.

Molly rose.

"Want some coffee, Captain?" Hamm said.

"Sure, Major. But, you can call me Molly. Everyone else has since we landed here. OK?"

"Fine. And if you're comfortable with it, you can call me Hamm, at least outside the operating room."

They walked back to the mess tent, which was now almost empty. Hamm got two mugs of coffee and carried them to where Molly had taken a seat with some of her nurses. When he got there, the others smiled, gathered their things and left. Hamm didn't know if they were finished eating or whether they were giving Molly and him space to be alone.

After their brief hand holding, the other nurses leaving them alone made him uncomfortable, probably because he found her so attractive and had a few more stray fantasies than a married man ought to have. Either way, they sat there for a while just sipping the hot coffee—black and bitter—and saying nothing. Their visit to James had taken a toll on them both, and he reminded himself that visits to those doomed men were among the most important things he could do.

Chapter Eighteen

1 July 1944, 0800 Hours
Field Hospital Charlie-7, East of St. Lô, France

Schneider, Hamm and McClintock sat around the wooden table in the mess tent. Most of the team had cleared their places and were beginning their own shift in the ORs. Hamm clutched his coffee mug between two hands, warming them in the morning chill. McClintock was on his third cup of the strong black brew. Schneider sorely missed his super sweet coffee with the heavy cream he used to have at home. Instead he stuck with tea now rather than give in to the bitter brew the army served up.

Hamm said, "I can't believe it's only been three weeks since we landed. Feels like years, doesn't it?"

"It's the constant packing up and moving that's getting to me," Schneider said. "The scrambling to keep up with the front lines, and all these casualties. I never expected anything like this."

"Well, we're in a war, Steve," McClintock said. "What did you think it would be like? Office hours?"

"Oh, screw you."

"I just meant we need to be as near to the action as possible. It's all about how long it takes to get these poor bastards on the operating table from the time they're hit, so you can cut on 'em."

"Oh, really? I never knew that. Thanks so much for letting me in on that, pal."

"Jesus, guys," Hamm said. "Give it a rest. We're all on the same team."

Schneider looked at his watch. "Okay. So let's go do it. Hamm, let's see about the autoclaves we've been waiting for. Maybe Molly knows something."

"And a good opportunity to see Captain Molly, eh?" McClintock said.

"What's with you today, Ted?"

"Enough, you guys," Hamm said. He took his coffee mug to the dirty dish rack and turned to leave. "C'mon, Steve. Let's go. See you in the OR, Ted."

McClintock stayed where he was, nursing his coffee in silence. Hamm and Schneider left the mess tent and walked over to Molly's office outside the operating tents.

"What the hell's McClintock got up his ass?" Schneider said.

"Just let it go, Steve. Everyone's under a lot of pressure. He's okay."

Molly's nurses were keeping the operating rooms turning over at an astounding rate, meaning more men were making it to the operating table alive. The field hospital had done over nine hundred cases in the first weeks, and the nurses were pitifully overworked and sometimes underappreciated.

Hamm and Schneider turned the corner to Molly's tent and saw a hand-lettered sign on her door:

EX NULLO, NON FECES

Hamm translated, "No Shit From No One! Whoever wrote that got it right."

Schneider laughed. "She's fighting a lot of big egos around here."

Hamm looked at Schneider and raised his eyebrows.

"I know! I know! I'm one of them," Schneider said. "But it's so easy to blame the nurses when things go wrong."

"Damn right, so don't be one of those." Hamm said.

"Molly's tough though. She doesn't let her nurses get bullied by the surgeons, or anyone else for that matter. And anyway that should be Ex *Neminae* Non Feces."

Hamm just shook his head, knocked on the tent post and entered. "Hey, Captain," he said.

"Good morning," she said to them both. "What can I do for you?"

"Well, first, any news on the extra autoclaves?"

"No. The same old stuff. 'They're on the way.' But no one seems to know where or when."

"Anything we can do to speed that up?" Hamm asked.

"Well, you could drive back to Omaha Beach and see if they're… Sorry, I'm getting cranky lately."

"You're in good company," Schneider said.

"Look, Captain," Hamm said. "It's only been a couple of weeks. Your WACs have made a hell of a difference around here. We moved three times in four days. It's exhausting. The packing and unpacking. But, your nurses are really doing the lion's share of the work."

"Thank you, Major. It's good to know we're appreciated."

"No question about it. We're heading over to the OR. See you there, probably."

"Definitely," she said.

July turned wet and miserable. Conditions were demoralizing. Living outside week after week might have been bearable under beautiful, dry, peacetime conditions. Barely. But in the wet and the cold of that summer, it was awful. Even in the big tents it was awful. Water seeped in and soaked the sleeping bags. Some of the men and women dug trenches around their tents, but they, too, inevitably filled with water. When they dug foxholes they were only dry until the first rain. Team members lost their toothbrushes, combs and family pictures in the mud. So, after several awful days camping out under incessant downpours, the group finally found farm buildings to use, and life dramatically changed for the better.

There had been a series of moves, first south and then to the east toward Paris. Names like Ste. Mère Église, Carentan, Isigny, and St. Lô stood out in Schneider's brain, though he had barely known of them before. Sometimes he could recall them clearly, like the total devastation at St. Lô, or the church steeple and the hedgerows around Ste. Mère Église. But the others became a blur of muddy villages with shattered stone fountains, partially-destroyed homes with shutters hanging askew, and bloated cattle lying in the roads with their feet pointing to the sky. The mix of smells was burned into his mind: the odors of rotting and burning flesh and meat commingled with the freshness of the summer vegetation. It was so bizarre that he knew he would never be rid of it.

Then there were the children in the villages, ragged in their country clothes. They stood staring out the windows of their shattered homes as medics passed by in the trucks and jeeps, or they ran alongside the vehicles collecting stale chocolate from the soldiers' C rations, yet enduring it all, the way only children could.

The teams pushed on as the battle and the front lines moved east. Finally, when they were just about at the end of their collective rope with the wet and the cold and the mud and the dying, there was a lull in the battle. Their good fortune extended to setting up at a lovely farm west of Paris.

Schneider didn't know how far it was because here too, the Germans had taken down all the road signs. But there had been lots of talk about getting to Paris someday. Always someday. Perhaps that day was coming.

This particular farm had been deserted for some time. Weeds choked the untended fields. The cattle roamed freely thanks to the artillery-blasted holes in the fences and hedgerows. The main house miraculously had escaped the shelling, and the men quickly converted it into quarters for the officers. They converted the barn for the enlisted men. It didn't take long to get the hospital up and running. By this time, the forward movement had stalled, so they settled in for what they expected to be a long haul. Long, at that time, might be as much as a week.

The operating tents were still fitted with the white liners to give better light and keep dirt from falling off the canvas into the open wounds or onto the sterile instruments. There were two post-op tents now and an evacuation tent where the convalescing soldiers awaited transport to the rear. They set up the tents in the shape of a cross, with the OR at the center. Everything revolved around the OR. The mess tent was near the farmhouse and tended to be the place away from work where everyone congregated. The mess tent was always filled with an entire shift of men and women trying to get some food before sleep. They worked twelve hours on and twelve hours off, when they could. Sometimes it was twenty-four hours on, or thirty-six or forty-eight if the fighting was really intense. After forty-eight hours, though, nobody was much good for anything, and they forced themselves to try to sleep for at least a few hours before they began making fatal errors.

So, to allow the off-duty people some undisturbed rest, those on call sat up and socialized in the mess when they weren't operating. It was warm from the cooking stoves and always smelled of coffee. The coffee smelled better than it tasted, but then Schneider had always felt that way about coffee. Like the smell of cut grass: sweet and pungent, and it always made him smile.

The downside of the farm was that, for some reason, it seemed to be on the Luftwaffe's target list. It was bombed and strafed with regularity. At first, everyone was terrified. Surgery would stop when the bombs started. Nurses and surgeons dropped to the floor, with no pretense of trying to maintain sterility. But, after a while they got philosophical and just kept operating. Somehow, the hospital never took a direct hit at that farm, and there were no tragedies such as the collapse of the surgical tent at the field hospital that killed so many and nearly buried Schneider alive. The sidewalls were ventilated with bullets and shrapnel a few times, but mercifully nobody was injured.

The other side of all of this was the total lack of privacy. There were always lines and small crowds for everything that needed to be done. Everyone showered with company, went to the latrine with company, ate with company, and slept with company in the same room. There were constant nocturnal noises: farts and groans and screams caused by nightmares. It seemed impossible to be alone even for a few minutes. It was dangerous to stray too far from the guarded periphery of the field hospital because there were still snipers around, and the battle lines kept changing all the time anyway. They never knew how close they were to an actual German position.

One afternoon, just after a long shift, Schneider couldn't stand the crowds any longer and took a walk away from the OR tent. He left the area, but instead of going to the mess tent or the officer's quarters, he just walked in a straight line away from everyone.

He found himself at the periphery of a field just beyond the farmhouse in the shadow of the trees that served as a windbreak for the once-cultivated land. There he saw a giant sawed-off tree stump, and there also, to his surprise, sitting on the stump, was Molly.

He was about to call out so as not to frighten her by his sudden appearance. She seemed to be laughing almost uncontrollably. When he got a little closer he realized she was crying. Actually, she was sobbing uncontrollably, long wrenching spasms of grief. Her shoulders were hunched with the effort, the tears cascading off her cheeks like rivers. She didn't even bother to wipe them away. The flood just continued, as if her soul were being wrung dry to rid herself of some grief, some longing, some loss. She was so completely submerged in her sorrow that Schneider thought, even if the Germans strafed and bombed and overran their position, she would have been unable to move from that stump.

Schneider moved to her side. When his hand touched her shoulder, and when she should have jumped out of her skin with fright, she kept crying, as if refusing to be interrupted in her grief.

"Captain?" he said softly.

She only continued to convulse. He decided to say no more until she was ready. He kept his hand on her shoulder, trying to comfort her in her grief.

Finally, she turned, wiping the tears from her eyes, shaking herself free of her thoughts and coming back into the present. Back to the awful war.

"I'm OK," she said and touched his hand where it rested on her shoulder. He didn't take his hand away. There was something startling in the intimacy of the touch. Perhaps it was the wetness of her tears still on her fingertips.

He started to walk away then, to leave her to her thoughts when she said,

"No. Don't go just yet."

He came back, and began to sit down on the ground. "No," she said quietly, her voice interrupted by the last residual spasms of her sobbing, "it's too wet. There's room here."

She moved over, and he sat down beside her. Their bodies touched, hip to hip, shoulder to shoulder. Schneider realized that this was the first time in nearly three years that he had felt a woman's body this close to his. He could sense her heat, and it felt good. Maybe too good.

"It's hard, isn't it?" he asked her. "The dying and the pain. You just can't get away from it, and God knows how long it's going to continue. I don't think we're anywhere near the end of this war."

She seemed confused.

"It's not the war. I'm doing OK with that. That's my job, and I can handle it. It's just...."

"Look, Molly. I'm intruding. You don't have to tell me anything. I just saw you out here, and I was worried. We're still a little too near the front for you to be so far from camp. These lines change so fast that there could be Jerries out here. I actually thought you were laughing when I walked by. It was odd to see you here by yourself, laughing uncontrollably. Then, when I got nearer, I realized you were crying. Funny, isn't it, how crying and laughing are so similar? You can mistake them so easily...."

He stopped abruptly. He realized that he was rambling because he was nervous being this close to her. He felt embarrassed and stupid and unsympathetic for being so preoccupied with her.

She nodded, still struggling to suppress her sobs.

In her silence, he went on.

"Anyway, I feel as if I'm intruding...so I'll go on back. Just don't stay here too long, OK?" He rose to go.

"Don't go...Steve." she said suddenly. "Please don't go."

He sat back on the stump, this time still closer.

"I'd like some company right now," she said with a sigh. "We'll just change the subject, OK?"

"OK."

"So...what's the new subject?" she said, letting out the first laugh of the day.

He laughed, too, and the two of them sat in silence for a few more minutes.

"Well, for one thing," he said, "I still haven't figured out where a woman with flaming red hair, freckles and green eyes gets a name like Ferrarro. Doesn't exactly fit with Molly either. You just don't look Italian. Scottish. Irish, maybe. Sicilian? Never!"

As she started to speak, they heard the sound of artillery at their backs, and turned to see how far away and from what direction it was coming. It was very far to the east. The delay between the flashes just over the horizon indicated they were in no danger. They had gotten good at estimating the distance from the front this way.

"Irish, actually," she said. "And Scottish. My maiden name was Molly Fitzgerald. Doesn't get more Irish than that. My father was Irish, my mother Scottish. A Campbell, she was. And she has more freckles than I do." She laughed. "And greener eyes, too."

Greener than hers? It was impossible to imagine. Schneider could hardly stop staring at them.

"Ferrarro is my husband's name." She was choking again, but she forced herself to go on. "Nick Ferrarro. And from Brooklyn! Can you imagine anything more Italian than that?" She seemed to be holding back again, but Schneider couldn't tell what.

He pulled back a bit, physically at least.

There's no point in dragging this out, he thought, but she just plowed on, for better or for worse.

"Steve…Nick is dead. I'm going to keep his name forever, but he's dead."

"I'm so sorry, Molly. I didn't know…I'm…sorry."

"No way for you to know. Nobody around here knows. I just can't talk about it without crying. Happens every so often. But, I'm doing pretty well right now, so I may as well…."

"You don't have to say anything. It's OK."

"No. It'll be good for me. That is, if you don't mind."

"Of course not."

Molly took a deep breath as a shudder passed through her.

She said, "He was Navy. OCS. I met him in New York, when I was working the OR at Bellevue. He was having his appendix out. One thing led to another, and we were married just before the war. Then he volunteered, and I did too. He was sent to Pearl, so I requested Tripler Army Hospital, and since they were short of OR staff anyway, they granted my request."

She sat silently for a moment. Schneider was keenly aware of her body heat now, and he was very uncomfortable. Or maybe too comfortable. But still, he didn't move away.

"He was killed in the Japanese attack. The *Arizona*. I don't know the details, and I really don't want to know because then I would picture him dying and suffering… and I just want to remember him as I knew him. I can still picture where the *Arizona* went down, and the flames and the men in the water trying to escape, and… Oh, dear God." She stopped again and buried her hands in her face trying to blot out the images in her mind.

"Anyway, I couldn't stay at Tripler any more after that. I couldn't be so near Pearl knowing he was down there. Under the water…."

This time she couldn't stop the sobs that welled up again. Schneider held her and she turned her head into his chest. Her warm tears soaked his scrubs, and it made him giddy and guilty all at once.

She wiped her eyes and took still another deep breath. She pulled back only slightly, finding comfort in his closeness. She looked up at him for a moment then she continued.

"I transferred out of the Pacific. You can understand why. Requested Europe and got it. And here I am. Spent a long time in England waiting for the invasion. And you know the rest."

"I'm sorry, Molly. That shouldn't happen to anyone. The fact that it happens to someone every damned minute out here can't make it any easier for you. I'm just so sorry."

She pulled back, seeming a little embarrassed at having cried on his chest. She touched the wet stain on his scrubs and gave a weak smile. They disconnected themselves and stood.

"Thanks for listening to me. It's the first time I've told that story all the way through. It's been two and a half years since he died, yet that's the first time I've said it out loud. Thanks for just listening to me."

They walked back to the farmhouse and the tents with the noise of the artillery still dominating the night. Schneider could barely stand it when they got to the fork in the path and he had to leave her side. He wanted to stay with her forever.

The next few weeks got busy again, so they were back on the move. The stay at the farm had spoiled everyone. Living in real rooms with walls and a roof seemed so civilized, despite sharing everything with crowds of others.

Now Schneider spent almost all his time in the operating tent or somewhere nearby, so he was always with Molly, or Hamm or McClintock and the rest of the team. The abilities of the surgical teams varied greatly, but there was no question that their group was among the best. Schneider and Hamm took more pride in that in front of Molly than either cared to admit. From the surgery to the anesthesia to the pre- and post-op preparation, their team never missed a trick.

Schneider spent a little time with Molly between cases, mostly at meals. But, there was nothing again like the day she poured her heart out to him sitting on that stump in the soggy field near the farmhouse. He thought they had forged a kind of bond then, but maybe, he admitted, he was just kidding himself.

In the operating room Molly treated Schneider as she did everyone else. She called him "Major" in front of others, maintaining formal army protocol with him at all times.

Schneider didn't know whether he admired her for her self-control or was disappointed that she showed no attraction to him. He was hoping for more.

There was that wedding band on his finger, of course. He didn't know who of the two of them was more aware of it. Finally, he gave up on the thought of romance with Molly and somewhat reluctantly returned to their purely professional relationship. He began calling her "Captain" again, and stopped trying to find ways to spend off-hours with her.

One night, after a very long stretch without sleep or rest, he was tanking up on food in the mess tent, refueling for the next onslaught. It was nearly two in the morning, and he couldn't remember when he had slept last. It hadn't been within the last twenty-four hours. He was trying to eat some dreadful concoction on his plate that was swimming in grease. He gave up and pushed the whole tray away, rescuing his coffee—the tea supply was gone—and some hard crackers.

He was considering melting part of a chocolate brick into the thick hot brew, when his tray disappeared and a fresh one was plopped down in front of him. On it was the best looking steak he had seen in years. Slightly charred on the outside, rare in the middle. A pink juice surrounded the meat. He couldn't believe it. He actually drooled. Then he looked up to see where this treasure had come from and found himself looking into Molly's smiling face.

Molly sat down right next to him on the bench, even though there was by now not another soul in the mess and all the other seats were empty.

"Holy shit! Where did you get this? And it isn't even Christmas," he said. He tried, not too successfully, to keep from salivating some more, and they both laughed as he wiped the drool at the corner of his mouth with his sleeve.

"What an elegant guy," she said.

"You know how to make a guy feel wanted."

"I brought you this didn't I? You want me to whisper sweet nothings in your ear, too?"

"Oh yes!" he said without hesitation. God! What am I thinking?

"OK," she said. "But, help me finish this steak first."

"Really, Molly, where did you get this?"

"There's a heifer out there in the back. *Was* a heifer. Now she's dinner. One of the GIs passing through bought it for two thousand francs. About forty dollars. Got it from a French farmer along the road somewhere. They shot it on the spot and have been carrying it around in the back of a jeep trying to find a real cook. So, they came upon us and figured they could get some good food, showers, and female company by bringing us the heifer. Pretty neat, huh?"

She didn't wait for him to reply. She cut a piece and speared it with a fork, lifting it to his mouth for a taste. Schneider opened his mouth as she placed it gently on his tongue. That simple gesture was the most sensuous thing in his life in the last three years, maybe ever, and it made him blush. Molly pulled the fork back and fed herself a piece. She used the same fork and made no gesture to wipe it off. Sharing that fork and the meat was for Schneider and Molly, somehow, a line crossed. It was both intimate and loving. It sent a message that needed no words. They never talked about it, but there it was.

And she started it.

For the next several weeks, the staff were up to their elbows in casualties and blood. Antonelli, Marsh and Higgenson seemed never to sleep. They were on the move day and night, bringing in the casualties, administering first aid, assisting in the pre-op and the OR and then back out into the field again.

It wasn't unusual for the hospital to do seven or eight hundred cases a week. Sometimes more. And that didn't include bringing in the dead. The Jerries may have been retreating, but they were putting up a hell of a fight as they went, not ceding an inch of ground without blood. As American boys fought their way east and inland, the surgical teams followed as closely as they could, sometimes to within a mile of the fighting. A few times the lines changed so fast that they were caught on the wrong side.

When they moved so fast, it was hard to get everything packed up in an orderly way. The serious abdominal cases and a few of the chest and neurosurgical cases were so unstable that they couldn't be transported. At those times, they would move the hospital with the rest of the wounded and recovering GIs, but leave a detachment of nurses and doctors behind to care for those patients until they could be moved. It was dangerous work because the lines were not always moving forward. When the Americans were retreating, it was crucial to get the patients and their medical teams out of harm's way as soon as possible. Small convoys of ambulances and supply trucks were constantly on the move.

The push east toward Paris continued. The Germans were moving away, and except for the high number of casualties pouring in all day and night, there was little evidence of any major counteroffensive. The medical group was burdened with hundreds of patients. Ambulances were running day and night to take the transportable cases west to the evac hospitals as the medical team moved further east. Always east toward Germany.

In this, their latest move, Schneider was riding with Hamm, McClintock and Molly in an ambulance truck carrying mostly medical personnel and supplies. It was not usual for the surgeons to be in one vehicle now, because they had moved out so fast, it just ended up that way. By chance, Molly ended up sitting with McClintock, and Schneider was visibly pissed. Each time Ted leaned closer and said something quietly to Molly, her laughter steamed Schneider even more.

Higgenson was up front with the driver. Marsh and Antonelli had stayed behind with a group of surgeons and nurses to care for the last of the wounded GIs until they were stable enough to evacuate. And this time the convoy had no infantry with them. Those soldiers were all far ahead chasing Germans or remained behind to protect the rest of the staff and patients.

"I don't think I'm going to miss Cherbourg or any of Normandy," Hamm said as the trucks bumped along the now deeply rutted and potholed road.

"Really?" Schneider said, with mock surprise.

"I don't know. I guess I just associate it with a hell of a lot of death and dying—such a waste of lives. I don't think I could ever come back here. I mean after the war is over...."

"Y'all can have this whole damned country if you ask me," McClintock said.

"It's so beautiful, though," Molly said, looking out at the countryside. "I would have liked to have seen it before the war."

"I did see it before the war," Schneider said, "and it was wonderful."

"You did?" she said.

"In college. I spent a whole summer in France learning French and pretending to be cosmopolitan. My friends said I was an insufferable bore when I got back to school."

"You're still an insufferable bore, Steve. You just can't help yourself." said McClintock.

Everybody nodded in agreement. Even Molly.

"A bore? Moi ?" Schneider laughed, but he was not good at taking a ribbing, especially in front of Molly. In the weeks since they had talked on that stump and then shared the steak in the mess tent, nothing more had happened. Their damn schedules were so completely out of sync. He would be up working, and she would be asleep. Or vice versa. For many days at a time, they hardly saw each other.

Schneider did a lot of fantasizing during those hours.

The trip dragged on, with stops and detours and reversals. Everyone was getting tired and cranky, dozing off in fits and starts. But, to their credit, they bore it pretty well. Schneider found himself rocking to the sway of the truck. He had changed seats—not very subtly— and now being next to Molly helped his mood a lot. But his mind kept going back to somewhere else. Try as he might, he could not let it go. Finally, he gave in and let his mind wander where it would.

Schneider's thoughts dwelled on one of his fights with Susan. It was weeks before he actually left, and more fights were still to come. But none stung him as much as that one.

Back in their kitchen, when he told her he was going to enlist, when she spoke those words that wounded him so, the words he would never forget: "What are you going to do when someone starts shooting at you? What are you going to do then?"

The memory of it took him back to where she had wanted it to take him, where it would hurt him the most: that night; so many years ago.

He was almost seventeen. Susan had just turned sixteen. By high-school standards, they were an item. They had been dating for four months and were in love as only teenagers can be: total, consuming, frustrating, and heartbreaking first love.

They had been to the movies and had taken two buses back to Susan's street. They were walking the last street to Susan's house. It was a quiet and sultry evening. Schneider could hear the wind in the many trees along her street. He was tired, dreading the long bus rides home back to his own house. At this time of night, after midnight, the buses ran only once an hour. He would be standing there in the night, alone, for a long time if he missed the next one.

But there was the promise of some necking on the front porch if he got lucky. They had done their share of smooching in the balcony during the movie, but Susan was always uncomfortable kissing in public, even in the darkness of the theater. When Schneider had begun to explore how far she would go, she had pushed him away. He felt hurt. After a few minutes, she had leaned into him again and whispered, "Later." She took his hand, which had been around her shoulders, and moved it furtively to her breast. Schneider was stunned. She had never allowed him that far. The night was looking up.

On the street to her house, Schneider started to smile. He had been so excited during the movie that he now had no idea which one they'd seen.

Susan looked at him as they walked and squeezed his hand tighter.

Just as they reached the house next to Susan's, a huge animal leaped from behind a row of chest-high hedges and directly into their path. It was black and fierce and growling. Schneider remembered looking directly into the animal's eyes and big white sharp teeth. Without any thought or planning, he reacted on pure instinct. His heart was racing as he placed both hands on Susan's shoulders and shoved her in front of his own body, between the Great Dane and himself.

Expecting a scream, Schneider was dumbfounded when Susan put out her hand and said, "Hi, Duke. Good dog."

She patted Duke on the head and was rewarded with a great sloppy kiss—from Duke—not Schneider.

It took several minutes for Schneider's heart to calm down. It would take a lifetime for him to forget the shame of his cowardly instinct. He had failed every test he could think of.

It was so horrendous an act that, for a moment, Susan thought he was joking. No one would push the girl he loved in front of a dog he believed to be attacking them. But when she realized what he had just done to her, she was at first speechless, then furious.

After loving up Duke, and scratching his big ears—the loving affection that Schneider had hoped for later—she turned her pent up rage on him.

"You son-of-a-bitch! You cowardly son-of-a-bitch!"

Then she turned and stormed into her house, furious and hurt. And terribly disappointed. She would never forget, and never quite forgive him.

He didn't tell a single person about that evening, until almost ten years later when he admitted it to Hamm.

Schneider came out of his reverie as the convoy slowed, then stopped at a bend in a small river. There was nothing around to suggest that they had arrived at the new field hospital site, so everyone jumped down to see what was going on. There was an American jeep parked off to the side. Hamm's driver was talking to the sergeant in the passenger seat. The sergeant's driver, an MP, had climbed out to stretch his legs, carefully taking his rifle with him. The rest of the doctors and nurses strolled over, happy to stretch their legs even in the mud and the light rain.

The sergeant was speaking. When he saw all of them, mostly officers, he turned his attention their way and began to explain again.

"I'm Sergeant O'Reilly. Like I was saying to your driver, you guys may wanna just turn around right here. There's a whole shitload of Jerries about eight hundred yards down the road and moving this way. They'll be here almost any time now."

"Well, where are you going, Sergeant? And what do you suggest we do?" Hamm asked.

"There's a little side road back there on the left, Major. I'm pretty sure it'll take us back to our lines. Not really sure what to tell you, sir. But anywhere is better than what's ahead of us. You got any protection here? Anyone armed?"

"I'm afraid not," Hamm said.

"Well, you can have my sidearm if that's any help," the MP said, slinging his M1 Garand rifle and reaching for the standard army issue .45.

Hamm waved him off again.

"We're not supposed to be armed. Though that doesn't seem to matter to the Krauts. I think that gun will get us in more trouble than not."

Schneider stepped forward, forcing Hamm to step aside. He held out his hand.

"I'll take that, if you're still offering it."

The MP handed Schneider the gun, grip first, and then took out two more clips of ammunition and handed them across as well.

"You never can tell, Doc. Might just save you after all."

Hamm blew out a deep breath. "Jesus, Steve. Or you might just get us killed."

He turned to the gathered group and said, "Looks like we don't really have a choice here. Let's get back in the trucks and How Able out of here. Follow the sergeant."

How Able was the military phonetic alphabet for H and A. It meant Haul Ass.

Everyone scrambled for the trucks. The MP climbed back in and wheeled his jeep around, heading back toward where they had come from. The two-truck medical convoy followed him closely because they had no idea where they were going nor what lay ahead of them.

"I don't like this," Schneider said.

"Me neither," said McClintock.

"Those guys aren't much protection," Higgenson said.

They were all keenly aware of how vulnerable their little convoy was. The three vehicles moved along slowly for about thirty minutes without encountering any Germans, before abruptly stopping again. They all jumped down as soon as the trucks ground to a halt. To their surprise, they found a small group of Americans in the field at the side of the road. Maybe eight of them. In a couple of seconds, they realized that six men were wounded. A lieutenant came out to the road and approached the jeep, talking with Sergeant O'Reilly, where everyone had gathered again. He saluted and received a bunch of very unmilitary, unenthusiastic salutes in return.

"Hey, majors. Name's Cantrell." He said. "I'm sure glad to see you guys." Then to Molly, "Hello, Captain."

Hamm took the lead again. "What's happening, Lieutenant?"

"Well, my platoon—what's left of it—got ambushed here in this field last night. We've got six men really badly wounded. No medics. I stayed here with one other GI while the rest of the platoon went for help. That was around midnight. They tried to slip out of here in the darkness so the Krauts wouldn't know they were gone. I haven't seen the Krauts or anyone else since."

"So where are they?" O'Reilly asked, looking warily around at the tree line.

"Don't know. There was some sporadic rifle and machine gun fire last night—around two in the morning—then nothing since. Must have slipped outta here in the darkness. Maybe they thought we had reinforcements on the way. Just don't know."

He shrugged, his body visibly straining with the effort.

"Look," Hamm said, "we'll take care of your wounded. Why don't you leave us one man with a gun. I guess you only have one man with a gun," he said, pointing to the GI who was still sitting with his wounded buddies out in the field. "You go with Sergeant O'Reilly here in the jeep and get us some more help. OK? Some medical supplies would be good, too."

"Yessir," the lieutenant said, still looking over toward the private with the rifle, "but I'm not sure how much use he's gonna be. Hang on a second."

Cantrell jogged back to the field and spoke with the private. Then he came back and jumped into the back of the jeep with the MP and O'Reilly. The three of them roared up the road as the group slogged back to their trucks.

And then they were alone.

In a matter of minutes, the quiet made everyone very uneasy. Even nature's sounds had disappeared into the stillness. Everyone pitched in to ferry supplies from their vehicle over to the ambulance truck and started organizing a makeshift hospital.

Again, Hamm took charge.

"Look, there's no way we're going to be able to drive these trucks into that field to get closer to those wounded guys. We'll just get bogged down for sure."

"Where should we set up?" McClintock asked.

"Well, there's a whole area over there with clusters of boulders, probably useful for shelter and defense." Hamm said.

"And a few depressions in the ground over there," Higgenson said pointing, "that we could deepen with some heavy digging. Make trenches and fox holes."

"And we'll be glad to have your strong young back digging with us, Dick," McClintock said.

So Hamm, McClintock, Molly, Higgenson and Schneider walked the hundred yards to assess the damage. The wounded men were clustered together in a small depression in the earth, and they were all in bad shape. It was amazing they had lived so long.

Hamm delegated the cases, and they split up. The one uninjured private left to guard them with his lone rifle never looked up or reacted. Nor did he offer to help at all. So they left him alone. His glassy-eyed gaze into the distance suggested he would be of little use anyway. The "thousand-yard stare" they called it.

Higgenson started IVs while Hamm and Schneider catalogued the injuries. McClintock began organizing the anesthesia supplies into working units for each of the wounded. Molly was preparing each of the surgical packs for the upcoming operations.

"I don't know if we have enough surgical packs for six cases here."

"I don't think we're going to get to do six cases," Hamm said, shaking his head at the severity of the injuries. "Let's just get going, one case at a time, and do the best we can."

Higgenson finished setting up an IV with plasma on the first man and hung it from the tree branch over the man's head. At a field hospital, the GI would have been on the operating table already, but there was nothing Hamm could do just then in that muddy field to speed things up.

"This guy's got a single gun shot wound to the abdomen. Seems stable, but…" Hamm said to Molly, who had stopped for a moment to apply a dressing and some sulfur powder to the wound.

Hamm looked at the man and could picture the bullet holes in the intestines leaking fecal contamination into the peritoneal cavity. Every hour without surgical treatment would bring this man closer to a painful death from peritonitis.

Schneider was looking at another soldier. "Jesus! This poor guy's peppered. Seven or eight abdominal holes and one chest wound. I don't know.…" Helpless to do anything but give morphine to the man, Schneider moved on.

Hamm set about assessing and treating the next man's injuries: dressing the wounds and starting some plasma. They had no penicillin in their packs. All of that precious drug was with his main supply in the trucks that had left the field hospital hours earlier. He shook his head wearily, feeling terribly helpless.

Molly knelt next to Schneider as he bent over yet another wounded man. A boy, really. The body was propped against a tree. He wasn't moving, and his eyes were shut. Schneider shook his head. "He's dead."

Molly followed Schneider to another GI who was alive, and writhing. Schneider knelt and pulled away the shreds of the GI's uniform. Both he and Molly gasped involuntarily. Even after all they had seen in the past many months, they still had to forcibly stop themselves from shutting their eyes against the terrible sight. The poor man had been opened from his pubis to his chest. His intestines had spilled out onto the ground like the gut pile of a butchered deer. There were bullet holes throughout the intestines, and a foamy green bile-stained liquid dripped onto the ground. Schneider was reminded of the froth he once saw at the edges of a horse's mouth after it had eaten ripe grass, especially with the dirt and debris sticking to the once glassy surface of his wounds. Flies crawled over the man's intestines. Although Molly and Schneider impotently waved the flies away, the flies won the battle. The man had a large bullet hole in his chest, and fine pink froth bubbled there.

Schneider shook his head in despair. He didn't try to dress or cover the wound. The man was still writhing and groaning, his voice taught and shrill. His eyes were pleading with Schneider at first. Then a look of relief came over him as if his salvation were suddenly at hand. As if Schneider could possibly help him. The young man managed a brave smile for Molly and in a hoarse whisper, said, "Ma'am."

Schneider reached into his kit and took out two Syrettes of morphine. He pulled both needle covers off at once with his teeth then injected the morphine into the man's thigh, right through the pants. He started to get up and then thought better of it. He reached back into his kit and got out another morphine Syrette. He looked at Molly for a moment, then gave the man a third shot. Schneider took off his own field jacket and covered the soldier, who was now shivering as shock mercifully began to deepen and send the poor man into a quiet, gentle, pre-death coma; his experience of the pain diminishing with each passing minute as the morphine took over his brain.

Schneider stood and moved on to the next soldier who had a single abdominal gunshot wound. Molly lingered behind for a moment, holding the dying man's hand. When Schneider looked back, though he didn't want to look at the man again, the GI didn't seem to be breathing.

Of the six wounded men, three of them might survive long enough for surgery.

Two hours later, inside the ambulance and it's jury-rigged operating room, Hamm and Schneider were just finishing the third of the primitive field operations. In spite of the cold and dampness outside, the small space inside the ambulance truck became quickly hot and dank with the sweat and breath of the whole surgical team and the patients. The smell of open-drop ether was overwhelming.

The first operation had been the single gunshot wound to the abdomen. Schneider was operating with Hamm assisting. Higgenson was holding a flashlight in one hand and helping pull on an abdominal retractor with the other.

Schneider sutured six holes in the small intestine and one in the colon, all made by a single bullet.

"Here's the goddamned bullet," Schneider said as he tossed the mangled piece of lead on the floor. "One shot, and look at all this damage!"

Higgenson was leaning in close so he could see every step in the procedure.

As Schneider sewed shut the seventh hole, he looked up at Hamm, and his eyes crinkled over his mask.

"So, Dick," he said, "we ready to close?"

"Yes, sir. Guess so."

Schneider and Hamm nodded to each other.

"Okay, wrong answer. We close now and he'll be dead before dawn." Schneider said. "First rule in gun shot wounds. If you can find the bullet free in the abdominal cavity, there's got to be an even number of holes. In, out. In, out. Right? So far, we've found and repaired only seven. We close this guy now, he's going to leak intestinal fluid from another hole we missed, and he'll be dead before morning."

Higgenson narrowed his eyes in thought. Then he said, "Of course, I get it."

"Good man," McClintock said, joining in the teaching session.

"And so if the bullet is still inside the intestine, there's got to be an odd number, right?" Higgenson asked.

"Yeah," Hamm said, "but don't get cocky. See, you can find an even number of holes and still be missing two more. Or four. So you need to run the bowel. Examine every inch of it from the jejunum to the rectum. And then back again to be doubly sure. And the stomach and duodenum, too."

Schneider was running the bowel as they spoke.

"Here it is, tucked behind the duodenal ligament. Could have missed that easily. Good thing I learned to count."

Hamm continued to teach as Schneider finished the operation.

"There's remarkably little contamination considering the magnitude of the injuries. But still, this man's going to need a colostomy to protect a repair job Steve did on his lacerated colon. We'll put him back together in a couple of months if he heals up all right."

Hamm and Schneider sewed the other holes closed, and used a major portion of what saline they had left to clean out the peritoneal cavity.

Between cases, Higgenson was assigned to do a lot of the minor surgical procedures required by the wounded men. There was also a lot of debriding of skin and muscle wounds, as well as suturing to be done. Higgenson did much of it, and he did it beautifully and meticulously. He took a lot of the work load off the surgeons.

"Y'all going to be a fine surgeon one day, Dick," McClintock said as they were moving the new patient onto the operating cot.

"Thank you sir. Seems like a long way off from here."

"It'll fly by, son. Don't y'all worry."

The second survivor had penetrating wounds of the chest. But the insertion of chest tubes did not stop all the bleeding or the air leak. So with some sense of disappointment, they had to open his chest to repair the holes in the man's lung, and stop a few arterial bleeders. But, this man, too, survived.

"Man, these boys are sure 'nuff tough!" McClintock said. "They're made of fine stuff, if you ask me."

"Sho 'nuff are," Schneider said, imitating McClintock perfectly.

"What about knife wounds, sir?" Higgenson asked.

"What about them?" Schneider said.

"Doesn't seem as if counting holes would work with those."

"You're going places, Dick. Absolutely right. With knives—or bayonets—it's a whole different ball game. You just have to run the bowl and not miss anything." Schneider turned to McClintock and said, "I think we got some talent here, Ted. What do you think?"

"I'm just hoping he doesn't get too crazy and want to become a surgeon."

The last man also had a gunshot wound of the abdomen. He had been saved for last, because it was a single through-and-through wound, with little bleeding. The man was the most stable, so he could wait the longest. Back at Charlie-7, all three would have had their operations at once with three separate teams. Not here.

All this time, Molly had been the scrub nurse, handing instruments and sorting out the many kinds of sutures for closing the intestinal wounds, the lung wounds, the arterial and venous wounds; and the giant stay-sutures—almost miniature ropes—that the surgeons used to close the abdominal walls and the chest.

She worked quietly and efficiently, and didn't participate in the OR banter. Between cases, she went off on her own to gather the dirty equipment, to wash and sterilize them in their primitive cooker so that she would be ready on time as soon as one patient was off the table and the next moved into place and asleep.

By the time they finished the last operation, it was full dark. They had been operating under the muted light of flashlights hand-held by Higgenson. The key was to be able to see well enough to complete the operation, without having so much light that they made targets for the enemy they suspected was out there. Higgenson's shoulders and back ached, as did the hand that held the big abdominal retractors .

Schneider arched his back painfully and stretched his arms. Everything seemed to hurt, but he said nothing. It would have been a sin, he thought, to complain in the presence of these young wounded men. He moved out of the ambulance and stepped into the chilly wet night, enjoying the fresh air and the room to breathe.

Schneider suddenly sensed someone at his back. Before he could turn around, the private with the thousand-yard stare draped Schneider's field jacket over Schneider's shoulders, then without a word, turned and walked back to his post. Molly came up right behind Schneider. She watched the private walk away, fading into the darkness until he was gone altogether. The two looked at each other. Her green eyes were so sad, sadder than he had seen her in a long time.

It was three o'clock in the morning by the time the group had the ambulance converted from an OR back to be able to carry the wounded in the side racks along the walls. They tied the tent and some cases of supplies to the roof and the hood. The rest of the equipment all went into the other truck. Still, there wasn't room enough for all of them to sleep inside, at least not without a lot of crushing and shoving.

Hamm rubbed his burning eyes and said, "I can't decide whether to move out right away and try to find the new field hospital, or wait here until light."

"I think we should move on now," McClintock said. "The longer we're all away from protection, the riskier it gets. Besides, we ought to get these casualties to the field hospital as soon as we can. They're going to need plasma and more IVs and penicillin too if they're gonna survive all this shit."

Molly, nodded her head and began to agree with Ted, when she was interrupted by Schneider.

"I don't know, moving around in the dark might be a hell of a lot more dangerous. Easy to get lost. We could get shot by our own guys if they're spooked enough. And who wouldn't be spooked out here? I think we should wait it out right where we are. There's been no firing for a few hours. Let's just keep our voices down and our lights out and bed down here."

Molly opened her mouth to speak, but was again cut off.

"I'm with Steve," Hamm said. "And I think we should dig some deeper holes in the cover of the trees and rocks over there and stay out of the truck. It's too damned good a target. Maybe drive down over there," he said, pointing east along the road, "to where we can pull up close to some cover, but still not sleep in the truck."

"You're right," Schneider said. "I don't want to be trapped in that ambulance either. And I think the casualties should be in the fox holes with us. If the truck is too dangerous for us, it's too dangerous for them."

Molly hadn't been able to say anything yet. She was incredulous that nobody seemed to care what she thought. But, everybody there outranked her. "Well, I think—"

"OK, let's do it," Hamm said, interrupting her. "Get everyone on board, and we'll pull on down to those trees over there."

"Well, shit!" Molly said.

"What?" Hamm said.

"I don't get a vote here?"

Hamm paused, then took a breath. "No, Molly. Actually nobody gets a vote here but me. I'm the senior medical officer and I was just trolling for ideas. Now, I've heard enough, and I've made a decision."

Molly pursed her lips and with a curt, "Yes, sir," as she stomped off to the ambulance to gather her things.

There were a few very tense minutes of silence, no one willing to cross either Hamm or Molly. Then everyone just jumped aboard, with Schneider scrambling not to be left behind. They ferried the trucks and the equipment and all the personnel a few hundred yards down the road toward Caen, where they found what looked like better cover for the night. It took only a few minutes, even in the inky blackness.

Then they got settled in again quickly. Their lonely shell-shocked private took his rifle and poncho and set off to find a place to guard his medical team and their wounded soldiers. The bodies of the dead had been wrapped in their ponchos and tied to the roofs of the two vehicles.

The three fresh post-op patients were carefully unloaded from the ambulance and carried far away to the deepest, best protected site they could find. They were completely surrounded by boulders. Higgenson camouflaged them with branches and leaves. Then he stood guard as their nurse and unarmed guardian.

Then the team unloaded their gear, clustering under the trees in the lee of the truck. They were only about twenty yards from Higgenson and his post-op GIs, yet all of them could just barely see each other in the darkness. It was foolish to be huddled so close together. A single mortar would have taken out everyone at once. But there was something about the darkness, and the cold, not to mention the Jerries in the area that made them instinctively huddle, in spite of their training.

Once they were settled in, Schneider took Molly's elbow and said, "Take this." He held the .45 out to her. "Put it in your shoulder pack. You're certainly a lot better shot than I am."

Molly took the weapon and said, "Actually, I am. But this thing won't do us much good beyond a few yards. And it might do a lot of harm. Like the muzzle flashes giving away our position. But you never know."

She shrugged, then checked the clip and rammed it home. She also checked that the safety was on and finally tucked the weapon into her bag.

Hamm watched, and weighed whether he should resist, but as he began to challenge Molly again, Ted grabbed his elbow and said, "You two have had enough angst for one night. Let it go, Hamm. She's probably the best shot on the team anyway."

Hamm could barely control his anger. He took a long breath and with a strained voice said, "Okay, everyone. Let's get away from these trucks and find some more rocks."

At Hamm's orders, they moved off away from the tempting targets made by the two vehicles, and found another natural rock formation a few yards beyond the wounded men and Higgenson.

"Let's just deepen this a bit, and settle down," he said.

Hamm had just dropped into the last of the trenches behind the rocks he'd dug with McClintock and Schneider when machine-gun fire tore the trees above them into splinters. McClintock tumbled in on top of Hamm, then rolled to his side and pressed his back against the rocky wall.

No sooner had the first volley ended than the machine gun opened up again and grenades were lobbed in their direction. Smaller trees toppled near their fortress. Hamm could hear the whistling of the rounds as they flew past; a bad sign, he knew, when he could hear the actual bullet passing by.

"Fuck this!" McClintock said, but he stayed frozen in place, seeing no better options.

Schneider, taking cover behind the rocks with Molly, grabbed her waist and muscled her to the ground.

"Don't move."

"Jesus!" she said. "You scared the hell out of me. And I can't breathe!"

It was then she realized that Schneider was shielding her with his body. He was practically smothering her with his weight. As soon as she realized what he was trying to do, she remained perfectly still. Their faces were close together, and he could feel her breath on his neck. She was still scared, and so was Schneider. But they felt at least a measure of safety in their newly dug hiding place.

"Where's the shooting coming from?" she whispered.

"No idea. Just stay put. All we have for protection are these rocks and that private back there. Lot of good he'll do us."

No one could tell where the firing was coming from. It continued more sporadically for a few minutes, then stopped altogether.

Now their medical team was clustered around a fifty square yard space, but safer than when they were near the trucks. Higgenson was nowhere to be seen, but of all of them, Schneider thought, Higgenson was the most capable of taking care of himself and his patients. Gun or no gun.

As if reading his mind, Molly asked, "Where do you think Dick is?"

"Not a clue. But I bet he's taking care of his patients."

Then, for about ten minutes, there was no more firing.

"Been quiet for a while," Schneider said. "I want to check on Dick. Something's not right. You stay here."

Then, as Schneider was about to get up, a staccato string of thuds and the shriek of ripping metal forced him back down. They peeked through openings in the rock pile and watched in horror as the ambulance was riddled with machine-gun fire; it rocked and bounced, dust and debris flying out of its sides like an exploding garbage can. Schneider expected it to burst into flames. But it didn't.

"Jesus!" Schneider whispered. "If we'd stayed in that ambulance they would have slaughtered the lot of us."

The guns stopped again. Shredded tree branches creaked as they swung above their heads. Then came the report of a solitary rifle very nearby. One shot. Pause. Another shot. Pause. Another shot.

They sank down again and waited. Two more shots fired from in front of them, but no bullets came their way. Then a few random shots were fired to the left. Then five minutes later from behind them, the bullets were flying outbound over their heads, or so it seemed. Then more firing from the right again. It was confusing, but as long as no more bullets struck near them, they didn't care.

"Think that's our private?" Molly asked.

"Don't know. Or maybe the Jerries have gotten behind us."

Another series of shots burst from the right, very near the truck. Then the blast of a grenade ripped through the air, sending up a geyser of flame from the truck's gas tank.

"Oh, God!" Molly gasped.

Again, they peeked over the top of the rock wall and watched as the burning truck lit up the night. Schneider started to duck back down just as he saw a figure back-lighted in the orange flames and smoke. It was their private—their lone defender—propped against the side of the truck, his rifle pointing straight ahead taking aim at the enemy.

He was the one answering the German fire. A solitary rifle trying to protect a bunch of unarmed doctors and their patients. Schneider wanted to call to him, to tell him to get under cover. Surely, the man could do no more. He must have been racing around behind them, always changing his location after every shot or two, trying to make the Germans believe they were fighting more than a one-man platoon.

Then the flames that had back lighted him crept upward and around him, engulfing him in a blanket of orange flame and black smoke. But the private did not move.

"Steve! He's burning!"

"No… he's dead, Molly. He's dead."

There was another brief lull in the firing. Then from the cover of rocks across from them, a large figure raced crouching toward the fallen private. It was Higgenson. He ran full tilt toward the burning man and threw himself on top of the body to smother the flames.

A series of three rapid-fire shots rang out again. Higgenson's body arched and bucked as the bullets tore into him.

Instantly, and instinctively—in spite of the danger—all four of the medical team leapt from their hiding places and raced the few yards to save him. McClintock and Schneider beat at the flames with their jackets and smothered the pyre with their bodies. Hamm wrapped his arms around Higgenson dragging him to cover, while Molly scrambled for their medical equipment.

The lone private was certainly dead. But Higgenson was still breathing. McClintock grabbed his instruments and quickly inserted an airway into Higgenson's trachea. Hamm cut away his medic's jacket and Schneider was trying without success to start a large-bore IV for plasma. All of Higgenson's veins were collapsed in his profound state of shock.

McClintock bagged air into and out of Higgenson's lungs while Hamm and Schneider tried to asses the situation. Only then did they see the three giant holes tight in the center of Higgenson's chest. There was a river of blood on his clothes and on the ground, but none was coming from the wounds. As they watched, all three holes began emitting pink froth with each breath from McClintock's anesthesia bag. Hamm lifted Higgenson's eyelids and in spite of the risk, shined his small flashlight into each eye.

Hamm slumped back onto his haunches and shook his head. He buried his hands in his face and sobbed. Schneider did the same, but McClintock kept working, only stopping when Hamm put his arm around him, gently pulling him back. McClintock slowly removed the endotracheal tube, and dropped it into his bag of supplies. Molly wrapped her arms around Higgenson and rocked him across her lap.

Schneider dropped the IVs and the plasma bag. He reached out and took Higgenson's hand in his, the tears still streaming down his face.

"What did you think you were you doing, Dick?"

Hamm sat up, wiped away his tears and put a hand on Schneider's back. "He did just what he always did. He did his job."

They kept Higgenson with them all night. Molly could not let him go. The ensuing silence was as frightening as the firefight had been. At least while there was shooting, Schneider felt he knew where the danger lay. But now, in the silence, he imagined German soldiers creeping up in the darkness, only yards away, ready to lob a grenade over the top of the rock wall. He saw in his mind a single silent enemy troop; then there were two, then four, then a platoon, a whole company overrunning their position. He saw the slaughter and his own death and his inability to save himself or Molly. And who would he save first? Would he give his life for this woman? For anyone? What would he do when the time came? Schneider had covered Molly's body with his own when the firefight started, but was it an effort to protect her, or an action forced upon him by his history of guilt? And when he thought about what Higgenson had done, knowingly risking and then losing his life for the very slim chance that he could save this young GI, he could not even conceive of such bravery in himself. Ever.

Molly and Schneider stayed next to Higgenson and the burned out truck until dawn. They neither moved nor spoke. All through the night, she never took her hands away from Higgenson's body. She was exhausted from the terrible strain of the events of the night, and Schneider was drained by his own fear and more than anything, his overwhelming sadness at the loss of Dick Higgenson.

The three wounded men still lay under the cover of the camouflage that Higgenson had built for them. Hamm and McClintock had dug in next to them, enlarging their little fortress of dirt and stones. They would watch over and care for their patients; changing IVs; administering morphine; checking on the chest tubes. All in the darkness.

The wounded had survived purely on damned good luck and perhaps some decent medical care. Perhaps the private had scared off the Germans after all. Perhaps he had made them think he really was a fighting force rather than one soldier and a bunch of noncombatants. Perhaps the Germans had killed enough for one night.

Whatever it was, the morning brought quiet to the field and the realization that the remaining medical group members were quite alone.

At first light, everyone cautiously rose from their positions. What was foremost in everyone's thoughts that morning was that Higgenson had given his life on the very small chance of saving the private who had saved all of them. The private who had tried to defend them had bought their lives with his own and with Dick's. Now nothing much remained of him but a helmet, a rifle barrel, and a burned brass belt buckle.

Hamm poked through the still warm ashes with a stick, searching for the boy's dog tags. After a minute, he pulled out a chain and shook it. There at the end of the chain were the tags, charcoal black.

Molly walked over to Hamm and asked, "Are you going to send those to his parents?"

"No, these go to graves registration. But, I want to copy down the details. He tried to save all of us, and perhaps he did. I'll ask his CO to put him in for a Bronze Star, maybe even a Silver Star. And I want to write to his parents and lie a little about how he died. I don't want them to know how it really happened. I want them to think it was quick. I'm not his commanding officer, but I'm going to write the letter anyway."

The whole group gathered at the remains of the truck. Hamm and Schneider carried Higgenson's body on their shoulders and placed him against a mound of earth and stone. Wrapped in the khaki blanket, and lying naturally against the side wall, he seemed to be resting there asleep, waiting for his ride back to the field hospital.

Molly moved among the critically ill post-ops from the night before, still amazed that none of the wounded had been hurt in the attack, and all were recovering pretty well. As well as could be expected only a few hours after surgery, hiding out in a camouflaged fox hole. Had everyone remained in the truck, of course, they all would have died horribly. She was fully aware that Hamm had made the right decision; and that he was, indeed, their commanding officer.

Hamm had just begun to collect the last of his medical kit when an American jeep rolled up the road. It scared everyone. Because of the heavy summer foliage they had not heard it coming until it was almost upon them. It could easily have been the Germans.

An MP private sat behind the wheel next to his sergeant. There were two more armed infantry GIs in the back. The sergeant jumped out of the jeep before the vehicle had stopped and saluted. Hamm waved him off and pointed to the recovering soldiers on the litters.

"Can you get us all out of here, Sergeant?"

"Yessir. But it'll take a bit longer before I can get you all out," he said, pointing to the small jeep.

"Well then, take the wounded, and maybe leave us some GIs with guns, okay?"

After the two most seriously wounded were secured to the hood of the jeep, the sergeant jumped back in. The two privates armed with their M1s and a bunch of grenades visible on their web belts, got out and stood on guard near the edge of the road. Then they lay the third wounded man, the most stable one, across the small back seat, leaning up against the side.

The jeep took off in the direction it had come from. No one had asked how long it might be before they were rescued. Then everyone sat down on the ground to wait. All the food had been in the truck, and in the excitement of the rescue and their hurry to get the wounded back to a field hospital, they had forgotten to ask if the sergeant had any rations to spare. By that time, they were very hungry. Unfortunately, there was nothing to do about it, so they all just sat down on anything dry they could find. Somehow they ended up in a little semicircle facing the remains of the truck and the remains of the private who had saved their lives.

Schneider finally asked, Hamm, "So who was that young man?"

Hamm felt around in his pocket and pulled out the dog tags dangling from the now shiny metal necklace. He handed them to Steve.

"Otis," Steve said. "Robert Simpson Otis. Private First Class."

Then he wiped the dog tags off and handed them back to Hamm.

Steve nodded his head slightly and murmured, "Thank you, Robert."

Chapter Nineteen

26 August 1944, 0600 Hours
Field Hospital Charlie-7, 100 Miles West of Paris

Nearly two more bloody months dragged on since their night under fire in that field. The German resistance was fierce in many places, and progress had been slowed for weeks at a time. Field Hospital Charlie-7 and its staff were almost constantly at work and under fire.

In the early morning light, a small group of personnel were gathered around the radio in the mess tent. Hamm and McClintock were drinking coffee while Antonelli and Marsh waited for their breakfast to be ready. Schneider was sitting next to Molly and trying to clear the static on the crappy radio that had been allotted to them.

"Sure ain't NBC," he said. "Maybe we can get Bob Hope or Jack Benny. *The Shadow, The Fat Man, Danger with Granger,* anything for Christ's sake! Something!"

Schneider was very frustrated, probably because he was hungry and tired and feeling somewhat guilty at how much he had enjoyed being so close to Molly for the past few weeks. Each day he waited for the OR schedule to be posted, and if she was not assigned to his team, he silently pouted. He didn't fully understand it, but when she was helping another team, especially Hamm's team, he felt like a jealous lover, scorned and discarded. It was so stupid. Juvenile. He was behaving worse than a teenager. It was really a lot worse than that because, whether he liked it or not, he still had a wife and two lovely young daughters at home, but all he did was moon away over Molly.

Schneider didn't think he was being very obvious. At least Hamm and McClintock hadn't said anything to him. But, why should they? They had been up to their asses in surgery almost every day for the past two months, and only in the last ten days had the pace slackened enough for anyone to breathe. In the first two months since the invasion, the group had done thousands of cases. That didn't include all the wounded and shock patients who didn't require surgery, just first aid or fluid management.

During this time the Allies continued to move east, at a slow pace at first, then accelerating, breaking through the enemy defenses and driving flat out for Germany. Scuttlebutt said that Patton was moving so fast he had outrun his own supply lines. That sounded just like Patton.

The first days after Normandy, the Allies only made a mile or two a day; now it could be a dozen or two dozen miles a day, and that kept the medical teams scampering to stay close to the troops.

As they drew nearer to Germany, Schneider began to think more and more about his uncle and his family. He still had no idea where they were, or if they were still alive for that matter. There were so many rumors about what was happening to the German Jews and the Poles. Some of what they heard was too outrageous to believe. At least no one wanted to believe it. What they were dealing with right there at the front was bad enough. No one wanted to think of anything worse.

With no news of his uncle since before the war, Schneider thought there would be little chance he could ever find him amid the chaos. Nevertheless, he held on to a faint hope. What a wonderful thing it would be to ride into Munich behind the troops to find that his uncle and aunt and cousins had survived the war.

By late August things were so quiet that on most days the medical teams were actually bored, though they hated to say it. The past night had been an all-nighter, commonplace before, but unusual lately. An armored personnel carrier full of GIs had hit a land mine about fifteen miles from the field hospital and were trucked back in three big ambulances. Teams were up all night putting those guys back together. There were fifteen casualties all told, and they saved every one of them. They had gotten very good at resuscitating the GIs in a hurry and speeding them though surgery. With all the medics scurrying to bring in the wounded, and with guys like McClintock at the anesthesia machines, they were a hell of a team. It was a family, really, and they prayed that some tight-ass in the war department wasn't going to get the idea that they should be separated. For whatever reason.

And not a day went by when they didn't think about Higgenson, and how he died trying to save an already dead GI, the second time in his young life and his all too short career as a medic. This man who saw his duty and did it every day. This Conscientious Objector.

So there they were, their little group, listening to the radio static when Schneider hit a clear patch on the dial. Out came the crystal clear voice of Free French Radio from Paris. From Paris! Schneider's French had radically improved over the past couple of months because he had taken care of a lot of civilian casualties and done a lot of reconnaissance translations with the locals and occasionally the Maquis, the French Resistance, known also as the French Forces of the Interior, or the FFI.

Often, the fighting guys would send for Schneider to conduct an interrogation of the farmers to gather terrain and logistics information. It made him feel as if he were taking a more active part in the war effort. Especially when he was helping with the Resistance, whose bravery he admired so much.

Schneider translated the radio news for everyone in the mess tent. Apparently, about ten days earlier, De Gaulle had called for a national resistance movement. The French had responded in spades. There was fierce round-the-clock fighting all over Paris. The Paris police had also declared a walkout strike against the Nazis. The entire city was engulfed in an insurrection, something they would never have dared to do before the invasion and the rapid retreat of the Germans.

But Paris wasn't yet free, and the call went out for help.

"What's he saying, Steve?" McClintock asked. Schneider waved his hand at him to pipe down so he could listen. His French was good, but simultaneous translation was still way over his head.

"Hang on. Hang on." Schneider tuned the dial a bit and listened carefully.

"The Second French Armored Division is closing in on Paris from the west," he said, "and the American Fourth Infantry Division is coming from... something, something...in the...south. Fighting in the streets…general insurrection…serious casualties…lack of medical supplies…yackety-yak…short of ammunition…pockets of Boche resistance."

Schneider struggled to piece together the sentences, but the meaning was clear. The end was in sight for the Germans in Paris, and within a day or two the city would be liberated. But everyone feared that the Germans would destroy the city before they left.

"Jesus Christ," said Marsh, "we're gonna liberate Paris! We're gonna fuckin' liberate Paris."

"So, why don't we go?" Hamm said. "I mean, why not? They're sure going to need medical supplies and surgeons. And nurses, Molly, nurses!"

Molly nodded a thank you to Hamm.

"So, why not go?" Hamm repeated into the silence. No one knew quite how to respond because Hamm was usually so conservative when it came to exposing his personnel to risk. He was beyond brave when it came to his own skin, as everyone saw on Omaha Beach and everywhere afterward. But exposing others to danger was another thing entirely.

"They don't need us here. There are more than enough surgical teams already, and business is slow enough, and it's going to get slower as the line moves east. We can catch up with the field hospital when they set up at a new position. Our GIs will have a radio. We can find out where to catch up with them."

Everyone sat silently staring at this crazy person. But only Hamm could have suggested it and not gotten booed off the stage as a nut case. He was the stability of the group. He was the rock. They all looked to him for reason and logic, whether it was a surgical decision or how to make the most of their supplies. Hamm wouldn't say something like this on a whim.

"Really?" Schneider said.

"Why not? We take one ambulance and load it with medical supplies and food. Skip the sleeping bags and the gear—we can sleep in the ambulance if we get delayed—and we're away. All roads lead to Paris, and there should be plenty of protection along the route. So… why not?"

"But, we don't have any orders, sir." It was Marsh.

"What they gonna to do to us, boy?" McClintock said in his soothing drawl. "Throw us out of the army? Send us home? Shit, they need us more than we need them. And we're not exactly deserting, are we? We're going toward the fight. We're gonna be heroes."

Everyone laughed. McClintock could do that at just the right moments. His southern drawl and his monotone were infectious. No matter how serious the subject, he seemed to make people smile.

Hamm brought everyone back to reality. "Give me a minute. I'll go see the CO and get us all passes. No need to piss off the higher-ups."

Without another moment's thought, everyone jumped up from the table and scrambled for the tents. Schneider grabbed Molly by the wrist and held her back. When everyone had gone, he said, "Molly, you don't have to go with us. This could get out of hand and become very dangerous."

She placed her other hand on his and said, "Steve, I've never been to Paris. And if I am going to go, there's nobody I'd rather go with than you guys." She looked down and added, "Mmmm...than with you."

Schneider's throat constricted. He took her by both shoulders and pulled her nearer. She came to him softly. He smelled her breath and her hair.

"Hey, Major! I'll get your surgical gear, OK?"

Antonelli. Shit.

"Go for it, Gene!"

Schneider let go of Molly's shoulders. She stepped back and smiled. Then she rushed from the tent, leaving Schneider with only her scent still in the air.

Antonelli was still there.

"I'll go get some clean skivvies, Gene. Don't want the Parisians to think we're cochons."

"Eh?"

"Pigs, Gene. Wouldn't want the French to think we're pigs."

"No, sir!"

Hamm returned with some papers in his hand and gave them a thumbs-up. "Said we could go if we took a few soldiers along. Not a problem, and they'll have a radio."

"Allons-y!" he said. Let's go. That was all the French Hamm knew. In less than forty minutes, the small volunteer group was on its way. The roads east were in pretty good condition for the first hour or so. Here and there were the remains of burnt out tanks, both German and American, and the occasional overturned truck or APC. Most were charred and in ruins. One tank lay on its side with the turret shredded as if something had blown up inside it. Schneider hated to think what had happened to that crew. When he saw it was a German tank, he sighed in relief. Then he felt guilty. He couldn't win.

Packed into the back of the truck were Schneider, Hamm, McClintock, Molly and two more WAC nurses, Marilyn and Jeanne.

Antonelli was driving with Marsh riding shotgun. Another nurse sat squeezed between Marsh and Antonelli. The rest of the nurses had decided to remain behind, in part because they were needed to run the post-op ward, in part because everyone knew the battle for Paris was not yet over.

These surgeons and nurses were an excited bunch, heading toward what they knew was going to be a special day in history. Something great was ahead of them, and they literally tingled with excitement.

As their little convoy, with two GI's in a jeep leading the way ahead of them, slowly covered the miles, the initial excitement waned a bit, and an awkward silence set in. It may have been his own conscience that was bothering him, but Schneider felt ill at ease with the idea of going to Paris with these single nurses. The three medics were all single, and—except for McClintock—most of the doctors in their field hospital were married men with children. A little imagination could go a long way toward some mighty uncomfortable territory. Schneider knew Hamm's wife and kids very well, and Hamm knew Schneider's.

Maybe it was only his own conscience. He was having some pretty vivid fantasies as Molly sat next to him, especially in the crowded conditions in the back of that truck with her thigh pressed firmly against his. He hadn't moved over to give her more room or make any separation between their bodies. Neither had she.

Because of the noise of the diesel engine, they had to lean their heads close together to be heard, and several times Schneider found himself talking right into Molly's ear, her hair touching his lips, the smell of her soap fresh in his nose. It was all too much for a guy who had been away from home for almost two years. Even after the terrible parting back in the States, Schneider had been an exemplary husband while he was stationed in England; he never went out to a pub alone with a woman; he was always in a group. All his socializing was done in the company of five or six other doctors and nurses.

But, there in France, Molly Ferraro came into his life like the thunder of rolling artillery, and his world had changed. So had his view of what lay ahead.

It was a tough trip that ride to Paris, in many ways.

After about two hours, the convoy slowed down. Schneider opened the little window that separated him from the driving compartment and asked Antonelli what was up.

"Checkpoint, sir. The last signs said we were only a few kilometers from Ver-sails."

Schneider remembered the sign for Versailles.

"That's pronounced 'Ver-sigh," Gene. Just so you can find your way back if you get lost and have to ask.

"Yes, sir. Hey, there's an MP waving me down," Antonelli said.

"Well, pull on up closer and get some information about what's going on."

"Yes, sir."

The MP strolled up to the driver's side. Like all the ambulances, the truck was a hard-sided vehicle with huge white circles and red crosses on the sides, roof, and hood: a welcome sight to most of the Allies.

Hamm was nearest the rear door and hopped out almost before the truck had stopped. Schneider couldn't see the exchange, but he heard the MP say, "Morning, Major." He could envision the salute and Hamm's own classic half-hearted return.

"Morning, Sergeant," Hamm said. "What's going on up there?"

"Well, sir, the Jerries are still holding out in a few pockets of resistance near the palace. Looks like they're prepared to die right there. And we're happy to oblige them."

"You have any casualties that might need our help? Prisoners?"

"No, sir. Not right now. We're really kicking the shit out of them, if you'll pardon me, sir. So, you may not want to go drivin' right up there in your ambulance just yet. Never can tell when a sniper or someone's gonna get out of control."

"Well, if you don't need us, we'd like to get on to Paris and see what's going on there. Any suggestions?"

"Yessir. I just came from there, and I would recommend taking that next left up at the crossroads—about a mile yonder—and then take the main road right on into Paris. Just bypass Versailles altogether." He said *Ver-sails*, too.

"Thanks for that, Sergeant. Good luck."

"Thank you, sir!"

Hamm climbed back in and sat down.

Antonelli shifted into gear and pulled out again. He leaned out the window and shouted, "That's 'Ver-Sigh,' sergeant!"

Schneider roared, "Way to go, Gene, You tell 'em."

"You heard?" Molly said.

"Yup," Schneider said. "So, let's go. Shouldn't be more than an hour from here."

"It shouldn't be," Hamm said. "Let's just hope it's that easy."

Molly leaned into Schneider's shoulder and said, "Paris! Can you believe it? Paris!" She smiled so hard that her eyes disappeared.

As the truck continued through the countryside, its occupants were astounded at the change from what they had seen around Normandy. It was as if the Germans had preserved everything for themselves and then, in their retreat, had bequeathed it to the Allies.

There were wheat and grain fields at the height of their season, golden in the warm August sunshine. The air smelled of ripe grains, of orchards full of fruit, of tilled soil and manure. In the intermittent silence, Schneider heard the bees buzzing, a sound that made him think of rejuvenation, of rebirth, instead of the constant onslaught of death and destruction. It made him ache for an end to the war.

Compared to the wet and dismal rains of June and July (it had been one of the wettest summers in memory) August was heaven. Combined with the lull in the fighting and the chance to see Paris with Molly, life could not have been better.

The truck was stopped by a French Gendarme, who said he was delighted to see them with their grande voiture chirugicale, their big surgical car. He assured them that the Partisans had driven the Germans out of Paris.

"Paris will be freed by the Parisians, n'est-ce pas?" he said, more a statement despite the rising inflection. Wishful thinking, perhaps.

However, he was the only one along the road of that opinion.

As they neared the outskirts of Paris, they came upon several platoons of American infantry. Hamm asked first if they needed any medical or surgical attention. None of them did. But, each officer had bad news.

The last one said, "Jerries are still dug in all over Paris, and there's some fierce fighting between them and the Resistance. The FFI are just entering the city now. But, if I were you guys, I'd turn around and go back where you came from. It just isn't safe around here yet."

"Thanks for the info, Captain, but I think we'll go on just a little farther," Hamm told him. "They might need us by the time we get there."

"Suit yourself, Major." Another salute, and they were gone.

Every time they stopped, someone told them to turn around and go back. Opinions in their own group grew divided.

"Are we being more than just a bit foolish about this?" Hamm wondered aloud, even though this trip was his idea in the first place. McClintock and Schneider were all for going on. McClintock was always for pushing ahead.

"Let's just keep moving carefully along," Schneider suggested. "We can look ahead at each opportunity to see if there are Jerries. We can always turn back if we see any trouble. It's unlikely we'll get cut off from the rear; I mean, we've seen nothing but American troops behind us all along this route."

Even as he argued his point, Schneider worried that he was following his desire for Molly more than his good sense.

They were still chewing on this when a French civilian bicycled up. He stopped and smiled, touching his fingers to the worn edge of his old blue beret in salute.

"Hiens! Vive les Américains!" he said.

Schneider walked over to the man and asked about the rest of the road to Paris.

"Paris?" he said with some amazement. "Non, messieurs. C'est impossible. Vous trouverez les chars, les snipers...les Boches!"

Schneider turned to the little band and said, "He thinks Paris is impossible. There are tanks and snipers and Germans all along the way. Sounds like he thinks we should turn back, too."

The others looked at Hamm in silence. McClintock was shaking his head, and Schneider could see he was terribly disappointed after having come so far. Schneider looked at Molly and found her staring straight into his eyes. It was so hard for him at that point. He wanted more than anything to show her Paris. He could speak French, and he knew his way around the city. Like a teenage boy, he wanted to show off.

And he would be risking her life, he knew, by listening to his urges.

"Well," Hamm said finally, "I can't make this decision alone. Give me some help, guys, and yes, from you as well Molly, if you would." Molly gave Hamm a knowing and appreciative smile, nodding her head saying, "Hamm, in this I'll pass."

After a short deliberation in total silence, heads popped up from their collective reveries and began to vote.

McClintock said, "I think we should just go for it. We can always turn back later."

Hamm said, "Well, we need to be very careful, if we go on."

McClintock just smiled, raising his eyebrows in assent.

The nurses were full of enthusiasm.

Antonelli and Marsh were already in the cab starting the engine.

Schneider nodded his agreement now that they had all voted and could not hold him responsible for acting irresponsibly. It was a total cop-out, he knew, but he copped out without hesitation.

They climbed into their seats in the back of the ambulance. Schneider sat nearest the cab, and when Molly slid in next to him, she pressed even closer than before so that he could feel the warmth of her body right through their uniforms. His heart was on fire.

They made their way carefully along the road, and with more than just a little fear. The route was strangely deserted. They expected a good deal more in the way of soldiers and equipment—either theirs or the Jerries'. But it was as if everyone had either fled or was gathering somewhere else for the big fight.

They entered Paris from the west, crossing the Seine near the Bois de Boulogne, then along the Allée de Longchamps. As they neared the Arc de Triomphe, they suddenly became ensnared in traffic.

Happily, it was all friendly: French men and women and children were everywhere. If the children were out playing, they assumed, it must mean that the pockets of German resistance were under control. They tried to push through, thinking that the red crosses on their truck would give them some clout. But it was no use. They turned around and tried a different approach, this time using some smaller streets, finally ending up on Avenue Victor Hugo.

Schneider banged on the wall of the cab and shouted to Marsh through the little window.

"Hang a left here; it'll take you right into the Place de l'Étoile."

"Where?"

"The Étoile. The Star. That's where the Arc de Triomphe is. That's where all the action will be."

"Yessir!"

Marsh laid down some rubber, or as much rubber as he could in that pathetic truck, and they moved in toward L'Étoile. They got jammed up again and decided to try a few more side streets. Schneider's memory of Paris was not as good on the Right Bank. As a college student, he had spent quite a lot of time there one summer, but the Latin Quarter on the Left Bank and the Cité Universitaire had been his hangouts. The Right Bank was too rich for his blood back then.

He leaned forward into the little window and said, "Maybe you ought to just park it here somewhere, Andy. We're not going to get much closer than this."

Marsh didn't answer, but pulled up onto the sidewalk with a big thump and cut the engine right there. He was driving like a native already after only thirty minutes in the city. They all climbed down from the truck, stumbling and pushing each other. They were elated and in total shock, disbelief, wonder.

God! We're in Paris on the day of its liberation from the fucking Germans, Schneider thought. He didn't know if it had struck anyone else as hard as it had him, but when he looked over at Hamm, he could see Hamm suppressing a tear forming in his eye.

Marsh and Antonelli were buzzing with excitement. For them, it was the fantasy of all the available French women, more than the historic moment, that had their minds engaged.

Schneider recognized the historic day for what it was, but it didn't take long for him to become totally focused on how he was going to get Molly away from all the camaraderie. He was nearly feverish with his desire for her, and words like "love" kept creeping into his brain. He could hardly bear to think of his fantasies for fear of jinxing it.

For a few moments, Schneider was oblivious to the noise of the crowds in the street, yet he could hear the metallic ticking of the engine as it cooled down in the shade of the trees.

"Hey, Steve," Hamm said. "What's the plan?"

"What? I'm the commanding officer now?"

"No," Hamm said, "but we have to stay a little focused and organized. We might be needed, and I don't want everyone scattered all over to hell and back. And you've been to Paris and know the geography."

Hamm and Schneider got together with McClintock and had a little huddle there on the sidewalk. The nurses and the medics were milling about, moving off into the crowd and coming back to the safety of home base, like little kids exploring a new playground.

"Look," Schneider suggested, "let's just leave the truck locked up here for a while. We can take a look around and then meet back here in a few hours. What do you think?" Hamm looked skeptical, but McClintock cut him off. "Hey, man," he drawled, "let's all take a little breather from this war. Ain't gonna hurt nothin'. Let's just enjoy this little celebration. Find out if we're needed anywhere, and then meet back here sometime reasonable. Like tomorrow morning."

Ah, fucking McClintock! Schneider thought. He could have kissed him. Hamm started to sputter, but McClintock just plowed right on.

"Ain't nothing gonna happen in that little biddy time, Hamm. We'll be back at the front soon enough, and then you'll wish we had taken the time to relax a little bit." He reached out and squeezed Hamm's trapezius hard with his meaty fist. Hamm winced even as he smiled.

Schneider thought McClintock was looking at him with more than a casual interest—maybe some jealousy too—but then the anesthesiologist turned and moved off into the crowd. Before he got ten feet, a French woman opened both her arms and smiled the biggest smile Schneider had ever seen. She said something in French that Schneider couldn't hear, and that McClintock surely couldn't understand, and then fell into his arms, giving him the most wonderful kiss. It lasted forever. The medical team stood staring in silence.

One of the woman's legs lifted from the ground, bent at the knee. Her stockings showed in the sunlight, and it rattled Schneider to realize he had not seen the seam of a woman's stocking in a long time. The woman wore a flowered cotton dress, and her dark hair was piled high wrapped in a braid. When they had finished their kiss, McClintock walked away with the woman on his arm. Before he disappeared into the crowd, and without even a backward glance, he raised his free hand, waving goodbye in their direction.

Antonelli and Marsh were chattering away with a couple of nurses in anticipation of free play. It was a high school outing.

The deal had been sealed. They would all meet back at the truck the next day. No time was specified. Schneider heard Hamm telling Marsh to check on the truck from time to time, and that maybe it would be even better if he and Antonelli took turns guarding it. It wasn't an order. Just a question.

Marsh looked at Hamm as if her were speaking Chinese. He nodded and stood there as Hamm, too, walked away. It had been a suggestion. No orders given. So, none could be disobeyed.

Then Antonelli and Marsh were gone.

Then Marilyn and Jeanne and Joan.

Just gone. Everyone blended into the crowd, hugging and kissing the Parisians who proffered champagne in celebration of the renaissance of their city.

Soon Schneider was standing alone next to the truck.

Alone? Jesus! Where's Molly?

He couldn't find her, and he panicked. Did she walk off with the nurses? Had he totally misinterpreted her signals? Was it really only his imagination?

Shit!

He began to scramble around the rear of the vehicle and shout her name when he ran right into her coming around the side of the ambulance. They slammed softly into each other. He grabbed her arms to keep both of them from stumbling and falling down right there in the street.

Molly looked at Schneider and smiled. Then, she released herself from his grip and reached up to put her arms around his neck. Schneider bent down and hesitated, but she did not. In a second, her lips were on his. Not tentatively. Not as strangers. But hard and bursting from the hours and days and weeks of frustration that had been penned up in both of them since they first spoke that morning after the strafing of the OR tent.

Molly pulled back after the longest time and smiled at Schneider again.

"Come on, Steve, show me Paris."

Where do I begin? Schneider wondered. This is Paris, the most romantic city on earth.

And more than that, it was Paris on the day of its liberation from the goddamned Nazis after four long awful years of captivity and death and war. And it was Paris with a woman who had taken hold of his heart in such a very short space of time, his heart that was now being squeezed in his chest by her soft grip. It was better than wonderful.

Schneider's mind was awhirl with thoughts. His brain felt like scrambled eggs. Molly took his arm, and they started down the side streets trying to avoid the crowds. It had been a long time since he had been in Paris. He remembered with a wild joy the excitement of sailing to Europe in the cheapest cabin aboard the Queen Mary so many years ago in college. The arrival at Southampton, the first days with his college friends in London, the sights, the concerts. A train trip out along the Thames for The Henley Royal Regatta. Then the boat train to Paris in time for Bastille Day.

It was all a far cry from his most recent trip across the Atlantic two years ago. His mind recoiled at the thought of it. This time it was the Queen Mary again, but now her holds were crammed with fifteen thousand GIs instead of two thousand luxury passengers. The carpets were gone and the rich wooden doors replaced with steel. The soft beds were gone, too, with bunks stacked six tiers high in their places. And the food. Oh, God! That crappy food!

The overwhelming stench of body odor and vomit flashed through his brain, requiring him to physically shake loose from the memories of that awful voyage. But he couldn't and thought of the towering wave that had struck the ship with such force that it listed until the upper decks were awash with sea water, a mere five degrees from capsizing with the possible loss of fifteen thousand souls—a disaster that would have dwarfed the sinking of the Titanic.

Punctuating the end of the voyage, with England in sight, they had collided with a British vessel, cutting her in half and killing hundreds of their Allies. Schneider watched men drown in the sea with land in sight, feeling utterly helpless and shackled by his own fear.

But now, back here with Molly, even in the throes of war, his mental gyroscope was very well tuned to the city that he remembered, as if it were his hometown, even from so long ago.

So long ago, he had come to Paris in the middle of the night, just two weeks after his nineteenth birthday, on the thirteenth of July, the evening before Bastille Day. The entire city was out in the streets, dancing and drinking and celebrating their favorite holiday. Paris then was almost as exciting as it was today. There was no Hitler yet, and the shock of the Depression was wearing off. There he was, a college sophomore, on his own with just enough money to last the summer…if he were careful. It was magic.

Now he was back again, and he could hardly stand it for the joy he felt. The magic again. He knew the war was far from over, and that this was just a break in the fighting. Soon enough, they would all be back at the front lines dealing with more death and injuries than he cared to think about. It didn't escape him that his and Molly's survival were still very much in question. He wondered who might be grieving his death if he were to die a year from now, a month, tomorrow? Susan? The girls? And who would grieve for Molly with her husband dead?

Still, he determined that he wouldn't think about the next day or the day after that. Who knew if they would come? He would take whatever moments the world would give him, alone with Molly in this island of peace in that sea of tragedy.

Even the Parisians were on his side. They were all in love from the looks of them.

Schneider's Uncle Mike, his father's brother, used to say to him, with a cherubic smile on his face, "When you're in love, my boy, the whole world is Jewish."

Yeah. So why not me?

Suddenly, he was no longer haunted by the thoughts of his wife and children at home. The truth of it was that he had been away for a hell of a long time. And he hadn't made love with anyone in more than two years, much less someone who had captured his heart as Molly had; someone who shared the daily fear and the pain and the dying. She knew him in some ways better than Susan, who had known him since their childhood.

"So, where are we going?" she asked, squeezing his arm tighter, interrupting his thoughts.

Schneider thought, that is a much bigger question, you know. Or else you're reading my mind.

"Well, let's head over to the Champs Élysées. We'll see the Arc de Triomphe. I bet that's where all the celebrating will be."

So they moved in the direction of the Champs, following Schneider's nose and his memory. They took a few wrong turns, but in that quarter of Paris, every street was worth the walk. There were lovely old homes and shady streets that seemed untouched by the years of war. Schneider wondered how many of those houses had quartered the Gestapo and the SS and the German Wehrmacht officers. But he shook the thoughts from his mind and continued to enjoy the beautiful summer weather. The streets were dappled with sunlight through the heavy foliage of the old trees. The air was warm and moist, heavy with the fragrance of the flowers still blooming along the streets.

After about ten minutes, they could just begin to hear the noise of the crowds near the Étoile. In a few minutes they were up to their necks in celebrating Parisians, but at that moment Schneider wasn't ready to share Molly with the crowds.

He stopped suddenly in front of one of the wonderful old town houses, surprising Molly and accidentally yanking her around by the arm. She laughed as she pirouetted into him, and in a moment he was lost in her lips again, and her hair, and her scent. He could feel her body sliding beneath her loose fitting khakis. She pressed herself to him almost as if she were reading the question in his mind, answering with her body: Yes, we will make love tonight.

Schneider could feel her presence all through his body, and it was nearly more than he could bear. She hugged him tightly, then released him from her grip and took his hand, pulling him toward the noises of the Étoile.

They made their way through the shady side streets where people were fewer and the going easier. Here and there were the remnants of burned German flags, the swastikas still smoldering on some of them. The French tricolor hung from hundreds of windows, fresh from their secret storage places of the last four years. There were even some American and British flags hanging alongside the French ones. Schneider wondered at the risks people took in keeping these flags hidden and ready throughout the whole Occupation. Many of the windows were open to the unbelievably beautiful summer's day. There was not a cloud in the sky. A light breeze moved the air.

The French were certain that God was on their side that Saturday morning in August.

Schneider and Molly heard later that the last week's fighting between the French Partisans and the Nazis had been particularly fierce. There were more than four hundred barricades erected all over the city to isolate the German groups and prevent the movement of tanks and armored personnel carriers. It was like the French Revolution, with cries of "Aux Barricades!" resounding throughout the city. There, lying behind pathetic fortresses of furniture, mattresses and burning tires, the French Partisans defended their posts with a terrible loss of life. Medical care was nonexistent, which might explain the welcome the Americans received as they came into town with their ambulance and their uniforms with their medical insignia. Quite unintentionally, they were the first of the Americans to arrive in Paris that day. The FFI, under Général De Gaulle had demanded that the French themselves, and only they, liberate Paris.

"Let's get over to the Étoile and see what's happening. Then we can find a place to stay for tonight," yelled Schneider over the noise of the crowd. "I think there's going to be a crush of people wanting rooms in Paris, and I don't know how many hotels are even open at this point."

Schneider was damned if he would spend this night on a park bench somewhere.

They walked faster as they neared the noises of the Champs Élysées, their excitement rising alongside the fervor of the French. They intersected the Champs several streets down toward the Place de la Concorde.

The crowds were in a frenzy. Marching through the streets was a column of French Partisans holding their guns on about fifty women with shaved heads. The crowd was now becoming more angry and violent, and only the presence of the Partisans kept them at bay. These women were collaborators who had given comfort, primarily their bodies, to the Nazis. Now they would feel the full brunt of the anger that had been pent up in the Parisians for so many years. The shaved heads identified their crimes, and their torn clothing (leaving some of them nearly naked) was a sign of the contempt in which they were held.

As the women passed, Molly drew nearer to Schneider and tightened her grip on his arm. She was shaking, and Schneider could see she was upset at the sight before her and the violence they both knew awaited these women. There was not long to wait.

Almost directly in front of them, amid shouts of "Putains! Les Salauds!" (Whores! Bastards!), a woman lunged from the crowd and spit into the passive face of one of the shorn women. The spittle dripped down her face, her hands bound behind her back. Her dress had been ripped from her, leaving her wearing only a tattered bleached slip and brassiere, exposing her shame to everyone on that crowded street. Molly buried her face in Schneider's chest, and even he, the supposedly battle-hardened surgeon, wanted to turn away. But, he couldn't. He was hypnotized and, in a way, fascinated. There was some kind of justice here, and he found himself, to his shame, almost enjoying it. He, like the Parisians, wanted revenge.

Behind these women came another band of captured collaborators. Schneider had no idea who they were, so he asked a Frenchman who was standing next to him. The man spit on the ground, and then explained that these were the male profiteers who had made money and curried favor from the Nazi occupation of Paris. Then he spit gain. The man paused for a moment, looking at Schneider's and Molly's insignias. He broke into a smile and grabbed Molly, kissing her on both cheeks. Without a pause, he turned and grabbed Schneider, kissing him too.

"Merci, mes amis. Merci beaucoup."

The man moved off and Schneider turned back to the spectacle of the captives. They were a ragged bunch, their clothes torn and their faces bloodied and swollen. Again, the crowds surged forward as these men were marched off to wherever the Partisans were taking them. Schneider knew that wherever it was, it wouldn't be pretty. Many of these men would not survive the night.

The Partisan captors were a ragged bunch as well, armed with a variety of weapons and wearing no uniforms. They had suffered greatly during the war, and at this moment they were not men and women to be trifled with. They prodded their prisoners ahead with their gun barrels. Occasionally, they struck a laggard in the back or head. Molly saw only the first such beating, for afterward she never took her head from Schneider's chest. This professional nurse who had seen, day in and day out, the worst that humans could inflict upon humans, could not bear to watch the revenge play out before her eyes.

Schneider never blinked.

One prisoner was dressed in a gray suit jacket, white shirt, and silk tie still knotted neatly at his throat. But his trousers were gone, making him a ridiculous figure standing there in his stocking feet and underwear, his tattered socks held up by garters. Schneider almost felt sorry for the man. Suddenly, a woman burst through the crowd and ran into the line. She shoved past a mildly protesting Partisan and struck the man in the temple with a cobble stone. She was so much smaller than the man that she had to jump to reach his temple. The man staggered and then received a second blow to the same place, toppling him to his knees. Only then did the Partisan guard gently take the woman by the elbow and lead her from the street and back into the crowd.

Another guard yanked the now bleeding man to his feet, shoving him back in line. The prisoners were made to keep their hands over their heads the whole time, though none could have put up any resistance at this point without being killed on the spot.

And so the shaven-headed women and the collaborator men continued down the violent and shame-laden gauntlet of the Champs Élysées and the Rue de Rivoli to whatever fate.

"Can we leave here, Steve?" Molly said as soon as the group had passed. "I don't want to see any more of this. This is…this is more like what I expect the Germans to do."

Schneider was struck at how the scene had shaken her, this woman who was in the presence of terrible wounds and pain and death almost every day of her young life. She was literally up to her elbows in blood twenty-four hours a day. There was something about the calculated brutality, even against the vermin collaborators, that offended her sense of fairness, her rules of fair play. At that moment, he wasn't quite sure what to think, but suddenly he, too, wanted out of there. The exhilaration of liberation day had been sadly stained by the public brutality, and Schneider wanted to get away as badly as Molly did.

They headed left, back up the Champs Élysées toward the Étoile. It was early afternoon by then. There must have been a million or more people crowding the two sides of the enormous avenue. Schneider had been impressed with the size and scope of the Champs when he was there during peacetime, but now, with this unending throng of people blanketing nearly every square foot of ground, it seemed far more vast than before.

Schneider and Molly were soon well away from the shadow of reprisals and revenge, for there in the streets again was the unbridled joy that had first greeted them when they arrived. Slowly, Molly came back to herself and seemed to put the scenes of a few minutes earlier behind her. As she emerged from her sorrow and fear, so did Steve. He held her tightly, for if he lost her in a crowd such as this, God only knew when he could find her again. They hadn't thought to set a meeting place in case they got separated—never even considered it.

The crowd seemed to be collecting itself as Steve and Molly neared the Arc de Triomphe at the Place de L' Étoile. Uniformed soldiers of the FFI, not the Partisans, were lining the avenue on both sides. Arm-in-arm they forced the crowd back into an orderly parade formation. Tanks of the FFI lined the route as well, with commanders in the open turrets. All along the route toward the Place de la Concorde on the rooftops, too, people were crowded seeking a good view. Schneider and Molly pushed and elbowed their way toward the front of the crowd. They expected some angry responses to their rudeness, but they wanted to see this historic moment whatever it took. Actually, each time they pushed past another Parisian, they were greeted with joy, and backslaps, and hugs, and even a kiss or two. Their American uniforms were like passports to the affections and gratitude of the French celebrants around them. It was a scene from one of the really bad war propaganda movies they had been seeing with shouts of "Vive les Américaines!" all around.

Then the crowd grew silent. A million people stood nearly speechless at the sight of their four-year-long dream coming true. Four years of unimaginable humiliation and shame, of deprivation and fear, of violence and torture, of unthinkable repression by their centuries-old enemy.

Now, at this moment in time, at this single event in history, Schneider and Molly would witness, along with a million Parisians, something they would never forget. Not one detail. Not a blink of the eye.

Général Charles De Gaulle was entering Paris for the first time since his flight in 1940. Molly and Schneider stood on tiptoes to take in the sight of the tall man in his immaculate uniform of the FFI, Kepi squarely on his head, his bulbous hawk nose and mustache visible even from where Schneider stood.

De Gaulle marched under the massive stones of the Arc de Triomphe to the music of the French National Anthem, the "Marseillaise." As he carried a huge wreath of red gladiolas, the anthem finished, and a solitary bugler stepped forward, raised his instrument to his lips and played the beautiful simple sad notes of "Taps." De Gaulle solemnly laid the flowers at the Grave of the Unknown Soldier while the bugler played. Symbolically De Gaulle then stooped to light the Eternal Flame which had been extinguished by the Nazis four years earlier.

Finally, De Gaulle stood, saluted the flame and the grave, turned, and began his march down the Champs Élysées toward the Place de la Concorde, heading on to the Cathedral of Notre Dame de Paris. The crowd burst into cheers. Shouts of joy and celebration filled the air as De Gaulle and his entourage proceeded before them. The military escort moved slowly down the avenue with De Gaulle at its head and Général Jacques Philippe Leclerc, nearly a head shorter than De Gaulle, one step behind.

De Gaulle and his FFI had made damned sure that the liberation of Paris would fall to them. Général Leclerc, commander of the French 2nd Armored Division, was returning nearly four years to the day since he set out on his journey back to Paris from the battlefields of African Cameroon to greet De Gaulle and make a show of unmistakable strength and solidarity. It was Leclerc himself, who, over the green cloth surface of a billiard table, had accepted the surrender of his beloved city from General Dietrich von Choltitz, the German commander of Paris.

The parade continued down the Champs, De Gaulle greeting the crowds with solemn waves of his hand. Although there was a definite military presence, there were no artificial barricades to separate De Gaulle from his people.

Molly and Schneider scrambled along the periphery to keep ahead of the mob, following the Général all the way to his destination at the Cathedral of Notre Dame. Schneider had been a history major in college and wasn't going to miss a second of this event. With Molly's hand firmly in his, they beat their way through the crowds, sometimes bypassing the parade route to pick it up again further along the way. When it finally dawned on Schneider that this was going to end up at

Notre Dame, he took a shortcut along the river past the Palais du Louvre, and to L'Île de la Cité via the Pont Neuf.

They came to the large square in front of Notre Dame just before De Gaulle arrived. There seemed no way they could get into the cathedral, but Schneider was dying to see the culmination of this journey. He asked a French officer of the FFI what was going to happen. Without turning his head, or his machine pistol, from the parade route, he said that Le Général would enter the church and participate in a *Te Deum* service to conclude the formal liberation ceremonies.

De Gaulle would make clear to everyone in France and the world that he, and he alone, was "the instrument of France's destiny".

Schneider asked the officer if there was any way he could get in to see the *Te Deum,* to which the officer blew some air through his pursed lips, the quintessential French response to almost any impossibility, and smiled, shrugging his shoulders.

But Schneider would not take no for an answer. He searched the crowd and the cathedral for a way in. Nothing. He had all but given up and was looking for a good vantage point for Molly and him to view the last moments before the Général entered the church when he saw another U.S. Army uniform, the first he had seen all afternoon. The man was wearing an army photographer's patch on his shoulder, and Schneider knew he had found his way in. With Molly's hand tightly in his, he pushed his way through the crowd and finally got next to the photographer, who was laden with equipment.

"Hey, Lieutenant," he said. "You look like you may need a grip."

The man looked puzzled for a second and then laughed.

"Sure can, Major. Love to have a superior officer carry my shit, uh, gear." He turned to Molly and the smile widened. "You too, Captain?"

"Me, too!" Molly said, a big smile on her face.

The lieutenant pounded on a door at the side of the cathedral. Just as the door opened, there were several rifle shots in the square. The enormous crowd fell to the ground en masse, and the threesome huddled for their lives in the cover of the stone arches of the cathedral. When Schneider looked up, the square was covered with cowering bodies trying to evade the gunfire. He scanned the area but could not place the source of the shooting. Then he broke into a smile, followed by a loud laugh. He pulled Molly to her feet, still maintaining the protection of the stone doorway, and pointed.

There in the middle of the crowd was a large bare circle, and in that circle was Général Charles De Gaulle, erect and unflustered, walking straight ahead to the entrance of the cathedral. He didn't so much as turn his head to see where the firing had come from. He just walked past the prostrate crowd, straight toward his destination as he had in battle for the past four years. Nothing was going to stop this man. Not even the possibility of a sniper's bullet in the back.

Schneider shoved his way in over the protests of the unkempt man who had opened the door, followed by Molly and the photographer. They made their way toward the pulpit, and set up the cameras off to the side with a terrific view of the proceedings.

"Hang on to these," the lieutenant said, handing Schneider and Molly some lenses and a bunch of flash bulbs.

Then they stood back and waited for De Gaulle. Schneider smelled the slight musty dampness of the old building, bringing back memories from very long ago.

As the main doors opened, they were temporarily blinded by the hot bright sunlight contrasting with the cool dark interior of the church. The gunfire continued outside as the FFI sought out and silenced the shooters. But if Le Général were aware of this chaos around him, he did not show it. He walked calmly into the cathedral and down through the center aisle.

The huge cathedral was completely filled with French civilians and soldiers. Fathers and mothers had brought their children to witness the great day. In the setting of the austere stone and stained glass windows, a reverent crowd of a thousand stood and waited for the great man to take his place.

Then, almost impossibly, gunfire erupted inside Notre Dame itself, ricocheting off the walls and sending shards of stone into the pews. Again the crowd ducked, taking cover behind the heavy wooden benches until there was not a face in sight.

Schneider grabbed Molly and pulled her back behind a stone pillar. He shoved her to the ground and covered her with his body, pressing them against the base of the column. Schneider peeked around the edge of the column to see not a soul visible in the cathedral. Everyone had taken shelter, mostly behind columns and beneath the sturdy wooden pews.

Everyone, that is, except De Gaulle again. The Général never flinched. Never ducked. Never broke his stride. He marched straight ahead to his destiny, erect, proud, and determined. Perhaps a little crazy, too.

Molly slowly pushed Schneider off her, and raised her head to see what was happening. The two of them stayed behind the column, and from that vantage point, would now witness this incredible historic event.

De Gaulle took his place to the left of the main aisle of the cathedral, opened his hymnal, and waited for the service to begin. The firing inside continued.

Behind De Gaulle, a general in the uniform of the FFI stood and shouted in French to the crowd, "Have you no pride? Stand up! Stand up!"

The crowd rallied, and with gunfire still sporadically punctuating the service, De Gaulle and his entourage recited the phrases of the Magnificat.

Then, with the service wisely curtailed, De Gaulle closed his hymnal, turned into the aisle, and walked calmly from the cathedral.

A final solitary gunshot echoed through the cathedral, and the firing ended. The FFI had found their sniper.

Molly and Schneider stayed hidden in the alcove until the Général was gone. They thanked the Lieutenant, handing him his lenses and all the unused flashbulbs. For in his awe, the lieutenant had not taken a single photograph. Then they slipped out the side door, once again back into the warm sunshine of that Saturday afternoon in Paris.

Molly and Schneider walked away from Notre Dame in a rapt silence. But as soon as they neared the river, Schneider turned and grabbed her by her shoulders and said, "Do you realize what we saw today? Just hours in Paris, and we watch De Gaulle liberate a city that's been under the Nazis for almost exactly four years! And we were here to see it! Can you imagine?"

Molly closed the space between them and threw her arms around his neck. She buried her face in his chest and held him. Then she pulled back just far enough to say, "These poor people! What they've been through. My God, it's unthinkable, Steve."

There was no more gunfire after they left Notre Dame. The FFI had apparently quelled the remaining German pockets of resistance. There were even rumors that most of the shooting was from celebrants firing their weapons into the air. Schneider knew that wasn't true because he had seen the stone chips flying off the sides of the cathedral, and he later found out that many civilians and Partisans were killed and wounded that day. But by late afternoon the city was free and at peace. Schneider had the rest of the day and night to show Molly around his wonderful city.

"Well? Where to?" she asked as they strolled toward the river.

"Let's see. Why don't we go get some lunch on the Left Bank and then walk up onto Montmartre to watch the sun set?"

Molly smiled eagerly, nodding her head. They crossed the Seine over the Pont Neuf again, this time turning left to go to the Latin Quarter. They took several small side streets and found themselves on the Boulevard St. Germain. Arm in arm, they headed up the boulevard past the old church of St. Germain des Prés, strolling leisurely, looking for a place to get something to eat. They had missed lunch entirely, and Schneider was damned if they were going back to the ambulance to eat C rations in Paris.

The cafés were teeming with people celebrating the liberation. Couples stared into each other's eyes over coffee and croissants. God knows where they got the coffee, or even if it was the real thing. But who cared? The sun was warm, and the Germans were gone from the streets. Paris belonged to the Parisians again…and to Steve and Molly.

The two took lots of little detours among the myriad side streets as Schneider tried to regain his bearings from his college days. The hotels where he had stayed then looked worn and tired. Part of him wanted to check into one of them. When he was there at age nineteen he had wanted more than anything to find some woman to share his bed. He never had. Now he was here again, but these small establishments seemed too down-at-the-heels even for wartime.

Schneider had dreamed about coming back to Paris some day with his love. He never had the time or the money after he and Susan married. Now he was there courtesy of Uncle Sam, and damned if he wasn't falling in love. His pockets contained French francs and American dollars, and he was feeling great.

They wandered, following an inadvertent circle, and found themselves back at the church of St. Germain des Prés. A throng of people milled about an outdoor café.

"Hey," Schneider said, taking Molly by the arm. "There's Aux Deux Maggots! My God! Let's see if we can get a table there."

"Even I've read about Aux Deux Maggots."

"I have no idea why it's called that, but it's a Paris landmark. Famous authors and poets have always come here to write and meet and argue. It was the place to meet for everyone, especially Americans who wanted to feel as if they had sampled the great Paris traditions. Anyway, let's go see if we can get in."

They hurried down the street, but things didn't look promising. There was a mob around the place, and every table was filled, inside and out. There was no line or place to sign in. No Maître D' to bribe and ease their way. Schneider had about given up hope of having lunch there when he heard his name shouted over the noise of the crowd.

"Major Schneider! Hey, Major Schneider! Over here!"

Schneider stood as tall as he could, trying to see over the crowd. There, at the back of the outside tables was Antonelli and two young women, obviously French. Schneider pushed his way through and onto the veranda, pissing off more than one person waiting for a table. Antonelli was standing when they got to his table and grinning from ear to ear. His face was flushed, most likely from the effects of the now empty wine bottle on the table, and he was slightly unsteady.

"Hey, Gene. How you doing?" Schneider asked, though it was obvious that Gene was doing great.

"Hey, Major. Hello, Captain," he said, nodding to Molly. "I'm doin' great!" and it was all he could do not to giggle. "This here is Collette," he said, pointing to the very pretty blond on his right, "and this is Monique." He pointed to an even prettier blond on his left. "I think."

"You think?" Molly said.

"Well, I don't speak any French, Captain. And they don't speak any English. So, I think that's their names. But, it's funny. I don't seem to need any French anyway." This time he did giggle.

"Hey, Major Schneider," he said, pulling Schneider slightly aside. "How do you say…" he hesitated, stumbling on his words like a love-sick high school kid.

"Say what?" Schneider asked, probably too loudly, embarrassing Antonelli.

"C'mon, Major. You know. You speak French."

"You want to know how to ask…?" Schneider said.

"Yeah, yeah." He was whispering now.

"Are you kidding?" Schneider said. "That would be like handing a four-year-old a loaded gun!" He patted Antonelli on the back and pushed him away.

"You'll figure it out, Gene. I'm sure."

Antonelli laughed.

"Listen, take this table. We're leavin' now. I'm gonna cut on down to the Champs," (he pronounced it as only Antonelli could, like the shortened form of champions) "and try and find Marsh. I think he was going to the Eiffel Tower or something. So you guys sit here."

Antonelli got up and took both girls by the arm, made a polite half-salute to Schneider and Molly, as good a salute as he could manage with both arms encumbered with women. He had to bend over so his forehead could reach his locked hands. Then he disappeared into the crowd. The last thing Schneider noticed was that Antonelli was definitely not heading toward the Eiffel Tower. He was about to call to him and point that out, but then just laughed and settled back into his chair as he noticed that Antonelli had also left Schneider with the bill.

"What? What's funny?"

"Nothing," he said, "squeezing Molly's hand. Let's order some lunch." He didn't let go of her hand once for the next forty-five minutes.

The rest of the afternoon continued to be magic. Feeling full from their first fabulous French meal together, and sleepy in the August heat, Schneider and Molly wandered all over Paris with only a vague sense of where they were heading. As Schneider had carefully planned in the recesses of his mind, just as it grew dark, they found themselves at the top of Montmartre, sitting on the steps of the great white church of Sacré-Coeur. With the famous domes at their backs, they watched the sun silently set in the crystal clear sky to the west. They sat there alone, oblivious to the hundreds of others, all lovers it seemed, arms around each other, enjoying the cool evening breeze and treasuring the respite from the terrible war. Neither of them said anything, but both silently dreaded the moment of their return to the ambulance and the carnage of the real war. They would plunge back into reality all too soon.

But, for a few minutes more, and in spite of the crowd around them, they remained up and above that war, in their own world, just the two of them.

Molly turned her head and placed a hand on Schneider's cheek. She drew his face to hers and whispered:

"Thank you, Steve, for sharing Paris with me."

Then she placed her lips over his and kissed him with such tenderness that he thought he might cry. Their tongues roamed carelessly over each other's mouth, and they stayed locked in that kiss and embrace long enough for the sky to turn from dusk to night. When they looked up again, all of Paris was dark, the stars the only source of light.

Just then, a miracle happened. For the first time since 1939, after four long years of war and occupation and terror, the engineers of Paris threw the switches that turned on the power once more to make Paris the City of Lights. All around them, the stars in the sky were extinguished by the stars on the ground, and from their high vantage point, they could see the street lights and building lights flood the whole city with a golden glow. The Arc de Triomphe, the Champs Élysées, the Tour Eiffel. The famous landmarks from millions of tourist postcards came to life in the blink of an eye. All around them the Parisians wept, and so did they.

Molly kissed Steve, then took his hand and said, "Come. It's time to find a place to stay."

They headed back toward the Champs Élysées, mercifully downhill most of the way. The streets were still filled with people, grownups and children celebrating their great day. They took a circuitous route, paying no attention to their direction, just continuing downhill.

Along the way they passed a synagogue where they learned a US Army chaplain, a rabbi from the 12th Regiment, was conducting a service to remember and honor the French Jews who were deported to the German concentration camps before the liberation of Paris. Schneider wondered if his uncle, too, had been deported to those same camps. He was sorry to learn that they had missed the service. For, in the short time he was at war, Schneider's Jewish heritage had surfaced almost without his consent. He had no idea where it had come from, but the threat from the Nazis, not only to him but to his German-Jewish family, had become very personal, and he was, without understanding why, ready to die in this cause. It came to him in a flash of insight that only an accident of birth had saved him from whatever hell his relatives were suffering now. An accident of history.

There were many Parisian Jews in the streets around the synagogue, crying with gratitude for their deliverance from the Nazis. Schneider and Molly were passing through the crowd, with Molly clinging tightly to Schneider's arm, when a hand tapped him on the shoulder. Schneider turned to see a small elderly man in an old black, pinstriped, double-breasted suit coat, which did not match his trousers. The jacket was faded from its original color, evident from the darker area over the left chest where a Star of David patch had been. Threads dangled around its the edges, as if the patch had been torn off in haste. And surely it had been.

Schneider looked at the man's face. He did not move an inch as Schneider inspected him. The man looked directly into his eyes and then reached out. In his hand was a piece of felt. It was yellow, and it took Schneider a long moment to realize that it was the very Star of David that the man had been forced to wear over his left breast for the last four years by order of the Nazis.

Schneider took the star from the man, numb with the horror of what it must have meant to have to wear this sign of his Jewishness all those years. He also realized the relief the old man must have felt as he handed it to Schneider, one of his perceived saviors, in a tacit act of thanks.

The man took Steve's and Molly's hands. He leaned forward, standing on his toes to reach up and kiss Steve on the cheek. Then, with tears in his eyes, he said, nodding, "Landsmann!"

The man gave Molly a kiss as well, then turned and walked away.

Molly turned to Steve and asked, "What did he say?"

"Countryman," he answered with tears now forming in his eyes. "He called me his countryman."

Molly started to speak, but Schneider interrupted. "Not Frenchmen. He meant that we are Jews, he and I."

"How could he know?"

Schneider smiled, now beginning to cry openly, and said, "Oh, we know. Somehow we always know."

Schneider stared quietly into the far distance. Molly took his hand and waited for him to return to her. He shook his head slowly as if pushing thoughts from his mind. Finally, Molly said, "Where are you, Steve?"

Schneider shook himself back to the present and then went on. "I'm thinking about my uncle."

"Who?"

"I have an uncle, my mother's brother, in Munich. A surgeon. We haven't heard anything from him since the war started. We don't know what happened to him and his family. They're the only ones of my mother's family who didn't leave Germany when the war started."

Molly waited, saying nothing.

Schneider said, "When this is over, I have to try to find him and my aunt. And their kids. He was like... hmmm.... Well, he wasn't really a father to me, but he was a role model. The time I spent in Germany was like the foundation of everything I thought a surgeon should be. He used to take me on hospital rounds with him. I was still in my teens then. I even fainted on him once," he said with a smile.

"What happened?"

"Oh, he was making rounds and took me in to see an older lady who had her thyroid out the day before. He took down the dressing and removed a Penrose drain from her neck incision. She let out a terrible howl. I got all flushed and hot in the face, and I heard ringing in my ears, but I didn't know what that meant then. The next sound was the banging of something hard on wood: my head hitting the side rails of the next bed as I slid to the floor. All I recall is waking up in the hallway with a bunch of faces staring at me and speaking in German. My uncle said, 'Don't worry about it, Stephen. It happens to everyone sooner or later. You'll get used to it.' I remember being so afraid that I would never be a surgeon. I had a similar reaction to my first autopsy. The heat in my face, the tingling. But by then I knew enough to sit down and put my head between my legs until I felt better. And he was right. I got used to all of it."

Schneider looked away again. "I can't even begin to believe he might be dead. God, if he'd only come to America with the rest of the family! He was so stubborn."

"Perhaps that stubborn streak has kept him alive," Molly said.

Schneider nodded. "I hope so, but...." He shook his head again. "I'll find him. I'll just stay here until I find out something. One way or the other."

Schneider reverently put the yellow Jewish star in his pocket and started to walk again with Molly on his arm. He looked again at the diminishing crowd around the synagogue. There were many of these poor people who had torn off the loathsome yellow stars, the symbols the Nazis had forced the Jews to wear, branding them as the Untermenschen. In these crowded streets, they were now handing them to the young GIs—Jews and Gentiles both—who had joined them in their services and had awakened them from the nightmare of the Nazi regime.

After that, it took Schneider some time to regain his equilibrium. The day had been so long and filled with so many ups and downs: the dangerous drive into Paris from the field hospital; the joys of the liberation; the beatings of the collaborators and the shaven women; the triumphal march of De Gaulle and the shooting at Notre Dame; watching the lighting of Paris from Sacré-Coeur; and now this, the French Jews freed from the death threat of the Germans.

Schneider was exhausted, and so was Molly. They tore themselves away from the synagogue and headed down toward the Opéra and the Place Vendôme. Schneider was determined to make this the most memorable day of the war. They would find a room at the Hotel Meurice or the Ritz or the Crillon or the Georges V—any one of the great Paris landmarks. He was not above using his rank to get them in, and there was no doubt in his mind that one of these grand dames of the hotel world would have a room for them.

When they arrived at the Rue de Rivoli, there in front of them at number 228 was the famous sign:

Hotel Meurice – Thé – Restaurant

Nothing had changed in the many years since he had met there, quite by accident, his Uncle Mike and Aunt Charlotte, walking down the Rue de Rivoli. They invited him into the Meurice, where they were staying, and treated him to dinner and a bath. The Meurice had then become his personal definition of opulence since, at the time, he had been staying in a two-dollar-a-night hotel without private toilet or bath.

So, Molly and Schneider stopped at the Meurice first.

But, it was not the place of his memories. The lobby was a shambles. The elevator cage, he learned, had been destroyed by a hand grenade the day before. The Meurice had been the headquarters for General von Choltitz and his staff, as well as some of the senior officers of the SS. The FFI took the hotel by storm. Bullet holes marked the marble of the lobby. Broken glass and shattered furnishings lay everywhere. A burned portrait of Hitler hung askew in a charred frame. Schneider later learned that the general and his staff were marched through the streets, caught by the FFI while trying to carry their booty in suitcases. They, too, were abused by the populace, and one of von Choltitz's officers was shot dead as a woman burst from the crowd and fired a small pistol into his temple at point blank range before being disarmed by the Resistance.

Although the concierge acted helpful and accommodating, Schneider could not shake the feeling that he and his staff had been too cozy with the Nazis. He pictured the soiled sheets and empty wine bottles, and his mind revolted at the thought of the SS screwing the now shaven-headed women in the rooms above on the very same linen.

He took Molly by the elbow. "Let's just try The Ritz. I think we'll be happier there."

Molly didn't argue. The Hotel Continental, just behind the Meurice, was in ruins, as were several other buildings nearby. They wandered over to the Place de la Concorde where the Hotel Crillon was located. It, too, had taken a pounding, apparently from the guns of the FFI tanks. They kept on walking.

From the Crillon, they walked up to the Place Vendôme where, happily, the Ritz was relatively intact. In fact, it looked quite appealing compared with much of the rest of the neighborhood. The Ritz was set in the relative calm of the Place Vendôme, with its ornate obelisk set in the center of the square. Couples were lounging around the monument, more reflective than the mobs along the Champs Élysées. Schneider glanced up at the mansard roof of the Ritz as they approached the arched stone entryway and walked through wrought iron gates. They went directly to the reception desk. Schneider looked around and saw that the place was jumping, but now with a mixture of Parisians as well as Americans. The bar and the restaurant were packed. Soldiers—French and American—drinking together, toasting the defeat of the Germans in Paris. The babel of several languages competed to be heard. Of course, German was conspicuously absent.

Schneider asked the flustered desk clerk if he had a room for the night, and to his complete amazement, the man said yes. In fact, he said, "Bien sûr, Monsieur Major." Of course.

Schneider had been fully prepared to bribe, cajole, or even fight for a room. Instead he signed the register with a flush of guilt. Checking into this famed hotel with a woman other than his wife felt like a greater betrayal than his physical infidelity. Odd that it should be that way, but there it was.

There were no porters around, but they had no luggage anyway. Schneider took the key on its huge brass pendant and made his way to the staircase. He stopped before starting up and asked Molly, "Do you want to stop at the bar for a while before we go upstairs?"

"No, thanks," she said, tucking her chin toward her chest and grinning. "Let's just go right on up."

Schneider was relieved not to have to spend any more time among the crowds. Even more, he was relieved that they were now unlikely to run into any of their colleagues in the mob at the bar and the restaurant, as they had at the Café Aux Deux Maggots.

Food had not entered Schneider's mind anyway. He was hungry only for Molly now and had reached the limit of his tolerance. And so, it seemed, had she.

Schneider unlocked the door with the big brass key, and pushed the door open. He turned to Molly and kissed her gently on the lips.

Then he guided her into the room with his hand on the small of her back.

The two of them stood in the foyer and took it all in.

The room was larger and more grand than either of them had ever been in. There were floor to ceiling crimson velvet drapes on each of the tall windows, held open by golden tasseled cords. Paris was still dark, but the view of the city was still shockingly clear in the star-lit night. The large double bed had been turned down for the night, with four enormous pillows, plump and soft. Molly crossed her arms in front of her, holding her shoulders, and sighed. She dropped her bag to the floor and wandered the room, running her hands over the soft clean surfaces of the bed and the chairs and the small sofa. She pushed open the bathroom door with its gilded mirror and stood in the threshold.

Steve came up behind her and wrapped his arms around her. He tucked his chin into the hair on her shoulder. The two of them stared at the huge tub and sparkling clean bathroom with its mirrors and towels and even some small soaps.

"We're not in Field Hospital Charlie-7 any more, Dorothy," Schneider said.

Molly laughed. She turned in his arms and hugged him close to her. "I guess not. At least for tonight."

By the time they had settled into their magnificent, top-floor room, it was past eleven. Schneider thought they might be hungry before long, so he called down for some wine and a light dinner while Molly stood at the windows overlooking the city. He came up behind her again and put his arms around her waist. She folded his arms into hers and leaned back against him. With Schneider's face in her hair, they watched the remaining few street lights begin to go out all over Paris, section by section. The engineers had made their point in lighting up their city, and now it was time to go back to the safety of the blackout. Paris was not going to make itself an easy target for the Luftwaffe that night.

The two backed away from the window and drew the heavy ornate curtains to keep the room lights from showing through.

"I'm sorry now I didn't think of bringing my razor and a change of clothing," Schneider said, feeling for the first time the griminess of his body in this elegant setting.

Molly smiled and said, "Well, I didn't forget."

She walked over to the table where she had placed her shoulder bag, and emptied it out on the bed. There were all the goodies they needed to become human again. She had brought toothpaste and a toothbrush, a comb and brush, some shampoo in a khaki bottle, and even a change of underwear. There was a lipstick and a razor, plus a few other things Schneider didn't recognize. When he beamed at her foresight, she said, "Oh, you think I'm sharing these with you?"

"You certainly might be a lot happier if you shared that razor with me."

She hugged him again and said, "Go take the first bath. You need it more than I do, and I intend to take a very long time."

He kissed her and said, "Not too long, please. I don't know if I can stand it."

"It'll be worth it." She kissed him again, this time lingering to run her hands through his hair.

Schneider disappeared into the bathroom, which was bigger than the whole hotel room he had stayed in so many years ago as a student. He dropped his khakis on the floor and sank into the luxurious tub. He washed, changing the water twice, and then with Molly's razor he attacked his two-day-old beard while still in the tub. He dried with the biggest bath towel in history, then cleaned and dried the whole place like new. He brushed his teeth with Molly's toothbrush and dried it off as well. He didn't think he'd fooled her though, as the taste of her Ipana was very distinctive.

He came out into the bedroom again with the towel wrapped around his waist, feeling a little self-conscious. She touched him lightly on his bare shoulder before she disappeared into the bathroom. One light touch on his shoulder, and he found himself standing in the middle of the room with an erection and nowhere to go.

While Steve was bathing, room service had arrived. Molly had opened the wine and poured two glasses, setting them down on the little wheeled table. She had placed the table at the foot of the bed and put two chairs there for them, next to each other rather than across. Schneider was marveling at her organization when he realized that she was, after all, an operating room nurse, and organization was her forte.

He took a sip of wine then waited in the chair. He realized that there was no way he could eat that dinner with everything else on his mind, so he left the towel on the arm of a chair and crawled into bed with the covers pulled just high enough to maintain a semblance of dignity.

And there he sat, in the semidarkness of the room, listening to the sounds of this woman at her bath.

Then he paced, ending up at one of the windows, where he stared into the darkness trying to make out the silhouettes of the city. He sat again, then paced some more. Finally he settled into the arm chair and waited some more. With a sigh he moved to the bed. He slipped partially under the turned-down comforter and sat up against the pillows.

Then the bathroom door opened. Molly hesitated in the doorway and adjusted her eyes to the darkness. She was wrapped in a bath towel, with her hair down over her shoulders. Standing there in her towel with her hair that way made him dizzy.

She came to the side of the bed and removed her towel. Against his will, Schneider gasped. Then she slipped in beside him and put her head on his chest. Her hair was still damp, red and curling against his black chest hair. Even in the darkness he could see the whiteness of her skin punctuated with a light spray of freckles along her shoulders. For the first time he felt her body align with his: her soft warm skin against his thigh, her cheek and lips against his chest. He placed his hand on her back and let it slowly slide down across her buttocks to her thighs. Then he traced her body with his fingers, closing his eyes to intensify the sensations in his finger tips.

Molly nuzzled closer to him, running her hands over his chest and abdomen, lingering over his pubic hair and settling against his thigh.

An old, wind-up Victrola sat on the night table. Schneider leaned over and cranked the handle until the spring was tight. Then he placed the needle in the groove. At once a woman's husky voice began to sing in French of love and loss and passion. It brought tears to his eyes, and though she understood no French, it made Molly weep as well.

"Who is that?" she asked, barely whispering so as not to break the mood.

"It's Edith Piaf," he said. "France's most famous chanteuse."

They listened together for several minutes until the song came to an end, the needle circling endlessly in the last groove of the worn record, as Edith's husky voice whispered, "Toujours, toujours, toujours..." Always.

Schneider pulled the needle from the record and set it gently on its cradle, careful not to damage this national treasure.

They faced each other and fell into each other's arms with all the passion that had been building since the very first day in that mess tent. They lay on their sides holding tightly as their bodies sought out the curves and recesses that seemed to fit so well together. Every time her soft lips touched Schneider's body, he shivered and ached for more. Molly released her grip on his shoulders and planted slow, lingering kisses on a path from his chest down his abdomen. He wanted her to stop there so that this would not end so quickly, as surely it was going to. But, he surrendered to inevitability.

Then with the uncontrolled giddiness that followed, they lay head to toe, laughing at nothing and holding on for dear life.

Finally, Molly released him and crawled up alongside him to bury her head in his chest again. She was so quiet that he thought she was asleep. His arm grew numb beneath her, and when he shifted to move it she kissed him again and pulled him back, placing her head on the pillows and staring at him with a faint smile on her lips. Looking at her there in the nearly total darkness of the blackout, he could, this once, isolate himself from all the rest of the world and give himself over to this moment for the first time since they had met, with no intruding thoughts of life outside that room.

They dozed lightly on and off for perhaps twenty minutes or so, then began again to explore each other's bodies. Schneider traced all the curves and lines he could find until he felt he could draw her from memory. And she did the same to him. They never spoke a word. She stroked him until he was ready to enter her. Somehow this was more serious for both of them, more formal than the impassioned play that began their lovemaking. As he moved on top of her, Molly held him gently, as if he might break.

All at once, they entered a world that would change them forever, and though they both knew it at that very moment, neither of them could know exactly how. Together they crossed a line from beyond which they could not and would not return. A moment such as this, Schneider knew, rarely came a second time and never quite the same.

But none of it could stop him from drowning in his love for her at that moment.

They fell asleep together afterward, and Schneider woke first to the sounds of explosions outside their window. Molly woke just seconds after him. They both ran to the window to see what was happening. They pulled the curtains back, and in the darkness of the blackout, they could see the flashes of an aerial bombardment a couple of miles away, near the northeast edges of the city. Apparently, Hitler was having a temper tantrum over losing Paris and had ordered the Luftwaffe to destroy the city, an order that General von Choltitz had earlier refused to follow.

Once they were sure there was no threat to either of them, Schneider hugged Molly and then went back to bed once again. The clock showed two in the morning. Neither of them brought it up, but they were not about to dress and go down to some bomb shelter, if there even were such a thing. The night belonged to them, and Schneider, for once, was not afraid.

They were starving for something good to eat. Naked and happy, they uncovered the dinner trays and settled into a delicious meal of cold chicken in aspic, some fresh salad with a sweet vinaigrette dressing, new potatoes sautéed in olive oil and garlic, and a completely unidentifiable desert that made their teeth tingle. There was wine and real chocolate for a nightcap. They took the wine back to bed and fed each other the last of the chocolate while they began again to taste each other's bodies. They explored and played and found new ways to enjoy the chocolate.

They spent the rest of the night sleeping and waking and making love until they could no longer. Then they stayed awake in each other's arms, talking little and catching short naps without releasing each other from their protective embrace.

When morning came, the early light broke though a crack in the curtain, and the two lovers sighed with the knowledge that they were about to return to the reality of their war. They bathed again, this time together, and packed Molly's bag for the walk back to the ambulance. Neither of them brought up the one subject that had to be addressed. It was too soon for that. But it was coming.

' They finished dressing with intense sorrow at the end to their time away from the war. Then they went downstairs to the restaurant and had the best breakfast they had tasted in many months. There was real coffee and real eggs No ham or bacon, but the croissants were delicious with jam, even without butter. Then, quite unexpectedly, came the piece de resistance: Schneider couldn't believe his eyes. Sugar. And Cream! Real whole cream right out of a real damned cow. He stirred in way too much sugar in both cups. Then he watched as Molly took over and poured the yellow thick stuff, floating it onto his coffee and, again, he actually drooled. She wiped his mouth before he took a long, slow sip. Back in heaven, even if only for a single cup's worth. Molly tried hers, and made a face. Then laughed.

Schneider went out to pay the bill, while Molly lingered over a last cup of coffee and another croissant.

When the tally was made, Schneider handed over all his French francs as well as every U.S. dollar he had on him. It amounted to what he was supposed to spend for the next two months. Still, it was not nearly enough to cover the bill. He didn't know how much Molly had with her, as her salary was less than his. But, he didn't want to ask her for any money, so he just looked pathetic and turned his pockets inside out.

He said to the clerk, "C'est tout. Je n'ai rien de plus." That's it. I have no more.

The manager scowled at first, and Schneider thought he would be having a meeting with the Paris gendarmes or the US Military Police. But, in a moment, the man smiled and nodded his head. He told Schneider in French that his lady was so beautiful that even he would have spent everything he had for one night at the Ritz.

"Comme Cyrano, oui?" the man asked.

"Yes, just like Cyrano. When he gives a month's pay away for the woman he loves. It's all in the gesture," Schneider said.

The man thanked Schneider for his help in liberating Paris. He made it sound as if Schneider had done it single-handedly. Schneider reached over the counter and through the guichet to shake the man's hand.

"Au revoir, Monsieur le Major," the man said. "Á bientôt!"

Schneider said good-bye and that he hoped he would see the manager soon again someday, too.

Molly met him at the door and took his arm. She said, "Are you completely broke now?"

"More than you'll ever know."

She laughed, and Schneider laughed, and the doorman laughed at them laughing. They stepped out into the quiet Sunday morning and started walking back across the Seine to where it all had started. They had been in Paris less than twenty-four hours.

Chapter Twenty

1 December 1944, 1700 hours
Field Hospital Charlie-7, Belgium

Pushing the Germans back toward Berlin was like trying to stuff too many items into a duffel bag. Each step forward created a pressure wanting to burst back out. In the three months since their short Paris vacation, the field hospital had followed the Allies' relentless drive toward Germany. Now it was winter. The world was changing fast.

As the German lines compressed backward toward the fatherland, the battles grew increasingly fiercer, and casualties piled up on both sides. The German army was on the run, but it had cost the Allies dearly. Patton's Third Army was still moving faster than their supply lines could keep up. Almost everywhere the front was changing so fast that the medics often did not know which side of the lines they were on.

Since Paris, the field hospital staff recognized Schneider and Molly as a couple, though no one would speak of it publicly. Hamm kept his opinions to himself, and in reality their romance was very low on the list of his concerns. He had been awake for nearly three days without more than a catnap between cases, usually while sitting in front of a cup of coffee in the mess tent. The steady stream of wounded bespoke the intensity of the fighting as they neared the Siegfried Line. Hitler's war machine, the Wehrmacht, knew that once the Allies crossed into Germany in force, there would be no stopping them.

For the men and women at the field hospitals near the front, there was never enough of anything: never enough hands to do the surgery, never enough supplies, never enough time. They were all tired beyond belief, and the only thing that kept them going was looking into the eyes of still one more boy who might die if anyone took time off. How could they sleep knowing that one of these young GIs would surely pay with his life for that nap?

Hamm worried that fatigue was making him sloppy, not to mention cranky. He was just closing the last of six big cases that afternoon, when Diane, his scrub nurse, handed him much too small a needle holder with an equally small suture in it.

Hamm slammed the needle holder down on the drapes, where it bounced onto the tent floor.

"We always close these cases with stay sutures, Diane. Always! This isn't plastic surgery, damn it! We want these guys to stay closed, not dehisce and eviscerate on the way back home."

Diane already held the heavy stay suture in a large needle holder out for him. Her face was flushed and her hand shook slightly. Hamm took the needle holder, looked up at her, then stopped. He realized that the whole operating staff was looking at him. The only sound was the gas moving through respirators.

"I'm sorry. I'd never do that in real life. I'm behaving like a three-year-old. It won't happen again."

The outburst was so unlike him, that the staff didn't know what to make of it. But his nerves were shot just like theirs. He was the pillar that held the whole team together in the worst of conditions. If he folded, the whole structure of the team might collapse.

Having the front lines so close didn't help. They were never out of earshot of the shelling. And the shelling, incoming and outgoing, never stopped, day or night. Antonelli and Marsh, not to mention the dozens of other young medics whose names Hamm never learned, were coming and going constantly. They were out there under fire all the time. It irked and embarrassed Hamm that he never heard them complain about anything but the food. Never about the danger, the fear.

The food, for Christ's sake!

Bullets were whistling by the medics' ears all the time, mortar rounds crashing in on them, and yet the medics never missed a beat. Marsh and Antonelli even made time to drop into the operating tent and post-op to see how the victims they had rescued were doing.

Hamm half expected a chewing-out from one of these kids if one of their rescues died after they got them to the pre-op tent alive. Actually, if they did make it to the OR, the surgeons usually saved them. Most of the GIs died right where they were hit or on the rough trek back to the field hospital. It got to be very personal: if the wounded arrived alive, Hamm felt he should be able to keep them alive. There was enough plasma to go around, even if they were often short of whole blood. And they had plenty of penicillin. Still, it was a point of honor. If Marsh and Antonelli and the others could bring them back to the hospital alive, Hamm's team would move the earth to keep them alive.

To complicate matters, the front was constantly changing. It scared Hamm to death. He never knew when he might find himself on the wrong side of the battle lines. A couple of the nurses were captured by a German patrol, then freed by the U.S infantry again an hour later. It was that unstable.

Winter had come with a furious series of storms. There was heavy wet snow with mud, and wet cold without letup. Tents sagged danger-ously and had to be cleared of snow to prevent collapse.

The chill went through their bones. Tents were heated with pot-bellied stoves, which helped only a bit. But the close quarters quickly became muggy and foul with body odors. Setting foot outside for some fresh air in the cold was almost not worth the danger.

One afternoon, Marsh and Antonelli were sitting in their tents taking a sorely needed break. The two of them had cots very close together.

Suddenly Marsh sat up and said, "Jesus, Gene. Your farts are killin' me."

'Oh, right. Yours are like lilacs, huh?"

"Screw you, man. And take a shower for Christ sake!"

Marsh slipped into his combat boots and bolted from the tent. The air outside was fresh, and for a minute Marsh just stood there with his eyes closed just taking in deep breaths. He was cold, but the thought of going back into the tent with Antonelli repulsed him. So he just stood there. Until the first new volley of gunfire.

The first one came from thin air. Then, he heard the bullets impacting all around him before he even heard the plane's engine. He rushed to the cover of a nearby jeep, crawling in the snow and mud to get under the engine block. The strafing run lasted only a few minutes, but Marsh didn't move for a long while after it was over. The engine block was still warm, and he couldn't face going back into that tent. So he just lay there.

Finally he pulled himself out from under the jeep, and wiped off as much mud as he could. When he straightened up, he saw Antonelli standing in the entry to their tent laughing at him.

"I guess my farts are worth dying for, huh Andy?"

Marsh shook his head and walked away. He went into the mess tent and sat by the stove. There was nothing to eat just then, so the place was empty. Marsh looked around and saw a series of bullet holes lined up along the roof opposite where he sat. He could follow the path of the shots right into the wooden table and canvas floor. Just chance that no one had been in there when the planes came.

He thought about the nurse they lost, and was sad that he never knew her name. She'd only been there less than a week, when the bullets flew through the area. Marsh was helping Hamm close a chest exploration. She was standing six feet from the operating table, cleaning instruments, when the planes flew overhead. She died on the spot with eight bullets in her chest and neck from a strafing run.

Thankfully, winter meant the cloud cover was often so thick and low that they couldn't see the planes flying overhead, which meant the Germans couldn't see them either.

Nonetheless, deep down inside, the medical team was always waiting for it. Waiting for that terrible day when it would finally happen, as they knew it surely would. Hamm was unprepared both mentally and physically. His hands weren't shaking yet, but it couldn't be long.

On the day it happened, Hamm had nearly finished exploring a bad chest wound. The kid had multiple shrapnel tears in his right lung, and a piece of metal had caught an edge of the pulmonary vein. God only knows why he hadn't died in the field. This was a terrible injury, one they almost never saw in surgery because those patients didn't make it back to the OR alive. This GI got lucky. By going into deep shock out there in the mud, his low blood pressure had allowed the torn vessel to clot for a while as Marsh and some huge infantry PFC dragged the guy's body back to the hospital. Dragged him, literally. They were out of stretchers, and it was too far to carry him by his shoulders and ankles. So they each took a leg and just dragged him through the snow and the mud all the way back to the field hospital. Marsh figured it was better to drag him this way with his feet in the air, just like elevating the legs of shock patients to restore some of the blood volume back to the heart. The man never should have made it back alive, but he did. They had to scrape the dirt off him with an entrenching tool before they could put him on the operating table.

Exhausted, Marsh slid down to the floor of the tent to catch his breath, and wait to see how this guy would do.

Schneider was operating at the table next to Hamm, working on a multiple gunshot wound to the abdomen. The guy had at least thirty holes in his intestines made by about seven entry wounds. There was fecal and small bowel contamination everywhere, as well as gastric acid from holes in his stomach. Schneider held up a fistful of food from the C-rats the guy ate before he was shot.

"His mother should have told him to chew his food more carefully," he said.

"We'll take your word for it, Steve," Hamm said. "We really don't need to see that right now." Hamm was perennially grumpy these days. The tragedies of these wounded and dying young men had overwhelmed his defenses and submerged him in a near depression.

Schneider went back to work, cleaning out the detritus from the man's abdomen and irrigating the peritoneal cavity with gallons of sterile saline.

"The solution to pollution is dilution," Schneider sang tunelessly under his breath. The trauma surgeon's mantra.

McClintock shook his head.

McClintock was still with the group, though several other gas-passers had come and gone. Hamm was getting anesthesia for his patient from a nurse. Technically, an MD was supposed to be giving the gas, but they were so shorthanded that McClintock would only get the case started. He would put them under and intubate the airway. Then the nurses kept them asleep until it was over. At that point, McClintock would wake them up and extubate them. It wasn't elegant, but it worked. In surgery, as in flying, takeoff and landing were the most dangerous parts: putting them to sleep and waking them up. The flight in between was usually the easy part. McClintock got the plane in the air and landed it again.

Hamm, in his exhaustion, had been so focused on getting the patient's chest ready to close that he hadn't noticed the intruder. He asked for chest tubes, holding out his right hand as he made space in the drapes for the counter-incision with his left.

His hand remained empty.

He looked up to see what was taking Marie, the scrub nurse, so long with the tubes. Only then did he realize that all the activity, all the chaos in the room, had stopped.

The only sounds were the hissing and clicking of the anesthesia machines, passing the gas into and out of the lungs of the patients and, of course, the not-so-distant reports of gunfire.

All heads were turned toward the tent door. There in the doorway stood a man in the uniform of the Waffen-SS.

Hamm glared at the SS Death's Head insignia on the officer's uniform and flew into a rage.

"Who do you think you are?" he screamed at him. "Get the hell out of my OR! Now!"

All eyes turned to Hamm. He detected astonishment, a crinkling of the eyes above their surgical masks.

The officer stepped into the room and clicked his heels.

What a Nazi thing to do! Hamm thought. He actually clicked his goddamned heels!

"I am Obersturmbannführer Fuchs, Waffen-SS."

A lieutenant Colonel, if Hamm recalled their ridiculous military hierarchy correctly.

"Well, what are you doing in my operating room Obersturmbannführer Fuchs?" he said, with sarcasm. Even as he said it, he regretted it.

The mind is fast, and thoughts are usually quicker than words. But Hamm's words moved too fast to keep him out of trouble right then.

"I'm afraid this is no longer your operating room Herr...?"

"Major Hammer," he said. His voice cracked.

"Well, *Major* Hammer." He pronounced it My-yore Hemmeh. "This is now *my* operating room, and you are all now my prisoners."

As he spoke, Fuchs moved further into the room. Behind him, Hamm could now see a gang of Waffen-SS, standing in a file, machine pistols at the ready. They were in the pre-op tent, and through the open flaps Hamm could see the rest of his staff standing against the wall with their hands clasped behind their heads. One of the enlisted men was lying on the floor, a small puddle of blood running from his right ear.

Hamm's medical brain automatically made the diagnosis; blunt head trauma; bleeding from the ear equals basilar skull fracture. And no neurosurgeon nearby.

Damn!

Then Hamm was startled by a scuffle at the head of his table. He turned just in time to see McClintock—with blazing eyes—deliver a crushing uppercut to the jaw of a German guard who was apparently fondling one of the nurses. The Guard crumpled to the ground, and so did McClintock as another German decked him with a rifle butt to the back of his head. McClintock lay there bleeding from a laceration in his scalp while one of the new WAC nurses immediately took over his place to deliver oxygen to the wounded GI on the operating table.

Marie bent to minister to McClintock, but the guard who decked McClintock motioned her away with his rifle and left McClintock there still unconscious and bleeding.

The Obersturmbannführer followed Hamm's gaze momentarily down to the wounded GI by the door.

Then turning back to Hamm he said, "He resisted capture. It is better if no one resists. This entire field hospital is now under my command."

Fuchs's tone changed in the next second. He had been calm and almost friendly. Now there was command and a not-so-veiled threat in his voice.

"You will stop what you are doing this minute. Everyone! We have casualties among my officers who need immediate attention."

Hamm was boiling with anger now, the adrenaline involuntarily surging through his arteries. He recognized all the signs: increasing heart rate, elevated blood pressure, heart pounding in his chest, face flushed. Had he been able to see his pupils, he knew, they would have been so dilated as to make his irises nearly pure black. And he was ready to fight.

Schneider stared at Hamm. He looked down at his own hands, still holding a forceps, and watched his uncontrollable shaking. He squeezed the instrument so that it would not fall from his fingers. He found himself, to his shame, clenching his sphincters, afraid that he would soil himself in his panic. Which was worse, the threat from the German or losing his urine and feces there in the OR? He couldn't answer that question. He could not think at all. He was literally frozen with fear and horrified at his own relief that it was Hamm, not he, who was facing down the German officer.

But no one in the room even noticed Schneider. Everyone's eyes locked on Hamm.

So, Hamm did the only thing he knew how to do; the only thing that could make his own hands from shaking.

He returned to his work. He put out his hand and said, "Chest tube."

Marie immediately slapped a tube into Hamm's left hand and a knife into his right. Hamm tried to focus on the field. He was making a small counter-incision in the chest, when the German officer shouted so loudly that Hamm jumped.

"Shtopp!" he said. "Stop what you are doing and clear these operating tables for my officers! Now!"

He had moved to within a foot of Hamm's table.

Hamm put down the scalpel and the chest tubes slowly and deliberately. He leaned over the table, his face only inches from Fuchs's smug face. Suddenly, he was calm, his course clear. Inside, the adrenaline still surged, his heart still raced, his blood pressure remained frighteningly high. But now he was functioning with clearheaded resolve.

"No, Colonel. You listen. We are going to finish these cases. Nobody is going to let these boys die here on the operating table. Then we are going to surrender to you. I will remind you that, as prisoners of war, we cannot be made to do any forced labor. Your Fuehrer and his officers have signed the Geneva Convention, and if we are now your prisoners, so be it. Find some fucking German surgeons to operate on your wounded!"

The veins stood out on Fuchs's neck, a scarlet hue rising in his Aryan cheeks; the same surge of adrenaline that moments ago threatened to put Hamm over the edge of his own rage.

Fuchs's icy blue eyes pierced into Hamm. Hamm looked away, his eyes lowering to the Death's Head insignia on Fuchs's lapels.

Without taking his eyes from Hamm, Fuchs unclipped the leather flap on his holster and withdrew his nine-millimeter Luger automatic pistol. He chambered a round, released the safety, and cocked the hammer. He shoved the shiny barrel into the place between Hamm's eyebrows. He pressed hard enough that it hurt. Only a few millimeters of trigger play separated Hamm from death. And Hamm knew it.

"No, Major Hammer. I am in command here, and you will follow my orders exactly as I give them. Do not presume to quote the Geneva Convention to me. You, whose army is firebombing civilian targets in Germany day and night. If you do not follow my orders, exactly as I give them, you will die where you stand. Is that perfectly clear?"

It was funny to Hamm, the things he thought about at a moment like this, with maybe seconds to live. First, he wondered where Fuchs had learned such excellent English. It was too good to be schoolboy English. Then, instead of wetting himself, or worse, as he always thought he might in such a situation, he became very calm. He didn't know where it came from. He had drawn his line, and so there was perhaps the absolute certainty that he was going die right there, along with the conviction that there was nothing he could do about it. So, out of nowhere, and knowing he had nothing to lose, he began to do the only thing that made sense.

He negotiated.

"All right, Colonel. You have the guns, for now. Here's what we'll do. We finish these cases. No room for argument on that. I'm willing to die for that one, and then you'll be short one great surgeon, and you can't afford that. Then, I and my team will go on operating just as before. We have been operating on American soldiers and German prisoners anyway, according to the severity of their wounds. Everyone gets equal care here, though God knows your soldiers have been a royal pain in the ass from the start, and it was tempting to just let them die. What a bunch of cry babies!"

Fuchs stiffened, pressing the gun muzzle harder into Hamm's forehead. Hamm refused to back off in spite of the pain and the sure knowledge that his world might go black any second.

"We all took oaths when we became doctors, and we don't break them even here. You stay the hell out of my operating room, and things will go on here as usual. And if I were you, I would keep that Geneva

Convention in mind. You never know when you might be looking down the barrel of a Colt .45 yourself."

Fuchs lowered his weapon slowly, leaving what Hamm felt was a very deep circular impression in the skin of his forehead. He carefully released the hammer, and reset the safety. Then, he holstered the gun, and re-buttoned the leather flap.

Hamm looked down at McClintock. He noted that his friend was stirring, and that the bleeding from the scalp laceration had slowed, forming a jelly-like crimson clot. And thankfully there was no blood coming from either ear.

"Very well, Major. I do need your facilities and your skill. We will run this field hospital together, you and I. But never forget that I am in command here. It would be a bad mistake to forget that. Oh, and tell your friend there," he said motioning to McClintock with a turn of his head, "that he is a very lucky man. And stupid. Be careful. One day this man's—how do you say—temper might get you killed."

Fuchs turned and barked some orders to the guard with the machine pistol. The guard clicked his heels and said, "Jawohl, Obersturmbannführer!"

Fuchs turned and walked quickly out. The room was silent for a moment.

"OK, everyone," Hamm said, "go back to work."

And they did. McClintock was awake now, but confused. Two medics helped him from the OR and took him into the post-op area. Without orders from anyone they placed him on a stretcher and began to clean the scalp wound and sew it up.

Hamm put in the chest tubes and closed the chest. At about the same time, Schneider finished closing the abdomen on his patient and tore his gloves from his hands. He slammed them into the garbage bag and stomped from the room, still shaky from the experience, but a fire rising in his chest. He was furious with McClintock and with Fuchs, yet more furious with himself. He had been totally paralyzed. That damned fear again. Always there, always slapping him in the face.

Hamm followed quickly behind Schneider, brushing past the guard. He gave into a childish whim and made sure to brush hard enough to make the guard stagger backwards to catch his balance.

Stupid thing to do. Jesus! Hamm thought. But these God damned SS troops are the worst. And, he thought, the most dangerous of them all.

He caught up to Schneider in the post-op tent. He nodded to the medics as they wiped up the excess blood that had dripped from McClintock's neck, and applied a bulky head dressing.

Hamm knelt next to McClintock.

"You all right?"

McClintock nodded, then winced at the pain in his head.

"Yeah, I'll live. What happened?"

Hamm's face darkened.

"What happened is that your God-damned temper almost got us all killed, that's what happened! You do something like that again, I'll deck you myself!"

McClintock lay his head back on the stretcher and closed his eyes.

Schneider was furiously writing orders on the patient's chart. Fluids, pain meds, penicillin, vital signs. The usual. Hamm grabbed his own patient's chart and began to write. It was so routine that he could write the orders and talk to Schneider at the same time.

"Well, what do you think?" Hamm asked.

"What do I think? Jesus, Hamm, we're fucking prisoners of war! Kriegsgefangen!"

Hamm glanced up at the SS guards posted at both the tent doors.

"Don't let them know you speak German, Steve. It could be useful to let them talk among themselves thinking we don't understand them," Hamm whispered.

Schneider chewed on that one. It was calming to have something useful they could use in the way of resistance, meager as it might be.

"Yeah, you're probably right. But we're in a load of shit here, Hamm. You really going to treat this as business as usual?"

"I don't think we have a choice. I could see it in his eyes. That son-of-a-bitch was ready to kill me to make his point. He doesn't give a damn about the Geneva Convention. He's not worried about a war crimes tribunal. He's going to go down fighting, Steve. He's Waffen-SS, man. The Aryan gods. He's going to die anyway and go to Valhalla or wherever the hell the dead Krauts go. And if we show him we're prepared to die, he'll just change the rules."

"What do you mean?"

"If he sees that you or I are ready to die for a principle, he'll just point that Luger at someone else. You ready to let him shoot Molly or one of the nurses?"

Schneider squirmed and then dropped his chart to his knees.

"No," he said softly. "I'm not going to let someone else die for me. You're right. He's holding all the cards right now." Schneider moved closer to Hamm and lowered his voice. "How did you do that?" he asked.

"Do what?"

"Stand up to that prick while he was pressing a loaded Luger to your forehead. Jesus, Hamm, he chambered and cocked the damned thing!"

"What did you want me to do?"

"I don't know. But I was shitting my pants! Damn near literally. Hamm, I've been shitting since we took off from England. I'm scared all the time. It never goes away. And, I'm as scared about anyone knowing I'm afraid as I am about what might happen to me."

"You're not afraid of my knowing it."

"No. That's different. We've been through too much together. And I think you already knew about me. About my....well...let's say it out loud...my cowardice."

"'Come on, Steve. This is war. Everyone is terrified twenty-four hours a day."

"Don't beat around the bush, Hamm. I'm a coward. I always have been. Since I was a kid, I've been afraid. Every time there's a fight or danger or anything, my guts turn to jelly, my heart races, and my face gets red. I can feel my blood pressure climbing"

"That's adrenaline, Steve. It's chemical, and there's nothing you can do about it."

"But, I just want to turn and run."

"And do you?"

"Do I what?"

"Turn and run. Have you ever turned and ran?"

Schneider thought for a moment.

"Well, not really. Except that time with Susan. You know, with the dog. I didn't run, but what I did was—"

"Jesus Steve. You're still going on about *that*? You were a kid. It was reflex. Anyone might have done that. Stop beating yourself up over something that happened when you were sixteen."

"Almost eighteen."

"So you were seventeen. We all feel that way. It's normal."

"It's not normal, Hamm. It's cowardly."

"Steve, everyone gets those feelings in moments of danger. We're programmed that way. You're a scientist, for God's sake. You should know that. It's built in by evolution. It's the three Fs: Fright-Fight-Flight. We all get it at some time."

Schneider just sat there looking at the floor, shaking his head.

"Listen," Hamm went on, "I was once sitting in the dentist's office. He was going to fill a cavity. So he injects me with some Novocain, and I guess he got a little bit of adrenaline in the injection by mistake. Must have hit a small vein in my gums. So even this little bit of adrenaline in the Novocain—maybe one in a hundred thousand dilution—and I nearly went through the roof. My heart was racing and pounding in my chest, my eyes were so dilated I couldn't focus, and I was sweating and hyperventilating."

"So what? That's normal. That's just the adrenaline talking."

"But I was terrified! I could barely sit in the chair. I had to hold on to the arms just to stay put. And I knew—I really knew—it was all chemical. I knew just what had happened. There was no danger. But I could hardly stand it. I even said to the dentist, 'This is a chemical reaction, and I know it's just the chemical, but I CAN'T STAND IT, AND I THINK I'M GOING TO RUN AWAY!'"

Schneider laughed.

Hamm continued.

"So it doesn't matter what the situation really is. Once you're in the grips of a chemical like adrenaline, it's all fright-fight-flight. Everyone feels that way in the same situation."

"Well," Schneider mused aloud. "First of all, you're a good friend for trying to make me feel better. And second of all, you're full of shit. Most guys don't crap their pants when there's danger. Look at these kids: Marsh and Antonelli. And Higgenson when he was alive. They keep on going back out there with no weapons to tend the wounded under fire. Every day, they put themselves on the line."

Hamm paused.

"And you don't think they're scared?"

Schneider didn't reply.

"For God sake, Steve, you didn't run away or freeze when Higgenson needed you! You flew to his aid. Things were on fire. Bullets were flying around. And you never hesitated!"

"That was Higgenson, Hamm...."

"Listen, Steve. I can't talk you out of this. We're all scared. Me included. Let me tell you one thing. Everyone is terrified when their life is on the line. Everyone. The only difference between the brave and the cowardly is that the brave continue to function. The coward folds up and is incapacitated. You're not a coward, Steve. Some day you'll see that."

Hamm took his clipboard and went back to the OR. He passed the German guards in the passageway and shook his head.

Sometime later, Schneider and Hamm were back in post-op. They were seated on low stools near the doorway.

Schneider said, "Really, Hamm, what are we going to do about this?"

"Nothing we can do," Hamm said

"Well, what about an escape? Isn't it the duty of officers and men to try to escape when they're captured?"

"You've been watching too many war movies," Hamm said. "Don't let my lecture on bravery get you into trouble. You don't need a posthumous Silver Star to prove you're brave. Besides, we need to stay here with the post-ops. They can't escape, so neither can we. As long as there are recovering patients, our first duty is to them. That Kraut has us by the balls. We're not going anywhere unless we all go. Even if a few of us did manage to get away, these Nazi bastards would just execute some of the ones left behind in retaliation. They do it every time the French Resistance kills a Kraut; they retaliate by killing forty or fifty civilians in return. Nope. We're stuck here until we get rescued or sent to a German POW camp. And don't forget, if this guy finds out we're both Jewish, it could get a lot worse in a hurry."

Schneider shivered.

"I wouldn't take a leak anywhere too public, if I were you," Hamm added as he got up to leave.

"No shit," Schneider said. "I never thought I would envy McClintock's foreskin."

There was nothing more to say, so they made their way to pre-op where they could get ready for the next cases.

Of all the people to capture us, it had to be the SS! Hamm thought. Hitler's personal killers. Jesus Christ!

The field hospital became a well-equipped prison camp. With all the U.S. infantry disarmed and locked away, and German soldiers standing guard round the clock, the surgical group had little hope for rescue any time soon. Fuchs stayed out of the way most of the time. He would make surprise visits to the OR or pre-op or anywhere he felt inclined, but in general, he didn't intrude. The staff members went about their duties with a chip on each shoulder. They were all tense and frightened. Hamm was most worried about the WAC nurses at the hospital. The Germans had been eyeing them, and it didn't take a genius to know what they wanted. The nurses could barely function. They were all terrified. The doctors and medics made sure none of the women were ever left alone by keeping the nurses in the company of at least one man or several women at all times.

They were at the mercy of the Krauts for their survival now. When the tension finally became dangerous, Hamm called Schneider, McClintock, and Molly together into the pre-op tent during a break in the surgery schedule. A few of the nurses had been mildly man-handled, saved only by their rather savage reaction. Gail, an OR circulating nurse, had her breasts fondled as she walked past a guard. She was carrying a full bedpan when he made the mistake of picking on her. She whirled like a ballerina and smashed the bedpan across his forehead, knocking him to the ground and leaving him with a gash about three inches long, not to mention a veil of toilet paper soaked in urine and feces. Everyone who saw it was delighted. Before the guard could do anything serious, Marsh, McClintock and Hamm were on him. They helped him—dragged him—to the OR to have his wounds cleaned and stitched. With each of them holding his arms and shoulders, he was helpless, though it appeared as if they had come to the guard's aid. None of the Germans shot them, anyway. Although Hamm hated to admit it even then, he did a damned poor job of cleaning out that wound. Sewing it together was a real no-no for a wound contaminated with feces and urine. Within twenty-four hours, the guard had rip-roaring cellulitis of the face and head. Three days later, he was hospitalized for his severe infection. It could have been fatal in that particular area. This could very easily become a fatal infection so close to the venous sinuses in the center of the brain. Hamm took out the stitches, leaving an inch-wide gash in the middle of the man's forehead. It would not be pretty when it healed, if it healed.

As luck had it, the man survived, and Gail's life saved.

Hamm pretended to give him penicillin; at least, there was an order for it in the chart. They made a nurse's note that it had been given. But they weren't going to waste precious supplies like that on the guard. To them, he was just one more sick Kraut and one less guard to worry about. Word got around, and there was a temporary lull in the molesting and harassing of the nurses.

But it was short lived.

When the Germans started in again, Hamm decided that he had to make a stand before it got serious. Before someone got killed.

He took Molly aside to ask how bad things were.

"Bad! Damn bad. It's hard to get anything done. There haven't been any rapes yet, but the German officers are looking very hungry, and it's only a matter of time. Someone's going to get hurt, Hamm."

"Look," Schneider said, "we have to preempt this. I think we need to go directly to Fuchs. He seems to want to avoid trouble. He's an arrogant son-of-a-bitch, but aren't they all, these SS?"

"So?" Hamm asked. "What do we do?"

"We go as a group. All of us, McClintock too." Schneider said. "All the teams represented. Tell him the problem and give him an ultimatum. His guys lay off the nurses, or there will be trouble."

"No. No good," Hamm said. "We lay down ultimatums, and he'll balk. He's too arrogant to take anything like that from us. He's in charge. He probably knows you're Jewish just from your name," Hamm said, nodding to Schneider. "Mine...? He's not so sure. But it won't matter. He'd just as soon kill you and the rest of the Jews in the group, and any one else who pisses him off. He just wants to get back to the front. I don't know where or what he screwed up, but this is punishment duty for him. Being here where it's relatively safe is murder on his ego. And his career. I'm telling you, arrogance is his middle name."

"Well, what do you suggest?" Schneider said.

"I say we go to him and tell him we're worried about the instability of the situation. That we are afraid that there will be a riot if the women are manhandled, and that we are afraid that the patients, his and ours, will be hurt in reprisals. Make us the ones who are afraid. Make us the supplicants. If we do it any other way, he'll react badly."

"I agree," Molly said. "It stinks, but it's the only way to control his men. If he gives the order, it will be obeyed. Otherwise, the groping will continue. Gail was very lucky to have gotten away with what she did. As it is, I'm walking a fine line with my women. They're ready to strike back, and one of them could get hurt or killed. I'll tell you this, these are a tough bunch of women—some of them have tempers like Ted's here."

McClintock opened his mouth, but then closed it without speaking.

"And none of them is going to get raped without a fight. I've heard that a couple of them are carrying scalpels in their pockets. I've given them orders to return them to the OR, but I don't know. So when there is more violence, we'll ultimately lose."

They were silent for a while, everyone thinking it over.

Finally, Hamm stood up and said, "OK. Let's go see Herr Head Kraut."

They left the tent together and walked up to Fuchs's headquarters at the very edge of the grounds. The Obersturmbannführer was royally installed, with all the trimmings. Generators for heat and light. A shower all to himself. Very nice digs so close to the front. The guard announced them, though only Schneider understood what was said.

When the four of them appeared at Fuchs' desk, they were very formal. Schneider and Molly stood at Hamm's right McClintock on the left. All stood at attention until Fuchs gave him permission to speak. Just the way the SS liked it. Hamm was seething at having to play this Hun's game. There would be a time for revenge, he thought, but this was not it.

"We have a problem, Obersturmbannführer."

"Yes, Major Hammer? What is it?"

"As I am sure you know, there was an incident in which one of your men assaulted an OR nurse."

"Assault is a rather strong term, Major."

"An assault it was, Obersturmbannführer. Only the nurse's quick reaction kept it from becoming more serious."

"From what I have heard, it has already become serious, for the guard."

"That's true, but he brought it upon himself."

Fuchs waved his hand impatiently. "Get to the point, Major."

"We just want to make sure that something like this does not happen again or perhaps something more serious next time. Right now the hospital is running as efficiently as it can under such strained circumstances. But we are on the verge of chaos, and it will take very little to tip the balance. The nurses are vital to the well being of all the patients: yours and mine. It would be a disaster to lose their good will. Mistakes might be made under the strain."

Fuchs bristled at the veiled threat, but Hamm went on before the Nazi could say anything.

"Perhaps you could intervene. Maybe clarify the necessity for non-fraternization with the enemy?"

Ah, a stroke of genius! Schneider thought. Hitler would have agreed with Hamm. Pure genius.

Fuchs thought it over for a few seconds and then waved them away as if they were annoying children.

"Very well."

And with that they were dismissed.

"Where did you pull that one from?" Schneider whispered to Hamm as they left.

"Right out of my ass."

Apparently the word did get out because the molestations and the abuse stopped. But, it was not to be the end of the danger.

Late one evening, after a long two days in the OR, the team was making post-op rounds in the tents. There were a lot of recovering patients now, both German and American, as well as a handful of

French civilians, admitted at Hamm's insistence, over the mild protests of the Germans. The beds were segregated: Germans on one side and the Americans on the other, with the French alongside the Americans.

The doctors and nurses made their way along, seeing one patient after another as usual, writing orders, changing dressings, checking on fluid intake and output, and going over the little lab work that was available. Supplies were dangerously low. The Germans had contributed none, and the Americans were on their fourth day of captivity with no resupply. They had been used to getting new supplies almost every other day at that point and were reaching the end of supplies badly needed for further surgery. Sutures and bandages were scarce. Plasma was almost gone, and there was no whole blood at all. They kept a secret stash of plasma, penicillin and morphine for their own boys. The staff gave the Germans sugar water for their antibiotic and pain meds, and the phony morphine actually worked some of the time.

And there was also not enough help to go around. Much of the medical and ancillary staff had been out shuttling patients to the rear when the Germans captured the hospital. The staff were damned shorthanded now but made the best of it. Nerves were strained all around. No one was happy.

Hamm was very proud of their GI patients. They kept still and cooperated. They rarely complained. Most of their inquiries were about the condition of their comrades. The Jerries, on the other hand, were mostly a bunch of crybabies. After two days in that ward, Hamm and Schneider were thoroughly convinced the Allies would win this war.

Hamm sat on a cot next to a German kid, giving him a new clean dressing. He found it hard to sustain his disgust of the Germans when he treated the very young soldiers such as this one. Though hardly into his teens, this young man never complained, and even pitched in to help care for both the Americans and the German patients.

"You should be on our side," Hamm told him.

"Was? Ich spreche kein Englisch," the young man said.

"I know. You don't understand a thing I'm saying. It's okay. Thanks for helping us out here. What's your name?"

The young man cocked his head.

"Your name…Namen? Name?"

"Ah. Horst."

"Okay, Horst. Thanks. Danke."

Schneider was two beds away from Hamm. So, they were both on the German side of the ward when Molly walked in with a late dinner tray for a recovering German lieutenant. He was only three days post-op from an abdominal injury that turned out to be nothing serious. No internal damage. He had a lot of pain from his incision—the big stay sutures hurt—but nothing wrong inside him, so he could be fed.

Molly handed him the tray of food and had just released it into his hands, when the Lieutenant sat straight up in bed and spit in her face. Then he heaved the whole tray at her face, striking her hard enough with the metal edge to gash her forehead, sending a terrible mess of food and soup and blood down her face and uniform. He shouted obscenities at her in English as she staggered from the impact. He got to his feet and lunged for her.

Horst was closest to the lieutenant, and leaped from his bed to intervene. But he barely made it to his feet, and the lieutenant struck him in the temple with a powerful back-fist and sent the boy crashing unconscious to the floor.

Hamm dropped his clipboard, rising to go to Molly's aid, but he was slow compared with Schneider.

Schneider flew, literally flew, through the air, slamming the German in the back. He locked a forearm stranglehold around the lieutenant's neck and dragged him back onto the bed. The much bigger German struggled, but Schneider was like a lion locked onto a zebra's neck. Crazed with anger, Schneider pressed his forearm around the man's neck and dug the radius bone of his forearm into the soldier's larynx, squeezing it with all his might. It would be only seconds before the trachea cracked and the soldier asphyxiated right there in the hospital tent.

Hamm was racing across the intervening cot when a blast shattered the air. The bullet whizzed past his ear. He instinctively dropped to the floor. Doctors, nurses, orderlies, everyone hit the deck. Even the patients, sick and weak as they were, were scrambling for cover. One GI was in skeletal traction and had a full cast up to his hip, but he dove for the floor dragging the weights and pulleys with him. He ended up almost comically suspended in the air just off the ground, covering his head and trying to burrow deeper into cover.

Then there was silence.

Only Schneider was oblivious to the gunfire. Only he persisted in his task, trying with all his strength to crush the laryngeal cartilage of the German lieutenant.

Hamm peeked up over the edge of the cot. First, he saw Molly cringing next to the same cot he had ducked behind. She was covered in food and bleeding from her forehead. Some of the blood was clotting in her red hair. Then he saw Schneider with his arm still locked in a death grip around the German patient. Hamm started to get up to see whether the guy was salvageable or Schneider had killed him. But, he needn't have bothered. The man lay there completely limp, a red entry wound square in the middle of his forehead. The exit wound had taken out the side of his temple on the left, scattering brains and bone on the pillow and just missing Schneider.

Schneider wasn't moving, and he wasn't letting up on the pressure. He was going to kill the son-of-a-bitch no matter what. Never mind the guy was already dead.

Hamm looked back toward the door flap. There in the doorway, gun still leveled and aimed, was Fuchs. It wasn't smoking as in the movies, but there was little doubt who had fired the shot.

Hamm leaned nearer to Schneider. He whispered, "You can let go now, pal. He's dead."

"I know," Schneider answered in a trance-like voice. "I killed him."

"I think the Colonel over there shot him."

"No," he said. "*I* killed him. I broke his fucking larynx. He was dead when the bullet hit him."

Hamm put his hand gently on Schneider's shoulder, trying to calm him. And trying to keep Fuchs from shooting Schneider too. "OK. If you say so."

"I say so. I killed him. I broke his larynx…."

"OK…OK." Hamm backed away, hands raised in surrender.

Then, to everyone's surprise, Fuchs put the pistol back in its holster and refastened the shining leather flap. He turned and left the tent without a word.

"You think he was aiming for you or the Kraut?" Hamm asked.

Schneider shrugged, and the German's torso shrugged with him.

No one stirred until Antonelli raised his head above a cot and said with a perfectly straight face, "Man! Don't fuck around with Hoppy!" He was referring to Hopalong Cassidy, who always saved the day in the westerns. Hamm wondered if Antonelli had meant Schneider or Fuchs.

With Fuchs gone, Hamm backed off a bit. Schneider was still strangling the dead German. Then Hamm took Schneider's wrist gently in his hand and unwound it from the man's neck. Schneider resisted at first, his muscles still in spasm. Then, he slowly gave in and let Hamm pry him away.

As the German slid to the floor, Hamm put his fingers on the man's throat. He could feel the edges of the broken tracheal cartilages, and sensed the extruded air crinkle under his fingers. He looked at Schneider with newfound respect.

"I think you did kill him before Fuchs shot him, Steve." Hamm said. "Anyway, Molly needs you now."

As he dashed over to help Molly, Schneider turned and whispered, "*I* killed him, you know."

The whole team was in the OR.

Schneider was getting the instruments out, when he said to Hamm, "I think you better do this repair, pal. I'm too close to Molly to do this."

"Good thinking," Hamm said. "No problem."

They switched places at the table. Hamm started a precision plastic repair of the laceration across Molly's forehead under a local anesthetic. Schneider played first assistant and scrub nurse, handing Hamm the instruments and medications while trying to calm Molly down. Actually, Molly was very calm. It was Schneider who was using her injury and his participation in the repair to calm himself down.

Hamm was using the last of the very fine sutures in their supply for the cosmetic repair.

"Can you believe what that snake did to me!" Molly was fuming. Even lying on an operating table with her face obscured by the sterile drapes, everyone could still see the anger in her eyes.

"Well, he certainly won't do that again," Schneider quipped, trying to lighten the mood.

"It's not funny!" Molly snapped. "We're risking our lives out here and treating them like human beings, and that's what they do?"

Schneider nodded solemnly and said, "I'm sorry, Molly. You're right. It isn't funny at all."

"Well, our young patient, Horst, did try to help you, Molly," Hamm said. "I'm glad he didn't get killed for his efforts. Just a big lump on his head."

Schneider had never seen Molly so angry. He was reminded of the expression "getting her Irish up." He would try to remember not to get Molly's Irish up any time again soon. Everything about the war was moving nearer the edge now. They all knew it.

"I guess you don't mess around with Fuchs," Hamm said. "That was a hell of a shot."

"But, the guy was already dead. I felt his larynx snap under my wrist. Wouldn't have lasted long, anyway."

To Schneider, Fuchs's appearance on the scene was superfluous. But, since it happened, Schneider had wrestled continuously with the question of whether his spontaneous act constituted bravery or not. He was terrified through it all. His heart raced, and his hands trembled even as he snapped the German's neck.

Is this bravery he wondered, or a primitive animal reflex? How can so much terror be called bravery?

"Either way," Hamm said, "even if he were aiming for you, Fuchs didn't have any choice except to look as if he meant to kill the Kraut. Would have lost face."

"Maybe," Schneider said, "or maybe he was just getting rid of a soldier who cracked up. Cracking up is not a Good-Kraut soldierly thing to do."

"Don't push it, Steve. The night is young. Killing a German officer—a patient—in a hospital ward might still land you in front of a Kraut firing squad."

At three forty-five the next morning, Fuchs's adjutant showed up at Hamm's tent, rousting everyone from a deep sleep.

Half dressed and in bare feet, they were herded along through the snow and mud in front of the adjutant. Hamm was furious at this middle-of-the-night outrage.

"What the hell are you doing getting us all out of bed at this hour? Whose orders are these?"

He swore and railed at the guard in English, confusing the issue of who was being called on the carpet. Molly was brought along by another guard, and she, McClintock and Schneider were pushed into the procession behind Hamm by two more guards.

"God damn it, get that fucking gun out of my face. You're gonna kill someone if you don't stop screwing around!" Hamm shouted.

The guard only understood the rage. He turned and struck Hamm in the face with the butt of his machine pistol. Hamm had turned his head to avoid the blow, but still took a nasty slam just below his eye.

"Schweigen Sie!" the adjutant shouted at them. Shut up! He threatened Hamm again with the butt of his gun. Hamm flinched and raised his hand to ward off any blow.

McClintock grabbed Hamm's wrist and yanked him out of the way.

"Cool it pal. I'm the hot head in this outfit."

Hamm actually laughed. Then he sagged and fell into line.

The four arrived at the command post and were shoved with rifles rammed into their backs into a line directly in front of Fuchs' desk. As Hamm studied Fuchs' face, he became wary, frightened by the smirk creeping across the man's lips.

"Well," he finally said, looking directly at Schneider. "Meine kleine freunde." My little friend.

Shit! This is bad. He's being too cute, Hamm thought. Hamm's face betrayed his horror, but in that brief moment he had firmed his resolve. This had to be about the killing of the German officer. The only question would be the magnitude of the reprisal. This could cost many lives. Not just Steve's.

"Herr Schneider, did you sleep well? Did you enjoy yourself tonight? The hero who saved his lover?"

Schneider just stared over Fuchs' head, at the blank wall behind the German. He knew where this must end, and for the moment, he found himself surprised at his calm. The outcome was inevitable. It was just a matter of when and how he was to die.

Fuchs was enjoying himself. "Do you think I didn't know that Herr Schneider is a Jew? Untermensche?" Fuchs smiled broadly now, enjoying the power.

Hamm winced. He could see the firing squad. He could feel the ropes that would tie Steve—perhaps all of them—to the execution post.

"And you, Herr Hammer? Might you also be one of his kind? Birds of a feather. Isn't that what you say?" And with that the Colonel began to slowly and methodically unbutton the flap of his holster.

Sweat broke out on Schneider's forehead. The pounding in his chest felt like a fist striking his ribs from the inside.

McClintock's eyes moved from side to side, scanning the room. He was looking for an opening; for a weapon; for a chance to get to Fuchs before Fuchs could kill Schneider. Anything to ignite the chaos that could buy their lives. But there was nothing The street fighter in him was raging with the wild passions of his adrenalin. But his brain was keeping the madness at bay...for the moment.

"Did you really think you could kill a German officer—a patient under your care—and get away with it?"

Schneider reflexively put his hand to his throat.

"No, no, no Herr Major. You won't hang. And we don't have time for a firing squad." He paused and smiled. "I'm going to shoot you myself."

Molly struggled to hold back her tears as she looked at Schneider and then to Hamm.

Fuchs paused, smiling the whole time. He eased his black shining Luger slowly from its holster. Slowly. Methodically.

Hamm's face had turned to stone. Fuchs looked at Schneider, who was now sweating profusely. Schneider's knees started to buckle. He looked to Molly who stood her ground. Her body never moved, as tears rolled down her cheeks.

As the Luger cleared its holster, the staccato of automatic weapons fire broke the quiet of the night all around the camp. Hamm's heart constricted as he visualized the now inevitable slaughter of his hospital staff and his patients.

He tried to turn and leap out of range at the moment he heard the first shots. Thinking he was about to die anyway, he made a last lunge for Fuchs, trying with all his strength to grab the hand that was bringing the Luger to bear on his friend.

Fuchs easily side-stepped Hamm's attack. Hamm fell helplessly to the floor, slamming his face on the edge of the desk, then landing prone next to Fuchs' feet.

McClintock dove at Fuchs, missing as Hamm had as Fuchs side-stepped him as well.

Hamm rolled to his back, and watched Fuchs' confusion. Fuchs wrinkled his forehead, staring out into the night. He didn't give Hamm or any of the others a second look.

Then as Hamm watched from below, Fuchs' head disintegrated, splattering the wall of the command post with blood and brain matter. Hamm looked toward the adjutant and saw exactly the same thing. The head exploded, and the man slumped to the ground.

Only Schneider stood rigidly frozen in place, still standing at the front of the desk. Soon after Fuchs dropped, Molly lunged at Fuchs' inert body and pulled the Luger from the dead man's grip. She mechanically chambered a round, and then turned to see what was happening behind her.

With no obvious targets, Molly, too, rushed to Hamm who was still on the floor, dazed from his head striking the desk, and now bleeding freely. She pressed her hand against the wound to stop the bleeding just as Schneider joined them to help Hamm off of the floor.

Then all of them turned and stared at the command post door. There, in the lighted rectangle, dressed in white winter camouflage and full battle gear, smoking gun still at the ready, was Sorenson.

Sorenson!

The lieutenant—no, a *captain,* now, Schneider saw from the bars on the collar—surveyed the room and brought his weapon up, pointing the muzzle to the ceiling.

"Evening, Major Schneider," he said, as if it were just another day on the job. "Captain Ferrarro, ma'am. Stay put here for a minute will you? Don't wanna get in the way of the cross-fire."

Sorenson limped out through the doorway and disappeared.

The attack lasted less than eight minutes in all. It had seemed longer to Schneider, but the shooting stopped soon enough. Outside they could hear groans and some swearing in German. Three platoons of American GIs were running around the camp disarming the few surviving German guards and locking them away. The American infantry were released from their cages and rearmed.

When it all ended, Schneider and McClintock, along with Molly, helped Hamm by the arm as they stepped over the body of the adjutant. They walked together out into the compound.

They soon met up again with Sorenson who was drinking coffee—real coffee—with the staff in the newly liberated mess tent. Just about everyone was there, their entire group as well as the commando platoons that had freed them. Schneider was thrilled to be alive, but his mind wouldn't let go of how near a thing it had been.

"We knew you were here," Sorenson said, "but it took time to get a rescue force together and coordinate it so that we could maximize the force and minimize our casualties."

"Well, that was one hell of a rescue, Captain," Hamm said. "What a stroke of luck you guys showed up when you did. We didn't have a lot of time left."

"Well, as you once told me," Sorenson said, "I'd rather be lucky than smart. We knew the Jerries were moving a lot of their people out of this area. So it made sense to get in here as soon as possible. The timing of the attack at 'oh-dark-thirty' was based on the time that the Jerries would be asleep, at their lowest efficiency and manpower. Just bad luck you guys were getting' rousted out by their CO."

"We weren't just getting 'rousted,' Captain," Schneider said. "Fuchs was getting ready to execute us. Me for sure."

"Glad we got here in time, sir."

"So what about your leg?" Hamm asked.

"Well, it isn't so great. Not that you didn't do a great job, Doc," he said to Hamm. "I recovered pretty fast in England, and they wanted to muster me out. I put up a hell of a fight, though, so it was easier to let me back into the fight than to deal with the mountain of paperwork I was creating. They assigned me to commando training, then shipped me back here for some selected operations. And guess what my first team's assignment was?" He smiled and nodded. "Yup. You."

Molly stood and reached her hand out to Hamm.

"C'mon, Major. Time to sew up that gash. We ought to be pretty good at this soon."

Schneider cleaned and sewed Hamm's head laceration, while Molly assisted, cutting sutures and handing instruments.

Later, they all drank more coffee and ate some real steaks and fresh potatoes with actual butter, which had arrived with the resupply a few hours after the rescue. It was heaven. It took them about four days to sort out the Germans. The few survivors were sent back as prisoners, except for a couple they kept around to bury their dead. Then they, too, were sent back as well. The Jerries complained and whined and bitched about doing labor under the Geneva Convention. But each time anyone made a real fuss, Sorenson would step up with his Colt .45, chamber a round, cock the hammer and ask, "Was wollen Sie?" What do *you* want?

There was a look in his eye that turned their guts to jelly. There was not much resistance after a few of those incidents. Schneider always wondered whether Sorenson would actually have pulled that trigger. He was glad it never came to that. No one tested Sorenson.

There were a lot of very young and very old German soldiers by this point in the war, conscripted at the last minute and sent off as cannon fodder. Hamm couldn't believe what he was seeing.

"Look at some of these kids," Hamm said. They're just reaching puberty! Who's sending them out to fight?"

"They're all that's left. So much for the great Reich," McClintock said.

"They're so pathetic. I could cry for them," Molly said.

"Well, they still have guns, so make sure they're disarmed before y'all start crying," McClintock added.

The Waffen-SS were even worse. Without guns in their hands, they, like most bullies, were spineless. They groveled worse than the kids. The Americans treated them badly, too. They just couldn't help themselves. The SS were worse than dog shit, to quote Antonelli.

After the near tragedy, Hamm had increased his hatred for the Nazis and even began to wonder about carrying a weapon himself. Him, of all people. He suspected that when the end of this war came, there would be a lawlessness that would supersede the Geneva Convention and its rules, and turn the place into Dodge City.

Before they moved on to their new location and reformed Field Hospital Charlie-7, Sorenson came to Hamm and said,

"You feel better if you had a weapon, Major? I can certainly arrange that."

Hamm hesitated. Then he said, "I appreciate the thought, Jim. But you're the soldier. I'm just the doctor. Probably best if we just keep it that way."

So Hamm remained as he had arrived: a man without a gun.

There was little time to relax and savor their rescue. Although they didn't realize it, they had not yet seen the worst of the weather or the fighting. December, 1944 arrived in earnest, and Hitler was getting ready to make life miserable for them once again.

They had survived very real danger. It didn't kill them. It had just made them all stronger and all the more determined.

Chapter Twenty-one

3 December 1944, 0530 Hours
A Concentration Camp near Weimar, Germany

Berg woke with the first light, as always. His neck and back felt frozen to the wooden desk chair where he had fallen asleep. He still spent his nights in the clinic office rather than go back to the barracks. The SS didn't seem to care one way or the other now. The war, they knew, was going very badly for them, and they had graver concerns than a decrepit old doctor.

Even Himmel had stopped pestering Berg about staying in the clinic all night. After so many months, he realized Berg was no threat to the security of the camp. In fact, though he dared not admit it even to himself, he was relieved to have Berg's expertise when his own men were sick.

The Germans kept a fairly well-stocked surgical kit, reserved solely for the use of the SS, of course. God forbid they should contaminate their bodies with instruments that had been used to treat Jews. In the four years of Berg's confinement, he had done a dozen or so operations on the SS. They usually sent for a legitimate Nazi anesthesiologist, but surgeons could not be spared from the front lines to do procedures at a prison camp. Berg's civilian reputation as a surgeon had survived the taint of his Jewishness. Nothing if not practical, these Nazis.

So, at first, Berg operated on them. Even though they were Nazis and his tormentors, he gave them his best. In the early days, several of the prisoners suggested to him that he might sabotage the surgery: make small inconspicuous mistakes that might prove fatal long after the surgery was over and the officer was far away from the camp. The idea began to intrigue Berg. Joseph Meyer was the instigator. He was an inmate—and a survivor—who would feign illness to get into the hospital from time to time, where he would harangue Berg for hours trying to convince him to give it a try.

"So, you think the rumors are true, Herr Doktor?" Joseph said as Berg cleaned a wound sustained at the hands of an irate guard.

"What rumors might those be, Joseph?" There were always rumors.

"They say that it's almost over, that the British and the Americans are winning the war."

"Well, what about all the reports of one smashing defeat after another by the Wehrmacht over the Americans. What of that?"

Joseph smiled. His skin wrinkled about his eyes.

"Have you noticed that each time the Americans are defeated, the defeat is closer and closer to Berlin?"

They both laughed.

"Actually, I have. But, still, there's not much the two of us can do to speed up these American defeats." He laughed again.

"There is something…." Joseph said.

Berg stopped what he was doing and looked around the room. This was dangerous talk.

"Joseph, what are you saying?"

"You could be like the Resistance, Doktor. There is so much you could do! I'm sure of it."

"Well?" Berg said.

"Yes, there must be something, something like a time bomb."

"A time bomb? You want me to plant a time bomb inside an SS officer?"

"Not a real time bomb, but, something equivalent: a surgical time bomb. Something that could go fatally wrong later on, far, far away from here. Think, Doktor, think!"

And Berg did think about it. It excited him. Perhaps he could do something to sabotage the SS, something to kill them when they were off at the front again. He wanted no reprisals against the inmates, so it would have to occur long after they left the camp. Joseph had lit his interest.

"Perhaps there is something," he said.

"Yes? What? Tell me."

"Well," he began, slowly working it out in his mind. "I could, for example, repair a major vessel, and instead of using a permanent suture, like silk or cotton, I could use plain catgut, which dissolves in a matter of ten days or so...."

"And?"

"Well, then at the first episode of elevated blood pressure, in combat—hah!—even during sex or something, the pressure might become too great, and the vessel might burst. It might not, but it might."

"There. You see? There *is* something you could do! What else? Think!"

"I could leave a sponge behind. That's really easy. It happens sometimes even when you're doing your best not to leave anything behind."

Jacob looked puzzled.

"A sponge," Berg explained, "is a piece of cotton gauze pad we use to sop up blood. We use hundreds during an operation. In the real world, they are carefully counted before and after the operation, but here, we skip that refinement. One or two would never be missed. An easy thing to do."

"And what would happen to the officer, if you did such a thing?"

"Well, he would be fine for a while, especially if it's a minor operation where he could recover rapidly and then be discharged. An appendectomy, a hernia repair. Then, in a week or two, the sponge would inevitably create infection. It's a foreign body, you see, and the officer would slowly become sicker and sicker. With the scant supplies at the front, he would need to be hospitalized and maybe require another operation."

"This's even better than the catgut arteries, Doktor!"

"You think so? Why?"

"Because it is better if they do not die"

"You sound too experienced in this, Joseph," Berg said, surprised at his friend's expertise and the thought that he had even considered these ideas.

"Yes, well...I am here for a reason. Unlike most of these people who committed no crime other than being Jews, or that they held the wrong political positions...I... I'm here because I was caught...well, let's just leave it at that. I was caught."

"But, if you were a Resistance fighter—I assume that's what they caught you at—why didn't they kill you?"

Joseph was silent for a moment, almost pensive. Then he looked Berg directly in the eye and said, "Doktor, I am not Joseph Meyer. Never mind who I am. I will not burden you with that secret. Joseph Meyer and his wife died in the cattle cars between München and here. I placed my identity papers on his body, and I took his identification, his clothes...I became him. There were so many of us in those cars; we were merely animals for the slaughter. There was no effort to identify the dead. Each time we stopped, we willingly handed over the bodies to make room in the cars, to rid ourselves of the dead, of the stench. And the SS had no time to waste. They threw the bodies in the ditches at the side of the tracks. The countryside is littered with the dead that were thrown from the train.

"The real Joseph died before he could ever reach this hell. It was a blessing for him, and at the same time, a mixed blessing for me. I was not shot as a spy or as a Resistance fighter."

Joseph, or whoever he was, stopped speaking and turned his eyes to the floor.

"I should not burden you with all of this, Doktor. It is dangerous for you and for me if you know too much. I'm sorry. You decide what to do. Perhaps you can help the war effort in your own way. It's up to you. They *will* kill you if you are caught at this. Make no mistake about it. Doktor or not, once you cross that line, there is no going back."

And with that, Joseph left, his wound now bandaged, straggling back into the muddy waste of the camp, blending in like an animal into his surroundings. Joseph was the kind of inmate who survived on the strength of his cunning. He might even live to see the end of the war...unless someone in the camp betrayed him. Berg hoped to God that he himself would not accidentally betray Joseph.

The seed that Joseph had planted grew like a tumor in Berg's brain. He even had headaches, an ailment that, until then, had never troubled him. He couldn't sleep and couldn't concentrate.

Berg knew that the SS laughed at him, at his pathetic struggles to help the poor souls who came to his hospital to die. He saved so few.

But, Joseph had given him hope. He felt a new power. Berg could be a soldier and actually fight the enemy. All these years he had hidden behind his profession's oath to never take a life, to never injure a patient. Could he now put that behind him and take up arms of a sort? All these years he shared the shame of a people who were led to the slaughter like lambs, who never fought back. Now he had his chance. Could he do it?

Verdammt, kann Ich! Damned right, I can.

Opportunity came less than a week later. Berg had spent so much time working it out in his mind that by the time the patient was on the operating table, it was almost easy.

The man was an SS Sturmbannführer. What a prize! He had developed the most mundane sort of surgical problem: a hernia. Probably too much constipation out there, or just a bad family legacy. In any case, he could not go back to the front because his hernia had become trapped, and his annoying problem turned into an emergency. The grandest gift of all was that Berg was to do the surgery alone. Grau was away, and Berg would be alone the whole time. He only hoped that the patient recovered quickly enough after the surgery to be far away from the camp when his infection set in. If they found Berg out too soon, there was no question he would be shot.

"Good evening, Sturmbannführer," Berg said, as the patient lay down on the operating table in the room reserved for the SS officers. This was a different building entirely, over near the SS quarters. This room was clean and well equipped with plenty of every kind of medicine and surgical instruments. Berg salivated with envy, like one of Pavlov's hounds. The room was kept locked and guarded at all times; it was never used for inmates no matter how sick they were.

"Good evening, Herr Doktor," the patient said, good-naturedly. "I hear that you were a well-respected surgeon in München before the war."

Berg nodded modestly. "Yes, Sturmbannführer, I certainly have done my share of surgery. Lately, not so much."

"Well, you haven't forgotten how to fix a hernia, have you?" he laughed. There was nervousness behind the bravado. Surgery and operating rooms are great equalizers.

"No," Berg said. "I've done several thousand of them. It's like riding a bicycle. I could do this in my sleep." Then he laughed. "But I won't. This shouldn't take long, and you can return to your job in a few days."

The man nodded again, but didn't speak. One of the SS medics prepared the anesthesia apparatus, while Berg tended to his instruments. He laid out the sponges, knives, sutures and clamps. In the real world, a nurse had always done this for him. When he arrived in the camps, Berg had to improvise a bit. He didn't have the luxury of a scrub nurse at the table. Today that would be to his advantage.

"Ready?" Berg asked the patient and the anesthetist.

"Yes," they replied in unison.

And so begins my life as a murderer, he thought, as he picked up his scalpel and waited for the ether to take effect. The smell of the gas made his eyes water a bit and brought him memories of his days as a real healer. He had qualms with what he was about to do to this man. But, oddly, the qualms were not about the risk to himself. Somehow, over the years in the camp, he had lost any sense of fear for his own safety. What could they do to him beyond killing him?

When the officer was asleep, the anesthetist nodded, and Berg began. It felt good to be operating again. There he was in a nearly normal operating room, his patient well anesthetized, and enough instruments to do what he needed to do. If only he had such opportunities for the rest of his patients.

Berg made the incision with care, then opened up each layer leading to the hernia: a defect in the abdominal wall in which the officer's intestines were now trapped like an animal trying to escape through too small a hole in a tree. He opened the thin, translucent hernial sac and pushed the intestines back into the abdominal cavity, holding them there with a wadded up sponge while he prepared the sutures for the repair of the defect. He was going to do the Halsted Repair, named after an American surgeon from Johns Hopkins, Berg remembered. He smiled at this little irony. Then, as if he did it every day, he placed a second small gauze sponge right against the femoral vein as it crossed into the thigh. He tucked it down neatly in place, and prepared to sew the hernial defect shut with strong silk sutures.

"Stop!" the voice shouted.

Berg was so startled that he dropped the needle holder to the floor. His hands shook, and he could feel his heart racing, beating against his breastbone like a hammer.

The anesthetist stood at the head of the table staring into the wound. Berg had not noticed that the man had been watching the operation.

"Why are you shouting at me, you damned fool?" Berg said, trying to regain control of the situation.

Before the anesthetist could answer, Berg reached into the wound and pulled the sponge away from the vein. He placed it conspicuously on the surgical tray, and then took another needle holder from the set of instruments.

The anesthetist stammered and said, "I thought you were leaving that sponge behind."

"Of course I'm not leaving the sponge behind! It is left in place until I am ready to repair the defect in the floor of the inguinal canal. Schwachsinnig!" Imbecile! "You've made me drop a valuable instrument. You'd better hope it is not damaged."

The man was cowed. He was not an officer, merely an enlisted man trained to give anesthesia. He started to protest, however. No Jew prisoner was going to give him orders.

"Listen to me, you miserable kike!" he shouted.

Just then the patient began to cough and buck. He was waking up, and though still unconscious, was responding to the pain of the incision. Berg quickly placed a handful of gauze sponges on top of the still unrepaired hernial defect in the abdominal wall and pressed down. He pressed hard to keep the patient from pushing his intestines out through the wound and turning the case into a disaster right there on the table.

"Put this patient back under!" he screamed at the German. "Pay attention to your anesthesia and let me worry about the surgery, you goddamned fool! If this man dies for your foolishness…!"

The anesthetist poured a steady stream of ether onto the mesh screen over the patient's nose and mouth. Still, the man strained and coughed, requiring Berg to do nothing but protect the wound.

"If this patient dies from your incompetence," Berg shouted, "you will certainly join him."

The anesthetist was more than worried, now. Berg was right. If anything happened to an officer of the SS because of an anesthetic error, the anesthetist would surely pay the price.

The room was literally filled with the vapors of the ether now, making everyone's eyes tear. Finally, the coughing and the straining stopped, as the level of anesthesia deepened, and the officer relaxed.

Berg carefully released his pressure on the wound, testing to see if he could proceed. Now that the officer was deeply asleep again, he removed the gauze pack and placed it on the tray. He peered stealthily at the anesthetist, making sure the man was not watching. Berg smiled behind his mask as he let slip another wad of cotton gauze, pushing it with his thumb down to the place next to the femoral vein, where it had been before.

The anesthetist was so busy trying to keep the anesthesia regulated that he never again looked up.

Twenty-five minutes later, Berg was ready to close the skin.

A good repair, if I say so myself. Even with such incompetent anesthesia.

That done, he nodded to the anesthetist to stop the ether.

"Now you can let him cough a bit as he wakes up. I want to be sure the repair will hold," Berg said. The hernial repair now hid the retained gauze pads. He had regained some of his equanimity, though he was sure that his mask and cap were stained with telltale sweat. He had come very close.

"Yawohl, Herr Doktor," the anesthetist said.

The stupid bastard hasn't seen a thing.

The sturmbannführer coughed twice, and the closure of the hernia strained against the sutures. But, there was no tear, no defect. It would be a strong repair. At least for a week or so. Then, if Berg were right, the gauze sponge would create an infection. The officer, hopefully back at the front with his other SS friends, would develop a fever, then increasing pain in his groin. If Berg were really lucky, the infected sponge would erode through the femoral vein and the man might bleed to death right there on the battlefield. Or, it would cause a thrombophlebitis, a clot in the vein, which could break off and go to his lungs and kill him on the spot. He'd just drop as if he had been shot.

Shot by me! Ha!

Better still, Berg mused, he would require some exploratory surgery to remove the infected sponge. He would become a burden to his army.

Whether they would ever take the trouble to trace it all back to Berg, he had no idea. If they did, Berg would be shot. Or gassed. Or something. One doktor for one sturmbannführer. A good bargain if Berg could raise the price by getting in several more operations before they shut him down. Good Resistance fighters don't last long in the field anyway. They only tried to take more enemy with them when they died. In his case, no innocent civilians would be shot for his actions.

Chapter Twenty-two

17 December 1944, 1200 Hours
Filed Hospital Charlie-7, Waimes, Belgium

It was the week before Christmas. Antonelli was at the front lines bringing in the wounded. Marsh was going back and forth between the front lines and the field hospital at Waimes. At the moment, there was a real shortage of medics.

A massive German counteroffensive had pushed a huge westward curve into the north-south lines at the German border. The Europeans called the counteroffensive the Battle of the Ardennes Forest. Americans called it the Battle of the Bulge. Marsh called it The Big Bug Out. Whatever it was called, from day one, everyone was running for their lives.

There were the usual rumors. The medical unit never knew what was real and what wasn't. Often only the sight of a German Panzer— a Tiger tank—firing down on them, or a convoy of German APCs, signaled the time to get out.

It all started on December 16th in the predawn hours. Rumor had it that whole divisions of German tanks and personnel were pouring into a highly concentrated area in the middle of Belgium and spearheading west. This was The Bulge. The Germans were trying to break through the American lines to the River Meuse to divide the American forces and then head north to capture the seaports to cut off supplies. They had diverted every last bit of manpower and machinery that they could. For Hitler, this was going to be the last battle. One way or another.

Medical groups were set up all over the area, generally within a mile or so from the front. There were field hospitals at Waimes, St. Vith, Buttenbach, Malmédy, and many others. What they all had in common was that they were constantly within sight of the fighting. They had plenty of supplies at that point and almost enough men and women to do the job. There were enough WAC nurses at all the hospitals, even those closest to the fighting. After six months on the lines, the men and women were comrades in arms. Everyone had gotten over the idea that the women were in need of constant protection. Still, when they had to evacuate, the nurses were sent out first with the litter cases. But that was the most effective way to do it anyway. The nurses were needed to take care of the critically injured pre-op and post-op patients en route. The surgeons stayed behind to keep operating until the last minute. The medics stayed behind to bring in the newly wounded cases from the front. It made sense to evacuate the nurses first then the doctors and the medics last.

Field Hospital Charlie-7 was now stationed at Waimes, Belgium. They had been there for some time and were set up in a real building. Pretty comfortable over all, compared to some of the places they had been. Most of the time, they were less than an hour from the front by ambulance, so the bodies kept coming in almost without letup. They treated the GIs there as best they could, then sent them further to the rear through Malmédy, Bastogne and Liège.

Antonelli and Marsh were still working together most of the time. But now the pressure was getting to them. Too many hours without sleep. Too many casualties. They were almost always at the front and the GIs were dropping like flies. The mortality among the medics was unimaginable. Some of the medics were losing a partner a month. Those boys were getting a reputation for bad luck. It had gotten so bad that some of them didn't want to know their new partner at all. They'd rather work alone. They were feeling as if they were jinxed.

"Stay away from me, man," they would say, "unless you want to get killed."

But Marsh and Antonelli were stuck with each other. They had survived.

Marsh found himself unable to remember the names of the other medics anymore, and the faces were all starting to blur together. Later that afternoon, he was out in the field trying to give first aid to wounded GIs and getting ready to bring them in. Suddenly, a voice was calling, "Marsh! Marsh!"

He knew it had to be a medic in his outfit because no other GI would know his name. The wounded would be shouting "Medic! Medic!" or "Corpsman!"

So when he heard "Marsh!" out there, he knew it was one of his medics who had been hit. He looked to see where the cries were coming from. And he was right. It was Jankowsky.

Jankowsky was a pretty good medic from what little Marsh saw of him. But they had been in the same group only a week, and Jankowsky had been in the field for only a month.

Marsh raced over to where Jankowsky was lying in the snow and writhing with pain. Apparently he'd received a chest wound while bending over a GI who'd been burned by a flame thrower. Jankowsky had been starting an IV and stood up a little too high to make the fluid run in faster when he caught one in the back. Straight into the chest and out the other side. He had a pneumothorax and bubbles were coming out his chest when Marsh got to him. Marsh plugged the hole, started an IV of plasma, and called for some stretcher-bearers. They got Jankowsky to the clearing station, and Hamm immediately put in a chest tube. Jankowsky didn't even need his chest cracked. That was his last day at the front with this team. Marsh never saw him again.

The badly burned GI died in a few days. They tended to do that.

So now, a week before Christmas, they were still in Waimes: another place Marsh and his young mates had never heard of. He had at least heard of Paris and Berlin, though he knew little about them.

Hammer, Schneider and McClintock were all still going strong. Plus there were other new surgeons and anesthesiologists who had joined them after the invasion, or had been with them the whole time. And many of the same nurses, too. Marsh happened to like a nurse named Katherine quite a lot, but she didn't know he was alive. He resigned himself to the fact that she was just out of his league. Still, it made him sad.

Sometime after midnight, the medical team all heard some activity along the road. This wasn't all that unusual since there were always a lot of jeeps and trucks and even tanks going by all the time. Marsh didn't know what it was about this time, but he sensed something. He had, in the months of constant fighting, developed a finely tuned antenna for danger. His stomach got queasy and knotted up. Just something about it.

Early that morning of December 17th, Marsh was sound asleep; Antonelli was out in the field helping with the incoming wounded. Staff Sergeant Donovan rushed into the tent and woke Marsh, rousting him out of bed. Marsh was awake anyway, but Donovan was more agitated than usual, which for Donovan was saying a lot.

"Marsh, get dressed and get your gear."

"What's up, Sarge?" he said.

"We're going over to Malmédy, to the field hospital there. We're packin' up here. The Jerries are mounting an offensive. A big push, coming right this way."

"Jesus! How bad is it?"

"Bad! Very bad. Get going."

"Well, how? Shouldn't I be here for the wounded guys we're gonna get from the offensive?"

"Yeah, yeah. Antonelli's already on that. You'll get plenty of work. Just pack up and help evacuate the place. Everyone's moving. Nobody stays here."

Donovan turned and went to the next room, rousting everyone who hadn't been awakened by all the racket. Marsh grabbed his gear and packed what he could carry. He had to leave a lot of stuff behind. More than usual. Something told him he wouldn't need it.

In a few minutes, Marsh was outside with everyone else, packing the gear. They were getting very good at bugging out of places. The trucks were loaded and ready to go in no time. They loaded the sickest first and sent them directly over to Malmédy. It was an easy uphill drive along the N32 to the Baugnez crossroads, and then a few miles to the Malmédy Field Hospital. Marsh, Antonelli, and the other medics had been back and forth between Waimes and Malmédy dozens of times ferrying supplies and wounded GIs. It was no big deal. So, Marsh stayed at the field hospital site until everyone was gone and all the supplies with them. By noon, the place was nearly empty, and Marsh was left with a jeep and one GI, named Jordan. Jordan was a new guy, and Marsh didn't know him very well. He was mostly a driver for trucks, jeeps, and even a half-track every now and then. But he liked Jordan, who was—in his own way—a lot like Marsh. Jordan was energetic and very conscientious. Not easy traits to find after so many months of slaughter and hardship.

They looked around one last time, and then Marsh said, "OK, man. Let's haul ass!"

Jordan was happy to be leaving. Marsh was too. Although his job was often solitary in the most dangerous circumstances, Marsh never liked being alone. It felt too spooky, and though he would never tell the guys in the unit, it was no different than when he was a kid and got left behind playing Hide 'n' Seek.

Marsh had been such a good hider, and so determined to win, that he would get into a hiding place and stay there as quiet as a mouse for hours. Meantime, the other kids would go home for lunch. The afternoon would roll by, and there Marsh would be, all tickled about winning the game, not knowing everybody had gone home. Then it started to get dark, and it wasn't so funny anymore. As soon as he found out he was alone, the fear took over. He would run home to his mom, crying until he was within sight of the house, where he would wipe his face and put on a show of being a big boy. Funny, he thought, it was no different here in Belgium. Or France.

The two men jumped into the jeep and set off up the N32 west toward the Baugnez crossroads. It was a hard-topped road, so they made good time. Marsh looked into the far distance whenever he could, but none of the other trucks or jeeps were in sight. The road was a long, gentle, uphill grade all the way to the crossroads, so neither Marsh nor Jordan could see very far ahead. Marsh's watch showed 1300 hours, so they still had more than three hours of daylight, even at this time of year. And at least they had each other for company.

BAUGNEZ CROSSROADS, BELGIUM
DECEMBER 17TH, 1944

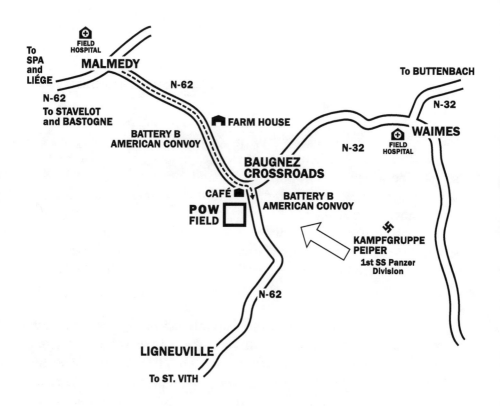

They drove a few more miles, and, as they neared the top of a hill, Marsh spotted a huge convoy of American half-tracks and trucks in the distance. He had heard that B Battery, of the 285th Field Artillery Observation Battalion, was moving down to Ligneauville, somewhere south of them.

He liked seeing the long line of his guys down there. He didn't feel so alone any more. As they drove on, Marsh complained to Jordan that they might be in for a long wait.

"That big convoy will probably tie up the crossroads. Maybe we can cut across a field down there. If it gets crowded, you might be able to cut around that Café right at the intersection. The old Frau will probably shit a brick when we drive across her field, but fuck her and the horse she rode in on. Never liked her anyway."

They continued down the N32 and were just coming up on the intersection, some two hundred yards away. Marsh was getting ready to wave to the troops when an earsplitting boom shook the ground and the jeep beneath them. It came from behind them, from the fields at the left of the road. Marsh turned in his seat, and his mouth fell open.

"Jesus Christ!" he said quietly, in complete awe of the scene he saw below him.

Jordan turned too, and nearly drove off the shoulder of the road. He slammed on the brakes and skidded, throwing up sand and pebbles as he hit the shoulder.

Below them in the fields were German Panzer tanks—"Tigers"—in battalion strength. There were so many of them, Marsh couldn't count them. They were cutting over from the N32, crossing the snow-covered field behind Marsh to attack the B Battalion convoy.

The Panzers had been right behind them below the road, but their eyes had been glued to the road ahead, trying to avoid the scattered snow drifts and puddles of snow-melt. No more than ten minutes separated the Germans from them. Jordan was driving faster than the tanks, but they had caught up by crossing the field to their left, attacking the B Battalion on the road going south.

Marsh and Jordan could see the whole battle now. B Battalion never had a chance. They were outgunned and outmaneuvered from the first shot. The barrage continued without stop. The tanks never even slowed down. There was nothing the GIs in the convoy could do. They had stumbled into the path of one of Hitler's most powerful Panzer forces, and they were doomed.

Marsh slapped Jordan on the back, and shouted, "Get the fuck out of here, man! Haul ass! Go! Go! Go!"

Jordan hit the accelerator and swerved back onto the hard-top. He careened right up to the intersection, where they then came under attack themselves. Shells from the Panzers burst everywhere around them. Because the B Battalion vehicles hadn't cleared the intersection yet, Marsh and Jordan were pinned down. Jordan turned hard and gunned it around the trucks, heading for the café, when a shell burst to their left and upended the jeep. Marsh leaped clear, his body crashing through the brush and splashing into a ditch full of snowy, mushy mud. Jordan tried to roll out but was scraped along the hard-top, shredding his uniform and badly abrading his palms and shins. Fortunately, since it was winter, he was dressed heavily, so the uniform absorbed much of the damage. The fall at such speed would otherwise have just about skinned him alive.

The Germans had stopped the American column completely, and the American GIs were surrendering or hiding in ditches and culverts at the side of the road. The Panzers lined up along the roadside, machine-gunning everyone who continued to resist or tried to run away. The American GIs were falling everywhere Marsh could see. It was a slaughter.

A German half-track pulled up alongside Marsh's jeep. Two officers aimed their automatic weapons, motioning for Marsh and Jordan to raise their hands. Marsh got to his knees with his hands straight up over his head; not a half-hearted sign of surrender, but truly reaching for the sky. There was no question about his surrender. And he was clearly unarmed. There were red crosses all over his helmet, and a red-cross armband on each arm. Still, he held them high.

The Germans had blood in their eyes. They wore the gray field uniforms of the Schutzstaffel and he was not about to fuck with them. He had been under fire day in and day out for six months, but he was never as afraid of anyone as he was of these SS men. After the short period as POWs in their own field hospital, Marsh had gotten religion when it came to the SS. He knew better than to cross them now.

One of the soldiers kept his muzzle trained directly at Marsh's chest, even though Marsh was unarmed. The other was screaming at

Jordan to get up, or so Marsh guessed. The German kept shouting, "Händen Hoch! Händen Hoch!"

Jordan was dazed, and the pain of his extensive abrasions was keeping his attention. With nearly no skin left on the palms, he couldn't use his hands to help himself up, and his knees were hamburgers. So he was rolling around trying to get to his feet, when the SS man shot him with a short burst from his automatic rifle. Jordan flew backwards and splayed out in the middle of the road. The German laughed and called to his partner, who hadn't taken his eyes off Marsh.

All Marsh understood was "scheiss," the German word for shit. Schneider had taught him that. Marsh had been kidding around with Schneider, yelling "Scheiss nicht! Scheiss nicht!" He told Marsh, "You mean, 'Shiess nicht.' You just said, 'Don't shit!' not 'Don't shoot!'"

They laughed a lot about that, and afterward Schneider was always yelling to Marsh, "Hey, Marsh. Scheiss nicht!"

Well, Marsh didn't know what that German was saying, but Jordan was clearly dead, half his chest blown to bits right over his heart. Marsh didn't move a muscle. He was helpless. The SS knew it, and they were enjoying it. The four of them were almost dead center of the crossroads at this point. The Kraut motioned with his gun and said something to Marsh in German. He was moving toward the café and the field beyond it.

Marsh didn't know how long the battle took from the beginning barrage to his surrender, but it all felt pretty quick. By the time he could see his watch, it was 1330, so it hadn't been more than twenty or thirty minutes from start to finish. As they walked to the field with the Kraut prodding the muzzle of his gun into the small of Marsh's back, he noticed that there was only sporadic firing now. None of it was from his side.

The fight was over and he was an SS prisoner. Again.

Fuck!

Marsh wasn't sure just how many GIs made it alive into the little field just southwest of the intersection, but it seemed like a hundred or a hundred and fifty. He had no idea how many bodies were lying out there in the ditches and the road. More than were now standing in the field. Even though the fight had ended quickly, the Germans kept shooting a hell of a lot of GIs, and Marsh could only think that he was damn lucky they were taking prisoners at all.

This could have been a real massacre, he told himself. These fucking Krauts.

The Germans herded everyone into the field. There was a barbed wire cattle fence four feet high, so climbing into the field with their hands over their heads was very hard. Many of the men were wounded and were being helped by their buddies. Some were being dragged, barely alive. One man was actually dead when they got him over the fence, but the GI dragging him just kept moving along, never looking back. Marsh saw it and had the feeling that the GI knew the man was dead, but he would not leave his buddy out there at the side of the road in the melting snow and mud. Marsh nodded to himself, knowing he would have done the same thing.

Sometime before 1400 hours, they were standing there in the field, a confused and defeated group of GIs still holding their hands high in the air. Marsh's shoulders were killing him, but there was no way he was going to lower his hands.

About twenty Germans came into the field and searched them. They took away guns, ammunition, almost everything. Then they began pulling off watches and dipping hands into pockets for wallets and money. Most of them were laughing the whole time and joking among themselves.

Big fucking joke, you cocksuckers. Your day's comin'....

Marsh was foundering in his fear, supporting himself only with hopes of revenge for the terrible slaughter that had taken place on the road in front of him, and hopes of getting revenge for Jordan.

The SS officers around the field were even grimmer than the enlisted men. They gave Marsh the creeps. Marsh never could locate the one who shot Jordan, but he didn't know what he would do if he did. He wasn't about to be a hero and attack the bastard. Jordan was already dead, and Marsh wanted to live. No matter what, he wanted to live. That thought didn't make him feel very brave. He wondered to himself what he was prepared to do to survive; who might die so that he could live?

Then, from nowhere, came that terrible feeling he had when the sergeant woke him up that very morning: the same tightness in the pit of his stomach. It was more than losing a battle, more than being taken prisoner for the second time, though that was bad enough. It was something else, but he just couldn't put his finger on it.

While they stood with their hands still high in the air, another convoy of Panzer tanks pulled up in the road alongside the field. The lead turret was open, and Marsh could see the commander dressed immaculately, almost as if he had just stepped onto the parade ground. His uniform was clean and pressed. He was the very model of a German officer. Hanging from his neck was one of those black iron crosses. From the way the other German officers ran up to him and saluted, Marsh knew this man was in charge of this whole outfit. He heard the name Piper or Peiper.

"Jawohl, Obersturmbannführer Peiper!" they said again and again, clicking their heels and snapping their idiotic stiff-armed Nazi salute.

So, Marsh thought, that's his name. Marsh couldn't remember the ranks of the German officers, but he knew from the insignia that the man was a lieutenant colonel.

Peiper's eyes scanned the prisoners standing in the field, staring for a long time as if he were considering what he should do with them. There were so many.

By then, Marsh was hopping from foot to foot. His heart was racing and he was sweating in spite of the cold. He was nearing all-out panic. It was all he could do not to cut and run, anything to get away from the intolerable uncertainty. Here is this lieutenant colonel of the Panzers and a whole army full of the fuckin' SS with him, and Peiper obviously is hell-bent-for-leather going somewhere, shooting and Blitzkrieging all over fucking Belgium. So what the hell is he going to do with a hundred or more American prisoners, Marsh wondered?

While Peiper considered all of this, Marsh remained with his arms high in the air. The pain in his shoulders was superseded by that terrible knot in his stomach. He just knew he was going to die there that day unless he did something about it.

A GI stood right in front of him. Marsh edged a bit to his own right, taking cover in the man's shadow, as if he were hiding behind a tree. Then he said in a very low whisper, "What do you think that Kraut Colonel's gonna do?" He didn't move his lips, imitating his favorite ventriloquist, Edgar Bergen, and his dummy, Charlie McCarthy.

The man in front of him didn't turn his head, but Marsh heard him whisper, "I'll give you one guess, pal."

"But, we're prisoners, for Christ's sakes," Marsh said through his teeth, trying to argue his way to a better outcome. "We aren't even armed anymore."

"Fuck that, pal. What's he going to do? Stop the whole offensive and baby-sit us here until reinforcements arrive?"

Marsh started to argue, but realized that it didn't matter what he reasoned out. All of their lives were in that colonel's hands, and Marsh didn't like the looks of any of it. If anything, he hoped that Peiper would stay in command rather than leave them to the SS grunts.

Another officer, this one also from the SS, walked over to the tank and climbed up onto the tread. Peiper leaned down and spoke quietly into his ear. Marsh really didn't like that. Most officers boomed out their orders in front of everyone. They loved command and the way they controlled everyone around them.

It was exactly then that Marsh was certain he was a dead man, and a dead man had nothing to lose. He was no less afraid.His stomach still roiled and knotted, threatening to spill his undigested breakfast over the snow and mud. Yet he maintained his reason and his ability to act. He had to have a plan. Make a plan and stick to it, he told himself.

He started to inch his way back toward the fence line as far from the road as he could. There were lots of men between him and the guards, and he thought they might not notice him if he moved very slowly, screening himself with the men in front of him. Yes, he felt shitty about that.

I didn't come all this way to lie down and die in some fucking field in Belgium.

He thought of his big brother dying on that beach in the Pacific (he still couldn't remember the name of the damned place) and he wasn't going to go down easily.

"Halt! Hände Hoch!"

The voice almost made Marsh shit. There was a Kraut guard, SS, right behind him. He had a machine pistol pointed right at Marsh's back, and he screamed in his ear. So much for haulin' ass.

Marsh moved a step away and stared straight ahead.

Just about the same time, the tanks started revving up their engines. The field filled with diesel fumes. All the tanks and some of the half-tracks started to move out down the road toward Ligneau-ville. It was very cold and damp, with mushy snow all over the field and mud everywhere. But the air was still, and the fumes of the tanks just hung in the air all around the prisoners. A few GIs started coughing. As soon as the main tank force was on its way, a half-track moved in along the road almost on top of the field. There was a seventy-five millimeter cannon mounted on it, and the gunner was lining up the muzzle right at the prisoners. Point blank range.

Marsh thought, oh fuck, here it comes.

Now there was a machine pistol at his back and some Kraut asshole was going to fire that big cannon right into the center of the mass of unarmed prisoners. FUBAR!

One officer jumped down from the half-track, shouting orders, waving his arms to his men. The enlisted men started to load the cannon. The seventy-five millimeter shell looked like a monster to Marsh. But what really scared him was that he saw the German guards, the SS who were in the field, including the one behind him, start to drift away and climb over the fences onto the road. They took up positions around three sides of the field, but were now out of the range of fire of each other and the seventy-five millimeter cannon.

The cannon—a totally inappropriate overkill weapon for close combat—was aimed over the heads of the prisoners, but the Germans were slowly depressing the muzzle. Then it stopped. It was still too high, the mechanism set so it could not be lowered any further. The German officer got very agitated and started yelling at the men on the half-track. They scrambled around a bit, but they still couldn't lower the muzzle enough to aim it at the prisoners.

Thank God.

Marsh knew they all should have started running right then and there. At least some of them would get away. But they didn't. There was no command structure. No one to give orders. No plan.

Finally, the officer shouted a few more commands, and moved the armored personnel carrier further back down the road. The Germans tried again. But the cannon muzzle was still a little too high. Now the half-track was blocking the road. The tankers and drivers of the other half-tracks were yelling at him. So, the officer jumped up into the vehicle and drove off. He was laughing as he disappeared out of sight after the tanks.

By that time, it was getting cold standing there, and Marsh's shoulders were killing him. They all still had their hands up over their heads. Until then, Marsh was focused on the muzzles of all the weapons pointed his way. He could see a slow motion preview in his brain of slugs coming out of those black holes and slamming into his chest. Like watching the movies back home.

He could barely keep his hands up for the pain. There was no reason to keep them standing that way, but the Germans were brutal whenever a hand came down even a little.

One man in the row to Marsh's left lowered his hands to right angles. A guard just shot him point blank in the face. Several men were beaten with rifle butts for talking or moving too much. The guards pantomimed that they were going to shoot if the prisoners lowered their hands, so pain or not, they all held them high.

Marsh had no idea how long he stayed like that. Another Kraut half-track passed by. The officer shouted at them, laughing. His English was nearly perfect.

"It's a long way to Tipperary, boys!"

A real joker.

There was some movement from the café. An older man came out the front door of the battered stone building. Marsh recognized him from the couple of times he stopped in there going to and from the front. Funny, he thought, how sometimes he would take a break at that café and have some terrible coffee for a few minutes to pretend there was no war. The man was always friendly enough to him, but Marsh suspected he was friendly to whoever had the guns at the time.

The man was dressed in a shabby blue coat, threads hanging from the sleeves, holes patched here and there. His head was bare.

The man walked up to an SS officer and began chatting away. It was as if they were out for a winter stroll. Old buddies. If a time ever came to get back here, Marsh promised himself, he was going to remember that man.

Then the door opened again, and the old lady, the one who owned the café, came out, too. She just stood there for a while looking around. Finally, she went up to a Kraut guard and led him away. Marsh could see them disappear behind the café and head toward a tumbledown shack that was barely standing up a few yards behind the café itself. He couldn't see what happened next, but the old lady came back, followed by two GIs with their hands held high, and the guard prodding them along with the machine pistol.

That bitch must have seen those GIs hide in the shed, and she told the fucking Krauts. I can't fucking believe it. If I only had a gun, I kid you not, I'd blow her away, right here, right now. I mean, we're here trying to free her fucking country. Jesus!

About this time, a few of the GIs fell to the ground. There were no shots, so Marsh thought they had been wounded earlier, or maybe they were playing dead. A medic who was with B Battery knelt down, and rolled one GI over onto his back. Marsh had never seen him before, but he knew the man was a medic because he had a red cross painted on each side of his helmet, and a red-cross armband on each arm, and he had kept his medical pack during the whole ordeal. The medic opened the kit and started to take out dressings and sulfa packets. Marsh couldn't figure out how the Germans had let him keep the kit this long, but apparently they had missed it. There were, after all, more than a hundred prisoners, and they had been drifting into the field in small groups for some time. The guy on the ground was bleeding from a gut wound, now staining the whole front of his coat. He must have been hit in the initial ambush and made it to the field.

The medic was plugging the wound and doing what he did best when a Kraut came into the field and walked up behind him. He put the muzzle of the gun to the back of the medic's helmet. Marsh could hear the little tick of metal on metal. The Kraut gave it a little shove, which pushed the helmet askew because the chinstrap wasn't fastened.

The medic slowly raised his hands and froze. The Kraut thumbed a switch on the machine pistol. Marsh thought he was putting on the safety. But he wasn't. He flicked the machine pistol to single fire and shot the medic through the head. The man tumbled down on top of the wounded GI and never moved again. The Kraut shoved the body aside with his boot, and put two shots though the dying GI's chest. Then he walked back out to the road.

Marsh was trying hard not to vomit. He was afraid if he did, they would shoot him, too. It wasn't the sight of the wounds or the deaths that got to him. It was the complete callousness of the act. The indifference. That Kraut might have been squashing a mosquito for all he seemed to feel. No, it was worse than that: he enjoyed it.

He fucking enjoyed it!

What happened next seemed to happen all at once, though Marsh knew even as it happened that there was a sequence to it. Still, it all crowded together in his mind as a single event.

One of the APCs pulled up close to the field at the southern end, the end farthest from Marsh and the café, which was right at the crossroads. The SS officer who had been speaking to Peiper stood up in the back and chambered a round in his nine millimeter pistol. He took careful aim. Marsh could see a slight grin on the officer's face. At first, Marsh thought he was trying to scare them again, but then he saw the flash of the twin lightning bolts on his collar: SS.

The officer fired three times in rapid succession, and three men in the front rank fell down. Almost at the same instant several of the APCs opened up with machine guns. Men were falling everywhere, all around Marsh. There were screams of pain and different screams too: screams of fear. After so long in battle, Marsh could actually tell them apart.

A lieutenant from B Battery, still with his hands up, yelled, "Stand fast! Don't run!" He must have thought that the Germans were only shooting prisoners who were running. But, they weren't. They were shooting everyone. It was a massacre.

The running and the panic continued. The screaming went on. Men were calling for their mothers, for God.

The Germans continued to shoot and shoot and shoot. How long? Marsh hadn't any idea. As soon as the first wave of men crumpled, he ran toward the trees between the field and the café. He wasn't going to head for that shed, but there was the most cover in that direction, and he knew there were culverts and shacks and places to hide. It was also the shortest route out of the field, away from the firing. If he made it that far, and they didn't find him by dark, he might have a chance of getting to Malmédy.

So Marsh ran. All the time he could hear the shouting and the screaming and the cries of pain and terror; he could hear the pistols and the automatic weapons. But, over all of that, what he remembered most clearly, what he would remember forever, were the voices of the Germans. They were laughing.

Chapter Twenty-three

18 December 1944, 0200 Hours
Baugnez Crossroads, near Malmédy, Belgium

Marsh was shivering badly, soaked completely through his clothing with snowmelt and mud. He could feel the cold grit of the mud rubbing the already sore spots where his clothing had let in the water and dirt. He hadn't moved in hours. When he crawled down into the culvert, he pulled a pile of debris over himself. He tried to cover everything, even his head. He lay in the culvert, less than a hundred yards from that terrible field. The café was just out of sight beyond the trees. He definitely wasn't going in that direction.

After the shooting started, Marsh had scrambled out of the field as fast as he could. The man in front of him, the one who was nearly shielding Marsh from the sight of the German guards, had turned to run at the same time Marsh did. The man was big, but fast and strong. He actually gained on Marsh and, in less than ten yards, was coming up on Marsh's back. Then Marsh heard a cry from right behind his ear, and at the same moment, there was terrible pain in his back. It ripped right up alongside his spine, just to the left. He felt the whole weight of the man's body slam into his back, nearly toppling him. Marsh turned in time to see the man slip to the ground and roll onto his back, his chest a mass of exit wounds no one could survive. He had almost climbed up Marsh's back to get away from the Germans, and Marsh realized all at once that the man had shielded him from the volley of bullets; the ones that had struck Marsh in the back had passed through the man first and then into him. The only reason he wasn't lying beside the now dead man in that field was that the bullets had spent all their energy going through the GI's body, tearing the life out of the man and having little energy left for Marsh. He had no idea how many bullets had struck him or how seriously he was wounded.

Thinking back from the relative safety of his culvert, it seemed as if he had stood there, over the man, figuring it all out, but he hadn't. Marsh never even broke stride, only glanced at the body, but kept stumbling and running. The farther he got from the field, the stronger he felt. Each step that took him further out of range and out of sight of those Kraut bastards gave him more determination to get away. But, the pain was worsening, and he knew how close he had just come to being spine shot. God knows he had dragged a lot of those poor bastards out of the foxholes and back to the hospitals only to later learn they would be paralyzed for life.

He clambered past the tree line to the northwest of the village and dodged across the little farm trail that led to the Malmédy Road. But he didn't dare go any farther. The Krauts were sure to send a patrol to search that road, which was the fastest route to the American lines. If there were any lines by then.

Marsh managed to get down into the culvert just as darkness was settling in. As the water wicked its way into his clothing, the heat seemed to evaporate from his body. At first he was lying in slush, but in a few minutes his body heat had melted the snow and slush all around him. It would have been better if it were ten degrees colder. At least then the water would have stayed frozen, and Marsh wouldn't have gotten wet inside his clothes.

From his little bunker, he could still hear firing. A few times he tried to peek out. His view was framed by the curved top of the culvert and his own chest at the bottom. It was like looking through a Kaleidoscope. Each time he moved his head to get a better picture, there was distortion in another edge of his view. He could never quite get everything at once. There didn't seem to be anyone coming to scour the trees in front of where he had hidden, but he could just make out figures, dark shadowy shapes, moving into the field. Only moaning and pitiful sounds came from the massacre site.

Massacre site. He finally had to say it to himself. For that's what it was.

Those fucking Krauts just murdered a hundred or more unarmed prisoners. My guys.

He didn't know how many made it out of the field, but it couldn't have been more than a dozen. Maybe twenty, tops.

As he peeked to see if he were still in danger of being discovered, Marsh saw the shadows again, moving among the bodies. He could only see part of a person at a time, and he was afraid to move too much because he knew from his own hunting days that movement will give your position away faster than anything else. That's why, he knew, rabbits and deer freeze when they feel threatened.

He couldn't see color or detail, but there was enough light to see the long gray coats and military caps of the SS. They walked casually among the bodies, kicking and prodding with their boots. Every few minutes there was an answering cry or sob, and then the unmistakable metallic click of a round being chambered. Then a single shot. They were shooting the wounded. They were killing every living being who had survived the initial machine gunning.

Marsh pulled himself down deeper into the water and made himself as small as he could. Then he just lay there, shivering. Finally, for the first time since the D-Day landing, he began to cry.

Sometime after midnight, Marsh heard what he hoped was the last of the trucks and APCs rev their engines and take off down the road south toward Ligneauville. Away from him. Away from Malmédy. In the stillness of that long winter night, he could hear the voices of the SS as they rode away. He couldn't understand the words, but the voices were of men who might have just left a party. It was again the unmistakable sound of laughter and camaraderie.

Marsh remained in the culvert for a while longer. For some reason he had stopped shivering, and had cried himself out as well. Now, he had to find a way back to his lines. He knew the road to Malmédy was probably his best bet. But, the Allies were retreating, and he didn't even know who held that road anymore. He didn't trust the Belgians now any more than the Germans. He knew that, at least around the crossroads, the Belgians would sell him out in a minute to keep the Krauts out of their hair. He saw that when that bitch snitched on the GIs hiding in her shed.

So, Marsh took one more careful look around him and decided that this was the best time to haul ass again. It was just after two in the morning. He climbed up out of the culvert and made his way along the shoulder of the farm trail toward the road. He walked in a crouch, in part for concealment and in part to keep warm. His muscles were cramped and sore, and he found himself staggering. No way could he outrun anyone. The pain in his back was starting to return as he warmed up. First, it was throbbing up and down the whole course of the left side next to his spine. In minutes, it was just a steady horrible stabbing. He felt wetness back there, but in the dark he couldn't tell if he was still bleeding or just wet from the culvert slush. He didn't know how much blood he had lost, but he was very weak. His vision was blurring, and he could feel his heart racing. When he began to shiver and sweat, he realized he was going into shock, just like the hundreds of men he tended to in the field. But, there would be no medic coming to his aid. He could not call out, "Corpsman!" and wait for help. He was on his own.

He prayed that he wouldn't collapse at the side of the road to become just another body like the thousands he had seen over the last six months. If he did, he hoped somebody would take his dog tags so his parents would know what happened to him.

He made his way across the first side road and then alternately crept and staggered toward the road to Malmédy. Before he came to the road, he turned left, keeping about a hundred yards between himself and the road; just enough to keep the road in sight and allow him to parallel its course without actually walking on the road itself. He didn't want to run into any Germans. Also, he knew from his trips back and forth that there were plenty of shacks and barns for him to hide in between there and Malmédy.

By about three in the morning, he was getting dangerously weaker. His vision was blurring, and he was shaking badly. He still couldn't tell if it was from the cold or the blood loss or both. But, he knew he might be dying. He talked to himself to keep awake and to pass the time. Then he became frightened, thinking he was going mad. Then he told himself that if he were going nuts, he wouldn't know it, so that being scared about going nuts was good. This all was very confusing.

Just about then, Marsh saw a barn, and he headed for it. He didn't want to collapse out there in the open, and he knew for sure that collapse was not very far off.

And he was right.

He made it into the barn, but he didn't make it into the hayloft.

The farmer and his wife found him lying in the mud and manure of the barn floor at the foot of the ladder to the loft. There was blood on the ladder half way up, so they surmised that he had tried to climb and fallen. They carefully carried him back to the house, hiding him there for three days. He woke up off and on for the first two days, enough for them to get some hot soup into him, and then on the third day he came around.

Their daughter, Nicole, was twenty-three. She was the only child of the farmer and his wife. She had married when she was very young, only seventeen, much against her parents' wishes. Her husband had run away to avoid the war, and they had not heard from him for more than a year.

Nicole had been strong-willed and defiant since a little girl. When Marsh was found in the barn, it was she who persuaded her parents— her mother most of all—who feared for their safety, to hide the young American from the Bosch.

"They will kill him," she pleaded.

"And they will kill us for hiding him," her mother said.

"But we aren't hiding him," her father said, now convinced by her pleas. "We found him in the barn, n'est-ce pas?"

"And if they don't believe us? What then?" the mother argued.

The father sighed, exasperated. "I'm not going to send that boy back to the Germans. That's final!"

They carried Marsh into the house, where Nicole insisted that he be placed in her bed. It was the warmest room in the house, backing onto the rear stones of the fireplace in the main room.

Several times a day, Nicole washed Marsh's wounds with strong soap and hot water. She bandaged him with shreds of her own clothing torn into strips and boiled to sterilize them. Then she piled as many quilts as she could find on top of him. He woke in a stupor at each dressing change, the pain just enough to penetrate his clouded brain. Then he fell back to sleep until the next time.

On the third night, a storm front passed through. In the aftermath of the wind and a short snow squall, the temperature dropped far below freezing. Even the fire in the main room could not stave off the chill that permeated the house.

Marsh rolled onto his back and cried out. He tried to change his position, but he was held fast by something. He could not struggle free. He could not, for some reason, move his arms at all. From down in the depths of sleep he forced his consciousness to focus. Had he been captured again? Was he tied up by the fucking Krauts?

He struggled some more. Slowly, as his eyes opened and focused, he was aware of the loosening of his restraint. Before he could see in the darkness of the room, he could hear a soft sound in his ear.

"Shhhhh. Shhhhh," she said. "Tais toi. Ne bouges pas." Marsh didn't understand the words.

When he felt fully awake, he found himself staring into the dark eyes of a young woman. She held her arms tightly around his chest, hugging him protectively to her. Marsh could make no sense of it. He relaxed, in part because he was so weak that it was doing no good to resist, but also because struggling only served to increase the pain in his back.

He took a breath and looked down. Only then did he notice that, except for the bandages swathing his chest, he was naked. As was she, whoever she was. She was talking to him now, quietly reassuring him in soft words in a language he knew must be French, but he could not understand.

Nicole was telling him to lie still, that he was safe. As she whispered, he was aware of the smell of her hair near his face. It was the first clean scent he could remember for months. He pulled back a few inches more. Without needing to look, he was aware that he was pressed against the naked body of this young woman. He could feel himself pressed against the warmth of her pubic hair, and it startled him. He nearly laughed (the first laugh in God-only-knew how long) as he felt himself becoming erect. He was embarrassed and tried to pull back, but Nicole held him tightly, pulling him gently nearer, pressing herself still harder against his penis.

Marsh could not take his eyes away from hers. He stared deeply, wondering, Who is this woman? Is this a dream? Am I dead?

This was not something that happened in Marsh's world.

Before he could process the answers, he felt her hand slide beneath the quilt and take his now fully erect penis, guiding it between her legs and into her wet vagina. She moved enough to let him enter her without his having to move, then rolled him gently back and climbed on top of him. She rocked softly back and forth, gently testing the limits of his pain. Soon they had found a rhythm that pleased them both and took them far from the war for just a few minutes.

When they had both come she pulled his body snugly to her, keeping him still inside her. The two fell into a light sleep, waking from time to time to share a kiss.

When the morning sun broke through an opening in the curtains, Marsh found himself alone in the bed. He looked around the room for the woman, but there was no one within sight. He knew then it had been the dream of a badly wounded man clinging to one of the recurring fantasies of his age.

But then he reached beneath the covers and found that his penis and pubic hair were matted and stuck to the covers. He frowned, then smiled. A wet dream? Either he was going nuts, or he had battle fatigue. That, or the war had just taken a turn for the better.

While Marsh was thinking about the miracles of life, the farmer sent Nicole to fetch help. She bicycled all the way to Malmédy. There she met up with the Allies, and they put her bike in a jeep. She brought the medics and a few armed GIs back to the farm, less than a mile from Baugnez Crossroads. Marsh had made it no further.

As the medics carried him out to the truck on a stretcher, he passed the young woman standing in the main room of the house. She was bundled in a ragged overcoat, a shawl still wrapped around her head against the cold.

Is she my dream? Marsh wondered. Was this the angel who gave me my life?

He could not recognize her in the bright light of day and the heavy clothing. He was bursting to ask her, but what could he say? What went through his mind almost made him laugh.

Hey, lady. Excuse me, but did we do it last night?

Just as he was passing through the door, Marsh looked over his head one last time. His eyes met the now upside-down face of Nicole, who looked quickly around the room then, with her eyes locked on his, she smiled, pursed her lips, and blew him a kiss.

Much later, Marsh couldn't remember anything he might have said to that family. He hoped he remembered to thank them. They had taken a hell of a chance for him. He knew there were a lot of civilians who did that throughout the war. Not all the civilians were like that bitch at the café.

With little ceremony, the GIs thanked the family and loaded Marsh into a truck, bringing him to the hospital at noon on the third day. They left the family what few food rations they carried.

Marsh could remember a bit of the trip back to Malmédy. His back hurt like hell, and he was running a high fever. They pumped him full of penicillin and some blood (his count was very low) and then his doctors, Hammer and Schneider, operated on him together. They didn't assist each other too often at that point in the war, but Marsh was a VIP to them. He received very special treatment.

Marsh remembered having felt about three or four bullets hit him in the back. Hamm showed him eleven slugs he took out of the muscle next to the spine. The incision was eighteen inches long. Marsh knew that the guy in back of him took the brunt of it. His death had saved Marsh.

After surviving eleven slugs in the back, Marsh felt indestructible. Hamm put him in for a Bronze Star and, of course, the Purple Heart. However, it would be some time before he would actually see the medals.

"You're going to be sent to the rear to recover, pal," Hamm said. "Should be a piece of cake."

"I hope it's Paris," Marsh said, "and not some shitty-ass tent city in the boonies. I mean, I'm gonna need some rest, but I'm not a litter case. Paris might be just the thing."

Hamm and Schneider smiled and shook their heads. That was Marsh, all right.

Marsh told his story over and over again. He needed to say it out loud. Every detail of the terrible massacre was etched into his memory, never to be forgotten.

"I never thought I'd get out of that field alive," he told Antonelli. They had so much firepower trained on us. And they thought it was one big joke! Those fuckers, if I ever get the chance…."

Antonelli said, "You'll do what? Shoot a bunch of prisoners? Murder some civilians? Maybe a few kids and their mothers? What the hell are you talking about, Andy. You don't even have a gun."

"You weren't there, Gene, so shut the fuck up. There were women and children and babies in that field, I heard. I never saw that part—I was too busy running. But, I heard from the MPs. Babies, they shot."

"Face, it, pal. The Krauts aren't the only ones killing prisoners. I heard our guys shot a whole bunch of German prisoners, too. Right after Malmédy. Twenty-five of them, I heard. So who the fuck are we to talk?"

Marsh was silent. He stared at the ground for a long time.

"What?" Antonelli asked.

Marsh let out a long sigh.

"I miss Dick. If we had been there back then, maybe he wouldn't've gotten killed. Maybe…."

"Andy, he had Major Schneider and Hammer and McClintock and Captain Ferrarro. What could we have done?"

"I don't know. Something. I just wish we'd been there."

When he was on board the ambulance the next day and heading west, Marsh could not stop thinking of the girl. Although he knew neither her name nor her family's, he knew exactly where that farmhouse was. He could have found his way from that killing field to the culvert and on to the farm in his sleep. Actually, he had already found it in his sleep. He could do it again. He would….

When the war is over…he thought as he fell asleep to the rocking of the truck. When this fucking war is over….

Chapter Twenty-four

8 May 1945, 0900 Hours
A Concentration Camp near Weimar, Germany

B erg gazed through the filthy glass of the only window in the room. It was May, and he should have seen sunshine and flowers and the fullness of spring. But his view was smeared and distorted by the muddy window and the cracked glass.

He stood next to the wooden table, his hands clasped in front of his waist. Grau—the SS doctor in charge of the camp—stood at the other side arranging the small tray of instruments. Grau was talking quietly as he laid out the syringes and needles. There was no pretext at sterility, of course. Infection wasn't a problem there. All the patients would be dead at the end of the day.

"I will load these syringes with either phenol or sodium Epivan," Grau said. "Only I will know which is which. A perfect double-blind scientific study. This should appeal to the scientist in you. You will inject directly into the left ventricle and push the whole dose into the heart as rapidly as you can, assuring a massive dose with the least dilution. Do you understand?"

"I can't do this, Sturmbannführer. Please don't make me do this. This is nothing more than murder. I..." Sweat poured down Berg's forehead into his eyes.

"Genug!" Enough! "You will be providing a merciful end for these people. You are saving them from Zyklon B and death in the gas chambers. And if you refuse me one more time, you will take their place, Herr Doktor. Then where will your patients be? Who will care for them?"

Berg's heart ached for the woman lying on his table. Grau was right, of course. These people were all to die in a short while anyway, and this death would be over in seconds if he did it correctly. But if he left it to the Kapos, they would surely botch the job, and the deaths would be agony. In Berg's hands, it would be a mercy killing, though he had sworn an oath never to do such a thing. Or was he just reasoning with himself into saving his own life? Would his survival make it easier for his patients? Did he just want to live one more day? Was he taking the coward's way out? If he died there and then, there would be no doctor to help any of the patients, little though he did for them. And the killing would be left to the butchers. For better or for worse, he committed himself to going through with this awful act.

Berg took the syringe from Grau and felt for an opening between the lower ribs just to the left of the sternum. It was easy to find, for there was no muscle and scarcely any flesh left on the poor woman's bones. Berg smiled at her. She looked into his eyes and nodded. She knew what was happening, and she was pleading silently for him to do it quickly, painlessly.

Berg took a deep breath, then plunged the long needle between the ribs and into her heart, pulling back on the plunger as the tip found its way into the left ventricle. Bright red blood flooded back into the syringe. He could feel her heart muscle beating against the needle's shaft. The woman squeezed her eyes shut against the pain of the needle irritating the heart muscle. Berg forced the plunger with his palm, rapidly emptying the contents into her heart. The woman shuddered for a moment and then her breathing stopped. There was no convulsion this time, so perhaps it was the Epivan for her, and not the phenol. A double-blind study indeed! Idiot!

Berg could smell the odor of urine and feces as her sphincters relaxed in the agonal moment of her death. He removed the needle gently from her heart, almost as if he believed he could spare her any more pain by the gentleness of his technique. Grau was smiling, nodding fractionally, pleased with the performance of his star surgeon, Jew though he might be. Grau wrote a few words in a little notebook, the results of his "experiment." Then, abruptly, he shouted to the Kapo at his side and the body was exchanged for the next patient.

The Kapos were prisoners chosen by the Germans to act as petty administrative functionaries. But over time they far exceeded their duties, for some reason becoming more and more egregiously brutal. It puzzled Berg that these men, mostly Jewish prisoners, could forsake their people so cruelly. He had many run-ins with them when trying to protect his patients. It usually ended badly for Berg or for the patient. Kapo Stein was among the worst. His presence in the hospital made Berg's skin crawl.

And so the day began, not to end until well after darkness. Grau left shortly after midday, but Berg was required to continue as the detested Kapos brought in body after body. Some died easily enough, though several suffered in their last moments on this earth, and Berg died a little with them.

Finally, the last patient was placed on the table. Berg lost count of how many he had executed; he still saw it that way, not as a mercy killing, but as an execution in which he was a willing participant. There had been many, and there would be more in the days to come.

He took up the last loaded syringe and began to palpate for the space between the ribs as he had done all day long. It was the action of an automaton. He was lost in his movements. He tried hard to treat each condemned inmate as a patient, showing them kindness and sympathy as he prepared them for death. He would struggle to maintain his humanity even in the face of such egregious barbarity until the final execution of the day was over.

Berg looked down at the patient as he had done all day long. He was determined not to let a single person go to his or her death without looking deeply into their eyes and recording the person's face, nor without transmitting to them the knowledge that their death had been noted and recorded. As he prepared this one last time, his own heart felt as if it had stopped. The pain could not have been worse had he inserted the long needle into his own ventricle and pushed the plunger down himself. Indeed, he thought for a moment that he should.

Berg started to speak, but his voice caught in his throat until he thought he would choke.

The man looked into Berg's eyes and smiled. He said simply, "Mein sohn."

"Vater!" he said, still choking on his words.

Berg was staring into the eyes of the dearest man on earth. Until that moment he had no idea what had become of his father, though he heard that he had been transported some years after he, himself, had been taken to the camps. How long had his father been here? Had he been within Berg's sight for days, months, years? If he had known, could he have made his father's life more bearable? Could he have saved him from the awful evil of that place? From even death?

"Father," Berg said again. But, he didn't know where to go. "Mother? Is she here too?" he finally managed.

The twinkle that appeared in his father's eyes when he first saw Berg's face vanished as Berg asked the question. He shook his head sadly and whispered, "She's gone, my son. Dead. We were in another camp, worse than this one. They sent me here two days ago. "

Berg looked at this living skeleton who had once been his father. He barely knew the man, except for the soulful dark eyes. Like all the others in the camp, he was gaunt and wan. His skin was so thin Berg could see the small vessels underneath. His eyes protruded under their lids, and when he took Berg's hand in his, Berg had to take care not to crush the frail bones. This was not his father. Not the one he knew all his life. Only when he looked into his eyes again was he sure it was truly the same man.

Berg squeezed his father's hands lightly. Tears flowed for the first time in so long that at first he didn't know what was happening. Crying was a luxury long gone from his repertoire of emotions.

Then from nowhere, Berg felt a stab of pain in his kidneys as the Kapo shoved his billy club into Berg's back.

"Beeilen Sie sich!" he shouted. Hurry up!

Without any thought, Berg wheeled at the Kapo and drove his fist into the man's face. Although, it was a weak and ineffective gesture, the man did stagger backwards, surprised by the attack. But Berg had no follow through. He was weak and pitifully ill equipped to fight. He realized he had never struck another human being in his life before that moment.

The next thing Berg felt was the club landing across his face, his knees buckling as he went down to the floor. Several more blows landed across his back and neck and arms. He cowered there on his knees, keenly aware of his pathetic inability to offer the least resistance, waiting for the storm of punishment to pass. Or better still, for death to intercede.

Then, he was hauled to his feet and thrust back to his father's side. Two Kapos were there now, pushing him back to the table. It was Stein who had bludgeoned him. Always Stein there to do the bidding of the Nazis. Berg could have killed him without a second thought. How impotent he felt with no weapons of any use, not even his own soft hands.

His father was weeping quietly now, unable to speak, unable to tear his eyes away from Berg's rapidly swelling face and broken nose. Blood trickled from Berg's nostrils. He wiped it away carelessly on his sleeve like a little boy crying in front of bullies. He turned back to his father.

"Do it, my son. Quickly. Please!" his father begged, his voice hoarse with terror.

"I can't, father. I can't," Berg told him.

But Stein was there with his club.

"You have your orders, Herr Doktor Berg, our famous surgeon from Munich. Or I can start breaking this old fool's bones instead! Do it now!" he screamed in Berg's ear. "Or I shall do it for you."

Stein waved his club over the old man's head. His father winced in terror, though Berg could see him struggling to be brave.

"All right! Enough!" Berg shouted at Stein with a force that actually made Stein take a step backward and assume a defensive stance with his club.

"I'll do it," Berg said in a choked whisper, hoping it would prevent any further attempt to terrorize his father or possibly injure Berg so badly that he would be unable to help the dear man to a more merciful death.

Berg stepped up to the tray, his hands shaking. He found the vial that he knew by now to contain the sodium Epivan, trying at the very least to spare this sweet frail man the agony of the phenol. He could barely get the needle into the vial until he saw his father's face.

The man was serene, his eyes closed. Though he was not smiling, all fear was gone. A resignation—no, more a look of release—emanated from him. His lips were moving, and though he made no sounds, Berg could see he was reciting the most sacred of Jewish prayers, the Shema

Yisroel. Berg recited along with him, his words aloud in synchrony with his father's silent prayers.

Shema Yisroel...Hear O Israel...

Berg felt for the space between the emaciated ribs.

Adonai Eloheynu...The Lord our God...

To Berg's surprise, he could feel his father's heart beating quietly and slowly beneath his fingers. No panic-driven rhythm. Only calmness. A serenity.

Adonai Echod...The Lord is One.

Although Stein fought and railed against him, Berg prevailed on the other Kapos to allow him to bathe and clean his father's body. He had wrapped the old man in one of his two remaining lab coats (there were no clean sheets anywhere to he found) and he managed to say the Kaddish over the body with a minion composed of patients gleaned from the few men on the ward still capable of standing long enough to utter a prayer. Berg hoped to get permission to bury his father himself when Grau or Himmel returned to the hospital.

Berg fell asleep in his chair that night. At precisely 0800 the next day, he still was in his chair when Standartenführer Himmel walked into the room. He cocked his head to one side and said, "Guten morgen, doktor. A terrible night for you, I heard."

Berg nodded. It was no surprise that word had gotten to Himmel. He knew everything that went on in the camp.

Berg could only sigh. Words were beyond him.

"This may bring you some comfort then," he said. "Kapo Stein will join his relatives today."

Berg's mind was confused and muzzy, without any reference as to what Himmel meant.

"Yes, Stein will be gassed with the eight o'clock group this morning. He is on his way to Oven Number One as we are speaking."

Berg should have rejoiced, shouted, smiled. But, it meant nothing to him. Kapos had a short life expectancy anyway. After a few months, they knew too much or enjoyed too much power, so the SS generally gassed them with some regularity. It didn't really affect the rest of the camp one way or the other.

But his own beating at Stein's hands and the news of Stein's death that morning as punishment were nothing compared to what Himmel said next. Himmel told Berg that he was sorry to hear about his father. Berg would never forget the way Himmel looked at him: there was the hint, just the hint of a smile, the suggestion of sympathy. But, there was also an ambiguity, an unexplained nuance that would haunt Berg every day for the rest of his life. And he was sure it was deliberate.

"Herr Berg," Himmel said, touching him lightly on the shoulder, "Why didn't you just come to me? Why didn't you say something?"

Then he shook his head in mock sorrow and walked slowly from the room.

Chapter Twenty-five

8 May 1945, 1200 Hours
Field Hospital Charlie-7, Leipzig, Germany

B y the time the biggest and bloodiest battle of the war—soon to be known as the Battle of the Bulge—was over, the Americans had suffered almost 90,000 casualties, with nearly 20,000 dead. With that terrible part of the winter war now almost six months behind them and little more than a terrible memory, life was again actually becoming a little boring at the field hospital. There had not been much in the way of fighting for several weeks. They had reached Leipzig now, deep into the heart of Germany, only a little more than two hours south of Berlin. The medical teams were used to losing so many soldiers in such a short time that any lull in the fighting seemed like peacetime.

And Marsh was back, though God knows how he managed to prevent getting shipped home after such a terrible injury. But he was the same Marsh they had all grown to love and admire.

Pockets of resistance remained, but the troops encountered none of the massive assaults they had met in Belgium near Bastogne last winter. Once the Allied armies had crossed the Rhine, everyone knew it would not be long before the war was over.

Schneider and Hamm were writing notes on some post-op patients. "Rumor has it that Patton publicly pissed in the Rhine to show his contempt for the Nazis." Schneider said.

"I wish I'd been there to see that," Hamm said.

"With the Russians coming from the east, and our guys moving in from the west, the Krauts are pretty well surrounded by now," Schneider said.

"And they are a pathetic bunch. So much for the Master Race and the Thousand Year Reich," Hamm mused.

"They'll all wish they'd surrendered to us when the Russians arrive. Rumors are they're damned brutal."

Hamm nodded.

"Some of those German kids I hear," Hamm said, "they're just reaching puberty! Who's sending them out to fight?"

"They're all that's left. So much for the great Reich," Schneider said.

"They're so pathetic. But, I could also cry for them." Hamm said.

Schneider thought for a moment, and then went on. "The scuttlebutt is that Hitler married his mistress a few days ago. Eva Braun, I think her name is, and then they committed suicide in his Berlin Bunker. As of now it's still scuttlebutt, but if it's true, I'm actually sorry to hear it. I'd have liked a little revenge, and it would have been nice to take that son-of-a-bitch alive."

The men were war-weary and anxious to get home. For days the rumors flew that this or that army had surrendered. Or that they had not.

Most of the surgery was on German prisoners now, and most of those were old men and children. They saw few SS prisoners, either because the SS were fighting to the death, or because the Allies weren't taking too many SS prisoners alive. Nobody lost much sleep over that. Hamm felt sorry for the old guys he saw in uniform. They were too old to be of much use to anyone, and they surrendered as soon as they saw a GI with a gun...or even without a gun. One group even surrendered to Antonelli. The most dangerous things he carried were some morphine Syrettes. He didn't know what to do with the prisoners, so he just led them back to some MPs and turned them over. He looked like the Pied Piper.

"In some ways it's sad to see the German army reduced to old men and teenagers," Hamm said. "Their guns are dirty and rusted, and their uniforms look like something out of a Bill Mauldin *Up Front* cartoon.

"Then there are the German civilians. They were just as pathetic. Half of them claimed to have never heard of a Nazi."

Schneider scowled as he spoke. "Yeah, 'What's a Nazi?' Imagine that!' Phhh! I had more respect for the ones who at least admitted what they were and surrendered to history. But these others: 'Nazis? Where? Who?' Like they'd been asleep for the last five or ten or fifteen years. Well, I'm not going to lose any sleep over them either, and I certainly won't waste my good time hurrying to their aid. It doesn't bother me one bit," he added.

But it did bother Hamm. He was uneasy with their diminishing sense of humanity toward their patients, Nazis or not. Schneider was more sanguine. He had lost that sense of obligation to come to the aid of the sick and injured. He was drawing lines in his mind, making categories.

Then, of course, there was the other big question: Where would they go when it was over in Europe? Home? Stay there in Europe? Be shipped to the Pacific?

The Pacific.

"God forbid!" Schneider said to Hamm when the subject came up. "Those Japs really give me the creeps. The things I've heard about the treatment of our prisoners over there make my skin crawl. Of course, the Nazis weren't so great either. I guess seeing them up close is different than the rumors of something unknown like the Japs."

When the German surrender finally came, different people heard about it at different times. At Field Hospital Charlie-7 they got the news later than most, because their only radio was broken. They finally liberated a German radio, a Kleinfunksprecher, and, though Schneider hated to admit it, it was a fine piece of equipment. At least it worked.

They were all in the mess hall, this time a real room in a real hotel in the center of Leipzig. Schneider was eating alone with Molly, agonizing about their own personal problem now that the end of the war was in sight. The surrender might come at any time. But coming, it was. And with it, the decisions that they both had been talking about for several months.

The question had become an irritant, an interruption in an otherwise fairy-tale romance. That was the whole trouble: It was too much like a fairy tale. Falling in love in a war zone, at the very front battle line, was just not real life. If Schneider had been single or, at least, had no kids, it would have been easy. But he was married, and Anna and Emily were young, and everyone at home was counting the days until Daddy came back to them. Here he was at the front lines of the biggest war in history, in love up to his ears, and longing to spend his life with this woman next to him. This woman who had been through the war with him night and day for nearly a year. Through everything.

Schneider finished his meal and watched Molly as she picked her way through hers.

"We do need to make a decision, you know. It could happen any day. I mean this war is ending," she said.

Schneider lowered his voice, and said, "I love you, Molly, and it wouldn't matter if we were here or in Sheboygan or Gary, Indiana. War or not, I fell in love with you against my better judgment. I know about married men falling in love. It's stupid and self-destructive. And it never works out. And, to tell you the truth, I never thought we both would survive the war. When we were under fire every night back there in France and Belgium, there was no way I thought we could survive. So, I didn't have to think too far ahead. Then when the Germans captured the field hospital and fucking Fuchs took over, my God, who could have believed we would survive. But, here we are, and I'm a hopeless romantic and—"

He stopped and turned his head away from her, trying to collect his thoughts. "I promised myself I wouldn't do this." Then, as if he were taking off one mask and replacing it with another, he turned back and said, "I just don't know, Molly. Maybe I need to go back to the real world and see Susan and the kids before I decide." He actually choked when he said Susan's name. It wasn't lost on Molly.

"I need to go on with my life as if you aren't going to wait for me," he went on. "I can't do anything else. I can't ask you to sit around waiting, hoping I'll come back to you. It isn't Susan's fault, this war. If it hadn't been for Hitler and the Nazis...."

He stopped, not knowing where he was going with this. Once again, his nervous confusion was making him babble. So, he remained silent then, feeling that he had gone too far; that perhaps he might say more than he meant to say. He felt and saw her slipping away from him, moving her heart toward a safer place 'back behind their own lines,' as they used to think of their safe havens from the Germans. It was all too startling to behold in those now darkening green eyes of hers.

"Is that what you really want?" she said, with a cold edge in her voice and a rigidity in her body. She wanted him to tell her that he wanted her so desperately that he would go home and divorce Susan and marry her. Hell, not even marry her but just stay there in Europe and live their lives together. It was a romantic dream, but she had been living a dream for so many months that it was hard to get ready to go back to the real world.

Molly had made the war into something to live for: a dream instead of a nightmare. It was, after all, Steve's fear for her safety that kept him sharp and alert, that made him kill the German patient without a second's hesitation and without any remorse. His only shame was the memory of how much he enjoyed it. Yes, he admitted to himself, and to her, and not without shame, that he actually enjoyed it when that man's larynx snapped. He still regretted that Fuchs had also shot the man. He wanted all of the credit for himself. But now was not the time to go back there.

The two of them sat, numb and mute, staring at the scrubbed wooden table top, when Antonelli burst into the room shouting. All heads turned toward him.

"It's over! It's over! The Krauts surrendered. Eisenhower signed the Nazi's surrender papers in Reims."

He called it Reems.

"Damn! It's officially over!" Antonelli was jumping up and down, hugging everyone within reach. Most of the room burst into cheers and laughter. They all knew it was coming, that the end was really there already. But, hearing it from Antonelli—the perpetual bearer of all news, good and bad—made it real.

Victory in Europe Day! It was over.

Soon all the personnel of the field hospital were pouring into the mess hall. It was noisier than New Year's Eve. They were singing "It's A

Long Way To Tipperary" and "There'll Be a Hot Time in the Old Town Tonight." Two GIs from Montana were singing, "Home on the Range."

Schneider was speechless. He didn't know what to do or say. He just stood there looking at Molly, and she stared back at him. There was no delaying any more. He had to say something. Do something.

Without a word and before he could speak, Molly turned and walked quickly away. Schneider tossed his tray onto the pile of dirties and tried to run after her. But he was caught in a mob of exuberance, of hugs and kisses, back slaps, and more hugs. Marsh was there, messing Schneider's hair, and then even Sorenson managed to lose his perpetual air of seriousness and authority. He was next to Schneider, hugging Mary Doyle, and then Shirley, and Pat, and just about every female who got within reach.

Schneider struggled to break free of the crowd. He tried to get to Molly, fighting his way through the throng of cheering GIs and nurses. But it was hopeless. He found himself carried back into the tent, smothered in a mob of celebrating officers and enlisted men and women. Just about all of his friends in the world were there in that tent with him. But not the love of his life.

He stood high on his toes in time to see Molly fleeing as if she were being chased. She ran as fast as she could, faster than if the Germans were after her. In his heart she was running from him and any life she might have had with him.

She just kept on running.

Schneider pushed and bullied his way back toward the door, accepting hugs and kisses as he went. But he wasn't making any headway. It was like one of those dreams where he was running through molasses, unable to evade a pursuer or catch his prey. The crush and the exuberance were just too great. Finally he surrendered to the crowd as he watched Molly disappear from sight, perhaps from his life.

Out of nowhere, Hamm stepped into his path. His face, and his alone, was as serious as Schneider's. Schneider was puzzled for a moment and he stopped trying to rush after Molly.

"What's up, Hamm?"

"War's over," he said, without a smile or any enthusiasm. "What's up with you?"

"What do you mean?" Schneider said.

"Want to talk to me?"

"About what?"

"C'mon, Steve. It's me, Hamm. Talk to me."

"Yeah. All right." Schneider knew just what Hamm was after. "Not here. This isn't the place right now."

"OK," Hamm said. "Later, pal. Go talk to her, but then come find me. We're all going for a little ride. The whole group."

"Ride? Where to?"

"I had some jeeps and some passes lined up before the news broke. We'll keep the hell away from Berlin and head down toward Prague to have some well-deserved furlough."

"OK. When do you want to go?"

"Soon as we can pack up a few things. I'm going over to post-op and make some rotation assignments. We'll leave a skeleton staff to hold the fort here. Maybe take three or four days, then rotate back and give the others a few days off."

"Right. I'll meet you back at the room. I need to go talk to Molly." Schneider said.

"I know." Hamm said.

"Think she'll come along?"

"I don't know. I was going to assign her to our leave group. Is that what you want?"

"Yeah, I do. Damn me, I really do." Schneider said.

"Well, you better OK it with her first."

They said no more and went in different directions, Hamm to post-op, and Schneider to find Molly. He hated to burst into the nurses' quarters, but there was no other way.

Chapter Twenty-six

8 May 1945, 1300 Hours
Field Hospital Charlie-7, Leipzig, Germany

Schneider headed toward Molly's tent, stopping as infrequently as possible to shake all the hands and share the general good mood of the field hospital. The heavy pall pressing down on his chest, when all the world was celebrating the great day, made him feel as if he alone bore the weight of defeat in his heart.

He got to the tents where the nurses were billeted and found the door open. There was a crowd inside there too, and a real party was going on. He was shocked to see Marsh standing on one of the cots, pouring champagne from a huge bottle. God knows where he got it. He even had champagne glasses. It was like New Year's Eve there, too.

Schneider scanned the crowd, and when he couldn't see Molly, he pushed his way to her cot. She wasn't there. He waded through the crowd again, and a third time, but she was nowhere to be found. Suddenly there was a tug at his sleeve. He turned expecting to find Molly there at his back. But it wasn't. It was Mary Doyle. She pulled Schneider down to her level and said quietly into his ear, "She's out there," and pointed to the rear entrance to the tent. He nodded and started to go, when Mary pulled at him again.

"Careful, Major. Gently."

He nodded to her and squeezed her hand. She squeezed back and smiled. He left the room by the back door.

Almost directly behind the nurses' area was an open field. There at the edge of the field was a stump, and on the stump was Molly. It was an exact replica of that encounter they had so long ago in France when she told Schneider of her husband's death at Pearl Harbor. She was sitting facing away from him again and looking west. This time there was no sunset and no dramatic scene. Just fields, and a lightly overcast sky. It was hard to tell what time of day it was, for the sun was obscured, though the day was bright and a little blustery. Spring in Europe had been wonderful much of the time. The coming of the new leaves and the early flowers; endless fields of something bright yellow, though Schneider had no idea what the crop was; endless rejuvenation following on the heels of death.

Schneider walked up behind her, making enough noise so that he wouldn't startle her. He could see her stiffen. Even without turning around, she knew who it was. Who else would be out there instead of joining the celebration back in the hospital?

"May I join you?" he asked quietly.

She shifted to her left and made room for him on the stump. But she didn't turn around; a bad sign, he thought. Schneider sat down next to her, moving close, trying to feel the warmth and softness that he had grown to love. Molly made no effort to move away, but she wasn't the same. Schneider had become accustomed to her melting into him when they touched, so that their bodies became inseparable, without clear boundaries between them. At that moment, though they touched, there was a subtle demarcation. Again, he didn't like it.

"Molly—"

"Don't talk just yet, Steve. Just sit here for a minute."

That was something, anyway, he thought.

She hadn't told him to beat it or leave her alone, as he had feared she might. No flare of that Irish temper he had seen when anyone, American or German, had gotten between her and her nurses or her and her patients. She never took any bullshit from anyone.

Ex nullo, non feces. She still took no shit from no one.

So they sat there in silence looking into the far distance. Not so different from the thousand yard stares of the shell-shocked GIs they treated. Schneider kept going back and forth between his choices. He had only two, really. He could avow his love for her and his determination to end his marriage to Susan. Or, he would go back to Susan and the kids, and try to start his life over again just the way it was before the war.

But who am I kidding, he wondered? Nothing in the world was ever going to be the same after the war. Nothing.

Schneider had no idea what he really wanted. He was operating out of fear. That much he knew. Divorce was alien to him. But his life with Susan seemed to come from another lifetime. Out here it was different. Lives ended in the blink of an eye. It made every moment precious. Everyone there in the war zone knew how little it took to snuff you out.

There had been a definite loss of spark, of passion, between Steve and Susan over the years, but maybe that was normal. None of his friends talked about their marriages, and he'd never thought about it before. It seemed only reasonable that passion would wane with time. Then Molly came along, and, all of a sudden, he was behaving like a teenager again. He was walking around with an erection every time he saw her or thought about her. And their lovemaking had exceeded his fantasies. He couldn't ever recall feeling that way with Susan, even in the beginning. They met, they courted, and everyone just assumed they were right for each other. Even they had bought into that one. So they married, and that was that. Schneider just couldn't remember the romance, the passion. Was he too sophisticated back then? Too jaded? Was Susan?

Then he wondered again if that were the natural course of things. If he settled into a real life with Molly, would their passion dwindle, too? Would their love-life become routine? He couldn't imagine it at the moment, but who the hell knew?

It wasn't just the sex that concerned him. He was also fearful of the realities of life. He was just starting out in surgery, and all of a sudden he would be saddled with alimony and child support and a new wife who would probably want what his ex-wife had. Molly had never said anything to indicate her own expectations, but it made sense. That one night in Paris was going to be hard to live up to again, what with a busy practice and the expenses.

The world of war just wasn't real. They had been taken out of their normal lives, lives where they had been taught never to kill, and then thrust almost overnight into a daily battle for their lives, living like animals. They were doing the unthinkable and witnessing the unbearable every day and night without letup, and now they were supposed to go back home just because Ike said it was over. Hitler was dead, and there were no more Nazis left to kill. So, it was supposed to be like when he played Ringalevio in the streets back home when he was a kid.

"Fins! Truce! Time to go home for supper." Everyone picks up his marbles and goes home.

So, how do I go home and forget everything that's happened here? Do I tell my family what I did here? What the Nazis did to us? I still haven't come to grips with the joy I got from killing that Kraut. To me, he was less than human and deserved to die. But he was also my patient, under my care and protection. So, what did that make me?

In the silence, Schneider labored under the burden of what had happened since he left home. All the horror and the killing and the pain and the sorrow. They would never understand it back home.

If I go back to Susan, do I confess to her my sins with Molly? Do I keep it my secret, and then find myself fantasizing about Molly while I am with Susan? Or do I go on and make a new life with this woman who shared so much with me here in France and Belgium and now Germany? Is that enough to build a life on? We had an awful lot in common with our work in the operating room. I never really felt that Susan understood what I did when I disappeared into the OR. I tried to get her to come with me one night, but it never worked out.

Ah, Jesus! What a mess.

They sat there on that tree stump for a long time. Schneider wanted so badly to put his arms around Molly and hold her tight. But, he couldn't, and he didn't know if she would have let him. He decided to wait for her to speak. It was a long wait.

"You need to go back, Steve." She finally said.

He had no idea what she meant. Back to the barracks? Back to Susan? Back to where?

"I don't know what you mean, Molly."

"I mean home. Back to your family when this is really over. We're going to be here a while longer. We aren't all going back just because a surrender was signed. I've heard it could be months, maybe years. But, one way or another, at some point, we're going to go home, and home for you is with Susan. And the girls." She paused, but Schneider had nothing to say at that moment, so he waited for her to go on. She took a breath and continued.

"This whole thing...this place...none of it is real. This isn't the real world, and we have to go back to the real world. I've loved what we had here, and I wouldn't take a moment of it back. But, when we get home, this is going to be like a dream, and dreams get forgotten fast."

"Can you just let it go, Molly? Just like that?"

"Isn't that just what you did?!" Her voice was just short of shrill. "I'm struggling, Steve, and you're not helping me. I know this much: I let myself fall in love with you, and I haven't the vaguest idea of who you really are. Nobody is the same out here, and I won't know anything until we're back in the real world again, and neither will you. So, let's just go back to work now, and behave like...I don't know... grownups."

She turned to Schneider for the first time and reached up to touch his face. He lowered his head and closed his eyes because he knew that this was good-bye. She cradled his cheeks in her soft hands and then kissed him on the lips, lightly and without...without something. He didn't know what, but it wasn't the same person who had kissed him the night before. Then she got up from the stump and walked back to the barracks, leaving him sitting there with his head now buried in his hands, and his hands slowly becoming wet with his tears.

Chapter Twenty-seven

9 May 1945, 0700 Hours
Field Hospital Charlie-7, Leipzig, Germany

The next morning, after an early breakfast, the teams loaded themselves into three jeeps and one ambulance truck. Hamm had arranged everything: passes, food, even a few armed infantrymen to accompany them along the way. He was very unconvinced that the ceasefire would hold. And as much as Schneider wanted to believe that the war was over, he was glad to see those young guys with their guns.

Schneider knew he didn't want to, or shouldn't want to, ride in the same jeep as Molly. He grabbed a small pack full of what he expected to need for a few days and started toward the motor pool. Then he saw Molly standing there at the side of the nurses' tents. He was so confused by then that he didn't know whether to hug her or ignore her.

He walked a few steps with her in silence until they were out of sight of the others. Then he melted. He couldn't help himself. He reached out and took her hand, squeezing it as hard as he could without hurting her. He felt as if he were back on one of those side streets in Paris. He could barely take his eyes off her.

However, it was she who spoke first.

"Oh, Steve. The war's over. I still love you, and God knows when we'll be going home."

All his resolve drained away, and he gave in to it all, moving closer, putting his face next to hers and whispering into her ear, "I didn't sleep at all last night."

"Me neither." Her breath near his ear gave him chills right down to his knees.

"I couldn't stop thinking of you," he said. "Every logical bone in my body tells me we have to end this. That I have to go back to work things out with Susan. But it's not what I want to do."

"I know this is not what I'm supposed to say, but just for the record, I cried all night last night."

They lapsed into silence, holding hands, leaning into each other. Back to the starting line. And where this was going to end, he couldn't even imagine. But, he *was* imagining a nice hotel in Prague, if they got that far. It wasn't Paris, but it was a hell of a long way from yesterday.

Then the sun came out, and they both headed off for the jeeps. They climbed into the back seat together, lay their heads back, and felt the warm rays burn into their faces. The jeep jerked into first gear, and they were off. God only knew where they would end up.

Molly slept for a while with her head on Schneider's shoulder. He could feel her fidget from time to time, changing positions and stretching to get comfortable. His arm was getting numb, but he didn't care. He didn't want to move from where he was. He couldn't wait until they got to Prague or wherever they would spend the night. It was such a long time since they had really been alone. Schneider couldn't think of tomorrow or the days after that. For so many months, the war had controlled his thinking, and he had gotten used to taking his life one day at a time.

By noon, they were all weary. The roads were potholed and difficult. The way was studded with destroyed jeeps and tanks and trucks, both German and American. The villages were a horrible sight. There were piles of dirt and wreckage as large as sand dunes. There was hardly a building that wasn't damaged or a window left with glass in it. Corpses of dead horses and cows lay along the road as well, bloated and rotting in the sun, their limbs sticking straight out like upside down table legs.

The smells were grotesque. Mixed with the fresh clean spring air were the horrible odors of rotting flesh, burnt rubber, and scorched metal, as well as a mixture of old cordite and motor oil. Schneider wondered if he would ever get the odors out of his brain. He recalled how sensitive he was to smells of all kinds. As a child he was repulsed somehow by odors that lingered in his family's bathroom: not only the basic smells of bodily functions, but even the smell of fresh toothpaste in the sink. As a surgical resident, he experienced a new genre of human stink; bending over the face of a drunk in the emergency room, he would suture messy facial lacerations as the patient spewed back breath befouled with a combination of alcohol and pungent food, mixed with the metallic odor of fresh blood. It was an experience so engrained in the olfactory centers of his brain that years later he could hardly bear to be too close to anyone who had been smoking or drinking scotch, or bourbon, or rye. Although as a physician, he quickly grew inured to the sight of the destruction of the human body, the smells still evoked a visceral response in his primitive brain, making his gorge rise and his throat gag. The smells of the air on that warm day brought it all back.

Along their way, crowds of Germans greeted their little convoy, begging for food and even medical care. The walking wounded appeared in the streets, stopping the jeeps and trucks when they saw the red crosses on the sides and the hoods. The doctors obliged whenever they stopped, doling out medicines, changing dressings, and making occasional diagnoses right there in the street.

At a small village later in the day, a young boy, perhaps twelve years old, stopped the convoy by hobbling out into their path on makeshift crutches. The arm pads were made of rags, and wool stuffing was coming out at the seams. Hamm stopped the jeep. They all climbed out to see what was wrong. Molly awoke in a groggy haze. The boy lay down in the road in front of the jeep and began to cry. He pointed to his knee, which was bandaged in dirty rags and stained with green pus.

Schneider approached the boy and wondered if they were still inside Germany. He didn't recall crossing any borders, but then again he might have been asleep when they did. The voices he heard were speaking German.

Molly came up alongside Schneider and knelt. She cradled the boy's head in her lap, but the boy still cried. Schneider gently unwrapped the bandages and threw them away into the dusty roadbed. The knee was badly swollen, though there was no sign of a wound. He spoke to the boy in German for a minute, and then turned to Molly and said, "He hasn't injured it, he says. It just swelled up one day a few weeks ago and kept getting worse. Looks like a septic joint to me. Believe it or not, this could be a septic joint from gonorrhea."

"At his age?"

"This is war time, Molly, all bets are off."

Molly continued to hold the boy while Schneider signaled for a medical kit. The driver fetched one from the truck and gave it to Schneider. Hamm came over to help. A crowd of locals had encircled them, making the infantry escort very nervous. There was still almost nothing in the way of law and order in the countryside, and snipers as well as assassins were a real threat. Nobody liked being surrounded by these country people, many of whom carried hoes and rakes. Somehow they were a more menacing rabble in their way than armed soldiers. Seeing this, their own infantry soldiers dispersed the crowd as Schneider treated the little boy.

"Wie heisse Sie?" Schneider asked him.

" Franz," the boy said in a quiet and frightened voice.

Schneider told Franz that there was an infection in the knee and that he was going to drain out the pus. Molly held the boy tighter as he began to sob long before anything was done to him. Schneider didn't take the time to try to find Franz's parents, if there were any, to obtain permission. He just went to work doing what the boy needed.

A man had wandered back to the edge of the road and was shouting something at Franz, who by now was nearly hysterical.

"What did he say, Steve?" Molly asked.

"He's telling Franz to stop crying and behave like a man! What an asshole! Hey, Corporal," Schneider called to one of the infantrymen. "Get that prick out of here, and shoot him if he comes back or tries to interfere with us."

The corporal drove the man back with the butt of his rifle until the man scampered away to the protection of a burnt-out house. Schneider returned to Franz. He now had a giant 100 cc syringe loaded with a number 14 needle—the kind of needle big enough to draw thick pus and the sight of which scares even grown men. Molly took Franz by the face and pulled his head into her chest to keep him from seeing the needle. Schneider quickly stuck the needle into the inflamed knee joint. It was all Molly could do to keep Franz under control. They were out of Novocain, so a quick needle stick was the best Schneider could do. He pulled back on the plunger, and gobs of green pus came oozing slowly back into the syringe. It was amazing to the circle of infantrymen to watch the knee deflate as the pus was pulled out. The syringe was completely full, but the knee still obviously contained a great deal more pus. So, Schneider detached the syringe from the needle while holding the needle carefully in place so as to avoid having to stick Franz again. Just as he squirted the pus out of the syringe and onto the dirt at the roadside, Franz snuck a peek from inside Molly's restraining hand.

Franz saw the needle still in his knee, slowly oozing green pus from the hub, and at the same time he must have seen Schneider squirting the disgusting stuff onto the road. The sight made even Molly swallow a few times; it was just too awful for Franz.

As Schneider was about to reattach the syringe to the needle, Franz let out a terrible cry and struggled to his feet.

"Nein! Nein!" was all Schneider heard as the boy wrenched himself free from Molly's grasp. Molly and Schneider simultaneously grabbed for Franz to stop him, but he was too quick. Even with the needle still in his painful knee and no crutches to help support him, his terror made him faster than anyone could have imagined. He scampered away, knocking Schneider to the ground as he escaped. Then he tore the needle from his knee as he ran. With a dribble of green pus still oozing from the hole in his swollen knee, he ran with amazing speed. His fear must have dulled the pain, for he never hesitated as he went. He climbed a fence at the side of the road then began to run again.

Schneider regained his feet and chased after the boy, with Molly trailing just behind. As Schneider approached the wooden fence, he heard screaming in German and English all around him.

And there it was. A big white sign with black letters and a skull and crossbones:

Achtung! Minen!

"Oh my God! Halt! Halt, Franz!" he shouted. "Minen! Minen!"
The whole crowd—Americans and Germans—were shouting now.

"Stop!"

"Halt!"

"Mines!"

"Minen!"

"Franz, stop!"

"Halt!"

Schneider was shouting, screaming as he ran. But Franz ran as if he never heard a word. His terror of that needle drove him farther and farther away over that terrible field.

Before Schneider could stop her, Molly was over that fence and running after Franz. She seemed to be concentrating on his footsteps, placing her feet where Franz had placed his. But it was hard going, with all the shouting and the confusion and the erratic pattern of the boy's staggering gait. His steps were uneven, but Molly wasn't gaining. Franz had outdistanced her because she was being so careful to step only where he had stepped. Franz was running as fast as he could, oblivious to the danger of the mines.

Above the shouting of the crowd, Schneider called to Molly. He pleaded with her to stop. She turned to look at him as he climbed over the fence and began to follow her path into the field. Molly stopped in her pursuit of Franz and turned back to Schneider.

"No! No, Steve! Go back! Don't come out here!"

But he closed his ears to her pleading. He walked toward her as fast as he dared, eyes fixed on the ground, placing each footstep into hers and Franz's steps as best he could. Then he stopped for a second and looked up. When he looked toward Franz, he could see the boy frozen in his place, now somehow keenly aware of where he had gotten himself. He was like the proverbial deer in the headlights, perhaps fifteen yards ahead of Molly in the muddy field, not a muscle moving, his eyes wide with fear.

Molly was looking back at Schneider as he rapidly closed the distance between them. His eyes must have betrayed the wildness in his brain for she called to him, with an unreal calm in her voice:

"Don't. Don't, my love. I'm OK. I'm OK."

Schneider stopped and settled into the footprints Molly had made for him in her walk across the field. With Franz immobile, he thought, maybe they could get the demolition crews out there to rescue them.

Schneider stood frozen in his place, and Molly in hers. Neither of them dared to move once reality had set in. Schneider couldn't see Franz because he was hidden behind Molly some yards farther into the field. But, since he hadn't heard any explosions, he assumed Franz was standing still, too.

Then he saw Molly's eyes fixed on his as she carefully started to retrace her footprints back toward him.

Although Schneider was more than thirty or forty yards away from Molly, he could see the fear in her eyes, the pleading. She never took her eyes off his, nor he off hers. Franz was on his own now. Schneider had to admit that right now he no longer had another thought for Franz or his safety. Someone else would have to rescue the boy. His mind was entirely focused on getting Molly and himself out of there in one piece.

"Don't move," Schneider said as calmly as the situation would allow. His voice carried over the muddy, cratered field.

Others must have come to grief here, he thought, looking at the jagged craters.

No one outside the field was speaking. They just stared. Although Schneider couldn't see him, he knew that Hamm would not be standing there doing nothing. He was almost certainly arranging some form of rescue by the mine removal squads who were so busy these days.

The trouble was, his was a medical group, and they weren't supposed to go across mine fields. They didn't have any mine removal experts with them. Or anywhere nearby, for that matter. Who knew how long they would have to stand there? It had been only a few minutes, but already his legs were shaking. He could see that Molly was in a half-stand-half-squat, trying to relax her legs as well. Neither of them was doing very well at remaining calm, for the shaking was getting worse.

Schneider tried to look back to the roadside, where the crowd had gathered like spectators at a sporting event. He tried to find Hamm but couldn't see him anywhere. It gave him hope that Hamm might be off organizing a rescue. But not much hope.

The minutes dragged on. Schneider had no idea how long they had been in the field. He tried to get a look at his watch, losing his balance as he did so and actually having to catch himself from falling by moving his foot to regain his balance. He could hear Molly gasp as he did.

His foot hit something hard in the mud, and he was sure it was all over. There was no click, and no explosion, so it must have been a rock or something. Or maybe a dud mine. He would never know. One sound came through to him over the rest, though it was soft and distant. He cocked his head, afraid to turn his body to look. Then it came to him: it was Franz, weeping and sniveling in a low monotone.

Schneider was tiring rapidly, and so was Molly. They didn't speak, each trying to keep focused on maintaining balance and taking no more steps. It was absolutely amazing how hard it was to stand exactly in one spot.

Finally, after what felt like a lifetime, Schneider saw Hamm appear at the fence. He had pushed through the crowd and cupped his hands over his mouth. His voice was calm. Too calm. Schneider knew Hamm all too well, and where his personal calm could still the fears of the most frightened patients, the tone of his voice now—it's total lack of concern or emotions—filled Schneider with fear. Hamm had the surgeon's ability to maintain control in emergencies, a skill that made him incredible in the face of life-threatening trauma and illness. The worse the situation, the more hopeless the injuries, the calmer Hamm became. He would shift gears, and while everyone else was moving faster and faster, too fast for safety, Hamm would slow down imperceptibly to the most efficient rate of action and deal with the trauma in a cold, calculated efficiency that had saved many lives that would otherwise have been lost.

What sent a chill through Schneider now was that he was hearing the very same tone of voice and seeing the totally calm demeanor that Hamm assumed in the face of unthinkable danger. It meant only one thing. The situation was very bad.

"Steve. Molly. Listen to me," Hamm said in that unmistakable voice. "There are no anti-mine personnel anywhere near us now. So here's what you have to do: you need to walk out of that field, one by one. And you need to keep at least thirty yards apart. That means no helping each other. No crowding.

"Steve. Can you hear me?" he asked in the lowest voice that would reach his friend. "Pass this all on to Franz. You need to go first. Retrace your own footsteps exactly. Their weight might have saved them, and yours might be too heavy. You need to go back in your own footprints.

Schneider tried to listen, to interpret the words. But his legs were shaking and his mind could not turn the instructions into action. He was still frozen in place.

"Don't answer me," Hamm went on. "Just do it. Molly, you stay put until Steve is out of the field. Then you go. I don't want you concentrating on Steve while you're walking. Just focus on yourself. I know it's hard, maybe impossible, but you've got to try. No other choice. OK?"

Molly and Schneider nodded. Then Schneider translated what Hamm had said into German for Franz, who only nodded his head, the tears streaming down his cheeks. Schneider turned his body, slowly pivoting in the mud and trying to stay squarely in his own tracks. Then, as he noted the sweat trickling down his back, just as it did in that glider so many months and miles and operations ago, he took a deep breath and studied the terrain. He was about fifty yards from the place he had entered the field. Shorter if he went straight to the fence, but, tempting as it was to take the shorter route, that would be suicide. So, he began.

He examined each footprint. He identified his own from Molly's from Franz's. That wasn't too hard. His were clearly bigger boots and deeper imprints, which gave him no comfort. If these were antitank mines rather than antipersonnel mines, his added weight might not make the difference in setting them off. He didn't know. He didn't wish either Molly or Franz anything bad, but he envied their lightness compared to his own weight.

And so it began. One foot after another. Holding his breath with every shift in weight. It seemed silly to do it that way. If he had to die, it would be better to be quick. Certainly, if he tripped a mine designed to destroy a tank, it should take him out quickly and painlessly. He knew that the antipersonnel mines could be rigged to bounce crotch high before exploding. He had operated on enough poor GIs to know the horrible carnage of those terrible mines.

But, clinging to life is universal, if not logical, so he went along one breath at a time, one step at a time, his life before his eyes every minute of the way. So many thoughts of so many different things raced through his mind as he walked his desperately slow pace. He thought of Molly; he pictured his children and Susan receiving the news of his death; his parents; even the Phillies' opening day.

At least his brain was transported away from that field for split seconds. From nowhere, he thought of the myth of Orpheus and Eurydice. He wanted desperately to turn around and see with his own eyes that Molly was safe. However, he dared not turn, not only for fear of losing his own balance but more from some conviction that, if he turned, Molly, like Eurydice climbing from the depths of Hades, would disappear. Lost forever. He was her Orpheus, and he must not turn to look at her.

After such a thought, he took a deep breath and cleansed his mind, focusing on the next step. And he did not look back.

He placed his heel into the toe-print of his boot, since he was going in the opposite direction from where he had come, and then carefully rocked forward to step into the silhouette of his boot print. He thought about retracing his steps backward to make a perfect print, but ruled that out as too tricky in his exhausted state. Surely if he stayed in the boot print, it didn't matter which direction he was going.

Schneider didn't know how long it took, or how many steps, for he counted one at a time and started at one again after each step. When he was within ten yards of the fence, people began to move back. That was wise, but it didn't make him feel very good. Everyone moved, that is, except Hamm. Hamm waited there at the very edge of the field nearest the fence.

"Don't be a hero, pal," Schneider said quietly. "Move on back."

Hamm looked forlorn, but he saw the logic. He took his sweaty hands off the fence rail and wiped them on his pants. Then he backed away. Not as far as the others, but far enough so that he would probably be safe if Schneider triggered a mine.

The last ten steps were excruciating. Schneider was exhausted and dripping with sweat. One step from the fence remained. He leaned forward looking for another boot print, but there was none. He was puzzled for a moment, looking behind himself at his tracks. He had followed his own path exactly, but somehow he was out of safe stepping spaces. One footprint short. Then it dawned on him. He envisioned himself vaulting the fence in his panic for Molly and flying a good three yards into the field from the top of the fence rail. He had cleared the first several yards in the air. Now there was no map for him to follow back, and he couldn't leap the last few yards from a standstill.

Schneider looked at Hamm for help. His mind was blank. He was out of energy to solve this seemingly unsolvable problem. Who knew what the odds were for a mine so close to the fence? But, he had come this far. Schneider just stood his ground. Hamm moved forward, a puzzled look on his face. He lifted his chin in a silent query.

What is it?

Then Hamm noticed that there were no more boot prints on the ground. "Damn!" he said. "Son of a bitch."

Schneider could see Hamm's mind racing. But, it was no use. There was no answer to this one. Schneider would just have to take that step and hope for the best. There were a hundred random boot steps behind him, twice traversed, with no mines under them. So why should this one be different? What were the odds that in that one tiny place, on that very last step, he would step on the trigger to a mine?

"God's got a sense of humor, eh, pal?" he said to Hamm.

Hamm nodded with that insouciance that had frightened Schneider before.

"Don't give me that look, Hamm," he said. "I'm not one of your patients…not yet. Just back up a bit more, eh?"

Hammer backed up a step. A useless gesture.

Schneider took a breath, picked a spot, straightened his back—he would not die cowering—and stepped toward the fence.

As his foot contacted the muddy ground, and he felt himself sinking into the depths, Schneider's mind pictured the little steel trigger spikes that bristled like a hedgehog from the surface of the mine. He lost all self-control and leaped toward the fence before his weight could sink his boot any deeper. This was pure unreasoned panic on his part, for the sudden extension of his legs to create the leap must have certainly pressed his foot deeper into the earth than had he carefully stepped forward. Whatever was there beneath his feet, mine or no mine, he reached the fence alive, and pulled himself over the top.

He tumbled to the other side—the safe side—and fell to his knees. Hamm was there in a fraction of a second, for he had started to move the very instant Schneider did. A stupid response on his part, too, but as unavoidable for Hamm as Schneider's leap had been for him.

A moment later, Schneider was cradled in Hamm's arms and spilled the partially digested K rations out of his guts and onto the edge of the road. Schneider hung there on his knees and looked at the mess on the ground.

As Schneider gasped for breath, he shook loose of Hamm. He was embarrassed that in his relief to be alive, he had, for the shortest moment, forgotten that Molly was still back in the field waiting her turn to step her way to safety.

And he never even thought about Franz at all.

Now they all gathered at the fence again. Schneider had moved along the posts to get as near to where Molly was and cut off the angled distance between them. Molly had already started moving back along her own tracks, taking each step as Schneider had done. Schneider inched along the fence, tangentially to her progress, keeping her as close as possible. Molly made her way slowly and painfully back. She had many more yards to cover than Schneider had. Nothing in his life had prepared Schneider for this, not even the worst of the emergencies in surgery. None of them had been about someone he loved so passionately as Molly. And to make it worse, this had all happened because some little boy had panicked at the site of a needle in Schneider's hand.

Hamm and Schneider hung over the rails, shoulders touching, breathing controlled. They whispered so as not to distract Molly from her long walk home. They shouted no words of encouragement. Nothing.

"Isn't there any way to lift her out of there, Hamm?" Schneider pleaded. "A crane from the combat engineers? One of those Sikorskys? Anything?"

Hamm shook his head. "We've tried them all. We've been in radio contact with the other division headquarters nearby, and nobody can get anything like that over here in time. Molly will have to walk out of there just as you did."

And so they watched every step by painful step, every meter of distance separating Molly from safety. Schneider stared into her eyes, watched her red hair as she moved closer to him, closer to safety. There was no doubt in his mind what he would do when he pulled her over that fence.

He would never leave her side again. Never.

Molly stayed focused. She stopped to rest. She straightened up and stretched her aching back. She was now thirty yards away from the fence. Hamm and Schneider kept pace with her movement. She looked at Schneider and smiled, nodding slowly up and down, as if to say that she could do it. That she would do it. For him. For them.

None of that relieved the tension in Schneider's neck and back. His heart still raced and his stomach knotted with each new step she took. As her weight shifted forward, he held his breath. Twice, Hamm placed his hand on Schneider's neck and squeezed, his fingers digging into the knotted muscles.

And she took another step. Twenty yards.

Hamm nudged Schneider. But Schneider could not take his eyes off Molly. She was close enough now for him to see every detail of her face. She had a fixed half-smile, which he knew was for his benefit. She was trying hard not to show the fear that was surging through her. Her red hair was plastered in strands across her forehead and cheeks, stuck in place by the glue of oils and sweat that were forming on her skin. Each time she stopped—every single step now—she looked up at Schneider with hope and longing in her eyes. The light breeze was blowing toward him, for he could smell her familiar scent. He knew that she wanted to be standing on his side of the fence, holding each other tightly and putting their ordeal into the past.

As she crossed more ground, more potholes and craters, she would stop longer to catch her breath. The distance between them seemed to Schneider to be negligible, to be crossable, if he could just reach out to her. She looked at him and said with her lips, "I love you, Steve." Although he couldn't actually hear the words, he could feel them the way he did when she would whisper as they lay in each other's arms, he inside her and all around her. It sent a chill into his ear and down his body to see her mouth the words.

At that very same time, exactly as she said those words to him, there was a commotion to the left. People, Germans and GIs, were shouting all at once.

"Halt!"

"Stop!"

"Nein!"

"No! No! No!"

Schneider looked into the field to see what they were shouting at. It was Franz. For whatever reason, whatever seizure of fear, Franz was running from the field directly toward the fence nearest him. He was not following his footprints or Molly's steps or Schneider's. He was in a blind crazy run for the shortest route from that field of death. He would not be left there alone. Nothing, not all the shouting in the world, would stop him. They all watched frozen at the horror of the inevitable.

Beyond any stretch of reason, nothing happened. Nothing at all. Franz ran through at least forty yards of mined soil and managed to escape totally unharmed. The local farmers tried to grab him as he vaulted the fence, but he evaded them like a broken-field runner. He raced toward the village with shouting Germans running after him.

Meanwhile, Molly never stopped—not once—fixing her eyes to the ground with each step as she moved closer and closer to safety. Schneider scrambled to the fence. Reaching over, he grabbed Molly's hand and arm, and yanked her across the fence rail. She flew over onto the safe side and landed in the mud next to Schneider. For a long moment, they both sat there numb and motionless. Then she grabbed his neck and pulled herself onto his body. She wept and shivered and squeezed the breath out of him. Then Hamm was there hugging them both in his arms.

The three struggled to their knees, barely able to walk. No one could speak.

Hamm helped them into a jeep and said something to the driver. The jeep roared away down that muddy road back in the direction of Leipzig. Neither Schneider nor Molly looked back.

Chapter Twenty-eight

19 May 1945, 0800 Hours
A Concentration Camp near Weimar, Germany

W hen Himmel came through the door, there was no doubt in Berg's mind why he was there. It was quite early in the day for him to make his visit. It couldn't be good. And since so little had changed in the camp other than that the Americans and the Russians were rumored to be on their way into Berlin, and if Berlin, then here as well. Berg knew his days were numbered.

"Well, Doktor Berg, you certainly have done it, haven't you?"

Berg sat quietly at his desk, alarmed by the look on Himmel's face in spite of his calm voice. Himmel's lips were curled into a smile, but his eyes were cold and dead.

It's all in the eyes. The rest of the face means nothing. This I have always known.

"We have had word that one of your former patients has died at the front."

It had to be the Sturmbannführer, Berg thought. I can't even recall his name. But, I can see myself placing the sponge next to his femoral artery just before I closed the tissues and repaired his hernia. Yes, he is dead. It has to be him.

"You remember, surely? Sturmbannführer Heinzel? Such a nice job of surgery, hmmm? I wasn't here that day, was I?"

Berg was beginning to sweat.

Even now, after so many years and months of surviving day by day, Berg couldn't still the racing of his heart. He wanted to live more than he wanted anything. He had nothing of the serenity his father had shown at the end, when his death was inevitable. Berg knew he would do anything to live another day. Another hour. And it made him ashamed.

"Do you want to tell me how you did it?" Himmel was smiling again. Just the mouth. Not the eyes.

When Berg did not answer, Himmel went on, "Heinzel died at the front, of course, but there was something strange. He went into shock, you see, just as we were engaged in a major battle near Berlin. One minute he is running with his men, and the next minute he is lying on the ground in shock. They dragged him to safety, expecting to find a bleeding wound. But, guess what?"

Himmel waited for Berg to respond, his head cocked, eyebrows raised, like a teacher expecting the correct answer in a classroom. And still the smiling lips. Berg just stared back into his eyes, hoping vainly to bluff his way out.

"Well, of course you know the rest. There was no wound at all. When they undressed him though, they found a massive purple swelling in his groin, right under that nicely healed hernia incision you made. The swelling went down into his thigh and up his abdomen. Of course, they rushed him to the operating tent. We haven't much left up there in the way of supplies right now, but he was alive when he got there, so they opened the hernia incision, and guess what they found?"

Berg cocked his head this time. He would play this game out. Himmel could accuse him of carelessness, but there would be no proof of murder. But, what was he thinking? Himmel needed no proof to do anything. He was an entire system of justice himself. He killed thousands of people every day who had committed no crime at all. What would stand in the way of his killing Berg right there and then?

Himmel drew out the silence. Berg's head cocked painfully to the side, Himmel's smile rigid on his lips.

"Very good, really," Himmel said finally. The smile disappeared. He stepped toward Berg. Berg slumped further into his chair in a pose of surrender.

"Only our surgeon's curiosity found you out. Very close to getting away with it, you know. How many more are out there, Doktor? Not many I suppose. You didn't get that many chances, did you?"

Berg looked around his little office. There was no escape from this room. And so, he did the only thing he could. He pulled himself up and smiled back at Himmel. Then he straightened his soiled white coat and nodded. And the funny thing was that his smile and his silent confession freed him from his own fear. He was completely calm; his thoughts were now with Rachel. And his father.

At that very moment, Himmel's lips curled down, and his brows furrowed, and his teeth showed like an ape. He reached down and unbuckled the leather flap that held his nine-millimeter Luger in his holster.

He slid the gun from its polished leather sheath. Berg could smell the oil and see the glistening surface of the meticulously maintained instrument. As Himmel pulled back on the receiver, Berg flinched at the metallic sound of the cartridge entering the chamber.

Berg involuntarily stepped back, stumbling as his knees struck the front edge of his chair. He fell into the seat, overwhelmed with the smell of his own fear and despair and shame. Himmel raised the Lugar, pointing it straight at Berg's forehead. Himmel was still smiling as he pulled back the hammer with his thumb.

Berg closed his eyes and, for the first time in all those years in hell, he prayed for himself.

Chapter Twenty-nine

20 May 1945, 0800 Hours
A Concentration Camp near Weimar, Germany

The day was warm and clear; the sky held not even the trace of a cloud. Schneider, McClintock, and Hammer walked three abreast down the battered road toward the camp, helmets back on their heads, the sun warming their pale skin. The red crosses on their helmets were now scuffed and marred by rough use over the past many months. The crosses were only symbolic now that the war was officially over.

The road's muddy surface was deeply rutted from the treads of trucks, jeeps and tanks. Along the shoulders lay the skeletal remains of the burnt-out engines of war. A Panzer tank stood on its side, staring down the twisted muzzle of a Sherman tank, both dead from shooting each other at close range. Inside the German tank were the burnt remains of the crews, sealed in their coffins by the horrendous temperatures of their final conflagration. Charred American jeeps were recognizable only by their square shapes and the faint outline of the insignia on the hood, burned black against the remaining olive paint. Twisted hulks of blackened steel defying identification arched from solidified pools of melted rubber.

No fires remained. No smoke. All the wasted rubble was now cold. Most of the American bodies had been removed some days ago, taken to processing depots for identification and burial. The familiar smell of cordite was gone. The only odors that remained were of burned rubber, steel and paint.

The three men walked down the center of the road, hardly looking at the debris. Over the past many months, they had seen more than enough of the same scenery everywhere the war took them. They had followed immediately behind the fight, always arriving in time to witness the resulting carnage and the destruction, but rarely any more of the battle itself. It was an odd perspective from which they witnessed the war. It reminded Hamm of his interminable ER duty in civilian life, where he saw the results of the violence, but rarely the actual acts of violence.

It had been ten days since Molly and Steve had their adventure in the minefield. To Hamm, they both seemed changed somehow, but it was not something he could put his finger on.

What a hard act for Susan to follow now, he thought, even if they did get back together.

Susan would be struggling to regain the love of her husband, fighting against the romantic memories of a fairy tale romance and a heroine's act of bravery. It seemed impossible to Hamm. But, he thought, you never know. Maybe when Steve gets back to the real world, everything that happened here will be like a dream, quickly forgotten…or only a dim memory.

"How far now, Hamm?" McClintock asked, interrupting the train of thoughts.

"Yeah. How far?" Schneider echoed in a lifeless monotone.

"You guys sound like my kids. 'Are we there yet, Daddy? When are we going to be there, Daddy.' I'm not your Daddy," Hamm said to McClintock. "And I'm not yours either," to Schneider.

"Easy, Hamm. Take it easy," said McClintock. "Don't get your yoogies in an uproar. It was just a fucking question."

"Well, I don't have the vaguest idea. And while we're at it, I'd like to know why we're walking. Where's our jeep?"

Just as he spoke, the roar of an engine made all three of them jump and turn sharply around. A battered jeep marked with a red cross skidded around the turn behind them, grinding gears, coming to a stop just short of running them down. McClintock and Schneider jumped to one side. Hamm just turned, planted his feet, folded his arms, and stood his ground. He was so pissed at having to walk all that way, he was damned if he was going to jump out of the way of his own jeep. Or maybe he was just angry at what he had seen along the walk. Or the memories…of what? He didn't know, but he was in no mood to screw around.

The front bumper of the jeep came to rest against his shins. Hamm stared into the eyes of Gwerski, his driver, who seemed totally undeterred by his officer's glare.

"Sorry, sirs. Had a little traffic back there. Refugees. They're all over the fuckin' place. I've never seen so fuckin' many people on the fuckin' roads. Fuckin' good thing they're not armed."

"Gwerski, you think you could say a whole sentence without 'fuckin'' in it?'" Schneider said shaking his head from side to side.

Gwerski shrugged. "What? Oh, yeah. Absa-fucking-lutely, sir."

In fact they were thrilled to have Gwerski as their driver. He was new to the group, but had proved himself capable and fearless. He planned ahead and took no chances. But, at the same time, very little deterred him. Apparently, he had grown up in Brooklyn and had never left there until he embarked for Europe on a troop ship. And just as thousands of other GIs, he puked nearly all the way over, but he recovered and hit the ground running.

The three docs climbed silently and sullenly into the jeep. Hamm took the front passenger's seat. McClintock and Schneider vaulted into the back.

"Let's go, Corporal," Hamm said, slapping the dashboard with his palm. "Straight ahead. Let's see what this is all about."

Half an hour later the jeep slowed to a crawl. McClintock and Schneider had nodded off, chins on their chests; McClintock was drooling a little. They had all grown proficient at sleeping deeply in the noisiest places and most uncomfortable positions imaginable. Hamm, like the captain of a ship at sea, remained awake, sitting forward in his seat, one hand on top of the windshield frame.

As they reached the crest of a tiny hill, Hamm reached back without looking and shook Schneider's knee. Then he nudged McClintock as well. Both men bolted awake, confused and muzzy-headed.

"What? Where are we?" Schneider asked.

Hamm pointed ahead down the center of the road. McClintock and Schneider were now awake and alert—another legacy from their surgical training as well as the war. Schneider's mouth sagged, but he said nothing. McClintock slowly moved his head back and forth in stunned disbelief.

Gwerski stopped the jeep, turned off the engine, and pocketed the key. None of them moved. Minutes passed. Still, all four remained motionless in their seats.

Finally, it was Schneider who rose to leave the jeep first. He swung his right leg over the side of the rear seat and hopped to the ground. Then, in a single motion, the others stepped from the jeep and began walking slowly forward.

They were a hundred yards from the camp. A large black sign with the name of the camp had been torn down and was now a smoldering pile of ash. Behind the destroyed sign, a brick wall bore German words painted in black gothic letters.

Arbeit Macht Frei

Some men dressed in gray rags were slashing at the rugged sign, trying in vain to obliterate it.

Gwerski stopped in front of the jeep. He would not, could not, walk any further. He leaned, half sitting, against the muddy bumper.

Hamm knew it was only his own pride that kept him from jumping into the vehicle and driving back from where they had come. That was exactly what Gwerski wanted to do. Nothing could have prepared him for this. Nor the rest of them.

Schneider, McClintock, and Hamm began to walk forward, paying no attention to Gwerski.

"My God," Hamm said quietly to no one. "My God."

"What do the signs say?" McClintock whispered to Schneider.

Funny thing, the whispering, Schneider thought. It was as if normal conversation would have been disrespectful.

"Don't know the name of the camp," Schneider answered. "I heard of a Buchenwald somewhere around here, but I don't think this is it. Saw it on the map once. Still...I'm not sure where we are. 'Arbeit Macht Frei.' That means, Work makes you free...or makes freedom, or work liberates, I guess. Something like that." He thought for a moment more. "Yeah, it's Work Makes You Free."

"So, what's it mean?" McClintock asked again.

"Beats the shit out of me. I don't know."

They moved slowly forward toward the barbed wire fencing. The gates were open, and it seemed as if hundreds—no, thousands—of people were milling about in slow motion. There was no pattern to the movement. It resembled a dusting of snow blowing across a black tarmac road in amorphous swirls. Hypnotic. Disorienting. As many people were still hovering around inside the camp as were drifting around outside the gates. There seemed to be no destination, only aimless movement. It was the Brownian motion of human molecules. But, these were like no humans that any of the men had ever seen before: not the most dangerously sick from civilian days, nor the most pitifully poor. These were ghosts from some other world. An asylum filled with demented souls of war. Crazed. Mute. Drifting with the breeze like dead leaves in the fall.

Hamm started for the gates and was soon surrounded by a small mob of maybe fifty of the ghosts. They spoke to him in words he could not understand, in voices he could hardly hear. It was Babel. But worst of all, he recoiled from them. He actually drew away. In that very moment, he was as ashamed of himself as he had ever been. Ashamed of his reaction, of his lack of humanity. Of his own revulsion.

I should rush to them, he thought. I should offer my aid. I should care for them. I should embrace them. I should feed them. I should clean their wounds. I should show them love.

But, he could not.

Instead, he stood frozen in his place: repulsed, horrified, unable to move, unable to reach out. This was not a rumor. Not scuttlebutt. Not any longer.

"I'm a doctor, for God's sake!" Hamm said aloud, but to no one. And no one answered.

For the rest of his life, he would recall with shame his emotions at that particular moment; not a day would go by without some memory of this. But he would never tell another soul.

A few seconds later, Schneider was at his side; he, too, was paralyzed by his revulsion. The crowd moved closer. Then, suddenly, both men were overwhelmed by an odor they had never before experienced.

It was not even close to the worst of the surgeons' vast repertoire of foul smells: not the gangrene of infected limbs; not the feculent odor of the cholera ward; nor the sickening sweet smell of kidney failure. Not even the intangible smell of death that they all knew more of than they would have wished.

It was something else. Something they could not quite define. Something....

The odor clung to their noses; it stuck in their throats and became part of their being. It permeated their clothes, their skin. It reminded them of their days in the anatomy lab when the smell of the embalming fluid became part of their life for nearly a year. But this.... this was something new. Something vastly more terrible. Unlike medical school, new clothes and a shower were not going to expunge this terrible haunting odor.

The crowd took on form now as the bodies pushed closer. Neither Hamm nor Schneider saw any people. They saw bodies. Bodies were drifting, floating around them. Most were naked, and though the day was still chilly, these bodies did not shiver nor did they cower with their arms folded about them; there was no covering their genitals as Hamm knew he would have done were he naked outside among strangers. Instead, they walked in their nakedness as if that were the normal way of life. And then it struck Hamm as it did Schneider: this was their normal life. The nakedness and the smells and the starvation, even their internal anatomy visible through the thin veil of skin, with their bones protruding through translucent parchment. Their mouths were without teeth or had teeth blackened through crusted lips. Their skin was covered with running sores. All the horrors of the pathology books assembled there to meet them in a giant diorama of the complete degradation that humankind could survive; worse, that humankind could inflict.

Hamm never felt it coming. One moment he was focused on the sights in front of him, the next he was on his knees, retching and retching without letup; he paused only long enough to catch his breath, cough, gag, and vomit again. When his stomach was empty, his abdominal muscles contracted hard, painfully trying to empty his body of something. Anything. When there was nothing at all left inside him, he began to sob. He had not behaved like this since that very first day of this war; the day he dropped to the sand on Dog White Beach after seeing the first of the terrible slaughter on D-day. But that day was nothing compared to this. He might, he thought, with the passing of decades, forget some of the horror of D-day. But the memories of this day would be with him, he knew, until he died.

In all his years of training, all the nights in the emergency rooms, all the months in the battlefield, all the human detritus of war, none of the terror and agony before this moment had caused him such depth of grief.

Schneider sank to his knees next to Hamm, taking him by his shoulders and holding him as only Hamm's mother ever had. And Schneider began to cry, too.

The crowd, maybe twenty souls now, for some of the others had lost interest and drifted on, pushed closer. Those who stayed paused in reverence at the sight of the two men—their rescuers, their heroes—down on their knees, crying. A small naked man stepped forward and kneeled down next to Schneider. The man was an anatomy lesson: every bone in his body showed through his skin. Schneider could count the bones and see the insertions of ligaments into joints. The man's penis was contracted and invisible into a swollen and inflamed scrotum. The man's bare feet were edematous, red, and ulcerated. He was completely bald. And his teeth protruded as if there were no room left for them in his mouth. The teeth were black.

The man placed a calming hand on Schneider's shoulder and motioned to Hamm. "Er wird in ordnung sein?" He will be all right?

"Ja," Schneider replied to the man, "Ja, Er wird in ordnung sein."

The old man stood and nodded sympathetically toward Hamm. Then he moved off to look for something to eat.

When Hamm recovered his control, they went to find McClintock. They found him leaning against the fence, breathing hard and white as a ghost. Tears were streaming down his face. Hamm and Schneider each put a hand on McClintock's shoulders, but he didn't move.

Hamm took some water from his canteen and soaked his handkerchief. He wiped the remains of vomit from his own lips, then used what was left of the water to wet down his neck. He nodded to Schneider.

"I'm OK. I'm OK." Then, after a deep breath, he said, "Alright. Let's do it. Let's do what they pay us for."

Schneider said, "We need to find the commanding officer here. Seems to be a command post setting up over there." He was pointing to the main wooden building in the compound where GIs were moving furniture.

McClintock quickly pulled himself together and the three of them set off across the open space toward the building, weaving to avoid some of the inmates who were still wandering around in their perpetual daze. So far, Hamm had touched no one.

Several times, people came toward them with their hands outstretched, begging for food. After only a few yards, the three doctors had emptied their packs and jackets of the scant rations they had on them. Candy bars. C rats. K rats. Some cigarettes. Hamm watched one man open the pitiful beaten up green K ration with the little metal opener that came with it, then carefully divide its contents with another man whom he supported with an arm around the waist. After that, the doctors could only shake their heads sadly as they walked past the starving masses with nothing left to give them.

As they neared the compound headquarters, they came upon a small gathering in the middle of the yard. Noisy inmates, not naked, but wearing some semblance of clothing, although rags by any definition, were milling around a tall stocky American officer, whose back was turned. The officer was very calm, but the crowd was visibly agitated.

When the three approached the officer, they saw that he was a major, wearing the medical corps insignia on his lapels. The major took no notice of Hamm or his men, or of anything going on around him. He was completely focused on the man in front of him.

Standing directly in front of the major was a German officer wearing the black uniform of the hated SS. Hamm couldn't recall the German insignias of rank, but the paired lightning bolts of the Waffen-SS were clear in his mind. The man still wore his long black leather coat, opened so that the battle decorations across his chest were plainly visible. There were dozens of ribbons and medals. His high stiff collar was neatly buttoned and dressed with a ribbon bearing the Knight's Cross.

The shining leather holster on his wide black belt was unclipped and empty.

The major was saying something to the German officer, they could not make out the words. What was clear, however, was the fury in his voice. The contempt. The utter outrage. His control was only contained by sternest discipline. The crowd pressed closer and closer until the major waved them back without taking his eyes off the German.

Hamm's trio stood in a wide circle, spotlighted by the sun as if they were on stage at an outdoor theater. Hamm pushed his way to the front of the crowd of inmates, who were now totally silent.

"Keep smiling, Fritz," the major said in a cool level tone. "Your time is coming." Hamm suspected that the SS officer understood every word, though he did not respond at all.

"Where is your Reichsführer Himmler now when you need him?" the major said. "Eh? And little Adolph. Took some cyanide and left you holding the bag, didn't he, the little prick?"

No response.

"One more time, Fritz. Your name, your rank, and your serial number."

The SS officer stepped forward, straightened his back, and said, "Schwein!"

Without warning, the German spit a huge gelatinous glob into the major's face. The yellowish fluid rolled down the officer's cheek and began to hang toward the ground in a thin disgusting string.

Hamm and Schneider winced. McClintock moved back a step.

The major carefully wiped the spit from his face with his handkerchief. He dropped the soggy rag to the ground. Then he unclipped the holster of his sidearm, chambered a .45 caliber round, and pressed the muzzle of his gun deeply under the German's chin. The German refused to yield an inch.

A small smile turned into a sneer on the major's lips. Finally, he shoved the muzzle forward with extraordinary force, knocking the German backward, splattering him into the mud. Before the fallen man could move, the major fired his gun, missing the German's head by inches, throwing a small geyser of mud up onto the German's face. The blast caused everyone in their little tableau to jump and step backwards.

The German rolled to his side, curled into a fetal position and stayed that way, waiting for the final shot.

The major holstered his weapon, and said, "Get this piece of shit out of my sight before I kill him. Take him over there, and turn him over to the MP company commander." He motioned to the area where some of the MPs had the remainder of the German staff cordoned off behind some barbed wire, "and make sure I never see his pathetic ass again!"

"Holy Shit!" Gwerski had appeared out of nowhere and was now standing behind Schneider. "That Kraut just fucked with the wrong boy."

"I guess he did," McClintock agreed. Then he turned to Hamm and Schneider and said, "I like this guy. Let's go introduce ourselves."

As they left to follow the major, the crowd closed in on the still cowering SS officer and began to strip him of his boots and clothing. Then, when he was naked, they began kicking and beating him until—after several minutes of just watching—the MPs intervened. All the time the inmates beat him, they never made a sound.

When Hamm's group entered the wooden command post, they found the major scrubbing his face with soap and water at a small basin. His skin was inflamed with the friction of his effort. He dried himself with a khaki towel and looked up, surprised to see three new medical officers.

"I'm John Hammer," Hamm said, holding out his hand. Hamm probably should have presented himself in a proper military manner, but he thought: What the hell? The war is over, and we're all just doctors.

"This is Steve Schneider and Ted McClintock. We're from the Evac Field Hospital. Detached for the moment to help you guys over here."

Hamm motioned to Gwerski, who still had a stupid grin on his face, and added, "This is Corporal Gwerski, our driver, who will do whatever you need him to do."

Gwerski nodded his agreement, standing from habit at stiff attention.

"Gentlemen," the major nodded, "Good to meet you. I'm Jerome Green." He shook hands with the three of them, and then motioned to

Gwerski. "Go on out there, son, and organize that chaos in the court-yard. And help the MPs keep all those Krauts away from the dead inmates. I plan a decent burial for those poor souls."

"Yes, sir!" Gwerski said and left the room.

Green motioned for everyone to sit down. No further mention was made of the mock shooting as Green brought them all up to date. Hamm noticed that the major was wearing a sidearm. He wondered where Schneider's had finally ended up. Not on his hip, anyway. He reminded himself to ask later but never did. Hamm shrugged to no one but himself.

"Well, as you can see, this is one major SNAFU. I don't know what we're going to do for all these poor people. Most of the guards took off about three days before we liberated the place. And we've only been here less than two days, ourselves. Some of the healthier inmates, the ones who've been here only a short while, went out and captured some of the guards. Tore most of them to pieces out there; they brought back a few live ones and hanged them while we were still getting organized. They borrowed some weapons from us and shot the rest. So, we don't have to deal with any of them now. There were a few collaborators inside the camp. Sondekommandos. They've disappeared, too. And I don't have the time or interest in finding them or wasting manpower on finding out what happened. That's over now. Period."

Hamm and his group sat in silence, waiting for Green to finish. From outside came the muted sounds of disparate activities. Men wandering the grounds; soldiers organizing the camp; and from far off, voices rising from the streets of the nearby town.

"The biggest problem is that this is a pretty mixed bag of prisoners. Some Jews, some politicals, and a whole bunch who want to kill each other for some damned reason I haven't figured out yet. But, that's not my problem. The Third Army MPs will deal with that. We have to set up mechanisms to save the ones who're still alive, though I don't think many are going to survive no matter what we do for them. We're still losing a couple of hundred a day."

"What's the prevailing medical problem here?" Hamm asked.

"Well, of course there's plenty of cholera. But the biggest problem right now is typhus. Place is crawling with lice. Every damned one of the inmates is infested with 'em. It'll be amazing if we don't get lice ourselves. I've got a pretty good supply of DDT and ordered some more, for all the good that'll do, but we've got to organize the enlisted men to get out there and burn most of the bedding and mattresses, scrub out the barracks, and delouse the people by shaving them and spraying every damned one with DDT. And there are thousands of them out there. The barracks aren't worth shit, but it'll keep them out of the rain and the cold for the time being. Do the best we can, anyway, until we get some more good tents."

Schneider said, "You know, we're actually surgeons, sir, Hamm and me. McClintock here is an anesthesiologist. Where do we fit in?"

"You're all doctors and you're warm bodies. As far as I'm concerned, everyone here is qualified to do everything. Christ, I was a gynecologist myself before this war started! Now I do just about anything. If we have any surgical cases, of course, you'll do those. Amputations, debridements, and so on. But, mostly, we've got to get this place cleaned up. There are thousands of infected ulcers. Most of these people have bones exposed, so there's a heap of osteomyelitis; oozing pus everywhere. It's awful. It's a medical nightmare. I've seen some pretty bad shit in my lifetime, but nothing I could have dreamed of comes close to this. The people who did this..." Green stopped. He shuddered and his voice choked. He suppressed what might have been a sob, then balled up his fist and said, "Goddamn them! Goddamn them!"

He hesitated a moment more, then slammed his fist into the desk. "You know those Jews out there? It ain't about Jews. They just happened to be handy. They had any Negroes in this country, they'd have been in here instead. Makes no difference to the Nazis. Right now, I could kill every fucking one of them Krauts...." Then he collected himself and took command again. He let out a long breath.

Schneider said, "Well you sure scared the crap out of that SS officer."

"Scared him? I missed. I'm lousy shot. I was shootin' to kill."

"What!" Schneider said. Then he smiled as he saw Green's pursed lips and the laughter in his crinkling brown eyes.

"Easy, son. Keep your sense of humor. I never miss."

"They've got a little hospital over there," he said pointing behind the barracks. "Most of the patients there have died since we got here. It seemed to be just a holding area for the nearly dead. There is a doctor, too. We found him sitting in a chair when we got here. Just sitting there like he was waiting to make rounds. So far, he hasn't spoken. Seems healthy enough. Maybe one of you guys could try to talk with him. One-on-one. Major Hammer?"

"Yessir, I will. Right away. Steve Schneider here speaks German, so we'll send him in to give it a try."

"And see if you can get him to eat something. Won't react to us. But his food seems to be gone a while after we leave it for him. I don't know whether he eats it or the inmates come along and steal it. Anyway, see if you can get him to talk to you. I'd hate to lose him after he survived all this."

"We'll try, major," Hamm said.

"Good. And, oh yeah, I found a notebook when we cleaned out this place. I think the doctor was keeping a record of all the deaths. He made notes of who killed each inmate. I'm going to hang on to it. Never know when we might get the chance to settle some scores around here. Nice to have a little documentation, know what I mean?"

Green looked wistful for a couple of seconds, and then snapped back to the present. He just stared.

After a minute of strained silence had gone by, McClintock asked, "What about nutrition?"

"What nutrition? You ever in your whole life seen anything like this? Most of those folks are going to die of malnutrition in the next few weeks no matter what we do. We've got barely enough to sustain them. I hate to talk this way, but as soon as a few thousand more die, the rations will go farther. For now, we carefully dole out everything they send us and hope for the best."

"What else are we dealing with here?" Hamm asked.

"Well, aside from the typhus and the cases of cholera, as if that isn't enough, we've got TB everywhere. Every one of 'em seems to cough up blood sooner or later. Then there's some scurvy. Scurvy!

"We've got dysentery. Diarrhea everywhere. I think that's why some of them don't wear pants even when we give them some. I mean this is your worst medical nightmare. Who the hell's ever equipped for something like this? Don't forget the Third Army is trying to take care of all the German civilians down here, too. Civilians got nothing to eat either. Son-of-a-bitch Hitler and his pals all killed themselves, so they get off easy. We gotta clean up their fuckin' mess.

"MP's are doing a great job keeping some semblance of order. Their company commander is doing all the right things. Best he can with the manpower he's got.

"So, you guys find a billet outside the camp. We'll set up some medical tents and ORs. Don't want to use the crappy little hospital at all. Too many germs in there we don't want to be mixing with our clean cases. Engineers arrived this morning to try to get a clean water system going and a latrine that'll isolate the feces from the water supply. Maybe control the cholera epidemic. We sure don't need any more of that on top of all this."

Gwerski came back into the room and stood at attention. Green nodded in his direction. "Yes, son?"

Standing at attention, Gwerski said, "The scum bag has been placed with the other scum bags as ordered, sir."

Green smiled. "OK. Good. Now, Sergeant—I'm giving you a field promotion. I'll put in the paperwork later. Find yourself some stripes." Then he turned to Hamm, McClintock, and Schneider and said, "Gentlemen, as of now I am the senior ranking medical officer here. In all matters that pertain to the health and well being of everyone in this area, my word is the law. So there will be no need to get higher approval for anything, if it's a medical matter. MP commander takes care of everything else."

He turned to Gwerski and said, "Get a detail of at least twenty men. All armed. Round up every civilian you can find in this goddamned town and make sure the mayor and the city councilmen are among them. Get someone who speaks German to go with you. The Krauts have known about this place all these years, and by God, and I am going to shove their noses in it. Bring them all into the camp with shovels and any wheeled vehicles you can find. No exceptions. Men and women. Old and young. Nobody who can walk gets out of this. Bring them in here and make them take every one of those bodies out there—there have to be thousands of them—and dig regulation military graves. I want the bodies cleaned and wrapped in sheets. Take sheets off the beds in their homes if you have to. Every last body will get a resting place and a head marker. The townspeople will make the crosses and the Jewish stars themselves. Every damned one of them. I'll arrange for the chaplains to perform appropriate services. Graves Registration will try to identify as many as they can...." His head drooped. "For their families. Now, get on it, Sergeant."

"Yessir!" Gwerski turned and left the room.

Green turned his attention back to Hamm, Schneider, and McClintock. "Questions?"

"Guess not, Major," Hamm said, trying to suppress a smile, thinking, I really like this guy.

They picked up their gear and started to leave. Green sat at his desk and attacked the pile of supply requisitions that he had spent most of the night filling out, without saying another word.

"I'm going to see what's ready in those medical tents," McClintock said, setting out across the main compound.

Hamm and Schneider picked up their kits and started across the dirt enclosure toward the hospital.

"What a pitiful excuse for a hospital," Schneider said, looking at the ramshackle building in front of them.

"Yeah, but it's better than nothing, I guess. Imagine trying to treat patients in there?" Hamm said. "It's the stuff of nightmares. Well, let's see what we can do for this old guy."

The two climbed the rickety steps and pushed through the door into the anteroom.

Schneider stopped so quickly that Hamm nearly ran into him.

Berg looked up from his desk where he had been staring into space. His eyes widened, somewhere between fear and wonder.

"Stephen," he said, "meine Neffe!"

"Dear God!" Schneider gasped. "Onkel Meyer!"

Schneider ran to the desk and dropped to his knees in front of Berg. He took the old man's hands in his and kissed them as he broke into tears. Schneider's head fell forward onto his uncle's knees and Berg caressed his nephew's hair. Then Berg began to cry as well, staining his coat with his tears. He shook with long gasping sobs that left him unable to speak.

Hamm stood watching for only a few seconds, then backed quietly out the door and left the two men alone.

After several minutes more, both Schneider and Berg fought back their tears. Schneider rocked back on his heels and looked at the remains of his once robust and powerful uncle.

"Oh, God, Onkle Meyer, what have they done to you?" he said in German.

Berg did not answer, but only stared back at his nephew. "So you are a soldier now, my boy." Then his eyes went to Schneider's medical insignias. "A Doktor and a soldier...."

Schneider shook his head. "No, Onkel, not really a soldier. It's just a uniform to me. I'm a surgeon, though. That I really am."

Berg looked so frail and so tired. Schneider took both of his uncle's hands and lifted him to his feet. He supported the old man under his arms and walked him to the cot in the corner of the room. He pulled back the clean, new army blanket, which he realized had been left there by Green's men, and arranged the pillow with its clean case. Then he eased Berg into the bed and pulled the cover to his chin.

"Rest now, Uncle Meyer? And what happened to your forehead?"

"Oh, that. A German officer thought he might like to see me dead. And he would have except that a moment before he would have pulled the trigger, the Americans came. When the shooting started, the Colonel ran away like a rabbit. I don't know what happened to him"

Schneider nodded. He patted his uncle's shoulder and said, "Rest now. I'll get you some food, and then we'll talk. We have all the time in the world. I am here for you now, finally."

Berg closed his eyes and, in seconds, was asleep.

Over the next several days, almost nobody in the rapidly growing medical group slept at all. While operating during a raging battle carried with it an inarguable urgency, taking care of those wretched souls should have been a more leisurely and orderly process. But, it was not.

Everyone worked day and night in a desperate attempt to keep alive those camp inmates who had survived their terrible ordeal. The success rate was pitifully low, however, and hundreds more died every day despite the doctors' best efforts. It was nothing like working on the healthy GIs they had treated in battle. Nothing in the world could have prepared them for what they found in the camps, and nothing would stop them from using everything in their power to stop the dying. They requisitioned, they borrowed, and, mostly, they stole the supplies they needed.

Schneider and Hamm set up a clinic in one of the newly sanitized empty barracks. It was good therapy for all of them to be so busy. Other than a few amputations, there was hardly any major surgery to be done at the time. But, there were endless infected wounds to be debrided and cleaned. Thousands of patients had running sores with underlying infection in their bones. Others had partially healed traumatic amputations of their limbs. The lines at the small clinic were endless, and at the end of the day, it seemed as if they had accomplished nothing. The lines of sick people never grew shorter. The burden of work never diminished. Always, there were still more patients to see, more human beings in need of help. There was no way any of them could look into the eyes of the next person in line and say, "Sorry, we're closed until morning." For that person, morning might never come.

At night, they would roll into their cots and fall immediately to sleep, only to be awakened an hour or two later by the orderlies to resume their duties. The lines were just too long, and the need was too desperate to keep a single patient waiting.

While the medical personnel worked through the night, engineers set up latrines to divert waste materials away from the drinking water supplies. Identification teams were set up to catalog the long list of the dead as well as the living. Although it seemed counter-intuitive, it was terribly important to learn the identities of the dead, for the living could ultimately insert themselves back into the lives of their families and friends. They knew who they were. But nobody wanted to allow the dead to disappear into the earth unrecognized, unremembered, leaving their families to search for them forever.

The job was impossible. Yet, it would be done. They would do it.

Gwerski, now wearing real sergeant's stripes on his sleeve worked with his men to round up teams of civilians from the surrounding villages and assemble his own forced-labor battalion to sort and bury the dead.

To everyone's surprise, out of nowhere, Marsh turned up, working with a vengeance, embarrassing everyone around him with his energy.

Hamm and Schneider knew Marsh's wounds still bothered him for they could see him grimace many times during the day as he straightened up and stretched his back to relieve the pain and the stiffness.

Antonelli didn't show up, and Marsh said he had no idea where he was, as they had gone different directions weeks ago.

Armed with shovels and wagons, and under the angry eyes of armed GIs, the reluctant German work force carried the foul, rotting bodies of the naked victims, laying them out in orderly lines in front of graves dug with military precision. It wasn't heavy work, for most of the bodies weighed less than eighty pounds and some considerably less.

The bodies were cleansed with precious clean water and soap, carefully wrapped in sheets, and lowered one by one into their resting places. Final prayers were offered by the military chaplains. Gwerski oversaw the dignity of the proceedings as if these were all members of his own family. He also oversaw the markers. Crosses and Stars of David were individually carved and set in place at the head of each grave. The graves were numbered, and careful records kept wherever possible. Some of the bodies still had readable numbers tattooed on their forearms, which were also recorded. The Germans had been meticulous record keepers. For the vast majority, however, there would be no name, no number. Only anonymous remembrance.

Then, one day, the medical team received the best present they could ask for. Amid the never-ending horror, the only time Hamm smiled in those weeks was that Sunday morning two weeks after they had arrived.

He was just dragging himself out of his tent, feeling the same dread that greeted him every day. He had just awakened from some escapist dream of normalcy, to find himself in hell again, when a beat-up ambulance rolled into the compound. The vehicle was so covered with mud that the red crosses were barely visible and the canvas cover was little more than a rag. But it was one of their ambulances and that meant more supplies and perhaps more personnel.

Hamm made himself the unofficial greeter of all newcomers, so he detoured and headed over to meet the new arrivals. He got there just as the rear flaps flew open, and a bunch of nurses and medics jumped to the ground. They looked as grim and depressed as he had been feeling since he arrived at the camp. He later found out that they had been doing the very same work further inside Germany. They had come from a place called Dachau near Munich. Hamm hadn't heard of it, but from the looks on their faces, it was no better than his own hell, maybe worse.

He was looking over the supplies stacked in the rear after everybody was off the truck, hoping for some boxes of clean bandages. They were going through gauze pads at an impossible pace. The passenger side door of the cab opened, and another nurse hopped down into the mud. He turned and put out his hand (saluting was truly a thing of the past by then) and nearly fell over with delight.

"Hey, Hamm," Molly said, throwing her arms around his neck and giving him an almost painfully tight hug. And then she was crying into his neck. Her tears wet the collar of his scrub suit. He shrugged his shoulders and waved his hands all around him, mutely indicating the surrounding horrors. And in a moment, he was crying, too.

He pulled her gently away, holding her by the shoulders at arm's length. She smiled at him with the tears still wet on her cheeks.

"My God, Molly, you look wonderful." He was lying. She looked terrible. She had lost too much weight and had dark bags under her eyes. Her once milky Celtic skin now sallow and wan.

"Liar," she said quietly. "I know just how I look." Then she hesitated, looked around and asked, "Steve here?"

Hamm just nodded, motioning with his head. "He's over in that tent, the one with the flaps tied open. Go ahead and wake him. It's time to get him up anyway."

Not that he could have stopped her. She turned before he was finished speaking and ran to find Steve.

Hamm's heart ached to see her, for he knew too well that she and Steve were in for a great deal more pain.

389

Hamm walked back toward the tent trailing slowly in Molly's wake. He didn't want to interrupt them, but he also needed desperately to get out of his filthy scrubs he'd been sleeping in. Besides, the truth was he really did want to see their reunion.

Molly bombed into the tent without hesitating just as Steve was getting up from his bed. She slammed into him and knocked him back onto the cot, nearly rolling off the other side. Then she was crying, and laughing, and hugging Steve almost before he could figure out what had happened. In another minute, they were locked in the longest, deepest kiss Hamm had seen in a very long while. After which it was time for Hamm to turn around and leave them alone. His clean scrubs would just have to wait.

The next day, Hamm sat at the edge of his cot, rubbing his red eyes. Schneider stirred and tried to force himself awake. He swung his legs over the edge of his cot and stepped automatically into his boots. He made a foul face and then sniffed at his own clothes, now soiled and stained with an unnamed oily residue.

"I think it's time to burn these," Schneider said, pointing at his clothes, "and get some new ones. It's getting hard to tell us from the inmates anymore."

Hamm nodded and struggled to make a small smile. But he was just too tired. In the long months of battle, he had never felt so defeated, so depressed. Never could he have dreamed of such cruelty, such depravity. For the first time in his life, he felt the urge to kill. He reveled in dreams of revenge against those who had perpetrated such atrocities against these poor helpless souls.

It was only with the greatest effort that Hamm could focus on treating one person at a time. Only by seeing each person as a special individual could he stay with what he was doing. Each time he allowed himself to glance up at the lines forming at the clinic door, or the bodies endlessly shuttled to the graveside, his heart sank, weighted with the futility of it all. He wanted to get up and walk home.

"I have to pretend every minute that this is my private practice, Steve," Hamm told Schneider one day. "I pretend that each one has a family out in my waiting room, watching the clock and hoping I'll come through the door with good news, just like at home. If I don't do that every time, with every patient, they just become numbers. Something less than humans. The Nazi's 'Untermenschen.' These poor people—*our* people— they all need us. And there's not enough of us to go around."

Schneider nodded. He admitted that he was struggling with the same thing. "You know," he added, "these really are my people. These are the ones I ran away from. They're mostly Jewish, and they're German. Back home I didn't want any part of them. They embarrassed me. Now I can't see leaving here until the job is done. The battlefield was one thing. I kept telling myself that as soon as the last gunshots were fired, I'm out of here. No more Army. No more of any of this bullshit. But I can't leave, Hamm. Not yet. I mean, I don't know when we're going to get orders sending us home, but I'm not ready to go. Not yet."

"I know." Hamm waited for Schneider to continue, and when he did not, Hamm said, "I think I will go home when they send me. I know they need us here, but there's going to be thousands of GIs going home who need more surgery. Colostomies to close. Amputations to revise. Chest fistulas that don't heal. There's going to be floods of surgery for us back there. I may just postpone rejoining my practice. Maybe go with the veterans' hospitals for a while. These are the guys who fought with us all these months, Steve. They died for us. There's so many like them who need my help. I'm going to put in for extended duty. For them. I guess, for Dick really."

Hamm saw a sadness in Steve's eyes, but he said nothing. He realized Steve was thinking of Molly. Before he could say anything, Steve said, "I have to make some decisions, Hamm. About Molly. I still don't know what I'm going to do."

Hamm wondered if Steve would find the courage to go back to his family, his life. It seemed easier to stay there under the pretext of finishing the job than to go back to repair his damaged marriage; harder to put Molly in the past. He didn't envy him. Steve and Molly had survived the ordeal in the minefield, but Hamm didn't know how they would survive the end of the war.

"Steve, listen to me. You know what I think of Molly. And you know I'm your friend. So would you just hear me out?"

Steve looked at Hamm with a wariness that said he didn't want to hear what Hamm was going to say. But Hamm persisted before Steve could interrupt. He was risking his friendship, but he had to say it.

"This isn't the real world, pal. This is a war, and nobody at home is going to understand the smallest particle of what we saw here. What we did here. What the Krauts did here. Mark my words, when we get home, all anybody will care about is that we're back safely, and they're not going to want to hear the details. And I am not going to want to tell them about this. I'm going to take off these God-awful clothes and get back into my civvies and back to my life. Even if it's in a veteran's hospital, it'll be different back home. I'm telling you, Steve, it's going to be another world. They don't really want to hear about this."

Schneider stared out the tent door for a moment and asked, "What does that have to do with me and Molly? That's really what you're talking about, isn't it?"

"Yes, it is. The war stuff is one thing, but not much different. You two guys fell in love out here like a scene from a movie. You were having trouble at home with Susan for a couple of years, and then you're alone in England, happier there alone than at home with Susan. Molly's lost her husband to the Japs at Pearl, so she's devastated and lonely. Mix that all together with the fear that neither of you might live long enough to go home. I mean that minefield, for Christ's sake. If that wasn't a nightmare, I don't know what is. So you guys fall in love and had...I don't know." Hamm struggled to find the words without getting too graphic. "Paris for one thing. It was a fairy tale. And fairy tales aren't real. They all end."

"So, you're saying we're not really in love? This is just all make-believe? We're not going to live happily ever after?"

"No, I'm not saying that. I'm not sure what I'm saying. And I'm sure I don't have the answers. Jesus, Steve. We all love Molly. Not the way you do, but I couldn't love her more if she were my sister. But you made some vows a few years ago, and there's a family back there that has been counting the days for years. They have dreaded every knock on their door. They think, when the war is over, you're coming home to them. Susan hasn't a clue that anything else is going to happen but that you will come home and resume your life with her, however tough it might be. She deserves a chance to put it back together."

Steve had been sitting on the edge of his cot with his elbows on his knees. Now he buried his face in his hands. Hamm didn't know if he was crying or not, for he made no sounds. Steve shook his head back and forth in a way that was both so pathetic and defeated that Hamm could barely bring himself to look at him. It felt as if he had now intruded too far into his best friend's life.

In his embarrassment, Hamm started to rummage through his duffel for something resembling a clean outfit when Gwerski walked through the door.

"You guys heard the news?"

Steve quickly wiped his face. He looked at Hamm and then said to Gwerski, "What news?"

"Bürgermeister Kimmel. The Mayor."

"Ooh, I like your German accent, Gwerski," Schneider said. "Keep it up."

Gwerski frowned, and then went on. "Hanged himself last night from the rafters in his office. I guess he couldn't take looking at all the bodies. I had him on burial detail the last couple of days." He looked down at his feet, oddly saddened by what had happened. As if it were somehow his fault for forcing the man into burying the dead.

"You know what?" Schneider said. "I couldn't give a shit about him or any of the rest of them. They all knew what was going on here. Every last one of them. You could smell the burning bodies for miles around, for Christ's sake. Still can. They could see the smoke. The ashes must have fallen on their houses. Jesus! Listen, Sergeant, you've got nothing to be ashamed of. The creep deserved it."

Gwerski looked directly at Schneider. "What could he have done even if he did know, Major? I mean, the Krauts, the Nazis, the SS ran the show. It wouldn't have mattered what he knew or didn't know. He couldn't have done nothin' about it. Any of them. What's one man gonna do?" Hamm stood up, putting on some reasonably clean pants. "Look, it just doesn't matter right now. Nothing matters now but getting the dead people identified, and buried, and out of the way. And we've got to try to keep the rest of them alive. These German civilians are a work force. Nothing more. They bury the dead, and that leaves more of us to take care of the living ones. Nothing more, Sergeant. It isn't your responsibility. Just do as you're ordered."

Gwerski looked at Hamm and Schneider and started to leave. There was a terrible look on his face. As he passed through the door, he muttered, "Yeah, yeah. That's what the Krauts keep saying: 'Just following orders.'"

Chapter Thirty

S chneider stared into Berg's eyes again as he had been doing for countless days. Every morning before going to the clinic, and every evening before sacking out for the night, he sat with his uncle in the older doctor's office. They had moved Berg's cot permanently into the office, hoping that the familiar surroundings would help ease him back into the real world. Since their reunion, Berg had lapsed back into a near catatonic state. He spent most of his time staring into the far distance, devoid of focus and emotion. He hadn't spoken since he said Schneider's name on the very first day.

They had managed to spoon-feed him enough food and fluids to keep him alive, if not actually thriving. He was as emaciated as some of the inmates, and his color was deathly.

Hamm, Molly, and Schneider sat in a semicircle about his bed. McClintock had gone out to get fresh coffee, and Gwerski was still doing the best he could, following Green's orders to bring some semblance of normalcy to this wretched place.

This particular evening, Berg was sitting up in his bed, leaning against pillows Molly had fluffed up behind his back.

Molly looked at Berg and said, "We can't put him back into that, that..." she said, pointing vaguely at the camp outside. "I don't know what to call it. But we can't let him go back there. This has been his home all these years, and I think we have a chance if we keep him right here."

"I have no problem with that, Molly," Schneider said. "I just don't think we're doing him any real good."

Hamm stood and paced for a second. This usually meant that he had something important to say, for he always paced when he was making a decision.

"Here's what we need to do," he began, his eyes squinting as if he were reading his plan off a distant backboard. "There's no psychiatric help coming any time soon. That's one thing we know for sure. This man is our colleague as well as your uncle, Steve. He stayed here and took care of the sick with nearly nothing in the way of supplies. He defied the SS from what I heard, and he took a lot of chances. He kept a log of the atrocities so we could prosecute the bastards who did this. If nothing else, we need him to testify and certify his diary.

"But more than anything else, he's one of us." Hamm looked at Schneider. "He's a doctor. He is one of our own. You know how every time one of us or one of our family members goes into a hospital or gets sick, our colleagues fall all over themselves to give us the best treatment. Nurses, doctors, administrators. Everyone. They bypass waiting rooms, they get special rooms and the best meals. You know. It's just what we do for each other. I'm not letting this doctor fall through the cracks and go back out there. And I'm not going to give up. We're going to take care of him until he's better, even if it means taking him into our own quarters until he's recovered. Period! No arguments!"

"No arguments here," Schneider said. "I've loved this man all my life. I'm with you."

"Me, too, Hamm. I'm with you guys," Molly said. "So? What now?"

They all remained silent, the only sound being their heavy breathing, Berg included.

Then Hamm said, "OK, here's how we start. We've already done all we can with his nutrition and his general health. He isn't exactly thriving, but neither is he slipping backwards, and I really think he's better than when we found him. What we do now is we continue the same medical regimen—I don't want to get off the winning horse at this point—but push harder from the psychiatric point of view. I think he is just shutting out the horror of all these years. Let's see if we can surround him with normalcy. Pictures of home. Find personal items and make his quarters here, more like a place he would want to be in, not a prison or a death chamber. We can move him into our quarters as the next option."

"I saw some stuff in the desk and in the back room as well," Molly said. "I have time right now. Let's just do it."

So without any delay, they ransacked Berg's hospital and office space. There was damned little stuff anywhere, but Molly came up with some hidden family pictures that were torn and faded. She showed them to Schneider, who pointed to each in turn. "That's my Aunt Rachel. These are the children, Max and Aaron. They would be older now. This was before the war, of course." He choked on his last words as he realized how little chance there was that his aunt or the children were alive.

Hamm cleaned out all the traces of Berg's other world: anything to do with the concentration camp part of his life. The logs and diaries which had been carefully removed from their septic hiding place, sanitized and stashed in Major Green's office safe, along with the identification papers of the dead prisoners. Instruments and clothing were all removed and replaced with as many "normal" items of daily life as they could find. They even came up with some respectable pictures of Germany before the war and hung them on the walls.

Berg seemed to be paying no attention, so after about an hour's worth of redoing his quarters, they tucked him in, and turned out the light. Then they all left for the night, completely exhausted but somewhat optimistic. They had, after all, done something.

Schneider turned to Hamm as they left the room and closed the door.

"We always say 'primum nole nocere.' Above all, do no harm. But it's embedded in the soul of every surgeon that doing something is better than standing around with your thumb up your ass. I feel as if we have to remove our collective thumbs and do something, but I just don't know what the hell to do."

Hamm put his hand on Schneider's back and gently propelled him to the door. "Let him rest, Steve. One day at a time. He doesn't need a surgeon now. He just needs a family and a lot of rest. And you're his family."

"Dear Daddy," the letter began as always. It was in pencil, printed neatly on deckled-edged paper with yellow daisies along the borders. It was from Emily, of course, and Schneider could picture her carefully composing each sentence with Anna looming over her shoulder and suggesting sentences faster than Emily could write them. He laughed at the image of his two little girls flopped across Emily's bed and squabbling over the letter, with Emily playing the role of the older and wiser sister.

The letter had come in a bunch with several others from Susan. But he always read Emily's first, in chronological order, because her stories, her enthusiasm for life, lifted his spirits.

"I can't wait 'til you get home!!!!!! I have so much to tell you and show you!!!!!" Emily's whole life was balanced on the tips of exclamation points.

"Anna is here bugging me to tell you she has a new teacher this term because her other teacher got sick. Really important, right??!!?? Anyway...."

And she would go on for pages in her precise handwriting, telling her father of nearly everything that happened since the last letter. Schneider knew that when he got home there would be nothing new for him to learn, but she would tell it to him all over again. Oh, the joys of having daughters!!!!

Emily was nine now, in the spring of fourth grade, and knocking them dead, according to Susan. She was beautiful and ebullient about almost everything. She was also way ahead in her reading. Anna, seven years old, lagged behind a bit since Emily did a lot of the reading and writing for her. They had become inseparable since Schneider went to war. Susan sent new pictures regularly for they were growing up so fast that he actually might not have recognized them after the years of separation. He made a mental note to bring some of these pictures to his uncle in the morning. And then he felt a sadness, since Berg knew nothing of the terrible struggle Schneider was having over the possibility of leaving his family.

Each new letter also brought sadness beyond bearing. He was in a constant state of guilt and sorrow since he and Molly had fallen in love. There were so many questions that he dared not ask himself; he was left in a self-made limbo, struggling between his passion for Molly and a longing for his family. Like a spoiled child, he wanted it all. For all the difficulties that Susan and he had been having before he went to war, he still had a family back there who were expecting him to come home to them and start their lives over now that the war was over and won. They had every reason to think that all would be just as it was before he left them; that he would be just the same. It was hard enough to imagine what he was going to say to Susan, who didn't know Molly even existed. But, far worse, what would he tell the girls? How could he even begin to explain it, if he were to leave them? Only then did he realize that his thoughts were almost exactly the words that Hamm had said to him.

Molly once asked him if she could see a picture of Susan and the girls. He lied at first, telling her that his photos had been lost in one of their fast evacuations during the Battle of the Bulge as everyone was calling it now. That, too, left him feeling empty and guilty, for now he was lying to Molly as well. Eventually, he showed her some of the pictures, and he could feel a sadness in her as great as his own. He thought the fact that she had been married too had sensitized her to the idea of loss, whether it was from death or desertion. And he thought she saw herself as the culprit in all of it.

It all made him wonder, night after night when he was alone with his thoughts: Who was he and what had he become? Was lying a way of life with him, now? Would lying be his stock-in-trade forever? Even Hamm had plowed his way into the quandary, and Schneider had been rude to him far beyond what Hamm deserved. Perhaps the level of his guilt made Hamm's questions all the more painful.

"So what are you and Molly going to do when this is over, Steve?" Hamm asked still again one night as they were sorting out their gear. It was not long after they had walked into that hellhole of a concentration camp, and neither of them knew whether they would be there for months or longer. The question of when the war would actually end for them was completely unsettled, except for the daily ration of scuttlebutt. "I don't know," Schneider mumbled back, hoping Hamm would just drop it. But he didn't.

"Susan have any idea about all this?"

"Of course not!" Schneider snapped. He was really afraid that Hamm assumed he had told Susan, and that Hamm might have written home something in a letter to Allison. So Schneider asked him directly.

"You talk to anyone about this? At home, I mean? Allison?"

"Take it easy, Steve. I haven't had a single conversation about it, not even with Molly. I doubt there's anyone in the entire Army of Occupation who doesn't know, but nobody out here really cares. Everyone has just one thought right now, and that is when are we going home? So, no, I don't think that Susan will ever hear anything from this side of the Atlantic."

Schneider cooled down a little, but he could feel his heart racing, whether from anxiety or embarrassment he couldn't decide. It was as if he had been caught at something. Perhaps it was a projection into the not-so-far-off future when he might be having this conversation with Susan. But, Hamm wasn't his superior officer. He was a friend, and Schneider realized his questions were out of concern for him and for Susan. And for Molly. Everyone in the group, he realized, was in love with Molly in one way or another. Even Hamm. They would die for her if it came to that.

"I don't know...I just don't know," Schneider said. "When we were so close to dying at the hands of the SS—when they captured the whole field hospital—I couldn't think of anything else but how I was going to save Molly. There wasn't anything else. I lived every day the way we did all through France. I just hoped to live one more day, and I would take what was given to me."

Hamm said, "It isn't about taking, Steve. We're well beyond the taking stage of things. You have a hell of a lot of responsibility back home: Susan and the girls, a home, a whole life you built. Are you going to throw it all away on a battlefield romance?"

Schneider turned to face Hamm, furious at his relegating what Schneider felt for Molly into something transient and sordid.

"What the hell does that mean, a battlefield romance? You have something to say on that?"

But Hamm never blinked. He never backed down. He just kept his usual calm, the same calm that he had when the whole world was going to hell, when tents were falling down and the OR was ventilated by shrapnel. No matter how bad it was, Hamm always just kept his head down, put out his hand, and asked for another clamp. Or needle holder. Or suture. Schneider usually admired his steadiness in the worst situations; Hamm was the rock. Now, his friend's steady calm just pissed him off.

"Steve," Hamm said without a pause, "I know you, and I know Susan, and I know Molly. I'm in as good a position to see this in a realistic light as anyone. And this is not the real world. It's no more real than the midnight emergencies we used to do back home. Remember? The car accidents, the gunshot wounds, the ruptured aneurysms; everyone running around trying to save lives in the middle of the night."

"What does that have to do with anything?"

"It has everything to do with everything. We have spent a lot of our lives in a surreal environment. We're dealing in life and death, up at two or three in the morning, dressed in pajamas with colleagues, men and women whose adrenaline is surging and their hormones buzzing. You know what I'm talking about. You've been there. How many quick romances have you seen after a big night in the OR? Trips to the unmade bed in the on-call room. You know just what I mean."

"So, you're saying—"

"I'm saying," he cut Schneider off, "that this is no different, except there's even more adrenaline and more craziness. People are trying to kill us, and none of us know when our number's coming up. So we throw our values out the window because life seems so short. Why deprive yourself of anything when you may not live to get back to the old world?"

Schneider had no answer, and by then he knew exactly what Hamm was talking about. He started doing busy work organizing his stuff, folding clean clothes and arranging his bed.

"I understand falling in love with Molly. She's young, and smart, and brave, and beautiful. She's a wonderful woman. Who wouldn't fall in love with Molly? If I weren't married I would be first in line! The issue is that you are married to Susan, and you have made promises to her, and indirectly to Anna and Emily, and you now have to keep those promises. I won't insult you by saying that you're thinking with your dick. I know there's a lot more to this than that. But for God's sake, Steve, you're married! Susan is your wife, and you now need to end this with Molly and go on home again."

"I—"

"And don't leave any doors open with Molly," Hamm said, cutting him off. "You have to be clear. Don't give her false hope. That would be too cruel. She has already had one terrible tragedy in her life, losing her husband. Don't drag this out and give her false hope, like, 'Let's just go our separate ways and think this over.' None of that crap. She needs to start her life over clean and find a man who loves her and have a family—just like the one you already have."

Schneider had nothing to say. He didn't want to agree with Hamm, but he couldn't argue with a single thing Hamm had said. He was totally deflated.

He nodded weakly and said, "I know, Hamm. I know. Thanks, pal."

A few days later, Schneider was sound asleep in his cot when he felt someone pushing him. He started to tell them to beat it when a hand covered his mouth, a small warm hand that smelled of…what did it smell of? Of Molly.

It was pitch black in the tent, so Schneider still couldn't see her. But he knew that scent, and it made him crazy.

Molly pushed in and crawled under the light army blanket alongside Schneider. He was wearing skivvies, and she had on a scrub suit. This was not going to help his resolve. Her head had barely touched the pillow before he had an erection, and she was doing nothing to stop them from going down that path. Then he realized they weren't exactly at the Ritz in Paris.

"What about Hamm?" he whispered into her hair.

"He's operating. Just started a thoracotomy, so he's gone for a couple of hours. I just had to see you, Steve. We haven't had a second alone in this place since I got here."

Schneider could feel every part of her body stretched out along her scrub suit and his shorts did nothing to separate them. She was down lower in the cot than he was, so her breasts were pressed against his stomach, her head into his chest. He was quickly losing control. He wanted her so badly right then that he had to squeeze his eyes shut in an effort to refocus on what Hamm and he had talked about. But, if she asked him right then to go AWOL with her and start their lives over together somewhere, he would have been packed in seconds and gone. Nothing Hamm could have told him would have stopped him.

"I spent the last several hours listening to a lecture from Mary," she whispered. "She told me it was time to leave you, to get on with my life. She said when they let us go home, you're going straight to Susan and the girls, and you're not even going to look back. Said this is all a combination of fairy tale and nightmare all rolled up into one. A romance and a horrible war. That none of it's real. Said I should cut my losses and run."

"She sounds like Hamm. I got the same lecture."

"I'm not doing it, Steve. I'm not just walking away without a fight. This isn't some one-night stand, some teenage quickie in your father's Chevy."

"Oldsmobile."

"Oldsmobile?"

"Yeah. My dad had an Oldsmobile."

"Who makes love in an Oldsmobile?" she said looking at him as if he were from Des Moines.

Schneider laughed and pulled her head back onto his chest. "Actually, nobody. I never did get laid in that car. But I sure made a lot of plans."

They laughed and then were quiet for a minute. Then he asked, "How is anyone back home going to understand what went on here, Molly? How can they possibly know what we've been through together?"

"They're not going to understand. The war changed everything. It's changed us. It's changed the whole world, and everyone thinks we're just going home, and everything's going to be just like before. But it's not. Not for me."

"Me neither," Steve said. "I just don't know how..." He stared into the darkness of the tent.

"How what?" Molly asked him.

"I don't know how we can return to that same life. I can't just pretend that you and I never happened."

"All of this happened, Steve. All of it. Nick was killed at Pearl. He is dead. We did meet and fall in love, and there's no denying any of it. I'm in love with you, and I don't care what Hamm or Mary or any of them say we should do. I'm not letting you go without a fight. I've fought my way through this whole war, and I'm not giving you up. I love you. I want to be with you for the rest of my life, and I'm not going to make it easy for anyone. Not Susan. Not even you."

Then she pursed her lips. He could feel her shaking, but he had no idea if it were from the fear that he might leave her or her rage to fight for him. Either way, it didn't matter. There was no argument that was going to settle it. No choice they could make was going to be good. It was like the war itself in a way. No matter how hard they tried to choose the very best paths, there was always wreckage in their wake.

And no matter what path I choose now, oh dear God, what havoc I'm going to create.

Molly stayed silent as Schneider thought of all the heartbreak ahead of them. Then, she wriggled up, nuzzling her face into his neck and kissing him gently along the edge of his jaw. But as he moved closer to her, if that were possible, he felt her tears streaming down his neck and onto his chest. Her crying was silent at first, followed by sobs that shuddered her whole body. She soaked them both.

When she stopped crying, she took his face in her hands and drew him into a long warm kiss. She rolled her soft lips around and around his until he released every thought but of loving her. Of loving her and making love with her. They scrambled out of what little they were wearing, pulling the scratchy blanket nearly completely over them. Molly pushed him gently onto his back and began kissing every inch of his body. He held her head and ran his fingers through her hair as he guided her kisses. She rested her head against his stomach and stroked his leg lazily, as if they had all night to be together. He could almost hear Edith Piaf again, the phonograph needle stuck in the last groove repeating toujours, toujours, toujours, toujours.

"We don't have forever tonight," he said to her, forgetting that she had no idea that he was back in Paris.

"Hmmm?" she said.

"I don't know how much longer we're going to be alone."

In response, she pulled herself up and climbed on top of him. She kissed him again and, with her hand, guided him inside her. This time they remained locked together in a dreamy slow passion, a long, long time, a simmer until she climaxed with barely a peep, falling finally onto his chest again and stayed against him as they both, against all good judgment, fell asleep.

Schneider woke from a deeply disturbed sleep, ready to tell her what he thought he needed to do. What they needed to do. He was tangled in the covers as he struggled to sit up in the pre-dawn darkness. He reached out to hold her again and pull her near him while they talked.

But she was gone.

When Hamm shook him awake later that morning, he leaped to his feet and scrambled for his clothes, thinking they were under attack. Hamm grabbed Schneider's shoulders and calmed him down. Schneider squinted into the light and shook his head, which caused a sudden pain. He must have been out cold.

"You've got to come see this, Steve!" Hamm was practically shouting and dragging Schneider at the same time. He had put his scrubs back on after realizing that Molly had left, so he slipped into his boots barefoot and followed Hamm out of the tent.

"What's happening?" he asked, still very muzzy-headed.

"Just wait and see. Just wait."

It was a brilliant, shining day, which only made Schneider squint all the more and intensified the pounding behind his eyes. They crossed the open field and headed for the remains of the prisoner's hospital, now empty except for Berg. The rest of their patients were all in the newly erected tents.

Hamm entered first, and as soon as they both adjusted to the relative dimness of the room, Schneider was shocked into immediate alertness, that ability that doctors develop after years of midnight emergencies. He couldn't believe his eyes.

Molly and McClintock were standing next to the wall, with Gwerski and Green on the other side. Seated at his desk was Berg. He was wearing a clean white coat over regulation U.S. Army scrubs. Over the left breast pocket of his white coat was a brand new nametag that said *Dr. Meyer Berg.* His hair was combed, and though he was still emaciated and sallow, he looked like a new man. And he was smiling! Everyone was smiling.

"My God, Uncle Meyer...." Schneider said. But he could find nothing more to say.

Green stepped forward.

"Major Schneider, I'd like you to meet our newest staff member."

Berg stood, slowly and painfully. He drew himself up to his full height, which Schneider could see was difficult for him. He extended his boney hand and said in his slightly accented English,

"Good morning, Stephen."

Schneider shook Berg's hand and then wrapped his arms around his uncle in a great bear hug. He could feel the bones through the thin skin and was afraid to squeeze too tightly. But Berg, too, held Schneider in his arms and did not release him. How long they held each other, Schneider wasn't sure. But it was all he could do not to cry. In his attempt to keep his feelings to himself, he was struck mute.

Berg sensed this, for he placed his left hand over Schneider's and squeezed even harder. He nodded his head as if to say, "Yes, I understand. I am overwhelmed as well."

Finally, when they released each other, Berg sat down quickly. He was clearly overburdened by both the emotional strain of the meeting as well as the physical effort of such a small gesture as standing and hugging his nephew. He leaned back in his rickety little chair and looked at everyone, one at a time. Schneider hadn't the slightest idea what Berg was thinking. Maybe what a ragtag bunch of saviors they all were. Probably not, though. He was looking not only at his long-lost nephew, but at his new colleagues, at others who knew just what he had been through and what he had to endure to stay loyal to his work, to his patients.

They all remained silent for a while. Then Gwerski slipped from the room with barely a sound. Green stepped to the side of the desk and squeezed Berg's shoulder. He nodded to all of them, then he, too, left the room with McClintock, followed closely behind by Hamm and Molly.

"Well," Berg said in perfect English. "We have a lot to talk about, don't we?"

"I think we do," Schneider said.

For the next several hours Berg and Schneider talked. Berg seemed never to tire now. He beckoned Steve to pull a chair closer to the desk

and began to tell his story. It started slowly like the soft patter of water at the beginning of a light rain. Then as the minutes and the hours passed, the momentum built until the stream of words merged into rivers, and the rivers into a torrent, until neither he nor Schneider could stem the flood of tears, and nothing would stop it but the telling and the hearing of all that had happened.

Chapter Thirty-one

26 May 1945, 0800 hours
A Concentration Camp near Weimar, Germany

That first day, Berg had begun talking as soon as the others had left the room. Slowly at first, choosing his words carefully. Stephen listened intently. He never took his eyes off his uncle's, never shifted in his seat.

To Berg, his cherished nephew would always be Stephen. Never Schneider or Steve as the other officers called him. As Stephen and Berg laughed together and cried together, they looked deeply into each other's souls. What Berg saw when he looked into Stephen's eyes; deeply, deeply into his eyes, was himself. They were two made into one. Their stories were different, but they were the same.

Over the next many days and weeks, Berg and Schneider talked in English and in German, and cursed and complained in Yiddish. Even a few words of French here and there when French expressed it best. Their languages bound them together almost as much as their blood, for they could use words in Yiddish that had no real equivalent in English. Some English words were senseless in German, and some words in German didn't have the same impact when spoken in English. Calling the Nazi's "pig-dogs!" just didn't resonate the way "Schwein-Hund!" did. And there was something about cocksucker and ratfucker that was just silly in German. Only in American English was swearing made sexual.

As Berg grew confident—not of his English, but of his story—he talked faster and faster until he had to stop himself and let Stephen talk for a while. The listening was hard. There was so much Berg wanted to tell his nephew. Should Berg not survive, he knew that Stephen would take Berg's story to the world, that Stephen must take his story to the world.

"When they brought me here," Berg said, "I looked upon the others...les autres...as something apart from me. I wasn't one of them. This was some horrible mistake. They were Jews, of course, like me. But I felt apart. When they took me to the clinic and put me to work, it made the separation even greater. But with time, a very long time, I realized that there was no difference. We were all the same. Each of us was a precious soul to someone out there. I noticed that those prisoners with no living relatives tended to die faster. They had nothing to live for. But for the others, each life had a value, a uniqueness that was sacred. Although I had skills and a value that was measured as greater than the others by the Nazis, it was all a myth. For if the time were to come when they no longer needed a doctor but needed more strong backs for the quarries, then I would join the lines at the showers. I would end my existence in some mass grave or as ashes streaming from the tops of the tall chimneys. My ashen remains would fall into the mud or onto the houses in that village over there. No, I was not very special after all."

Berg paused, for he was close to tears again and didn't want to cry.

"You said that every soul is unique, sacred," Stephen said. "I don't remember you being a religious man, Uncle."

"Religious? No. Not really. Do I believe in God? Before the war I didn't think about it much. I went to Schul on the High Holy days: Rosh Hashanah, Yom Kippur, Pesach. But these were family events. Social events. Times to be together. To eat, mostly. To hug and kiss our relatives. But God? No, not really in any deep or meaningful way. I was...mmm...agnostic? Is that the word?"

Stephen nodded. "That's the word, if you mean you don't know for sure one way or the other."

"Yes, yes, then. Agnostic. So, I didn't dwell on it. Later, here, when my life was in danger every day, every minute, I began to get some faith. Based on fear, admittedly, but faith nonetheless."

"There are no atheists in foxholes," Stephen muttered under his breath.

Berg hesitated, for he had no idea what Stephen meant. Then it came to him and he laughed. "Yes. There are no atheists in foxholes, or in prison camps either. That is a good one," he said with a smile to Schneider.

"Well, I regained some faith," he went on. "I prayed and made blessings over the patients. It was the only thing I could do for them sometimes, these barruchahs. I would have preferred your penicillin, but I had only the blessings, so I used them. I think they worked sometimes, too. Like penicillin. A miracle drug, you call it. So I had miracles, too. The miracle was that some of my patients actually survived. Not many, but some."

Stephen nodded but seemed to be caught in his own thoughts. Berg now waited for him to speak. There was a long silence, but Berg knew his nephew would say what he needed to when he was ready but not before.

Schneider looked at his uncle again, and said, "Uncle Meyer. Can I ask you something? Something very personal?"

"Of course, Stephen. You can ask me anything."

"Well, I have a problem. It might seem very trivial right now. With all the death and the suffering.... I'm almost ashamed to bring it up. But I have no one else left to go to." Schneider looked away and pursed his lips, considering if he should continue.

"Please, my boy. Go on."

"Some time ago I met someone. A nurse. You met her. Her name is Molly. We worked closely together, and after a while we began to have...feelings for each other." Schneider squirmed.

Berg waited, his face showing nothing. So Schneider continued.

"So, one thing led to another. Something about the war, the killing, the dying, the fear, all of it, I think, pushed us closer and closer together. And now I think we're both in love." He grimaced at what he had just said, and squeezed his eyes shut and shook his head. "I'm sorry, uncle, I shouldn't involve you in this."

Berg smiled. "Go ahead, Stephen, involve me." He gave a little laugh.

Schneider breathed more easily and said, "Well, now the war is almost over. We'll all be going home. I can't believe I'm saying this, but I don't want to go home. It wasn't good between Susan and me when

I left. Our marriage was a shambles. Had there been no war, it might have ended anyway. But, now?"

"Listen to me, Stephen. This is an old story. Older than you can imagine. And believe it or not, I once faced the same problem. There was a woman in my life, who also wasn't my wife. And like you, she was a nurse too. Before the war. Many years. And I had the same pain. Agony over what I should do."

Schneider waited a beat, wanting to hear the end of the story. Finally, he asked, "What did you do? How did you choose?"

"In the end, I followed my heart," Berg said quietly.

The two men stared into each other's eyes for the longest time. Neither spoke. Was Stephen's Aunt Rachel his Molly or his Susan?

But his uncle said nothing more.

Finally, Schneider took a breath and said, "From what I've heard so far, you are telling me the story of my own life, Uncle Meyer. Not about Molly. But our families. Yours and mine. My parents are German Orthodox Jews just like you were, of course. But I never embraced my past or my religion. Truthfully, I rejected both. I'm an agnostic, too, maybe even an atheist. Foxholes or not. Or at least I was. Then, even if I didn't start believing in God, I at least allowed myself to realize that there were some things out of my control. Along with that, I began to identify with my parents again, especially Mom. I realized how cruel it must have seemed to them that they embarrassed me so. That I never brought my friends home. That I denied their heritage, their religion. Now that I'm a father, myself, I can feel their anguish that their only son was ashamed of them for something that they could not control: who they were, where they came from. I feel so ashamed.

"Then, when I got here—especially in the last weeks when we marched into a defeated Germany—I had new feelings about my mother and father. It wasn't because of any fear of dying. I don't think it ever struck me clearly until I walked into this camp. It was just like being hit in the chest with a huge rock. It took the wind out of me, and it literally knocked me to my knees. I couldn't breathe; I couldn't stand up. I found I couldn't look around at what was here: the people, and the bodies, and the suffering. I shut it all out. All the death and dying I've seen since D-Day did nothing to harden me, to prepare me for this. Then, on my knees next to Hamm in that mud— my best friend vomiting out his guts—and a little naked man, a skeleton, really, comes along and tries to comfort Hamm. Comfort us! His saviors! That was the moment, I think. I knew where my heart's connections were, and I know now I can never sever them, even if I wanted to. I am connected to these people and to the generations of my people all the way as far as we can trace the family. And I can't cut that cord no matter how much I might want to. I'm connected to you; there's no need, no desire to cut that cord. I'm your nephew, and I'm a Jew. And I am a German."

Stephen stopped and lowered his head. It was the first time he stopped looking at Berg.

"I know that connection, Stephen," Berg said. "I am tied to our ancestors now as well. I even know exactly when I realized it. Too bad it had to happen as the result of something so awful. An evil beyond imagination. Too bad it doesn't happen as the result of something wonderful. Some miracle of God. Saving a patient who really should have died. Shouldn't that give us our faith every time? But it doesn't. The miracles become routine, and just maybe, the horror is required. Horror beyond belief."

Berg stopped then because the memories were flooding back, and he wasn't ready for them. But he knew that some floods he couldn't stop, and he couldn't stop this one. He talked and he sobbed and he told Stephen how he found his faith. It should have been something wonderful, but it was the most terrible thing that ever happened to him.

He told Stephen of how he had to kill his own father, Stephen's great uncle.

He told him in detail. Every intimate moment so that someone beside himself and that scum of a Nazi that made him do it (he would never speak that name again) would know. And Stephen listened and heard him and they both cried. Stephen barely remembered Berg's father, it was so long ago that they had met. But in the telling of it, Berg knew that the nightmares might now end. That, for the first time since that evil moment in the hospital when he had to plunge the needle into his father's heart, he might sleep through the night and not wake again drenched in his own sweat and tears. For a moment, with Stephen hugging his shoulders and comforting him, Berg was afraid that he had passed on a contagion to Stephen worse than typhus, worse than the plague—that he had infected Stephen with his nightmares. Berg wondered silently how Stephen would ever be cured of such knowledge.

When Berg could speak no more, the two stood and held each other in silence until the shaking and the sobbing subsided. Stephen backed slowly away and sat down again, and to his everlasting credit in Berg's eyes, he did not try to console him or rationalize what Berg had done. He did not tell Berg that it was OK because it ultimately saved his father further suffering. He did not tell Berg that he really had no choice, that he did the right thing. No, instead he chose to suffer with him and share the terrible weight in his heart and, by doing so, lightened it a fraction. Berg might never dream of that awful act again, but he would also never spend a remaining day of his life without thinking of it. Now, sadly, neither might Stephen.

However, there was something more. Something Schneider would not crystallize in his mind for several more days. Something had happened to him as he shared the terror and the horror with his uncle. He realized—no, more than that; he truly believed for the very first time—that there are many things worse than pain or death. Death, in itself, was a normal event in the course of living. Sometime after that day, Schneider felt the nagging fears that plagued his life slip away from him like a heavy burden falling from his shoulders. No, he realized, there are many worse things than death. With that threat gone, there was little left to frighten him.

Chapter Thirty-two

15 April 1946, 1900 Hours
Deutsches Theater Restaurant, Munich, Germany

The old restaurant was slowly filling up. The people milled about uncertainly as they entered the large room, finding their way to wooden tables set with military precision in long, parallel rows. The room had been cleaned meticulously, something of a rarity in Munich at the time because, now, even a year after the liberation of the camps, rubble and destruction were everywhere. The tables were set with clean dishes and silverware, mostly unmatched. There were water glasses and wine glasses supplied by the US Army.

Quiet dominated the room in spite of the fact that more than two hundred people were gathering for dinner.

"Hey, Hamm," Schneider whispered. "Where should we sit?"

Hamm shrugged his shoulders and looked over at McClintock. McClintock, moved into the room and began searching for an empty place. He roamed the room to find a table. Berg and Molly were sticking very close to Schneider. The group did not want to impose themselves upon the civilians there. They would be happy if any of the German citizens joined them, but this little medical team felt as if they were intruding into someone else's home. All except Berg, himself, who knew he was home. Finally.

They were dressed in their cleanest uniforms, pressed as well as they could be. Their shoes had been shined, and some of the battle-weary clothing long since replaced. There was a stark contrast between their own clothing, now replenished by the quartermaster corps, and the range of attire that surrounded them. Some of the civilian men and women were dressed neatly in suits and dresses. Most of the garments were clean, if a bit tired looking, with attempts made to repair the tears and the ragged cuffs. Some had not been able to do so. Many of the men were wearing tallit, Jewish prayer shawls, and all had their heads covered with black yarmulke, the small ever-present skullcaps. Schneider, McClintock, Berg, and Hamm had picked up their yarmulkes from a basket at the door. Schneider looked a bit uncomfortable when he put his on, but McClintock seemed to be enjoying it, as if he were incognito. Hamm took a tallit and folded it into his pocket. Berg was dressed in a dark gray suit and black tie. His shirt was new and stood out in contrast to the tired clothing of the other civilians. It was oversize, but clean.

They found an empty table not too far from the front of the room. There were sets of candles on every table, with matchsticks lying neatly next to each. The military precision and orderliness shone through the religious civility of the room. They sat down on the chairs and benches and noticed, as they waited, that no one else seemed comfortable enough to join them at the couple of empty places at their table.

"Who's at the head table?" McClintock asked, pointing toward the dais with his chin.

"I think that's the army chaplain, the Rabbi," Hamm said. "He put this whole thing together. Massive undertaking, from what I heard. They had to organize—appropriate, uh, steal really—everything, sometimes not exactly through Army channels."

"Like what?" Molly asked.

"Like everything!" Schneider cut in. "They scrounged the silverware, the glasses, and the tablecloths. Food. Kosher wine. They even had to find Hebrew type to print the prayer books. Almost all that stuff was destroyed by the Nazis years ago."

"So, Steve, you going to be my guide tonight?" McClintock asked. "I mean, this is my first Passover dinner. Probably Molly's, too," he said nodding in her direction.

"Seder, Ted. Not dinner. You may as well start out calling it by the right name. It's a Passover festival, but don't forget that Jesus's Last Supper was a Seder too. And he was a Rabbi."

"I know, I know. We just never emphasized that part of it in our family. Presbyterians don't really spend a lot of time on Jesus's Jewishness."

"I can only imagine," Hamm said.

"Well, tonight's Seder is very special," Schneider said. "It's the first one openly celebrated in Germany since Hitler and his goons took power. This is going to be one hell of a special event." He was barely able to speak by then, as he realized just exactly what a moment this was for the German Jews there that night.

An older man and woman entered the room, looking around for seats, which were rapidly becoming scarce as the time approached for the Seder to begin. Hamm saw the couple tentatively approaching the table. He raised a welcoming hand and waved them over. The couple nodded and, as if ordered, took seats next to Hamm and McClintock. The old man helped his wife off with her coat, and then settled himself into his own seat.

Hamm realized he couldn't tell how old these people were. Maybe in their sixties. She had the look of a scared sparrow. There was constant fear in her eyes, as well as an unbearable sadness. Hamm was, by then, too familiar with that look, those eyes. He thought she might jump up and fly away at the first word spoken to her.

The husband—he supposed the man was her husband—seemed to be holding it together for the two of them, though he was in no great shape himself. He, too, had that look. Hamm didn't know quite how to describe it, but when he looked into the man's eyes, he felt as if he had to look away. It was as if he might see in those eyes what the man had seen. Those scenes burned into the poor man's retinas might project back to Hamm like an image on a movie screen. He just didn't want to see them. He had already seen enough, and what his eyes had seen was nothing to what the old man's had.

As if to confirm his suspicions, the woman stretched out her left arm to steady herself on the table as she sat down. In doing so, she exposed her forearm, and everyone could see the serial number tattooed there in black ink. They all looked away quickly, and the woman seemed not to notice.

"Guten Abend," Schneider said to the couple. Good evening.

"Guten Abend," the man and woman said together. She was still looking down at the table. The man, at least, was able to meet Schneider's eyes as he spoke.

Though Berg remained quiet, Schneider knew that he could count on him to bring the couple into the conversation if necessary. Schneider's German was very good by now, but of course, Berg's was perfect.

"Sprechen sie Englisch?" Schneider asked them, and to everyone's relief, they did.

Their speech was somewhat halting, and heavily accented, but the evening was made immeasurably easier for everyone once they had a common language.

Berg reached across the table to shake hands with the husband. "My name is Meyer Berg," he said in English, "and I'm so glad to see you here." The man shook Berg's hand tentatively, and the woman nodded, her eyes still lowered.

"My name is John Hammer," Hamm said, "and this is Steve Schneider, and Ted McClintock. This is Molly Ferrarro." He purposely avoided using terms of military rank.

"I am Chaim Guttmann," the old man said, nodding to everyone at the table in turn. "And this is my wife, Bessie."

"We're so happy you could join us," Molly said, speaking for the first time since she entered the room. Molly had shifted her seat to be nearer Bessie.

Hamm, for his part, still feared that at any moment the tiny woman would flap her little wings and fly out the door, but Molly's presence seemed to reassure her. Then the group settled back in silence and looked at each other. It was a very awkward moment for everyone, that feeling that they had so little to say at such a momentous time in history. And yet there were so many horrible shared stories that they did not want to share, or even to remember.

Soon the tables were filled to capacity. GIs were bringing in extra chairs to fill up every possible place. They all had the same thoughts gnawing at their brains. They looked into the faces of the young GIs and WACs and saw there the faces of all the others who were gone now. Gone forever.

By the time the rabbi was ready to begin the service, every seat in the hall was filled. There were easily more than two hundred people there.

Hamm leaned toward the elderly couple. He still could not be sure of their ages because there was a timelessness in their faces obscured by something that spoke of stories almost too terrible to tell. He asked, "So, Herr Guttmann, are you and your wife from Munich?"

Great conversationalist I am, he thought.

Guttmann looked at his wife for a moment. She turned her face, but Hamm could see the tears forming on her cheek. She did not wipe them away.

"No, sir," Guttmann replied. "We are from a very small town in the east. On the Polish border." Guttmann did not mention the name of the town. Hamm suspected it would mean nothing to him anyway, and perhaps there was no longer such a place.

"Do you have family here in Munich?" Hamm asked, instantly regretting it, and wanting to pummel himself for his stupidity. Everyone had lost family in this war, and of all people to ask, Jewish refugees.

Idiot! he thought to himself. Leave it alone. I should stick to talking about the weather!

But Guttmann never missed a beat. He began to tell his story as if it were the most natural thing in the world. Bessie didn't look up, but kept her eyes fixed on the rabbi and the preliminaries of the service.

"When the Germans marched into Poland," he explained, "all the Jews were rounded up and moved to the resettlement camps. We were given a few hours to collect one small bag of belongings, and were told that we would be moved to a place where there were other Jews; that there would be some sort of work for us to do. Food and shelter would be provided." He paused and smiled the tiniest of smiles, shaking his head at his stupidity, his naiveté. "So, what could we do?" he went on, shrugging his shoulders and turning his hands upward as if to God. "What else could we believe? We packed a few things, and we went." His voice rose a little at the end of each sentence.

"We went to the railway station, and then it became clear that all was not as they told us...that something was wrong. There were hundreds of guards with guns, and uh hunds, uh...dogs, biting at us. We saw that the trains were cars for...for...."

"Cattle?" Berg offered, after exchanging a few words in German.

"Yes. Yes. For cattle. Not for people. They put so many of us in there that we could not sit down. We were shoulder by shoulder. Even the old ones had to stand up. There were no toilets…no heat…no water or food…."

He stopped and began to shake. Berg reached out and touched Guttmann's arm.

"This is hard, I know. But, it has been very good for me to tell these things. To say it out loud. But take a moment. It's okay."

Guttmann nodded. He looked to Bessie for support, but she said nothing. Then he gathered his strength, seeming to steel himself to tell the story that had to be told. Each time he told it, Hamm and Schneider realized, he was writing history. He, like Berg, like so many others, was insuring that there would be someone else—one more person, a witness—who would know what happened; who would hear the truth; who would tell the truth to others.

"It was the old ones who made me so sad," Guttman went on, "and the children. It was so awful for them, for they didn't have the strength. I was only thirty-eight years old at the time, and I could barely take it. But the children…."

Everyone at the table was horrified when they realized that this man sitting next to them was likely less than forty-five years old. The man looked as old as their grandfathers.

But Guttmann went on as if he had not noticed.

"We were on that train for nearly four days, in weather that was often below freezing. Several people in my car died, and their bodies were passed out the door whenever the train stopped."

The man stopped again and rubbed his eyes. Then he told some of the details of his imprisonment. Only at the very end of the story did he mention that he and Bessie had brought their three small children with them. When they arrived at the camp, the children were taken away and sent to a different enclosure. They would go to a children's school, the guards had said, reassuring the panicked parents.

"We never saw them again. We still look, but…."

"How did you survive in a place like that?" Molly asked. "And how do you ever get over it? How…?"

Bessie interrupted her. The table became quiet, and all the eyes were on the woman, for it was the first time she had spoken.

"You survive!" she said with a fire that was completely unexpected. "That's all you can do," she added, looking directly into Molly's eyes. She spoke each word separately, distinctly, as if to emphasize that every word counted; every word she said, they all must remember. "You do whatever it takes to survive," she went on. "Every person is capable of doing the most awful things imaginable, if it means surviving for just one more minute."

There seemed nothing more to say. But, quietly, Chaim finished their story.

During the past year they had been going from town to town, soliciting everyone from the International Red Cross to the Armies of Occupation to the relief organizations, searching through the various lists of both the dead and the survivors. There was still no word of their children. Their whole life's quest was merely to answer that one question. It would be better to find out the children were, in fact, dead, than to go on not knowing where they were, how they were, who was taking care of them…or not.

The rabbi moved to the center of the dais, his neat black robe open at the top button, exposing a glimpse of his army shirt and tie underneath its folds. On his head, he too wore the traditional black yarmulke and around his shoulders the tallit. He grasped the fringe hanging from the corner of the blue and white silk shawl and kissed it.

Hamm reached into his pocket and pulled out the tallit he had picked up when he entered the room. He kissed the prayer shawl and placed it around his shoulders.

While the rabbi prepared to begin the service, Berg leaned toward the Guttmanns. He said in German, "We must continue sometime, the three of us. Just us. It will be good for all of us."

Guttmann nodded.

The rabbi looked up at the congregation gathered before him. He started to speak, but stopped. Tears filled his eyes, and he paused to wipe them away. He cleared his throat and, in a voice hoarse with emotion, began the service with the most important of all Jewish prayers, the affirmation of the unity of God.

"Shema, Yisroel. Adonai eloheynu. Adonai, echod."

Hear, oh Israel. The Lord our God, the Lord is One.

All around the room, the voices of the Jews followed the Passover prayers in several languages. Schneider, too, was uttering the first Hebrew words that every Jewish child learned. Hamm realized that this was the first time he had ever heard Schneider speak Hebrew. Schneider looked at Hamm as he spoke, the trace of a smile on his lips painted over with a dab of shame.

Molly nestled close to Schneider's shoulder. Hamm could see a terribly sad look in her eyes. He felt as if he needed to pray for the two of them as much as for anyone else. Life was not going to be easy for them no matter what course of action they decided.

As the evening wore on, German remained the dominant common language. However, there was a polyglot mixture as well of Hebrew, French, English, Polish, Russian, Spanish, Czech, and even Italian. And these were only the languages Schneider and Hamm could pick out from the voices around them. Others, they had never heard before.

On the table between every two seats was a black book, marked on its cover with two concentric circles surrounding the familiar capital letter A, the insignia of the United States Third Army—by then known as The Army of Occupation of Southern Germany. Beneath the famous A were printed in red the English words:

PASSOVER SERVICE
Munich Enclave
Munich, Germany, April 15–16, 1946

McClintock shoved the book nearer to Schneider and gave him a questioning look. Schneider opened the first few pages and saw a woodcut design in Hebrew letters: Haggadah. He couldn't read the rest, but he assumed it had something to do with the artist and the author of the extraordinary text.

"It's the Haggadah," he whispered to McClintock. "The book we use for the Seder. It tells the order of the service, but basically it's the story of how God freed the Jews from slavery under Pharaoh in ancient Egypt."

McClintock nodded. He knew the story. He had, after all, read the Old Testament. Probably even more carefully than Schneider.

The next page was the title page for the book, which noted the place of the service: the Deutsches Theatre Restaurant. The rabbi's name was at the bottom. Neither Hamm nor Schneider had met him before, though they had heard of the work he was doing to restore the destroyed Jewish community, the She'erith Hapletah, "the few who escaped," or "the surviving remnant," as they were now called in Hebrew.

Hamm moved closer to follow the Haggadah with Schneider, McClintock and Molly. He pushed his own Haggadah over to the Guttmanns, thinking they needed to celebrate this on their own.

Schneider turned the page, falling further behind the chanting of the rabbi and the congregation.

The next woodcut shocked everyone. Instead of the traditional drawings of the pyramids and the other symbols of ancient Egypt, their eyes were drawn to the border of the page where there was a caricature of Hitler with a swastika armband. There were figures of emaciated men in the striped prison uniforms of the concentration camps, bent under the burden of heavy loads, presumably toiling for the Nazis rather than Pharaoh. The images of the victims of the Nazis evolved around the border of the page into pictures of fruit, and crops of grain, and a trowel to build a new nation: the foretelling of the coming of Eretz Yisrael, the Land of Israel.

The introduction, in English, also surprised them. The page began with, "And the khaki-clad sons of Israel commanded by Lt. General Truscotte gathered together as was the custom in Israel, to celebrate the Passover festival."

Schneider whispered to Hamm, "They seem to have left out Patton."

Hamm nodded, eyebrows raised, while Schneider turned the page.

More woodcuts bordered the pages, now showing the future in the Promised Land, a land of crops and farmers. The text went on to draw parallels between the liberation of the ancient Jews and the liberation of the camps.

Schneider turned the next page.

Everyone winced as they scanned the woodcut borders once again. At the top was another swastika and the words Brause Bad, the deadly gas showers of the extermination camps. More horrible still were the drawings of all the terribly efficient engines of death: the knives and axes, the gas chambers, and the crematoria. In the middle of the page, instead of the words that begin the traditional Haggadah,

"We were slaves unto Pharaoh in Egypt."

was inscribed alone on the page,

"We were slaves to Hitler in Germany."

And so this new Haggadah, "The Survivors' Haggadah," began, comparing at every turn the plight of the Jews under Hitler to the story of their slavery under Pharaoh. With each new page there was the suggestion, in drawings and in the text, that the bitter fruits of slavery would be turned into the fruits of the harvest; that the memories of the camps would spur the work of the future to provide the Jews with a place that was their own, just as Moses had led them to the Promised Land after their exodus from Egypt. Thus, the story that each Jewish father tells his sons and daughters every Passover, the story of the freeing of the Jews from slavery in Egypt, would now be joined by the telling of the story of their imprisonment under Hitler, and their exodus after their liberation by the Allied armies of Eisenhower. Woodcut after woodcut showed black and white images of the camps in the most chilling details: Nazi guards separating the children from their parents, soldiers shooting unarmed prisoners, laborers toiling under impossible loads as they were lashed by guards with leather whips, dark black chimneys spewing into the air the terrible smoke in which rose the souls of the tortured and the dead Jews. Among these were images of a brighter future of freedom, of plenty, of peace.

Those who were there would swear to tell the story forever so that no one could ever forget. No one. Ever.

Soon, nearly everyone in the room was either crying silently or straining to hold back tears. Even McClintock, and Molly were drawn into the collective sorrow of the Jewish service.

As the rabbi continued, Schneider explained the various elements to Molly and McClintock. It was a wonder for Hamm to see Steve shed his long-worn cloak of agnosticism and embrace his Judaism with fervor and pride. And tears.

Page after page continued to reveal woodcuts such as pyramids next to gas chambers and Pharaoh's slaves juxtaposed next to the camp victims digging their own graves. These were intermingled with the traditional Hebrew liturgy followed by admonitions to future generations.

With Schneider as their guide, Molly and McClintock learned about the Passover symbols. These very symbols had embarrassed Schneider as he grew up in an Orthodox Jewish home, driving him farther from his parents with every passing year; something only the war and its aftermath could reverse.

Schneider showed Molly and Ted the matzo, the unleavened bread that the ancient Jews baked on their backs by the heat of the sun as they fled across the desert; the bitter herbs to signify the bitter days of slavery; and the burnt lamb bone to recall the sacrifices. Molly crumbled the matzo as she took her turn, looking more like the Catholic she was, taking the host rather than the unleavened bread of the exodus. Berg lifted his piece of the matzo in a silent toast to Molly. She smiled at him and nodded.

The group heard the most famous of all the liturgy, the Four Questions, when the youngest child asks,

"Why is this night different from all other nights?

"Why is it on all other nights during the year we eat either leavened or unleavened bread, but on this night we eat only unleavened bread?

"Why is it on all other nights, we eat all kinds of herbs, but on this night we eat only bitter herbs?

"Why is it on all other nights we need not dip our herbs even once, but on this night we dip twice?

"On all other nights, we dine either sitting upright or reclining, but on this night we all recline?"

And the story began, as the eldest, this time the rabbi, answered the questions, reading from the Haggadah,

"We were slaves in Egypt unto Pharaoh..."

The child was told that the unleavened bread was a food of necessity for the fleeing Jews who had not the time to allow the dough to rise, that the bitter herbs are to remind them of the bitter times, and that reclining at dinner is the sign of a free man, no longer a slave.

And so it went that evening in Munich, as it was all over the rest of the world where Jews were free to practice their religion, free to ask these important questions.

At evening's end, the seven of them still at Hamm's table joined the service for the newly freed congregation of European Jews. Schneider rejoined his own faith; Hamm and Berg renewed theirs; McClintock and Molly celebrated for all of them. And the Guttmanns sobbed.

The shock of the revised Haggadah was just beginning to wear off when the service came to the chanting of the Dayenu, the Hebrew word signifying, "It would have been enough."

In the traditional Haggadah, the Jews thank God for his infinite blessings. In the traditional responsive reading, they say: if God had *only* freed us from Pharaoh, Dayenu! It would have been enough! If God had *only* led us out of Egypt, Dayenu! It would have been enough!

Each blessing was recounted and thanks was offered to God, for any one of those would have been enough!

But in the Haggadah of the Munich Seder, the Jews instead admonished God for plagues visited upon them by the Nazis.

"If he had given us the ghettos but no gas chambers and crematoria, Dayenu! It would have been enough! If he had given us the gas chambers and the crematoria, but our wives and children had not been tortured, Dayenu! It would have been enough! If he had tortured our wives and children...."

And so it went, on and on, reciting each and every horror of their lives under Hitler, every unthinkable, unspeakable plague endured under the SS and the Nazis, any one of which would have been enough!

By the time the Seder neared its end, the voices had grown hushed. Tears saturated every cheek and napkin. Schneider felt a desperate need to be by himself to assimilate the events of the evening. He knew that, for him, this would be a process that would go on for many years to come; the Seder was only the beginning.

This—perhaps the most unusual Seder since the Last Supper—unfolded in an ordinary restaurant before an extraordinary congregation. It reminded Hamm of how most of the great events in humankind's short history on the planet were played out in front of common, ordinary men and women.

As the evening wound down Hamm found himself focused on Molly and Steve. They had all been through years of war and all its horrors together, and he realized that in a short while they would all be parting. This Seder marked a special place in their lives, a line in time between the years of war and the years of peace. Hamm had a feeling that it might be a very long time before they three would be together again. For the past many months, they had worked together to clean up Hitler's mess: healing the casualties, civilian and military, left in the wake of the great armies of Europe. It once seemed as if they would be there forever. Now, on the eve of their departure, he realized that they were each going to travel very different paths.

Steve and Molly had been in their own world that night, their heads now close together as Schneider moved next to her and joined her in reading through "The Survivor's Haggadah." There was a connection between them so intangible yet so strong that it was palpable. Neither had said anything to Hamm about their plans after the war, but he was looking at two changed people. All of them were changed, of course. But these two lovers had much more pain in front of them. Whether they would stay together or not, Hamm wasn't sure. However, even he could see the connection between their hearts.

At the end, the congregation rose and silently shook the hands in turn of everyone at each table. "Next year, in Jerusalem," they repeated to each other. These the traditional words of hope and prayer of the Jews for as long as anyone could remember. The same words were on the lips of every congregant as the handshaking and hugging spread through the room. Even McClintock and Molly, the resident gentiles, found themselves caught up in this most important wish of Jews all over the world: to find a place of their own, a nation forever open to all Jews in need of a homeland.

Hamm could only wonder where each of them would be when it came time again for the Seder next year.

The crowd dispersed quickly when the Seder was finally over. The rabbi stood near the door, shaking hands with the German civilians as well as the army personnel as they left. Chaim and Bessie Guttmann stood uncertainly near the door. They seemed reluctant to leave the warmth and the safety of the restaurant. Berg approached them and spoke quietly in German.

He turned to Schneider and said, "I think I'll walk a while with the Guttmanns. They seem very uneasy to be on their own. I'll see you later at the rooms."

Schneider started to protest, still protective of his uncle. But he realized that the man needed to take over his life again, so this was as good a way as any. Here they could all recreate a kind of family: a new community.

Berg nodded to Hamm and lightly kissed Molly on both cheeks. He held his hand against her forehead for a few seconds as a blessing just for her. Then he hugged his nephew, Stephen, and disappeared with the Guttmanns.

Chapter Thirty-three

15 April 1946, 2200 Hours
Munich, Germany

Hamm, McClintock, and Schneider headed for the door. Molly took Schneider's arm and snuggled close to him as they walked out into the dark street. There was a chill in the air as the last remnants of the German winter held back the real coming of spring. The streets were wet and slick. Only a few streetlights were on, making glistening paths along the uneven and, as yet, unrepaired roadway. Hamm and McClintock walked a few yards in front of Schneider and Molly, hunched against the cold, hands stuck deep into their jacket pockets for warmth. The warm glow of the Seder and its camaraderie left their bodies as soon as they stepped out into the cold, wet Munich night. As they left the security of the large assembled crowd for the eerie emptiness of the rubble-strewn streets, an unease crept into their hearts.

Alone for the first time all evening, the group of four meandered slowly along the back streets of Munich, somehow reluctant to call it a night. The Seder had evoked many mixed emotions in all of them, a uniting of the spirit in many ways. For McClintock, it was a new look into a religion that had, for his whole life, seemed foreign and strange. The biases of his family had hardened him against the Jews when he was young. It was not until college, and then later in medical school and residency, that he had come face-to-face with large numbers of colleagues who were Jewish. Still, he had never really taken an interest in the religion itself, so his contacts were professional and social, rarely philosophical. He felt that something new and substantial had entered his life.

All lost in their own thoughts, the little procession followed no defined route, but rather slowly heading only in the vague direction of their billet, about a mile and half away. It would be only a twenty or thirty minute walk at their pace, but already Molly had begun to shiver from the dampness more than the temperature. The wet air seemed to cut through her army coat and knife straight into her bones. She tightened her grip on Steve's arm and pressed herself closer to his body for the heat she needed and out of the love she felt for him.

By the time they had walked no more than ten minutes, mostly in silence, the streets were entirely empty. Not a soul was in sight. Houses were dark, to save on the cost of electricity wherever it was available, to save on candles and lamp oil where it was not.

Hamm began to talk quietly to McClintock. Neither Molly nor Steve could hear what they were saying, nor did they try. Both still agonized over their own futures. Time was slipping away, and it was only a matter of days before they would have to decide what they would do. Molly was going to fight for Steve, no matter what it took. Steve was wavering painfully toward staying in Europe with Molly, at least for the foreseeable future. By not going home, he could delay the painful encounter with Susan. He rationalized his need to help resettle his uncle, but he knew in his heart that this was just an excuse. Berg was on his own road home, even though there was no home to which he could return.

About halfway back to the billet, Hamm and McClintock turned a corner, disappearing from sight for the few seconds it would take Steve and Molly to make the turn as well. Instinctively, the couple hurried their steps to catch up. There was safety in numbers, and though the Allies had definitely won the war a year earlier, the peace was still fragile: with the economy stalled, people were short of just about everything. Jobs were scarce. The menace of the post-war months was real, with bitter hatreds still active between the losers and the winners. To make it worse, there were illegal military handguns and rifles to be found nearly everywhere. Even grenades surfaced from time to time. The role of the military police had expanded considerably to restore order to the chaos. But it was taking time, and nobody was comfortable on the streets alone after dark.

As Steve and Molly neared the corner where they had lost sight of Hamm and McClintock, they heard a muffled noise, distinct but indecipherable. It was little more than a scuffling. But, there was something, something that made the hair stand up on the back of Steve's neck. Molly tightened her grip as Steve reached down to free himself from her hand on his arm. Instinctively, he wanted to be able to move. To fight? To run away? Something. But he didn't know what. In those short few seconds, his heart began to race, and even in the cold wet night, he began to feel the sweat breaking out on his forehead and down his back.

Steve and Molly turned the corner almost together. Steve reached out to hold Molly back, stepping forward to turn the corner first; to put himself between her and whatever danger might lie ahead.

Almost immediately he tripped, stumbling over the bodies of Hamm and McClintock. As he fell to the ground, he saw that his friends were prone, hands behind their heads, face down on the wet pavement. Two young German men—he couldn't see them well enough to guess their ages—were standing over them, the much taller man pointing an American officer's .45 at the back of Hamm's head. Molly, just behind Steve, rounded the corner, and before she too stumbled to the ground, grabbed the side of the building for support. Her stomach tightened and she cried out, "Steve!"

The sight of her created agitation and surprise from the two Germans, neither knowing where to point their weapons as they were now outnumbered by officers in uniform in this unexpected turn of events.

The man holding the gun on Hamm was dressed in a ragged German army greatcoat. The insignias were torn off, so the green color was deeper and richer where the insignias had protected the coat. The sleeves and hem were ragged, and there were tears in the front pocket.

A shorter man stood over McClintock, who was bleeding slightly from a two-inch gash in his forehead, the blood dripping over his left eyelid.

"Achtung, Kurtz!", the tall man shouted.

Kurtz was armed with a length of steel pipe, ready to strike again. In his left hand were two leather wallets dangling open, a few American bills protruding from the compartments.

Both men became increasingly agitated with the arrival of Molly and Schneider, and were now speaking frantically to each other in German.

Schneider tried to hear what they were saying. He could make out Ami, the derogatory German slang for the Americans. He also heard the German word, schießen, to shoot, along with the warning, Achtung!

Schneider rolled over and struggled to his knees to look around for Molly, making sure she was out of harms way. Just then Kurtz struck him across the temple with the pipe.

"Um Christus willen, schießen, Lange!

Hamm, right next to Steve on the ground, whispered, "Steve, what the hell are they saying?"

"Shit," Steve whispered, "He's telling him to shoot us! He's saying, 'Shoot for Christ's sake.' Can you fuckin' believe it?"

Lange, seeing them talking, kicked Schneider low in the left chest, knocking the wind out of him and momentarily paralyzing his diaphragm. Molly opened her mouth to scream for help, but nothing came out.

Schneider collapsed to the ground with the impact of the strike. He struggled to catch his breath, but it would not come. He had felt the distinct cracking of a rib, seizing him with intense localized pain and making his breathing nearly impossible.

With rising fury in his gut, and adrenaline coursing through his veins, McClintock started to leap to Schneider's defense. But Lange leaned down and whispered in a menacing voice, "Bewegen Sie sich nicht."

Though Ted had no idea what the tall German had said, he knew it's meaning in his gut. Schneider did know and was relieved that Ted did not move.

Steve shook his head to clear his mind, realizing he had not lost consciousness. He felt the blood from his lacerated temple trickling down toward his eyes. Everything in him screamed in fear and rage. Schneider thought: The fucking war is over. It's over for God's sake, but he couldn't get the words out in German or in English.

It was all a blur. Everything was happening too fast to make any sense. All instincts were set on high. Ted, Hamm and Schneider knew where this could end.

The Germans became more and more agitated, now faced with three soldiers and a woman instead of just the two men they had set out to mug. As Hamm turned over and struggled to get up, Lange pushed the barrel of his .45 against Hamm's forehead, forcing him onto his back.

Kurtz was losing it. He hopped from foot to foot. Hamm could see his eyes darting wildly from side to side, scanning the neighborhood for signs of soldiers or MPs.

"Erschießt sie! Erschießt sie! Lasst uns töten sie alle!," he said to his comrade, urgently, harshly.

Schneider wondered if Hamm also understood that the man was telling his partner to shoot everyone. To kill everyone. Hamm had understood the word for shoot but could do nothing, pinned down as he was by the force of the cocked gun against his head. It was that awful day in the operating room all over again; he was helpless in the face of a German's weapon, but this time it was an American made gun.

McClintock, still on his stomach with his face in the ground and Kurtz's foot now placed squarely on his back, had nowhere to move. Each time he struggled, the foot only pressed in harder, making it almost impossible to breath.

Schneider then heard Lange say, "Kurtz, Ich möchte dass Frau," that he wanted Molly for himself. And in that moment, Schneider's previously controlled outrage exploded. As Lange started to move in toward Molly, still standing a few feet away near the corner of the building, Schneider lunged upward. He drove his shoulder into Lange's chest, knocking him to his knees, while grabbing for the gun hand. At the same moment McClintock, feeling Kurtz's foot release from his back, charged at Kurtz, aiming for the pipe in the German's hand.

As Lange struggled to regain his footing, Schneider grabbed the muzzle of the .45 with both hands. He wrenched hard, twisting the gun away, swinging the muzzle upward. He had lots of leverage working for him as he angled the gun further and further up. The German's fingers and wrist began to crack. Then a deafening explosion filled the air next to Schneider's ear as the .45 fired. In a final adrenaline-fueled effort, the German wrenched the gun free and slashed the butt backhanded into Schneider's temple, striking the same place as was hit by the pipe. Schneider fell to the ground, sprawled helplessly on the wet street, barely conscious, bleeding profusely.

Lange aimed the .45 with both hands directly at the center of Schneider's chest. Then, there was another tremendous blast. The German's eyes widened in disbelief as he slumped to the ground in a heap, his chest instantly soaked with blood.

Schneider recovered in time to see Molly, her own .45 emitting a fine wisp of smoke into the damp night air. Shaking, but in complete control—rage in her eyes—she paused only for a second, assuring herself that the armed man was dead, then swung the gun steadily toward Kurtz.

Momentarily stopped by the shock of seeing his friend dying, Kurtz recovered and wheeled to his right. Filling his field of vision was Molly, the big .45 in her hands, pointing straight at him. She—this small woman in a military uniform—had killed his friend.

Molly, now registering the shock of her spontaneous act, did not want to shoot him, wishing for all the world that he would just run away. She was quietly whispering, "Don't move. Don't you dare move. Not one step." It actually sounded more like a plea than a command and the young man knew it, as did Schneider.

Taking advantage of her perceived weakness, he lunged at her, leaping across McClintock. He raised his pipe and swung it toward Molly as both Hamm and McClintock tried to get back into the fight.

A second blast shook the street.

Kurtz's chest exploded, showering all of them with blood.

Molly remained completely still, never taking her eyes off the dying Kurtz, never moving her gun from its target, tears beginning to stream down her cheeks.

Hamm moved immediately to Molly's side, while McClintock went to check on Steve. Putting his arm around Molly, Hamm took the gun and put it in his pocket. Molly said nothing, only now fully registering the shock of what she had done; she, who saved people from the very same wounds she just inflicted. She had just killed two strangers in the street. She, who shot animals only for food and never for sport, and never ever would have dreamed she could have shot another human being. Only minutes before, it would have been unthinkable.

Hamm, with his arm still around her shoulder quietly whispered, "Molly, it's OK. You're OK. Steve's OK." With that, she looked into his eyes, hugged him and said, "Oh God, Hamm, what have I done?"

Schneider was now sitting up, McClintock by his side. As Molly knelt and put her arms around Steve, Hamm reached into his jacket and pulled out his white and blue Tallit, the prayer shawl he had worn for the Seder. He wadded the shawl into a ball and pressed it against the bleeding wound in Schneider's temple, asking McClintock to hold it in place.

Hamm then eased Schneider down on his back and elevated his friend's feet across his own thighs, to help restore some blood volume.

As the three sat on the wet ground, McClintock and Hamm took turns maintaining light pressure on Schneider's head wound, while Molly hugged him to her chest, whispering quietly into his ear, trying to soothe him and herself, through her tears.

No one had time for even a glance at the dead Germans.

They all kept a wary vigil for signs of more trouble. Hamm now well aware that the gun was in his pocket, wondering if he could use it with the same cool expertise that Molly had just moments ago.

Soon the quiet of the night was interrupted by the wail of sirens. Two jeeps and an ambulance raced into their street. Some frightened German citizen, watching from behind blacked-out windows, had sent for help.

The MPs and medics helped Schneider into the ambulance while Molly climbed in alongside him. McClintock waved off the ambulance attendants, covering his own wound with his handkerchief.

McClintock and Hamm went together to talk with the MPs briefly and then climbed into the jeep to follow the ambulance back to the military hospital.

Kurtz and Lange lay where they died. The MP's gathered quietly and began taking notes. It took them less than thirty minutes. Then, with the bodies removed, they returned to their jeeps and drove off.

The rain began again just as they left. It would continue for several hours more, washing the street clean of blood until no traces of what had happened there that night remained. And the street was silent again.

Epilogue

15 April, 2004
The Home of Dr. Jacob Hammer
Philadelphia, Pennsylvania

I was seated at the head of the Passover Seder table for the very first time in my life. At sixty-four years old, it seemed kind of late in life. But, the happy reason was that my father, John Hammer, had lived to such a ripe old age that he had presided over these family holidays for more than sixty years. The unhappy part was that he had died recently. My earliest memories of these Seders start around the age of six, when Dad had just returned from War. Since then, the myriad Seders have melded, and only the last several are clear in my memory.

The crowd around our table had increased over those years. My newest grandchild, Noah, was only six months old and was serving as the table centerpiece in his little baby cradle. He was the second child of my son, Edward, who had just turned forty. A proud older father. Now there were sixteen of us seated for the dinner, crowded and noisy and jubilant. Only my younger brother, Richard, was missing. He was doing Passover with his wife's family this year. Mother was not happy about that.

My wife, Marjorie, had been busy all day, consumed with coordinating the many complicated dishes that would make up the Seder. I barely saw her until we all were seated around the table.

Soon I would open the Passover Haggadah and begin to read, "We were slaves unto Pharaoh...." However, we were still waiting for two more guests.

It was a noisy reunion. The young cousins were growing wilder by the minute in anticipation of the Seder. They ran from room to room, chasing and hiding from one another; and screeching with joy when they were found. They had not seen each other for many months, and a warm chaos and tumult everywhere filled my living room and kitchen.

Meantime, my mind drifted back upstairs to my study, where, on the old roll-top desk—the desk my father had used for fifty years—sat an old cardboard box I had opened earlier that day.

, We had buried Dad nearly three months before. After a long struggle with cancer and an agonizing several months for everyone, he had finally left us. It was a terrible end to a rich and full life. The long and painful process of dying from his cancer was something we all knew he did not deserve. His symptoms made his life miserable. As both his son and also a doctor, being unable to relieve his suffering, I suffered with him. After he died, I spent many hours alone wondering if I had really known him. He was a dear and wonderful man. His patients loved him and his colleagues respected him. He was always solid and unruffled, no matter how serious the event—a great virtue in a surgeon. Most certainly, he was a role model to me as I struggled through my own long surgical education.

My father's name was John, but everyone who didn't call him Doctor or Doc called him Hamm. For as long as I can recall, everyone has called me Jake. Most Jews do not name their children after a living relative, so I had not been named after my father. But we shared initials. I still have his old-fashioned black leather doctor's bag with his—our—initials monogrammed in fading gold leaf.

To have been his son was a great blessing, an honor. I don't know if I ever told him that. What a shame I missed the chance. I suppose I'm not alone in this. Maybe we should have practice funerals to remind us of what is important.

At Dad's funeral, throngs of people came to tell me how much they loved him and what he had meant to their lives and to those he had befriended and those whose lives he had saved. I wondered if they, too, had failed to tell him so while he was still alive.

Yesterday, my mother, Allison, flew in from Arizona to be with us for the Seder. She was doing as well as could be expected, for she loved him deeply, and I know she missed him terribly. The two of them shared a fairy tale life. They had married young and raised their family under the burdens of the Great Depression. They had weathered my father's long surgical residency and the years of separation during World War II. But they thrived together through it all.

Dad had been in surgical practice only a few years when America entered the war in Europe. He was just getting on his feet, paying off his education debts and building his home, a family, and a reputation. Life was starting to look good. But the war was so enormous and Hitler's evil so heinous that Dad, along with many of his friends, volunteered and went straight into active duty. After a short training period, he changed out of his long white coat and into the khaki uniform to become Major John Hammer, U.S. Medical Corps. He told me he never did get used to being called Major.

"They called me a few other things from time to time, Jake," he said once, "but I won't go into that."

I was only five when the war ended, so the odd part for me was that when he finally came home, he never talked about his war experiences. Never.

He was away for more than three years, and when he came back, instead of returning to his practice, he signed on with the Veterans Administration Hospital and took care of the men he served overseas. He could not leave the job unfinished, could not desert his men.

Over the years, as the war receded in everyone's memory, I never learned what he did over there. Of course, I knew he operated on the wounded, but I had no details. There were no war stories. As far as I knew, except for two of them, he never contacted his old war buddies either. We were waiting for them now.

Unlike my generation in Vietnam, where everyone came home with something to say about the war, my father's generation was reluctant to talk about their experience. While I knew well the horrors of war surgery—I served in a unit in Vietnam myself—I grew up knowing almost nothing about World War II except what I read in books. It was as if the soldiers simply packed up one day and left home to do a job that needed to be done. Several years later, they returned and said no more about it. End of story. There was no debate over the right and wrong of it as with Vietnam, no rioting between the hawks and the doves. I don't think there were many doves when it came to fighting the Germans and the Japanese. The country was not torn apart the way Vietnam tore my generation apart. To Americans at the time of WW II, Hitler was evil incarnate, and his Thousand Year Reich had to be stopped. Nobody denied that. When it was over, the men and women came home again, changed out of their uniforms, and went back to work as if they had never left. Oh, yes, there were the wounded and the sick who needed care. So, men like Dad took on the job. But for almost all who served, the war itself was a time that needed to be forgotten, tucked away in the dark dusty attics of their minds.

When I picked up Mom at the airport yesterday, she had two suitcases. While she was unpacking in the guest room, I helped her put things away. She emptied one suitcase and then asked me to put the second one on the bed. She opened it, revealing an oblong cardboard box inside. I thought she must have brought presents for the children and the grandchildren. But the box was not for them. It was for me.

"Jacob, I want you to see this," she said. She was probably the only person who still called me by my formal name.

"I was cleaning out the house a few weeks ago." She sat on the bed next to the old box, while she continued talking. "I need to lighten my load. I don't want you to have the awful job of going through my things when it comes time for me to die."

I started to speak, but she held up a hand.

"I know what you're going to say, but don't. It doesn't matter. What matters is this," she said, pointing to the box.

It was in good shape for its age. I was amused and puzzled to see the word Oxydol on the side, the name of a laundry soap my mom had used for forty years. I thought of other brand names from my childhood, like Ipana toothpaste, also long gone.

On the top of the Oxydol box were the remnants of tape, brittle and yellowed with age. Mom pulled off some of the new tape she had applied to keep the box closed. She carefully crumpled it up and placed it in the wastebasket next to the small writing desk by the bed. She had always been very neat.

Then she opened the flaps, stepped back, and pointed to the contents.

I was puzzled and more than a little anxious. I had no idea what to expect. Photos, perhaps? A will? What?

On the very top was a small leather case, like a jewelry box, clean and unscratched, although I knew it had to be very old. I looked at Mom and then opened it. Inside was a military medal that I recognized immediately.

"You know what that is?" Mom asked me.

"Yes, it's the Bronze Star. For valor in combat."

I never received one of those in Vietnam, and I had been jealous of colleagues who did.

"Dad's?"

She nodded.

"You knew about this?" I asked.

She shook her head no, and shrugged.

I put the precious medal on the nightstand. Deeper in the box I found little books, but they were not just any books.

"What are these, Mom?"

"Look at them, darling."

I reached in and took out the top one. It was a light brown leather-bound volume, heavily worn along its edges. Small pieces of the desiccated leather flaked to the floor like dry leaves. Mom bent and picked the little leather pieces off the carpet and deposited them into the wastebasket.

Near the left side of the front cover were gold-tooled letters, slightly worn as well.

**DAILY
REMINDER**

The edges of the pages were colored a faded red. Along the book's spine was the date, also in gold, worn and barely readable:

441

1943

On the inside of the cover was a calendar for that year, and I noticed that my birthday—my third birthday—had been on a Monday. I had no recollection of it, but of course Dad wouldn't have been home to celebrate it with me anyway. He was already overseas. Still, the date had been circled so that he would remember to send me something. I sniffed the pages, hoping there would be something of him there. A cigar odor, perhaps. Something. But, there was nothing. Not a trace. The book had been published by The Standard Diary Company of Cambridge, Massachusetts and contained a page for each day. The pages had blue ruled lines like a composition book. On the first page was the printed heading:

Friday, January 1, 1943
1st day—364 days to follow
New Year's Day.

The diary began in my father's familiar handwriting. Difficult, but not illegible.

Spent New Year's Eve at Evenlode with Steve. We did some 'pub chasing' and finished off our last Vat 69.

I was surprised to see my father write about pub chasing and Vat 69, since I never knew him to drink. I calculated that about that time he would have been in England, training and getting ready for the invasion of Normandy, then still a year and a half away, and Top Secret.

There were more leather bound diaries, exactly like the first, labeled 1944 and 1945. I closed the last book for a moment and put it down on the bed.

I found myself becoming inexplicably angry. Why was I only seeing these nearly sixty years after the war ended? Why hadn't Dad shown me these?

Mom said nothing. She only watched me go through the box. Beneath the diary was another book, also old, but not as worn, as if it had lived its life inside the box, protected from the world, rarely handled or read. The Khaki cover had a capital letter **A** inside blue and red concentric circles: the insignia of the US Third Army—the army of occupation in Germany after the war. Patton's army.

Beneath the Third Army insignia in red letters were the words:

PASSOVER SERVICE
Munich Enclave
Munich, Germany, April 15–16, 1946

"Oh, dear God…."

There were English and Hebrew words, with black and white woodcuts surrounding each page. I saw the now familiar pyramids and cremation ovens, Egyptian slaves and Nazi guards, gas chambers and fertile fields. I shivered and closed the book. Mom remained still. I put the book aside on the night table without reading any further.

"You knew about all of this?"

"Oh, no. Your father never showed me any of it. I didn't even know he kept a diary. I kept the letters he sent to me, of course…and the letters to you. They're in there, also."

She reached in and pulled out one rubber-band bound packet of letters. I recognized Dad's distinctive handwriting in blue ink on the top envelope. It was addressed to Mrs. Allison Hammer.

"The war was so painful for him," she said. "When he came home, he never said a word. None of them did. They wanted to get back to their lives and forget."

"But all those years…" I said. "I mean, I wasn't a child forever!"

"Don't get angry, Jacob. He just didn't want to expose us to what he saw. To what happened to him. It must have been horrible there."

"But, Mom, not to tell us anything. Not even let me see these diaries. I went to war, too. Surely he…."

"Oh, Jacob. You're so much like your father."

Mom nodded slowly to herself, and, without a word, slipped from the room.

I flipped through the letters, leaving them in their rubber bands without reading them. Then I picked up the first diary again and sat down in the armchair next to the window. I opened the diary to the first page.

New Year's Day, 1943

And I began to read.

It was getting late now, and our last two guests still hadn't shown up. There had been no phone calls. My mother was starting to fret. Again.

"It's awfully late, Jacob, you know. I mean, the children...."

"I know, Mom," I said. "Let's give them a few more minutes. There's probably a lot of traffic, and he's not the greatest driver."

"He's driving still? Your father stopped driving years ago."

"Yeah, he still drives." I laughed. "God help us all."

"Jacob, he really shouldn't be driving."

"I know, Mom. Maybe she drives for them now," I said, wanting to be done with this conversation." Yeah, she's probably driving."

"So where are they, then, if she's driving?" she said, hands out, palms raised. I would lose my fragile calm very soon if this kept up.

"Mom, why don't you see how the cooking's going? If everything is ready, we'll just start without them."

Marjorie was still bustling in and out of the kitchen and dining room. She knew enough after all these years to stay out of Mom's way. Peace at any price.

I called to my oldest son, Edward, "Go into the dining room and make sure there's a place set for Elijah."

Edward laughed. He was patronizing me. "Sure, Dad. I'll make sure."

I looked at my watch and wondered if I should really go ahead and call everyone to the table. If they'd only carried a cell phone, I could call and know for sure when they'd be here. But they were the last of the Luddites and had never given in to e-mail, much less cell phones.

By eight o'clock the natives were just too restless to delay any longer, and dinner was getting overdone. Mom was nearing hysteria. So I grabbed Edward and said, "OK, son, get all the kids to the table."

"Should I page Elijah, too?" he said with a laugh.

"Nobody loves a smart ass," I said. "Just round up the kids. Where's Rachel?"

Edward's four year old daughter was Jacob's favorite, even though he would never play favorites. At four, her Grandpa could do no wrong.

"She's organizing a Passover Rebellion. The kids are going to strike for higher allowances."

"Go get her, and make sure she sits near me."

"Okay, Dad."

"And get your sister to help Mom."

"Beth's been in the kitchen with her all evening—mostly keeping Grandma calm."

"Good."

We all took our seats. The little ones all jostled to get closer to me. And I loved it! I told them all to behave, but of course I was thrilled they all wanted to be near me. When everyone was seated and quiet, I reached for the Haggadah. The old book had been in the family now for three generations and was showing its age. The children all had new versions loaded with colorful pictures and large print.

As I was about to start the service, I heard a crunching of tires in the driveway and the tired squeal of old brakes in need of new pads. I let out a long sigh, happy now that everyone would be here for the start of the service, and especially that Mom would settle down and stop fretting.

I was just about to send Edward to greet them, but at the sound of the car doors closing, the kids all scrambled from the table and rushed to the front door. There was a flurry of activity and greetings and hugs and kisses. I sat back in my seat smiling at Mom, who wasn't going to give me the satisfaction. She pointed to her left wrist, which was funny, since she never wore a watch.

I nodded, I know, I know. Enough, already!

I knew she would never be rude; instead, she would take out her feelings on me. What else was new?

In a minute more, the room lit up with the high voices of the children now all like bees swarming around the last of the Passover guests. It might have been Elijah himself for all the excitement.

I got up and pushed through the little mob. The kids reluctantly gave way, allowing me into the circle. They drifted back to their seats. I gave Molly a huge hug and a big kiss on her cheek.

Molly kissed me back. "I'm so sorry we're late," she said. "The traffic...and you know how he drives!"

I looked at her carefully, trying as always to see any change, any signs that she was growing old. I had known her for as long as I could remember. But, no, her age had only enhanced her beauty somehow.

"Hi, Jake," Steve said, reaching for a hug. He nearly took my breath away. A great strong bear hug for a man his age.

I took their coats and handed them to Edward, who was waiting to take them away.

In a moment, we were all seated. The children each reluctantly moved down the table one seat so that Molly could sit next to me. Steve took his place next to Marjorie at the other end of the table. Then there was silence.

So it began again, as it has in Jewish homes all over the world for millennia. The story of the Jews as slaves; of the plagues visited by God upon the family of the Egyptian royalty; of the Angel of Death passing over the houses of the Jews, sparing their first born children from the touch of Death; of the Exodus; of forty years wandering the desert with Moses; of a new life in the Promised Land.

I read a few more lines, and my eyes began to swim. Tears welled up, and I could barely see. Hamm—Dad—should have been here reading, and no matter what anyone said, Passover would never be the same again without him.

It didn't matter though. I continued to say the words. After so many years, I knew them by heart. What Jew didn't? Passover was the happiest and most beloved holiday feast of the year because of the food, and the stories, and the gathering of the family. Many Jews who never showed up at synagogue all year long—like me—would not miss a single Seder if they could help it.

Everybody loved Passover.

I continued to read the story and made my way to the Four Questions. As the oldest of the clan, I would answer the Four Questions asked by the youngest child at the table who was old enough to read. Tonight, it was my seven-year-old granddaughter, Sarah, Beth's daughter, proud as she could be at her first reading. Holding her Haggadah, but looking straight into my eyes, she asked me, "Why is this night different from all other nights?" And she went on to ask me why, on this night, do we eat only unleavened bread, and on through all the traditional questions. She looked at me, pretending she had never heard the answers before.

Steve sat quietly though the service, and as usual, he hardly took his eyes off Molly. It was nice to see them apparently just as in love as Dad told me they were during the war when they met.

When dinner was over and the service finished, everyone rose to move into the living room and the den. The kids followed Edward to see who could find the Afikoman, the matzo he had hidden before everyone had arrived. The grown-ups all anted up dollar bills for the winner and some more booby prizes for the rest of the little ones.

I stayed at the table with Molly and Steve. My mother and Marjorie moved into the kitchen to help clean up.

"Another one," Steve said with a sigh. "One more Passover together. It's so good to be with all of you. But it's just so different without your father."

" I know. I know. How many is that?" I asked.

"Well, it's 2004, and we should count the one in Munich. So that's… uh…fifty-nine counting the first one, I think."

"Fifty-nine Seders," I said. "Wow, that's a hell of a lot of matzo and Manischewitz!"

Molly laughed. Then she said, "I'm sorry about your father, Jake. We all loved him so much."

"Thank you. I know. Everyone misses him terribly. It was a tough year watching him die. Not a way any of us want to end our lives. I keep thinking of all the cancer patients he treated, only to die of one of the worst cancers of them all."

Steve put his hand on mine and said, "It stinks. He held our group together over there. He was The Rock. He was a wonderful surgeon and a really good friend to me…to us."

I was trying not to choke up, so I changed the subject.

"How are the girls?" I asked Steve. "Emily and Anna?"

"They're great. They're having First Seder with Susan and her husband tonight, along with their kids…not really kids any more either. Lots of generations of Schneiders now. We're having Second Seder with them tomorrow at our house."

Steve looked away for a moment. Molly took his hand. The two of them had no children together. I don't know if it was by choice or something else. Dad never discussed it, and I never felt it was something I could ask Steve or Molly. While they were so devoted to my dad, I felt a bit as if I were their son-by-proxy. I was in their lives because Dad had kept them in his. He never let a holiday or a birthday or a wedding or bar mitzvah go by without including the Schneiders.

After the war, Steve had come home to his old practice. Molly resigned her commission in the WACs and became his office nurse and assistant. She actually ran the whole practice. Steve spent a lot of time teaching upcoming young doctors the practice and principles of surgery, especially trauma surgery. He always attended Grand Rounds and Mortality Conference at the hospital, and offered what wisdom he could from his long experience as a combat surgeon.

Steve had told me that he went to war burdened by a heaviness in his soul: a failing marriage; a fear of his own cowardice that ate at him during all the years under fire; his lost faith; and his alienation from his German-Jewish heritage and family. In the end, he came home a very different man, stronger in many ways. Perhaps a little wounded deep inside as well. I only wish that my own dad had told me as much about how the war had impacted him.

He and Molly married as soon as he and Susan were divorced. It was a messy time from what little my Dad told me. He thought Steve should have gone back to Susan. Steve was crazy about Molly, but Dad felt Steve owed his marriage with Susan a try. Of course, Mom had a lot to say about it, too, but it never changed anything. Apparently there were too many things that happened over there in the war that changed everyone.

Steve's Uncle Meyer searched for his wife and children for years. It was a long search, but he never found any trace of them, no evidence that they were either alive or dead. Nothing. As if they never existed. He had kept such careful records of his own patients, but apparently no one had done the same for his family. Finally, he left Germany forever and settled down not far from Steve and Molly. He died only a few years later...of something no one could name. Everyone said he had just lived too long without any heart for life.

And then there was a medic named Marsh. I heard Dad telling Mom about him. Shortly after he left the army, he called Dad to say he was on his way back to Malmédy to look for the young woman who saved him: the woman of his dreams, or perhaps, Dad thought, just the woman in his dream. We all wondered if he ever found her, but no one ever heard from him again.

Another medic named Antonelli showed up in Philadelphia not long after the war. He asked Dad and Steve for letters of recommendation. He was going to go to college and then to medical school on the Servicemen's Readjustment Act, now known as the G.I. Bill. Steve told him that he'd probably know more about trauma surgery than his teachers would. And it thrilled Dad.

Dr. McClintock came back to Philadelphia, too. He stayed single for as long as I knew him and continued to "pass gas" (as he always joked) for Dr. Schneider.

Dad came home and started a new life as a surgeon at the VA hospital, caring for the men he served in Europe. After about eight years he took a position as professor of medicine at a teaching hospital in Philadelphia, and he stayed there for the rest of his life.

This Passover, we spent a very quiet evening together. I tried not to see every gathering as possibly the last, but it was hard not to. I watched Steve age even as Molly appeared to stay so young. Looking back, they seemed to have made the right choices, though I'm sure it was never easy in the doing. I couldn't help but wonder what Molly would do when Steve died.

After most of the others had said goodnight and left, Edward drifted back into the den with us. He sat down between Steve and Molly and me and, for a while, just listened. Finally he asked, "When can I hear about it, Dr. Schneider?"

"Hear about what, pal?" Steve said. I smiled. Steve always called dad "pal," and he called me "pal'" too. Now Edward had been promoted to that name.

"I want to know about the war. About what happened there. About my Grandpa. And about you."

"You don't want to hear about all that, pal. It's old stuff. It was horrible. And it's history. Gone."

"But it's my history too," Edward persisted. "Dad told me all about Vietnam," he said, looking at me. "And some day the story of Grandpa's war—your war—will be gone unless I know all about it, unless I remember it and tell it to my kids. There's no one else but you now to tell me about it. This matters. It matters to me."

Steve looked at me and then to Molly. Neither of us moved or spoke.

"Fair enough," he said. 'Where would you like me to begin?"

I sat quietly with Edward, Steve and Molly in the den. I listened to Steve's voice as he told Edward the story of his, and his grandfather Hamm's, war.

It was hours later by the time Steve had finished. But, in spite of the late hour—nearly morning now—everyone was still attentive. Steve became more and more energized and enlivened with each passing hour. It was as if he had been just waiting for Edward to ask.

We hugged and kissed goodbye on the frosty front doorstep. Steve and Molly walked down the drive. Thankfully, I saw Molly take the driver's seat. I left Edward waving goodbye to them, and returned to my study upstairs. As I walked the hallway, I could hear Mom snoring lightly in her room. The little ones were sleeping together in one bedroom, all tucked into makeshift nests on the floor, all snoring like my Mom.

I made my way back into the sitting room where I had left the diaries and letters. It was chilly in the room, but I didn't want to turn up the heat. It felt better to bundle up in a blanket on the wing chair. I pulled the carton nearer to me and began opening the letters dad had saved in chronological order.

Soon, I sensed Edward at my side. He found himself a spot on the floor and looked toward the cardboard carton. I pointed at the diary and nodded.

Edward picked up his grandfather's worn leather journal and opened to the first page.

"*Friday, January 1, 1943.*" He read to me.

"*Spent New Year's Eve at Evenlode with Steve.*"

End

Tribute

*"The soldiers have been wonderful, never a whimper. Always "Yes, Sir,"
even with their last breath. It is the amazing courage of these boys that
spurs us on. We can't sell them short. They must always be our prime
consideration.*

*"This has made me a wiser man. It has imbued me with the real-
ization that petty things won't disturb me in the future, that there is an
indescribable beauty in just living.*

*"Thank you for your prayers. Somebody did take care of me, but I
am afraid many more deserving men have been sacrificed in the holo-
caust."*

From a letter home
Dr. Alfred Hurwitz
June, 1944

Author's Note

This is a novel, a work of fiction. All individual characters appearing in this work are fictitious. Any resemblance to real persons, is purely coincidental. None of them should be construed to represent any actual person, living or dead.

Events such as the D-Day invasion, the Battle of the Bulge, the events which took place at the Baugnez Crossroads near Malmédy, the liberation of Hitler's concentration camps, and the 1946 Munich Seder are all documented historic events. While the background and story lines are based upon true events, the stories are fictionalized.

None of the names of characters, field hospitals or surgical groups portrayed here are meant to represent any specific person, place or group. Names and military designations of field hospitals, ships and organizations have been changed, and do not represent the actual names or standard military numbering. Well known figures such as General Dwight D. Eisenhower, General George S. Patton, Général Charles De Gaulle, SS Lieutenant Colonel Joachim Peiper appear briefly as background to the documented historical setting.

Proof

Made in the USA
Charleston, SC
19 April 2012